TRO

He peered into the cloud of tobacco smoke and tried to see his life there. I have a reputation most men would envy, he thought. My name is recognized all over this part of the country. Everyone who hears it either respects it or fears it. I'm the most educated man in these parts. I have a profession that puts me on the side of right.

"Where's all that gotten me?" he mumbled at the smoke.

Even before he heard it, he knew the October rain had started. For him, rain held the promise of action. Hidden somewhere in the dark and the wet was the promise of adventure.

The rain still held its pledge of action and adventure, but he did not go searching for it. He knew it would seek him out. It was the kind of night and the sort of rain that means adventure if you are twenty-five, and action if you are thirty-five. But when you are forty-five it only means trouble. Randall MacLane was forty-five.

———⹁✦⹁———

Dear Reader:

Just a moment of your time could earn you $1,000! We're working hard to bring you the best books, and to continue to do that we need your help. Simply turn to the back of this book, and let us know what you think by answering seven important questions.

Return the completed survey with your name and address filled in, and you will automatically be entered in a drawing to win $1,000, subject to the official rules.

Good luck!

Geoff Hannell

Geoff Hannell
Publisher

AN ORDINARY MAN

J. R. McFARLAND

HarperPaperbacks
A Division of HarperCollins*Publishers*

HarperPaperbacks *A Division of* HarperCollins*Publishers*
10 East 53rd Street, New York, N.Y. 10022

Copyright © 1995 by John Robert McFarland
All rights reserved. No part of this book may be used or reproduced in any manner whatsoever without written permission of the publisher, except in the case of brief quotations embodied in critical articles and reviews. For information address HarperCollins*Publishers,*
10 East 53rd Street, New York, N.Y. 10022.

Cover illustration by Tony Gabriele

First printing: July 1995

Printed in the United States of America

HarperPaperbacks and colophon are trademarks of HarperCollins*Publishers*

❖ 10 9 8 7 6 5 4 3 2 1

For my parents,
John Francis and Mildred Pond McFarland

Table of Contents

Prologue

A group of about a half-dozen riders angled at him, trying to cut him off before he reached the mass ahead, to get the kill for themselves. They did not count on the rage of the man they rode against, however. They did not know how his horse felt that rage through his thighs, so that it ran with the strength of terror, trying to escape the power of destruction that sat astride it.

The Indians rode only for the joy of fighting, the hope of counting coup, the respect of their people, the urge for honor. Truly powerful motivations, but they were a flock of sparrows compared with the falcon of Randall MacLane's rage.

The Rain and Solitary Men

He sat in the dark, alone, staring out at the town through the rain. It was the sort of night his Scots-highland ancestors would have welcomed, to go out to make their murky way beyond the eyes of the docile, law-abiding, hearth-sitting lowlands. MacLane always felt a twinge of guilt when he remembered the stories from his boyhood about his ancestral clan. They were the brigand clan, those outside and beyond the law.

Now he sat in a darkened jail on a rainy night, but he wasn't there as a brigand. He wore the badge of the law. He was its keeper, not its breaker. He wondered how the ancestors would feel about that.

The rain took him back to the green hills of Indiana, so far away and so long ago. As a boy there he had dreamed of being an Indian fighter. When it rained, he stalked his father in the barnyard, slipping in the dark from woodshed to chicken house to grain bin, always a few feet behind and just out of sight and sound. Wasn't that what Indian fighters did?

Later, at the state college in Bloomington, he listened

to the other students complain about the rain. He could not understand why. To him, rain held the saturated promise of action. Hidden somewhere in the dark and the wet was the pledge of adventure.

The rain extended still its promise of action and adventure, but he did not go searching for it. He knew it would seek him out, as it had so many times before . . . on a Montana hill, at the wagon, in a dozen lawless towns where he had worn the badge no one else dared to wear. It was the kind of night and the sort of rain that means adventure if you are twenty-five, and action if you are thirty-five. But when you are forty-five it only means trouble. Randall MacLane was forty-five.

At forty-five, when staring through the rain, sensing the feeling in your increasingly creaky joints that action means trouble, even a solitary man begins to feel lonely. At forty-five you worry about your belt having no more holes and about your throat being raspy every time you puff your pipe and especially about the spots that float in front of your eyes on a sunny day. You wonder if you're too old for the job. You ask what else you can do, and you get no answers. Those, at least, are your thoughts if you are an ordinary man. More than anything else, Randall MacLane longed to be an ordinary man.

How, though, could a man ever be ordinary when he had been sent with a message to the world's hero, but had arrived too late? How could he be ordinary when he had tamed a dozen towns and killed a hundred people and saved a thousand more? How could he be ordinary when he was the one man an entire territory feared and trusted more than anyone else? That wasn't an ordinary life. Randall MacLane was not an ordinary man.

At least he could take refuge in the rain. Rain has always been the friend of solitary men. When you are not an ordinary man, however, you sit in the dark, alone, and stare at the town through the rain, and you know that the trouble will come.

A Message for Custer

Thirty years before, when he was fifteen, Randall MacLane had been a boy with a dream, a clear vision of what he would do and be. So little of what had happened to him, however, was a part of his dream. Strange events had circled around him and obscured that boyhood vision, the way storm clouds roil the horizon to blot out the sun.

It had all started with the message, the message entrusted to him by the congressman in Washington.

It was amazing that MacLane was in Washington at all. There was no place for new officers in the postwar army.

He was, however, one of the first graduates of the brand-new Reserve Officers Training Course. Some politicians had thought it would be a good idea to break the stranglehold that West Point and its traditions had on the army. They had fought for this program, to train officers in colleges across the land. They weren't about to bury the program just because there was no need for new officers.

So, shortly before his twenty-third birthday, Randall

MacLane received a commission in the army. He wanted to be assigned to the frontier, but was excited about being sent to the nation's capital. He was sure it would be fascinating to see how the decisions of the army and the government were made. He didn't know this appointment was just for show, until he arrived and found there was nothing for him to do and no future in which to do it.

In that vacuum, however, he met Lafayette Luquire.

Colonel Seeley, his commander, called him aside one day.

"There's this Congress donkey from South Carolina or some godforsaken place that wants to talk to 'a bright young officer about the future of the army,' or some such stupid thing."

He said "bright young officer" the same way most people would say "plague-infected rat."

"As though there's any future for the army except taking orders from idiots like him. Anyway, they picked you out, which proves something about how smart they are. Here's the directions. Go meet him there at one o'clock."

He handed Randall a folded piece of paper with an address.

"Who is it I'm meeting, and how will I know him?"

"He'll be the only person there that looks like a bigger fool than you."

With that, Seeley was gone.

Randall estimated that he had twice as much time as needed to walk to the rendezvous, but with nothing better to do, he decided to arrive early and see what he could learn. The address on the paper turned out to be a small tobacco shop.

There was a slick-haired young man, not much older than himself, dressed almost like a fop, standing in front of the shop, staring into the window. He leaned on a walking stick that sported a gold top shaped like a horse. As

Randall approached the door he turned with a flourish of his stick and gave Randall a wide smile.

"Ah, Lieutenant MacLane, I'm sure."

"Why, uh, yes . . ."

"Not to be surprised, Lieutenant. I am Congressman Lafayette Luquire. Among other responsibilities, I serve on the committee that oversees the army. I want to know what the bright young up-and-coming officers like yourself have to say about the direction we should be taking. Speaking of directions, let us walk as we talk. Does the digestion good."

He didn't offer to shake hands, just pointed down the street with his cane and began a slow stroll that didn't promise much for the digestion. Randall almost minced his steps to keep from leaving Congressman Luquire behind. He also felt a rumbling in his stomach as he realized the congressman already had dined, while he himself had missed lunch and had nothing to digest. That seemed a small thing, however, compared with the rumbling of his curiosity.

"But, how did you know . . ."

"That you'd be early? I counted on it, my young friend. Had you not been, I would not have trusted your judgment. I need to hear from someone who can get out ahead."

The congressman's answer surprised MacLane. He hadn't even thought about why Luquire was there so early. He had intended to ask how the congressman knew who he was and why he had asked for him in the first place. He decided it would be impolite at best, and probably rude, to mention that now, so he simply strolled along, answering the questions Luquire put to him about the army.

They were intriguing questions, but not because they were perceptive. They had little to do with anything of importance in the army, as best MacLane could tell. His companion, however, listened carefully to each of his answers, as though on them the fate of the entire army would hang.

After half an hour the congressman pulled a gold watch from the pocket of his brocaded waistcoat.

"Ah, I must return to my duties, and just as I was learning so much. But please, I have more to ask you. Let us meet at the same spot, and at the same time, one week from today. We shall continue our discussion then. You go that way."

He didn't wait for an agreement from Randall on the next meeting, just pointed with his stick down a narrow street, then turned his back and hurried off. Randall had no idea where he was. They had wandered the backstreets of a district he didn't know at all. He took off in the direction the stick had pointed, however, and eventually found his way back to his office.

He was back at the tobacco shop the following week, and so was the congressman. Once again they wandered backstreets. Luquire asked more and more questions, but fewer and fewer of them had anything to do with the army. Randall didn't mind, however. Most of the questions were about him, and this young man from Congress seemed fascinated by the answers. Randall began to think there might be some future for him in the army after all. Luquire could be a powerful advocate.

Their meetings went on for several weeks, always walking the backstreets of the capital.

The young lieutenant was flattered by Congressman Lafayette Luquire's attention. Luquire was only a few years older than he. Anyone could see, however, that he was destined to be a powerful man. The mantle of greatness had settled on him early, and he wore it with ease. The friendship of such a man was strong applejack for the poor farm boy from Indiana. It was a welcome break from the boring routine of a junior officer.

It was also a matter of suspicion to Travis Hamilton, another graduate of the college officer program.

*   *   *

Randall and Travis had little in common, except a dislike for Colonel Seeley, their commanding officer. The colonel was interested only in gambling, drinking, and women—in that order. That didn't bother Travis, who was interested in the same three, but in the reverse order.

The two lieutenants, however, shared a disdain for Seeley's cynicism. His motto was that nothing ever changed, so why bother with any of it? MacLane and Hamilton were sure the world could be turned if they were allowed a chance at the lever.

MacLane was putting on his hat, to go meet the congressman for one of their afternoon walks on Washington's backstreets, when Travis decided to attack the subject of his suspicion head-on.

"Look, Randall. What does Luquire want from you? The rich and powerful don't befriend the poor just because the poor are lonely."

"Has it ever occurred to you, Travis, that he might respect my knowledge?"

Hamilton made a rude smacking noise with his lips.

"Want you for your knowledge? Your knowledge of what, how to get elected? He's forgotten more about that than you'll ever know. The knowledge of the army you've gotten by sitting behind a desk and doing nothing? More likely he wants you for your ignorance."

It sounded too much like the truth. Randall really didn't have any useful knowledge. He must have been boring company, compared with all the others with whom Lafayette Luquire could spend his time. But why would anyone be wanted for his ignorance? So Randall MacLane did what most people do when faced with a truth that tastes like sugar-dipped lemons; he simply walked out the door and ignored it.

*   *   *

It was exactly one month before his enlistment was up that he was invited to the congressman's house. That had never happened before. Their meetings were always in the open, walking backstreets. The invitation to the Luquire house surprised and pleased him. Perhaps the congressman really had found a postarmy position for him.

There was no future in the army following the Civil War. They had kept him in Washington because of his education. That college degree he had so much coveted had become a stumbling block. He wanted to fight Indians. The army wanted him to fight supply-list bureaucrats. Colonel Seeley told him often enough that "the army has more junior officers that it's got jackasses. There's no place in it for an educated jackass."

Randall was glad enough to leave their do-nothing army, but now what if he had nothing to do? The congressman had listened to his complaints about the army and his future with great sympathy. He seemed especially interested in Randall's lament that he had joined the army to fight Indians but had been stuck in offices. He even promised "to be on the lookout." Surely Luquire must now have a line on a position for him. Why else would he invite MacLane to his home?

Randall's knock on the door was answered by a young man he had never seen before. He was dressed in the manner of a junior partner in a law firm. He was obviously not a servant, or even a secretary, but he knew his way around the house. Without ceremony he led Randall through the dimly lit hallway to a small back room.

Lafayette Luquire was there. So were five other men, three only a little older than MacLane, the other two in their late forties. Bottles mustered on the table, dead soldiers still at attention. Brandy snifters tilted in their hands. Cigars burned like torches in their mouths. They filled the room so completely that Randall and his guide could barely edge inside the door. The men looked like they were holding poses for some mythical photographer, as though they had been in the midst of a conversation that could not be continued in his presence.

The congressman jumped up and pulled him in with a handshake both nervous and powerful. It was the first time Luquire had bothered to shake his hand. His grip was much stronger than Randall expected.

"Welcome, Randall, welcome."

Lafayette Luquire bubbled like a pool of Pluto water. His cheeks glistened and his eyes gleamed with an unnatural brightness. Randall had never seen the upward-bound young congressman like this. He could not tell whether he was a little drunk or a little mad or both.

No one else in the room was introduced to him. No brandy or cigar was offered to him, but that did not surprise him. The congressman knew he neither smoked nor drank. Without preamble one of the older men addressed him.

"Congressman Luquire tells us you are a man of courage who loves his country and can be trusted to do his duty. Is that true?"

Randall's tongue stuck to the roof of his mouth and refused to move. How do you answer such a question? Who were these men? Was he being interviewed for a job? The men looked like they might be railroad executives. What job could he do for a railroad?

MacLane was grateful for the dim light, hoping it disguised the fast flush he felt pushing up his neck and over his face. His uncertainty seemed to hang in the air, suspended in the cigar smoke.

He was surprised to hear his own voice, much too loud for the small room. His mouth was speaking before his mind had decided what he wanted to say. It was a trait that often got him into trouble but also often pushed him to new possibilities. His voice, at least, did not question the right of these men to have an answer, even though he did not know who they were.

"I know I love my country, sir." He addressed himself

only to the man who had asked the question. "I can only hope that I am a man of courage who is worthy of trust."

The congressman glanced quickly around the room. No one else spoke, and that seemed to satisfy him.

"Randall," he said, his voice lowering to seriousness at the same time as his eyes glistened with excitement, "we have a mission for you. These men represent the best interests of our country. I don't need to tell you that the years following the war have been trying ones. You know personally in what disarray the army lies. I know that the Congress is not much better. If there were ever a time that we needed strong leadership, now is that time. This whole continent is ready to explode into a new economic paradise."

His voice did not rise, but the words sped from his mouth faster and faster, without a syllable out of place. One who did not know the congressman might think it was a rehearsed speech.

Without even a pause for breath, with no gap in the words, he pulled the handkerchief from his breast pocket, wiped his brow, and rushed on.

"Leadership, man, that is the key," he said, every spark from his eye flaming with urgency. "The muddle-heads in Washington are going to let this chance go by and it will never come again. But we shall not spurn this opportunity. All the lamps are waiting and ready to be lit. There is only one man who can light them. You are to take him the match."

The words of the congressman danced in the middle of the room like the flames from the lamps of which he spoke. Every man in that tight little circle seemed drawn to them, as moths are drawn to a lighted candle. Randall felt like he was being pulled in from beyond the circle of the light into the very center of the heat. His heart beat faster with the knowledge that he was on the inside of something big.

"Who is this man?" he whispered.

The congressman did not answer immediately. He waited, like an actor, allowing the tension in the room to build. Finally, when he spoke, he did not answer the question Randall asked.

"He is in the West. None of us can leave Washington long enough to take a message to him. We cannot trust any conventional means of communication. The message must be delivered personally into his hands. No one else must see it or even know that it exists. The courier must be inconspicuous. He must have a natural reason for traveling there. That courier is you, Randall. You must leave Washington immediately for the high plains. A military man on a military matter."

"But, sir," Randall blurted, "my military time is up in only four weeks. I'm due to be mustered out."

"I know, I know," replied the congressman. "But we have arranged for that. Tell Colonel Seeley that you must go west immediately on family business. He has nothing to gain by keeping you four more weeks. You can carry papers from him that will allow you to be mustered out at one of the Western forts. If you hurry you can make it before your time is up. It is urgent that you do. If Seeley balks, tell me. We can get him to give you what you ask. He is indebted to Mr.—"

Luquire was about to say the name of a man to whom he now gestured, the other older man, a big man with a gleaming pate. Just as he started to speak his name the bald man exploded into a coughing fit. Randall was not sure whether Luquire said the name and he missed it because of the coughing, or if the cough actually shut off the flow of the congressman's words. At any rate, Randall did not hear the name, and Luquire reddened as though he were the one coughing.

"Well, don't worry about that," he said hastily. "Just let me know if Seeley gives you problems. We'll take care of it."

MacLane did not question the obvious and heavy-handed attempt to keep him ignorant of the man's name.

After all, he knew no one in the room except Luquire. Randall was an army man. He understood that there are times when too much knowledge simply gets in the way of doing the job. Neither did he question why he was being ordered on a military mission by nonmilitary personnel. He was getting out of the army. Here was a chance to see the storied West, a chance at last to get some adventure, some action, some of what he had joined the army for in the first place.

The congressman continued. "You have no family here, so you can leave as soon as Seeley approves. That means tomorrow. The orders are already drafted. Just take them to him and get them signed."

One of the faceless young men at the table handed Randall the sheaf of papers for Colonel Seeley. Another, who sat at the left of the bald man, reached into his coat and pulled out two long envelopes, one buff and one blue. He handed the buff envelope to Randall.

"You now have authorization papers to speed you on your journey," said the congressman. "Those documents will get you onto any train or stagecoach. They'll get you a horse at any army post. Don't tell Colonel Seeley or anyone else about them. Don't use them unless you have to. As soon as you have delivered the message, destroy them."

Then the young man at the table handed MacLane the blue envelope.

"You will leave that envelope with a man in St. Louis," Luquire told him. "His name and where you can locate him are on it. It is only a prelude to the main message with which we entrust you. You could make better time going through Chicago than St. Louis, but before you deliver the message, the man in St. Louis must have this envelope."

Things were happening so fast, and Randall's hands were full of papers. He was actually turning to leave before it occurred to him that he did not yet have the message or the name of the man who was to receive it. He turned back to the room as his face reddened again. He hoped no one had noticed.

The last man in the room, one with huge muttonchop whiskers, reached down below the table and brought up a long, narrow metal box. It had no handle, but a small padlock held its clasp in place. He handed it to the congressman, who in turn passed it to Randall.

"Keep it out of sight," said Lafayette Luquire. "Deliver it to one man only. Do not contact us again. From now on you are simply an army lieutenant hurrying home because of family business. But board the first train that will start you to the Dakota. Take this box at once to the man, wherever he is. You are carrying a message of urgent importance to General Custer."

The "Grays" are Always There

Randall had no time to think after the meeting. He was carried along by a sense of urgency.

He returned to his quarters, packed his bags, and took them to the train station, even though it was past midnight. Colonel Seeley would be up early, and he wanted to be able to leave as soon as he had gotten his papers signed. He knew the colonel would not be surprised that Randall had the papers ready before approaching him. They worked that way anyhow, with as little contact as possible. Randall knew the colonel did not approve of him—his teetotaling, his churchgoing, his college education, his seriousness.

Randall thought he should bid good-bye to Travis Hamilton, but decided not to. Travis would only claim that he was right, that the congressman had only befriended him to be able to use him. Well, Randall MacLane didn't care. He was the one with the message to Custer.

He spent the rest of the night tying up a few loose

ends in the office until the colonel arrived. Colonel Seeley listened to his story of the urgent need to return to his family, snorted, and signed the papers without comment. He did not even return MacLane's farewell salute. Randall wondered if the unnamed man from the congressman's house had already contacted Seeley. That was no concern of his now.

He went to the station and boarded the train to go to Indianapolis, and from there to St. Louis.

His nervous energy finally drained out. He dozed on and off throughout the day as the train clicked and hissed and wailed its way west, content with the knowledge that his path led him away from Washington forever. He was finally going west, going to find the man who was the symbol of all he thought the army was about when he joined it. He experienced a pang of regret as he realized he was not going actually to join Custer. Well, at least he had one mission of significance before his army days were done. After that . . .

He had gone to the congressman's house the night before thinking he would learn what his future held. Now he had an assignment for only a month and no prospects beyond this. Lafayette Luquire hadn't planned a very long future for him.

The days as he traveled were almost more boring than his time in Washington. There was an endless succession of trains and stations and days and nights as he worked his way through the green summer toward St. Louis and the boat up the Mississippi. On it he would have to ride for days to find Custer on the plains.

Time. He had to use the time. Trains and people along the way did not seem to understand his urgency. He longed to be done with the journey, to have the excitement of standing in the presence of Custer, delivering the message with which he had been entrusted. Through the boredom of the days and the jarring of the trains, he at least had the satisfaction of knowing that he was doing something significant at last, something for which he had been especially chosen by men so important even their names could not be known.

When he crossed the line from Ohio to Indiana, the routine of travel had mellowed him into a mood of meditation and memory. His mind traveled also. It went back to the farm, some hundred miles farther south, where he had first stalked his father in the barnyard and dreamed of being a famous Indian fighter, someone like George Custer had become. He was only ten when the war reached into those Indiana hills and changed him from a simple and carefree milker of cows and hoer of corn and picker of berries into a man of rage.

The call had gone out for soldiers. It had come from the man who then sat in the White House, a man who had grown up on a farm like his own, only a few counties away. His father and brother answered the call, walking to Loogootee to join the Fourteenth Indiana Regiment, the "Gallant Fourteenth."

He wanted to go with them. No one told him he was too young. Instead they said that someone must stay to watch after his mother and sister and to help his grandfather run the farm. He knew, however, that it was just the accident of his birth date that kept him on the farm as a boy while the real men went off to fight the war.

He stalked stiff-legged out into the apple orchard and flailed at the fallen apples with a stick, enraged that he should be left behind with women and old men and little children. Such rage had never visited him before, a visit like a flung rock in the back of the head.

He trembled not only with rage, but with fright as well. His life was being invaded by strange forces over which he had no control.

*　　*　　*

The forces continued.

People told him that the war would be short and his father and brother would be home soon. But they never returned. No one ever told him exactly how they died or whether they were killed together. Perhaps no one knew.

The force of grief now invaded. Grief, however, could be faced and backed down through the use of his newly spawned rage. At least rage was one invading force that he could in turn use to his own advantage.

The worst invader of all was the knowledge of his own mortality. Children so young usually learn only that others die. Farm boys, however, are surrounded by death. Randall already knew that others die. Now it came home to him that he, too, would die.

This body was his, but in the most important way of all, it wasn't his at all. Would it continue to exist? Over that, he had no control. There were powers everywhere, in all sorts of gray uniforms, that would try to take it from him. Finally, even if he could beat down every one of them, he would not win. God was always waiting.

God! The loving and terrible God. Randall never understood whether he should feel exalted or terrified because of the presence of God.

One preacher who came to the Red Oak Methodist Church talked about how much God loved him, how God even sent Jesus to die on the cross for him. The next preacher who rode that circuit thundered out how God was lying in wait to catch him in even the tiniest transgression, for the express purpose of burning him in the fires of hell forever.

Randall compromised. He believed it all. The presence of God terrified and comforted him at the same time. It was his life, but God ran it. As he grew, both the reality of fear and the need for forgiveness grew with him.

Then another strange force invaded him, trying to take over his will.

Girls and women, who before had simply been creatures to serve, like his mother, or creatures to ignore, like
his sister, were now mysteriously fascinating. He wanted
to be around them, to be close to them, to know what their
bodies looked like under all those clothes. Then he wanted
to do more than simply see those bodies. He yearned to
touch them, feel them, hold them, enter into them.

He was ashamed and disgusted. That was surely the
quickest road to hell any devil ever devised! He was determined to thrust all such thoughts from his mind. As soon
as he threw them out the front door, however, they came
sneaking in by the back. If he pushed them out the windows, they thudded back in down the chimney. It was his
body, but he did not even control its desires.

The wars of the world outside him and the wars of the
world inside . . . he was an unwilling soldier in them all.
Why couldn't they just have let him fight in the "war to
free the slaves" and let him skip these others, these wars
in which he was the slave? Death, lust, and God contended
with one another, and he was the battlefield. He alternately
cajoled and raged at those gray regiments, unsure whether
either approach had any affect.

Finally came the day his grandfather died, the day that
changed Randall from hothouse boyhood to icehouse
manhood. He was much too young. Such days should
come only after the timelessness of childhood and the
pressured days of adolescence.

Wartimes, however, jumble the days into a shapeless
pile. The pages are ripped from the book and stuffed into
a pail, to be pulled out one by one without sequence. Wars
produce stories, but they destroy narrative.

The iron wheels clicked over the rails through that
part of Indiana that separates the prairies from the hills.
Randall sat staring out the window through the rain, seeing the past rather than the present. He had seen these

same maple trees and honeysuckle vines and rainwashed gullies in a hundred other places. They were there as he traveled to Bloomington to the university. They flanked him as he went to Washington to join the army. Most of all they had surrounded him every day from his birth. They protected him with familiarity, but they shut down his imagination and closed off the horizon. Finally he would escape them, to the flatness of the plains to the west. Now, however, they brought back unbidden the memory of that humid, summer day when the windows could no longer be closed against his grandfather's screaming.

Something was growing inside Grandfather. That's what Doc Turner said. Nothing could be done about it. An alien force had invaded the old man, just as alien forces had invaded the boy. The force and the man struggled in the ultimate conflict. Grandfather was losing. His mind recalled stories no one else knew. His tongue spat out curses the old man had never used before. Finally his throat screamed out cries of rage and pain as he lay upon his bed.

One morning their mother sent Randall and his sister outside with an unaccustomed urgency.

"Work in the summer kitchen," she told them. "Clean out the stove."

He would normally have complained. Randall did not think of himself as kitchen help. After all, with his grandfather sick, he was doing all the farm chores. Why should he do kitchen work as well? His mother's wild and deep-bruised eyes spoke to him somehow, though. He knew she wanted him and his sister to be together.

They had just begun on the stove when the old man's terrible screams began to roar out the window at them, propelled by a new and terrifying force. The awful power of the total agony in that horrible screeching swept over them like a flash flood in a yellow dirt gully. They knew no one could put so much force into such cries and still live. A new and terrifying knowledge hammered at Randall.

In a few more puffs of breath, he would be the last male in the MacLane clan.

His sister attempted to plug her ears against the fearful sounds with her fingers, but nothing short of the grim reaper's scythe could cut them off. She grabbed the lid lifter from the stove's top ledge and began to beat on the stove with it, trying to drown out the noise of death with her own furious sounds of life. Hardly knowing what he was doing, Randall seized the poker. Together they pounded out a cacophony of rage and fear upon the poor stove.

They whacked and beat and drummed until their bodies ran with sweat, until their arms were heavier than the legs of the cowering stove, until they slumped exhausted down beside the object of their misplaced rage.

It took a few moments of straining lungs and pounding hearts before they realized that the entire area had grown silent. Their wild stove sounds had overawed the entire farm. No birds chirped. Even the cicadas had gone mute before their onslaught. Most of all, no more screams issued through the open windows of the house. The old man was gone, his cries of death defeated by two children and a stove. If there were a man left to that house, Randall knew that he was the man.

Their mother burst out of the house. She stood now, legs splayed, gaping at them, mouth open in astonishment, arms hanging like dead cornstalks at her sides. Randall saw her, longed to run to her, as an iron filing flies to a magnet. He wanted to fling himself into her arms, either to comfort or to be comforted.

Instead, he turned away. His face flushed red again, not from exertion this time, but from shame. He could not stand the screams of death, so he had tried to cover them over with his own sounds of mad life. He had raged against death, but death won anyway.

Even in the flush of humiliation and the sweat of summer rage, a strange sort of chill crept over him, as when a spider climbs your backbone when your hands are full.

Now he was a man. He could no longer play the child, beating on stoves to drown out the sounds of reality. That did not work. It only exhausted him when he needed his strength to withstand the invading forces.

From now on, he knew, his emotions would be reined in, under strict control. Only children struck out in futile rage. The men who held death back were those who planned, learned, calculated, controlled. He would be that kind of man.

Before the day was out, he had decided to read every book in the county. By the time he left for the university, he had.

Teachers marveled at his knowledge. Adults praised him for being so disciplined. Boys shunned him because he was different. Girls ignored him because he was "no fun." He did not go to dances or parties. He worked and he read.

He developed a reputation as the most dependable youth in the county. That particular reputation endeared him to no one—young or old. He did not understand why dependability should be a fence, walling him off from everyone from his sister and his fellow students at college to Colonel Seeley and Travis Hamilton.

He didn't understand it now, either, as the trains pulled him from Cincinnati to Indianapolis to St. Louis. Surely it was his reputation for dependability that had earned him the chance to take the message to Custer, so how could it be wrong?

A Time for Dreams to Come True

<hr/>

A small bird with a crimson head flew up beside his open train window. It seemed to peer in at him, but who can tell where a bird is looking? Randall could not call the bird by name, but he had never been a man of the woods and hills, even though he lived in them. He preferred to read about birds rather than look at them.

For a moment it raced the train, trilling its call. Then it peeled off south and winged over redbud and dogwood trees and disappeared in a cloud the length of a river. It was only then that he recognized its song: "Bloom-ing-*ton*! Bloom-ing-*ton*!"

For a moment he danced about with the mad notion of simply jumping off the train to follow the crimson-headed bird. He had not seen Bloomington's spring redbuds or its autumn oaks since he left for Washington and the army. Perhaps he would never be so close again.

The cool metal of the message box reminded him, however, that there was no time for side trips. When you are "the most dependable man in the county," you are entrusted with messages that keep you on the main road.

Randall thought about his reputation, steady as the *click-click-click* of the iron wheels beneath him upon the solid rail bed. Surely it was this reputation for reliability that had earned him his task. He was pleased at that thought. His work and planning and control had paid off. It was he who was taking the message to Custer.

It didn't occur to him at all that he might have been chosen more for his naïveté than for his intelligence, more for his restlessness in Washington than for his usefulness in the West. Restless men take on assignments, for the sake of change, that a more settled man would question.

Nor did he wonder if he might have been chosen because he would soon be a civilian and would have no reason to return to Washington, or because he was without family ties, so that no one would come looking if anything happened to him.

He assumed, as he had from the day his grandfather died, that he could win his way in the world by suppressing his emotions, silencing the voices of the invading forces that constantly sought to wrest his life away from his control. That others might use his strengths against him in the way that God and lust and death used his weaknesses against him was a foreign thought.

On her sixteenth birthday, at supper, his sister, Elizabeth, announced that she intended to wed Ernest Dorfmann.

Randall waited until she was at the well, near the summer kitchen, before he said anything to her.

She was leaning over to pull up the bucket as he approached. Her legs were strong. Her bosom and hips were full. She was more woman than girl. She'd grown up while he was reading books. He resented her womanhood, resented Ernest Dorfmann for wanting her.

He got there in time to help her lift the bucket out and rest it on the rim of the well. They held on to the bail together. Her cheeks were flushed. There was an enticing line of perspiration on her upper lip.

"Lizzie, I . . . this isn't a good time for you to marry. Mother's not well. I'm going to go off to study someday, maybe even next year. And Ernest . . . Lizzie, he's . . . well, he's not good enough for you."

She tossed her head.

"He can barely speak English. The Dorfmanns can't even come to church at Red Oak because they can't understand the preacher. They have to go to that Brethren Church where they do the services in German."

Still, Elizabeth did not speak.

"They don't have two pennies to rub together. Look at the place they live in. It's like a pigsty. He'll be lucky even to get some farmer to take him on as a hired hand. You'll end up living in a chicken coop."

His sister looked down, but she continued to hold on to the bail. She absently rubbed her bare toe in the mud at the base of the well, making a little line between them.

"I thought maybe we could live here," she said.

"Here? Whatever for? We can hardly feed ourselves. Ernest must eat like a horse, big as he is!"

"He is big," she said softly. "He can work hard, Randall. If we live here, I can take care of Mother, and when you go off to school, he can do the farmwork."

"Lizzie, I've pretty well promised Douglas Farmer that he can crop the place when I'm gone. He'll get twice out of those fields what Ernest can."

"If he gets twice, we'll still have the same, 'cause he'll take half."

She was tugging a little at the bail now, glancing at the house, making it clear that she had other things to do.

"Liz, I know I'm only two years older than you are, but I'm the man of this place. You can't get married without my permission. I'm not giving it. Ernest Dorfmann is just looking for a good deal. He figures if he marries you, he gets a place to live and an easy ride on the back of the wagon. That's not going to happen."

She gave a sudden jerk on the pail and pulled it free from his fist, spilling half of it over the front of her dress. The cotton molded quickly to her flesh, emphasizing the fullness of her breasts and belly. She started for the house, her bare feet slightly splayed.

"You aren't the man of this place," she threw back over her shoulder.

Her words were like smoldering cinders pulled from a fireplace and thrown quickly out a window.

"There's been no man here since Grandfather died. Ernest is twice the man you are. We don't care what you think, or what you say. We've already started, anyway, and Mother says we can live here and have the farm."

Randall watched her retreat, hips and bucket swaying. His eyes began to fuzz up. It looked like there were two of her. The house began to move, up and down, side to side. He had to hold on to the side of the well until his vision returned and he could see his way into the house.

His mother was sitting in the parlor, as she always did in the evenings. Her gray hair was pulled into a huge bun. His father had believed a woman should never cut her hair. Hers had not felt scissors from the day they had married.

She was staring at a picture of Jesus, surrounded by sheep, holding a lamb in his arms. He looked very young.

"Is it true," he asked softly, "about you telling Elizabeth she could marry Ernest and have the farm?"

She looked at the picture, not at him, as she spoke. He could barely hear her words.

"Randall, you're not a farmer. You don't need this place. I don't know what it is, but you need something else. Lizzie, she's the kind that needs to marry, raise a family."

"But . . . I've been the man here ever since . . . I ought to have something to say . . . and Ernest . . . what kind of man is he for her?"

His mother didn't speak, just stared at the picture of the Good Shepherd.

He wanted desperately to go to her, to fold his arms around her, or to have her fold her arms around him. Instead, he turned around and walked out and went to his room. He tore all the buttons off his shirt as he ripped it from his body and threw it on his bed.

Reverend Wilkey of Red Oak Church came to the house to do the wedding. All of Ernest's large guttural-sounding family were there, acting like pigs around the round table of food Elizabeth and his mother had prepared, pointing at his sister's belly and clapping Ernest on the back.

Randall felt like a stranger in his own house. He had known that he would leave someday. His mother was right, he was no farmer. But he hadn't expected to be pushed out.

His mother helped less and less around the house. As the days went by she spent more and more time just staring at the picture on the wall, waiting for the young shepherd.

His sister and her new husband acted like he wasn't even there, as though they lived by themselves. Elizabeth set a place for him at meals, but never spoke to him. Ernest took over the farm. He consulted Randall about nothing, not that they could have talked much anyway. He didn't even try sign language with Randall, unless he needed another set of muscles to wrestle a wagon or a sow. Then he would make wild and impatient gestures with his arms.

Randall couldn't stand the way his mother stared at the picture, couldn't stand the way Ernest stared at Elizabeth, couldn't stand the noises that came from their room at night, couldn't stand the way the farm began to blossom under Ernest's husbandry, couldn't stand to face Douglas Farmer and tell him he couldn't crop their land when he left because he had nothing to say about what happened to their land.

He didn't say good-bye to anyone. He just packed up his meager belongings and struck out for the new state college in Bloomington. He felt very free . . . and very frightened.

His mother died the following year. Reverend Wilkey wrote to tell him. She died of influenza, according to Doc Turner. Randall knew the real reason. She died because she was too weak to fight off the invading forces.

The men in gray coats had cut off her husband and firstborn son. The growing gray thing in her father-in-law had made him into a crazy, shouting lunatic and made her into a graying, fading woman. A man with gray in his mouth had moved in and taken away her daughter. Finally, the gray dreams of death, those dreams of promised rest, had seduced her away from herself, made her cough and sneeze and cry her life out bit by noxious bit.

She was poor and weak, and the invaders always beat you if you were poor and weak. She had gotten too old too soon, just as Randall stayed too young too long and missed the war. If you were too old or too young, the invaders got you, just as surely as if you were poor and weak.

MacLane felt the guilt of all those deaths upon his soul. Had he not been too young he could have gone to war and his father could have stayed home. He could have saved his brother in battle and they would have come home together. His mother would not have grown old and his grandfather would not have given in to the growing thing within.

If he had been older, wiser, stronger . . . he could have kept Ernest out of his sister and out of their house.

It was all because he was poor and weak and young, just as his mother died because she was poor and weak and old. He made his vow. Never again would he settle for being weak and poor and young. He would become rich and strong. He would do it in the only way he knew how. He would learn. The road to strength ran right down the middle of the brain.

No one in all of Gibson County understood why the farm boy read, why he wanted to go to school, to the university yet. What use was such an education in the real world? Randall, however, no longer lived in their real world, their world of crops and sows and babies. His was the world of head, not heart; of knowledge, not glands. If you had no money or position or talent, the one way left to strength was education. He knew that.

When he arrived in Bloomington, he simply announced to the registrar at Indiana University that he had come to learn.

"Do you wish to enroll in the classical or scientific course of study?"

"Well, I'm not sure. . . ."

"I see. Hmm . . . tell me of your education to this point. Perhaps that will help."

Randall puffed up a little. This was his chance.

"I've read every book in the county . . . Gibson County, that is."

"Well, that's very admirable, Mr. MacLane, but I think you'll have to take the admission tests."

"Fine."

Randall stood and waited. The registrar waited also. Finally he said, "You mean you're ready to take them now?"

The first tests were in Latin Grammar and Reader, Caesar, and Greek Grammar and Reader. Randall hardly knew that such languages existed. He sat glued to his chair. How could he get up and tell the registrar that he could not even read the exams? What would he do if they did not admit him to the university, if he could not learn?

It was then that a man with a slight twinkle in his eye stepped out through the open door to an inner office. He entered the room as a man of knowledge, as one who always knew what was happening in any room long before he got there. He walked over to the table where Randall sat, his pen deathly still.

"My name is Wylie," he said to Randall.

He took the papers from the table and handed them to the registrar.

"I think there's been a mistake. I believe Mr. MacLane has come to enroll in the Preparatory Department. Please give him the appropriate exam paper."

Without another word he returned to his office.

The registrar presented Randall with a new set of papers—orthography, reading, writing, arithmetic, English grammar, and geography.

He failed arithmetic. The man named Wylie said it was all right.

"I'm sure Mr. MacLane will acquit himself well here."

He turned to the registrar again.

"Please help Mr. MacLane find inexpensive lodgings and appropriate work."

He didn't ask Randall if he needed work; he just knew.

In years to come, Randall would think often of the kindness and calmness of the president of the university. He would wonder from what source such qualities came, and why they never seemed to be a part of his own life.

Before the year was over, Randall had worked his way out of the Preparatory Department and into the regular classes. When he was a senior he won the first-place prizes in both the languages he could not read when he came.

He did not protest the elimination of the Preparatory Department, however, two years later, in 1870, even though he could not have entered college without it. He did regret the decision to end "the Preps," as the students called it, but he was too busy to give it much thought.

Like many of the other students, he worked hard to earn the three dollars a week for his room and board. In addition there was the daily round. Each day started with required religious services. Then there were three classes each day, religion lectures every Sunday afternoon, church on Sunday morning, and study . . . always study.

He had gone to the university to overcome the handicaps of youth and poverty and weakness, but even as a student, he found that victory still lay beyond. He was still among the most youthful, in terms of disciplined study.

Although the university discouraged any of the students having much money to spend, everyone knew the difference between the rich and the poor. The affluent did not work, even in the summers. In those vacation sessions, they traveled to Europe, returning to college in mid-September with tales of places Randall could only read about.

The only armor he could wear to mask the weakness of his inexperience and poverty was aloofness. He went his own way, kept his own counsel. He was polite, but accepted no friends.

He declined to recite orally, unless specifically called upon. His wide and undisciplined reading had given him a feel for written language, however, so he knew that his written exams and papers were equal to those of the best students.

If there were one thing that united the student body, it was the rain. In the fall and in the spring, just as classes started for the first and third terms, the rain clouds camped over Bloomington for days at a time, waiting until the students dared set foot outside the shelter of the buildings, then dumping on them with gloomy glee.

Even in this, however, MacLane stood apart. Every other student complained about the rain; he went walking in it.

He did not tell the others how he felt. He was not sure himself why he liked the rain. Was it recall of the feelings of adventure he had when he trailed his father through the barnyard? Would the rain have drowned out his grandfather's dying cries? He didn't know. Nor did he imagine that twenty-five years later he would sit in the jail-house in Middle Bend and think about the rain on the Indiana hills and find a strange sort of comfort in the memory. But then, the rain has always been a friend to solitary men.

Through the first three years in Bloomington, the study was enough, an end in itself.

The other students went to school with an eye to the future. They were to be ministers, lawyers, physicians, merchants. Those whose fathers owned land could return to it as farmers and gentlemen. Teachers, dentists, professors, bankers, editors, druggists . . . as Randall considered the futures of his classmates, he became uncomfortably aware of the gulf that separated them from him.

He had gone to college to become one with the strong and powerful and mature. No matter how strong he became, however, through his ability to work harder or accomplish more, no matter how powerful through the accumulation of knowledge, he was at one with no one.

In his last year, there came an answer to his unconscious prayer. A "Department of Military Science" was established. He was the only fourth-year student enrolled in it. Since it was new, in its first year only a basic course for freshmen was provided. But MacLane knew this was his chance. He could not enter into the sedentary life of a lawyer or teacher. He had no stomach for medicine, no interest in business, no money to get himself started.

The army was drying up after the war, but it was what he wanted. There were still Indians to fight, battles to win.

He threw himself into his military course with a zeal that amazed all who knew him. He spoke out, volunteered, grabbed the front at all times.

Major Hooper was the one and only professor in the Department of Military Science. A less jaded officer would have noticed MacLane's drivenness. If Major Hooper noticed, he did not care. His career was almost over. He had nothing to gain and little to lose. His one real ambition was to get out of Bloomington as soon as his pension was secured.

Who knew why Hooper recommended MacLane for a commission? Perhaps it was just to spite his superiors. Very few young men became lieutenants in the army that year, but Randall MacLane was one of those few. At the time that was all that seemed to matter.

A few of his professors and fellow students questioned Randall's desire to enter the army. It was a strange choice for an independent and solitary man. He had roomed with the same family throughout his stay at the university, but even they did not feel they really knew him. President Wylie wondered how he would do in an organization where orders must be obeyed whether or not they made sense. The army was always close quarters. Men depended on one another not only for battle support but for morale, for friendship, for meaning. How would a loner like MacLane fit in?

Randall himself, however, sensed what military outsiders never understand. The hierarchy and order and unquestioning obedience of the army are camouflage and protection. If you don't even know how to say hello, the military manual tells you how to do it, when to do it, and even to whom to do it, complete with hand signals. The military lets a man be as solitary as he wishes on the inside, because he never has to think about who he is on the outside. He can look at the shoulder of his uniform and learn all he needs to know about who he is as he relates to other people.

*   *   *

Finally now, after three years of putting up with Colonel Seeley and the insufferable, oppressive Washington humidity, he was headed west, to dry air and clear skies and enough room and few enough people for a man to take off his uniform. Now came the promise of action, an arena in which strength was measured by will rather than by wealth, by ability instead of age.

Perhaps now even God would let him be himself. Surely God owed him something by now, after all those chapel services and Sunday observances in Bloomington, and denying himself and worshiping every Sunday in Washington, the only man in uniform in the little Methodist chapel.

"God," he prayed, "I know I'm not supposed to ask for anything for myself. And I'm not asking for safety or anything like that. But, please, God . . ."

He did not know how to finish. He did want to ask for something for himself, but he had no idea what it was. The click of the wheels of the train on the tracks kept rhythm with his unvoiced prayer all the way to St. Louis.

Now he had to hand off the blue envelope to his contact there and get that boat up the river.

The message to Custer—that was all that mattered now. The time for thinking about the past was over. The past had been a time of preparation, but for what he did not know. Now he sensed that the time had come to know.

More Indians Than You Ever Imagined

Delivering the blue envelope to the man in St. Louis was anticlimatic at best. He was easy enough to find. Randall simply went to the Mississippi Palisades Hotel, the address given on the envelope, and asked for Mr. Sidney Johnson, whose name was written in parentheses beside the name of the hotel. The clerk checked his list and sent MacLane up to Room 311.

A bellman had been standing by. As soon as Randall asked for Mr. Sidney Johnson, the wiry little man scampered off to the end of the lobby and spoke hurriedly with a large man wearing a florid cravat and half chomping, half smoking a very large cigar. The man heaved himself up out of his chair as Randall started for the stairs.

MacLane had knocked twice on the door of 311 when the man from the lobby came puffing around the corner of the hallway and hurried up to him.

"I'm Mr. Johnson," he announced. "You got something for me?"

"Well, uh," stammered Randall, "uh, I have something for Mr. Johnson, but, uh, I . . ."

"You MacLane?" the man asked gruffly from around the stump of his cigar.

"Why, yes, I am," Randall answered. He had not expected the man to know his name.

"That figures," said the man, patting his bulging belly, as if reassuring it that all was well. "Look, you don't know if I'm Johnson. What did they tell you about me, how to recognize me? Nothing, right?"

"Well, uh, yes, that's right. They didn't say anything about you."

It struck Randall only then that it was a curious oversight.

"So, you can't recognize me, but I know who you are. I also know you have a blue envelope for me. That means I'm your man."

It made sense to Randall. He handed over the envelope.

The man ripped off the end of it with hamlike fingers, pulled the letter out, and began to read. Immediately his face reddened and his eyes took on a feverish glare.

"Hot damn," he exclaimed. "God Almighty."

Sweat broke out onto Mr. Sidney Johnson's florid face. He actually trembled so much the paper rattled in his huge hand. Randall was sure he was going to smash it into a ball just because his hands seemed to have a life of their own. Johnson looked up and right into Randall's eyes, but the young soldier knew the man had no idea he was even there.

"Hot damn," he whispered once again, to someone far beyond either MacLane or the hotel wall.

Whether Mr. Johnson was pleased or shocked was impossible to tell, but there was no doubt he was affected.

Without another word to MacLane, he dug into the pocket of his vest, pulled out his key, went into Room 311 and swung the door shut behind him.

Randall stood there for a moment, unsure what to do.

He looked around to see if anyone could possibly have seen them. He felt rather foolish and didn't want an audience. He saw no one.

Well, maybe Mr. Johnson had no time for him, even to say thank you, but Randall had no time for Mr. Johnson, either. There were more important things to do. He almost ran back to the river to make arrangements for the rest of his journey.

The trip up the Mississippi revived MacLane. Not only was he getting closer to Custer, but he had never before ridden on a paddleboat. The boat and the river and the towns along the banks intrigued him. He liked the sense of going somewhere against the current.

After the river, however, came waiting and frustration and anxiety. His time was running out. Why did he have to see the strange Mr. Johnson in St. Louis when he could easily have saved whole days by going through Chicago?

To make matters worse, no one knew exactly where Custer was. MacLane had to make his way from the Mississippi to the Missouri to the Platte. The waters got lower and the boats got smaller.

The only transport up the Platte was two little shallow-draft boats taking supplies to Custer and Terry. Their captains were afraid the river would dry up behind them if they went too far, so they decided to wait at Fort McPherson. If the army did not come for the supplies there, the boats would return downriver rather than risk being left literally high and dry.

Randall was forced to use his special papers to commandeer a horse from the reluctant fort commander so he could start across the plains with his message.

No one at Fort McPherson had any idea where Custer was. Maybe even General Phil Sheridan in his Chicago headquarters of the Military Division of the Missouri did not know Custer's whereabouts. He was somewhere farther north, in the Military Department of Dakota, trying to chase Crazy Horse back onto the reservation; that was the best information available.

"Yep. General Terry's got his whole damn command out on the plains takin' care a' them redskins," the sutler at the fort told him. "That damn Crazy Horse acts like he owns the whole damn country. Well, if anyone can put him in his place, Custer's the one, you can bet on that, an' don't think Terry don't know it."

MacLane felt a sudden tightening of his chest, a stiffening in the muscles of his neck, an immediate sensing that his time had finally come. Unbidden, a scene from his college days came into his mind. He saw himself sitting in the beginning Greek class, the professor at the slate board. The professor had written two words on the board, then stuffed his hands into the pockets of his perpetually chalk-dusted coat.

"Now, gentlemen," he said, "there are two Greek words for time. One is *chronos,* from which words like our 'chronological' come. It means the simple passing of the minutes, days, years. But there is also *kairos.* A *kairos* time is when all is ready, the moment when meaning comes. In the Bible it is translated as 'the fullness of time.' When all the preparations have been made in *chronos,* then comes *kairos.*"

MacLane was sure that for him this was a *kairos* moment. He would find Custer and deliver the message. That was the fulfillment of his time, for which all until then had been but preparation.

Strangely, he didn't even think about what might be in the message. That made no difference to him. All that mattered was who carried that thin metal box, and the one who opened it.

What would happen when the message was delivered, when the time was fulfilled?

He saw pictures in the waves of heat hovering above the plains grass. . . .

*   *   *

Custer opened the case, took one look at the message, and then clapped Randall on the shoulder.

"Well done, MacLane," he said. "From now on, I want you at my side every moment."

He waved his hat at his troops, then wheeled his horse and rode west, Randall at his side, Indians scattering in respect before them, blue-coated troopers riding in their dust.

Custer opened the case. His face fell.

"So you alone had the courage to bring this to me," he said to Randall, his mournful eyes avoiding the younger man.

Custer opened the case. His eyes sought Randall's. They were clear and pale and blue.

"You may have saved this entire nation, MacLane," he said, his voice trembling with emotion.

As his thighs began to chafe and his bottom ached, the pictures faded. Randall's enthusiasm and imagination began to drag. His month was almost up. He was in strange country, traveling by himself on horseback, unsure of when he would meet hostile Indians or where he could get help.

Actually, the Indian danger was minimal. Almost all the Indians who had gone out from the agencies to join Sitting Bull and Crazy Horse were already in place. Randall did not know that, however. All he knew was that Terry and Crook and Gibbon and all the other generals of the Department of the Dakota were trying to close in on that large and roving band of Indians that was determined to have one more fling at the old-fashioned life of the plains before the white men sealed off the Indian past forever. Custer and his Seventh Cavalry were with Terry. Somewhere in the vicinity of the Powder and Rosebud and Yellowstone and Bighorn rivers they would come together.

MacLane worked his way up the Platte. He had to stay close to the rivers because he had no guide. He needed to change horses as often as possible to make speed, but the only army post between Fort McPherson and Fort Laramie was the Sidney Barracks. It was too far from the river to take the chance. So he dragged into Fort Laramie, tired and sore and with a horse to match. There he got a fresh mount to take him on to Fort Fetterman.

At Fetterman he was once again required to break his low profile and use his special papers to commandeer the only Indian scout in the place, a happy old Crow who was drunk more than he was sober. But he knew the country into which they would ride, and he had no love either for Sitting Bull's Hunkpapa Sioux or Crazy Horse's Oglalla Sioux. He wasn't good company; his only interests were drinking and telling tall tales. Randall was disgusted by the drinking and not interested in the stories. At least he was not alone, and the man did seem to know the country.

From Fetterman they struck cross-country to the Powder River, up the Powder to avoid the Big Horn Mountains, all the way into Montana territory. It was at that point the old Crow decided it wasn't wise for him to get any closer to the Sioux. He decided to look up relatives instead. He pointed MacLane west toward the Tongue and Rosebud rivers and disappeared.

Randall wasn't sorry to see him go. He didn't want to be held back by someone who knew the way. He had a job to do, and he was going to do it. It was June 22, 1876, and he had only three more days before his commission ran out and he would leave the army.

He struck out west, always bending north when faced with a choice, hoping that route would bring him across General Terry's line of march. He knew from what he had learned at Fort Fetterman that Terry and Custer were supposed to be angling southwest from Fort Abraham Lincoln in Dakota territory. Gibbon was moving east along the Yellowstone from Fort Ellis in Montana, and Crook had left

Fetterman only a few days before. Those Dakota, Montana, and Wyoming columns were to converge in the Bighorn River area, having swept the "hostiles" ahead of them.

His first intention had been to follow Crook. The one great help his Crow guide had given, though, was to insist that they move northeast, away from Crook's route. The Crow was sure they could intercept Terry and Custer before they reached the Tongue River. He was wrong about that, but as it turned out, Crook's march had been halted by the northern Cheyenne. Randall did not know it, but that particular route to Custer and the safe fulfillment of his mission was closed off.

He rode from first light in the morning until darkness overtook him at night. He didn't want to risk a fire, so those three days were even more miserable than the rest of the trip had been. It was an unnecessary misery. He could have built a bonfire every night and not been any more obvious to the Indians than he already was. He was so totally ignorant of Indians and the plains, however, that he thought he was as hidden as he had been in his hill-country barnyard, stalking his father in the rain.

Saddle-sore, footsore, hungry in every pore, he plodded on, like some long-distance runner who has forgotten he's in a race but keeps going because his legs cannot stop. He was in the territory he had longed all his life to see, but he was not really seeing it. There was no time for that. Besides, his eyes were usually turned around to view the pictures on the inside, in his head.

He rode for miles automatically, with no real awareness of what was around him. Except as a general exercise in caution, he even forgot about the threat of hostile Indians. He had one thing to do, and time was running out on that. He could see the country later. Right now he had a message for Custer.

By June 24 he began spotting signs that there was some sort of activity involving a lot of people and horses on ahead to the west. Even his untrained eye could see that.

"Even a blind man could see it," he muttered.

The grass was eaten down for as far around as he could see. The ground was rutted by travois poles in what looked like a thousand narrow, little railroad tracks. Most ominous of all was a pall of dust that seemed to ride the western horizon.

MacLane was both puzzled and startled by all these signs. He knew that the plains Indians were different from the eastern Indians he had learned about as a boy. Washington was alive with the stories of Custer and the other Indian "tamers" in the aftermath of the Civil War. Nothing he had thought, read, or heard, however, had prepared him for the idea of thousands of Indians gathered in one place. Of course, in that he was not alone.

Randall didn't know whether the pall of dust was coming toward him or moving away from him. He knew it was getting closer, but he assumed that might be only because of his own efforts at pursuit. He was sure that one man on horseback could travel faster than thousands of Indians with their families, moving their homes and possessions by travois.

He was wrong again. The plains Indians were used to traveling great distances at incredible speeds, which mystified even experienced cavalry troops. As tired as he and his horse were, MacLane would never have caught up to them until they decided to go into camp. Once again, however, his ignorance proved no problem. The dust cloud was neither coming nor going.

It did not even occur to MacLane that he could turn around or try to avoid the mass of Indians he knew was ahead. Terry and Crook and Gibbon were converging on the Indians. Whether they had arrived as yet was immaterial. He had a message for Custer. Where the Indians were, Custer would not be far away.

On Reno Hill

———◆◆◆———

On the morning of June 25 MacLane was on the move even before the first gray light of dawn made it possible to see the ground beneath him. He sat slouched in the saddle, letting his weary mount pick its way at a slow walk over the rutted ground. Although every joint and muscle in his body ached, his spirit was reviving. There seemed to be a sense of anticipation in the predawn quiet around him. He was sure this would be the day when his mission was accomplished. Once again, he was wrong.

As the horizon turned from ash gray to dull lavender, he began to push his horse along as fast as the weary beast was willing to travel. He was making progress. He knew it. He could feel it.

Yet as the hours went by he caught sight of no one. All he could vouch for was that the dust cloud was getting larger. By noon he was hungry, had already put in eight hours in the saddle, and the adrenaline on which he was running was dry as a squealing wagon axle.

It was then that he topped a rise and saw the Little

Bighorn River, a short section where the river meandered on an east-west course instead of its usual north-south route. Not more than a mile ahead, a troop of cavalry was making its way west, away from him. Another troop was riding north, but it was two miles or more away already. He urged his horse down to the river, desperately seeking a place to ford.

The river crossings were the most difficult part of the journey for him. He had not yet learned how to read a ford. He had tried to cross the Tongue at a spot both too wide and too deep and barely got back to the bank with his life and his gear intact. Now he and his horse were both almost to the end of their strength. He knew he dared take no chances, but the troops were so close! Yet they were moving away from him, always out of reach. . . .

The horse soldiers must have crossed the river, though, so there had to be a ford. He decided it had to be upstream from him, since the northerly force was over twice as far away as the troop riding west. He turned his horse north, resigned to finding a decent ford before he could join the men in blue, in uniforms so dusty that the blue now looked gray. A line from an old church song came into his head, and he hummed it over and over, "One more river to cross, one more river to cross . . ."

Finally, he found the spot where the horse soldiers had made their ford, not far from where a small creek mysteriously petered out before it reached the river. He plunged his horse on, although he knew that it was useless to expect it to go any faster than the weary pace it now set. Into the water and over to the western side. Then there came the most important decision.

With which column did Custer ride? MacLane had no idea, so he did the logical thing. He rode for the soldiers he could reach more quickly. The two troops were bound to join together again sooner or later, and Custer was as likely to be with the one as the other. There was another reason for his decision. He had backtracked along the river to find the ford, which meant he was closer to the line of march taken by the soldiers headed north. Now they were long gone from sight. The ground was so badly rutted and tracked by Indians as well as cavalrymen that he was not sure his untrained eye could find them. Better to follow the soldiers headed west, he decided, since they would always have the river on their left. He could use it as a guide. If he rode along the riverbank and saw no sign of the cavalrymen fording back across, he was sure to find them.

As it turned out, he only needed to follow the report of the rifles. He had hardly crossed the river when he first heard them, a strange, sharp sound. It was not much like the firing range, more like the sound of corn popping in the heavy iron kettle when he had swung it back and forth on its hinged, iron hook over the fireplace as a boy. He rode down into a small, shallow, angled valley and followed the terrain as he listened to the firing.

In the two minutes it took him to reach the valley's end and ride up the hill there, the world had changed. He rode out onto a scene that not even the maddest artist could have painted. The entire horizon was smeared in one long swipe by the cloud of dust, now so near that he could smell it. It was like walking into a garden where only the flowers had been forgotten.

At last he could see the reason for the dust. Hundreds of Indians filled all the plain before him, riding left and right, back and forth, in no pattern that he could discern. They looked like honeybees trying to swarm and unable to find the queen. Here and there he could make out clumps of tepees and more Indians scurrying on foot around them. The dust cloud hovered far beyond the Indians and tepees that he could see, so he assumed there must be three or four times as many as were in his sight. Years later he learned that even that estimate was much too low.

He was drawn like a moth to flame. He had dreamed of battles with the Indians all his life. Now he was going to see one, be in it, just as he thought his army life and his chance for adventure were over. All because of the message to Custer. He blessed the day he had met the congressman.

He slapped the flank of his mare and cantered forward. Even the horse seemed caught up in the excitement, pricking up its ears and loping along with more energy than it had shown in days. He wished he had a sword to draw.

The possibility that he might be in trouble did not even graze his mind. In that, he was much like the man he was trying to find.

He hadn't ridden a hundred yards, however, before he saw that some of the soldiers were in trouble. On the far side of the river was a small group of troopers. They had dismounted and had taken shelter in a little wooded area. They were firing at Indians who were riding at them from every side. They hit their targets with surprising regularity, but it made no difference at all. They were simply overwhelmed.

MacLane splashed through a creek and continued along the river, not following its convolutions but simply letting it guide him. He came almost at once to a chain of little humpbacked hills, one following another, like pigs in a line looking for their mother. He rode up onto the first one and saw, just about a mile away, a whole hilltop of bluecoats. He could not see them well, but he could tell they had taken up a defensive position and were under heavy attack from a large number of Indians that seemed content to fire on them from a distance.

The hill was not surrounded, in part at least because another column of cavalry was coming from the east, apparently to relieve the men on the hill. They were galloping in a column of fours. Randall made a quick count and came up with around one hundred and twenty. That was obviously the place to be. He headed for the hill on as direct a line as he could lay out.

He arrived just after the head of the column rode up onto the hill. No one seemed to notice MacLane; he was just another white man, which meant he could be ignored. The attitude seemed to be: "Watch out for the Indians, but every white man can watch out for himself."

A wild and haggard-looking man, wearing the uniform of a cavalry major, staggered down the hill toward the column. A bandanna was tied around his head. MacLane could not tell whether it covered a wound or was there just to protect him from the sun. He grabbed the bridle of the lead horse, on which was mounted a rather mild-looking, large-featured captain.

"For God's sake, Benteen, halt your command and help me. I've lost half my men," the major cried.

"Where's Custer?" asked the captain.

"I have no idea. He headed downstream. God, he has five companies with him. Surely he heard our firing. I expected him to be coming to our relief by now."

The major's arms flailed about as he talked, while his eyes roved wildly over the terrain.

The sound of Custer's name sent a jolt through MacLane. Custer was not here, but he was not far. Perhaps he would see the famous general any moment, leading his troops upstream, flying along to sweep the Indians out of the way and coming to the aid of his subordinates. They obviously needed all the help they could get.

All around was confusion. Men were digging up breastworks with any tool they could find, but there seemed to be no plan, no organization to it. Some dug here, some there, with no definite perimeter and no clear angles for defensive fire in case they should be attacked. A few of the men lay behind horse carcasses. From the looks of the wounds to the horses, MacLane figured the soldiers must have shot the horses themselves. Some men were gnawing on cold biscuits and jerky as though nothing else was happening. The wounded lay all over the place rather than in an organized aid station.

No one was on picket duty. Quite a few men were watching the land around them, but, again, the scene was one of disorganization. There might be a dozen watching in one direction and none in another. No one even seemed aware of the little band being wiped out across the river, although it must have been part of the very troop that was now digging in on the hill.

The captain dismounted.

"How's your ammunition, Reno?" he asked the major.

"Terrible. He sent us out there against that village, like it was the Washita all over, but this time they came right at us, thousands of them. We tried to hold them off, but there were so many of them. We got into that little woods across the river, but they were all around. We retreated to here, and we lost men and ammunition with every step. The brazen savages, riding right up to us, firing right into us!"

The major's arms flailed ever more wildly as he talked, like a windmill gone berserk. His speech was slightly slurred, as if he were talking with a swollen tongue.

The captain turned to the man at his elbow.

"Sergeant," he bellowed, as though the man were a hundred yards away. "Divide the ammunition of our command with that of Major Reno. See that each man has at least half his normal ration. Then have Captain Weir station the men in defensive positions by company. The pack train should be coming up soon. When it gets here, fill out each man's ration from the ammunition packs on the train."

"Yes, sir," replied the sergeant, with a perfunctory salute, turning immediately to his task.

MacLane felt he needed to report. The obvious officer to report to was the major called Reno. He was clearly the superior in rank. The captain called Benteen was the man who seemed to know what he was doing, however. He decided to split the difference.

Striding up to where they stood, he snapped to attention and pulled out his best parade-ground salute, aiming it at the general area between them.

"Lieutenant MacLane, of Washington, sir. I have been sent with a message for General Custer."

The two officers gaped. You would think a horse just spoke to them, Randall thought.

"From where?" asked Benteen.

"Washington, sir. The capital."

Belatedly, MacLane wondered if he should be telling anyone else about the source of the message he had for Custer. It was not, after all, a message from military headquarters sent through military channels. He had not considered, however, that he might not be able to approach Custer directly and would have to explain to others what he was doing here.

"Why are you not in uniform, Lieutenant?"

Randall had the impression Captain Benteen asked the question simply because it occurred to him, not because he was really interested. As Benteen talked, his head constantly swiveled, scanning the horizon for something he did not seem to be sure he would recognize even if he saw it.

Now MacLane was in a quandary. How much should he reveal? He decided to fall back on a soldier's best friend.

"I was ordered to travel as a civilian, sir."

He did not say from whom the orders came. He knew a captain would assume they were military and came from higher than himself, so there would be no point in pursuing it, especially since under the circumstances he had considerably more important things on his mind.

"Well, it looks like you're going to have to wait awhile," the captain said.

His mouth was open to say more, but he was interrupted by the sound of firing downstream.

"Perhaps it won't be long after all," he corrected himself.

Then he turned his back on MacLane and bellowed at the nearest sergeant.

"Sergeant Culbertson, bring the officers up here. I'll need to talk with them."

Randall was fascinated by how quickly the captain had taken command of the hill, even though Major Reno was already there and outranked him. Reno was clearly shaken by what had happened to him and his men. Randall knew few officers, however, who would not resent the way Benteen took over, and who would not do something to reestablish their own authority, even if they were not fit for it. The major, however, seemed relieved.

Randall did not bother to ask to be dismissed but swung up onto his horse and fell in beside Culbertson as he rode down the line. The hill was large and the troopers were all over. Contacting the officers was a riding job. Besides, a cavalryman simply did not feel right walking.

"Do you think General Custer is coming back to relieve the command, Sergeant?"

The sergeant looked Randall up and down. Randall knew he didn't look like much to this rough veteran of Indian wars.

"Who the hell are you?" Sergeant Culbertson asked abruptly.

Randall tried to stiffen his spine and his voice as he answered.

"I'm Lieutenant MacLane, from Washington," he said. "The capital," he added, since no one around seemed to understand where he was talking about when he said he came from Washington.

"Beggin' your pardon, sir," said Sargeant Culbertson, with a casual swipe of a salute. "Just didn't recognize you as an officer."

Randall could not tell if the man intended to be insulting or not. He certainly didn't seem very repentant, despite his words. Just then an agitated-looking lieutenant mounted his horse, although he was now no farther than fifteen yards from them, and spurred his mount, although he immediately had to pull it up again to come to a sliding halt in front of them.

"What's the word, Culbertson? I can hear the firing. Are we going after them?"

"I don't know, Lieutenant Varnum," replied the sergeant, tipping his hat back and scratching his head in a move vaguely reminiscent of a salute. "All I know is Captain Benteen wants you and the other officers up there with him."

"Damn it, man, what's going on? It sounds like Custer's in it up to his ears. We don't have time for meetings. Let's get going."

"Yes, sir. I got to get goin' and tell the rest of the officers about the meeting."

The sergeant continued on his rounds. Varnum slumped into his saddle and began walking his horse toward what had become the impromptu command post. He made a loose, blowing noise with his lips. Randall rode along beside him.

"I just got here," he said to the other officer.

He decided to dispense with the salute and the news of his message and where he had come from. None of them seemed appropriate or helpful now.

"My name's Randall MacLane. I'm a lieutenant, too. Is General Custer in some sort of trouble? I understood from the major and Captain Benteen that the attack took place here and General Custer was on his way back to relieve this troop."

Lieutenant Varnum looked the thin, young man up and down with a glance Randall was getting used to but that still worried him. Did he look that out of place?

"First off, Lieutenant, you'd be better off not referring to Custer as a general around Reno and Benteen. That was only a brevet rank, good only in the big war. They resent that he was ever a general. They resent everything about him. Second, why should Custer relieve this bunch?

Look how quiet it is out there now. The Indians have hightailed it, but there's still a lot of shooting going on downstream. That's Custer down there, and from the sound of it, they're fighting every bloodthirsty redskin in the territory. If any relieving is going to be done, we'd better get to it ourselves."

They were almost back to where Benteen and Reno waited for the officers. Two others, Captain Weir and Lieutenant Edgerly, fell in beside them as they rode. Varnum introduced them quickly to Randall, referring to him only by name and title. He acknowledged them automatically, but half his mind was in Washington and half of it was downstream with Custer. It did not seem possible that Custer might be in trouble, might even be killed, but according to Varnum, that was the way it was.

The officers stood in a little semicircle in front of Major Reno and Captain Benteen. The captain got right to business.

"The redskins have fallen back for now, but there's no telling what they'll do next. Has the ammunition been divided up evenly?"

He looked around the crescent of officers, his gaze lingering on Randall for a moment, as if still trying to figure out what he was doing there and if he was going to be any trouble. An officer's first thought, whenever confronted by a new soldier, is, Is he trouble? There was an indifferent murmur from the other officers, acknowledging that the ammunition was now divided.

"All right," continued Benteen, "hold your positions for now. The pack train should be here soon. We can get more ammunition and reassess the situation then."

"But what about the firing?"

The speaker was still another lieutenant. Benteen flushed and spat out his answer.

"There's been firing, and there will be more. Damn it, we're in a battle. Who can tell what about the sound of firing?"

The lieutenant broke in, not angry, but almost pleading, his hands open wide, palms up.

"But, sir, that's a big engagement. Custer must be in trouble. I asked Lieutenant Hare if he could hear it when we were standing over there, and he could. Good God, you know how hard of hearing he is. If he can hear it, there's something going on."

MacLane guessed that the man standing to the speaker's left must be Lieutenant Hare. He seemed to be listening hard to the conversation but hearing very little of it.

"Damn it, Godfrey," Benteen replied, "I don't care what Luther Hare can hear or not hear. We don't have ammunition, and we can't be riding off until the pack train gets up here. Besides, we're all under Major Reno's command now. He's the senior officer here."

The major jerked a little, his red bandanna riding up on his head and then falling back around his ears. The announcement that he was in charge seemed to catch him by surprise.

"Uh, yes," he stuttered. "We have to wait for the pack train. And I've got to get some men and go down to the riverbank to recover Lieutenant Hodgson's body and get water for the wounded. Yes, we'll wait."

He made his decision as though agreeing with Captain Benteen rather than exercising authority as the officer in charge. Immediately he strode away and began to shout out names, gathering up what seemed to Randall to be a rather large troop for a body recovery party.

The captain called Weir trotted after Reno, with his own Lieutenant, Edgerly, behind him. For some reason, as though his body had decided what to do without consulting his mind, Randall went after them. They looked like a line of crows working down a trail of spilled corn.

"Major," Captain Weir called to Reno's back, "I'd like to request permission to move D Company down toward the sound of the guns."

"Permission denied," Reno called back over his shoulder.

Weir, Edgerly, and Randall almost collided as the captain pulled up short.

"Damn," muttered Lieutenant Edgerly. "What the hell do we do now?" He looked off downstream.

"I think the firing is slacking off," he continued.

"I'm going to ride down that way by myself, to see what I can see," said Captain Weir. "Reno denied me permission to move D Company, but he didn't say I couldn't be my own scout."

"I want to go with you," Randall said quickly.

"No, you'll get into trouble with Reno and Benteen."

"I'm almost out of the army, anyway," Randall replied. "I have a message for Custer. I'm not concerned with what Reno and Benteen think."

Captain Weir carefully pulled at his sweat-stained hat as he looked off toward the mountains of dust. Then, almost formally, he addressed Randall.

"I'm going to ride down through there. You stay with Lieutenant Edgerly. When the lieutenant sees where I'm headed, he's going to think Reno gave me permission after all. He was far enough behind me when Reno said I couldn't move D Company that he couldn't hear. So he's going to move the company parallel with me but over there behind that hill. If you go with him, you'd better buckle on a sword. Do you understand what I'm saying to this young man, Edgerly?"

"Yes, sir!" Edgerly replied.

He did not salute, but there was attention in his voice. He grinned at MacLane. Randall grinned back. This was what he was here for. Suddenly, he felt at one with these men he had barely met. It was a rare feeling for the solitary young man. It filled him.

A Rage to Deliver

MacLane and Edgerly hurried back to the D Company troopers, trying to look unsuspicious, automatically moving in a wide arc around the area where Captain Benteen still stood.

"Benteen's got plenty to keep busy with, and Reno's occupied with getting Lieutenant Hodgson's body back, so they probably won't notice us," said Edgerly. "Too bad Reno didn't worry more about Hodgson's body while it was still alive, and the rest of the men, too."

His voice was as bitter as old persimmon pudding. Randall wanted to ask more about the harried major, but there wasn't time for that.

Edgerly moved quietly among the men of D Company, telling them to mount up and follow him without noise and without dust. Silence was important, more for outwitting their own officers than for the Indians. The top of the hill seemed unnaturally quiet now. Even the groans and the steady, quiet cursing of the wounded sounded loud against the background thuds of thousands of horses' hooves a long way off.

Randall took Captain Weir's advice and gladly buckled on a cavalry sword that a wounded man had discarded. It completed something about him, but he wasn't sure what.

MacLane rode beside Lieutenant Edgerly as they walked their horses slowly down the hill and out of the direct sight of Captain Benteen. Major Reno could have noticed them from where he was advancing on Lieutenant Hodgson's body. He seemed, however, to be looking inward.

Suddenly the unnatural quiet was shattered. Indian sharpshooters had been lying in wait, hoarding their ammunition or, in the case of those armed with bows, waiting for the soldiers to get close enough so they could use their weapons. They now opened up on Reno and his men. One of the troopers fell immediately in a tangle of empty canteens he had slung around his neck.

"Damn!" Lieutenant Edgerly burst out. "Well, it's tough on Reno, but it gives us some cover. Benteen will have to take care of that. We've got other fish to fry."

Then he called over his shoulder.

"All right, then, men. Follow me. We're going to hook up with the captain and go get Custer."

There were a few muttered affirmations.

"Damn right!"

"Let's get to it!"

"Now let's do them redskins!"

Mostly, though, the men simply set their hats and their jaws. They checked their weapons, then silently and automatically began to spread out into a skirmish line.

Captain Weir galloped up, angling across the front of the line, pursued casually by a half-dozen braves a hundred yards behind. They quickly wheeled away when they saw the new line of bluecoats.

"Damn it, Lieutenant, get these men in order," Weir shouted. "We can't ride down in there in a line." Without waiting for Edgerly, he waved at the men and shouted, "Column of twos."

The men closest got the message and began to move back into column. Randall fell in beside Lieutenant Edgerly to make the first pair behind the captain. Now he was getting ready to fight, not just to deliver a message. He told himself that he was doing this only to be able to get to Custer, to fulfill his mission. For the first time in his military career, however, he really understood the unspoken motivation of the true soldier. He *wanted* to fight.

Randall looked behind him to watch the men of D Company falling into column. He was surprised to see Lieutenant Hare, Major Reno's adjutant, riding after them.

"Looks like trouble," MacLane said to Edgerly. "We'd better whip it up. The major must have seen us."

Lieutenant Edgerly wheeled his horse in a circle to get a view of the advancing Luther Hare.

"Too late," he said. "Riding off from the adjutant would really put our bacon in the fire."

They waited while the lieutenant spurred his horse on toward them. He was riding flat out, so the wait was only a minute or two. To Randall, however, it seemed like the sun was standing still, just as it had for Joshua. He did not know, however, whether the lengthening of the day was to assure the victory to Custer or to the Indians. Hare arrived breathless, as though he had been running instead of the horse. Without preamble he addressed Captain Weir.

"Major Reno says since you're out here, try to communicate with Custer. He's going to get the whole force together, pack train and wounded and everybody, and follow along behind. If you get into trouble, just come back to us."

Captain Weir could not hide a smile.

"Fine, adjutant," he said, snapping off a salute. "Orders understood. Lieutenant Edgerly, take half the column and head off down that ravine to the right. I'll take the other half and go up on the high ground to the left. We'll advance in parallel."

"Yes, sir," said the lieutenant, saluting smartly.

He immediately wheeled his horse and rode down the column to pick up its second half. No one had given Randall any order, so he continued to ride beside Edgerly.

Like a caterpillar cut in two, the column separated and began to slide over the rough terrain, leaving Lieutenant Hare sitting his horse, listening for something, it seemed.

Edgerly and his men rode down the ravine and then along a ridge that ran parallel to the river.

"There's Custer's trail."

He pointed it out to Randall as they rode.

"Off to the right there, along the far slope, plain as day."

Randall's eye was not trained to the plains, but even he could tell that it was Custer's trail. It was so different from all around it, a disciplined, clear, iron-shod intentional movement. The Indian sign all around them was without clarity, without cohesion. He felt a moment of pride as he thought of the difference, of the force the army represented, of its clear, civilizing influence in the midst of this savage land and its savage inhabitants. Then he realized uneasily that it was the savages who had so far carried the day.

"Lieutenant, sir," one of the men called. "Captain Weir is signaling us."

All turned at once to the left, to see the captain's signals. He was waving to them to change direction, to angle back toward him. MacLane felt a vague uneasiness. He knew he was out of place, but he spoke anyway.

"We really shouldn't go that way, should we? I mean, General Custer's trail is over there."

"Captain Weir's never fought the Sioux before, but he's the captain," Edgerly replied grimly. "Come on, men."

They had not ridden more than two hundred yards in the direction the captain pointed out before the reason became clear. A large force of Indians was trying to cut them off from behind. Weir was on higher ground. He had been able to see them before Edgerly.

Edgerly and his men came up onto the higher plateau already occupied by Weir, riding almost parallel but still apart, only gradually easing one column toward the other.

The Indians now fell back as they saw the two lines of troops converging, realizing they did not have the angle to wedge between them. It felt good to be in sight of the other soldiers, good to know Reno was advancing behind them. That did not, however, solve the problem of getting through to Custer, Randall with his message and Weir with his order to communicate. From his elbow Randall heard Edgerly's voice.

"Look up there, MacLane. See? Straight ahead, all those Indians riding back and forth. Must be a couple of miles. They're shooting at something, but I can't figure out what."

Randall strained his eyes to see. There was no problem in picking out the Indians. There were whole lines of them without a break, riding helter-skelter. Whatever they were shooting at, however, was hidden by the Indians themselves and the dust they were churning up. In the pit of his stomach Randall MacLane knew what they were shooting at—more precisely, *who* they were shooting at.

"Is there anybody else out there?" he asked, hoping against hope. "Do you think maybe Terry or Gibbon could be coming up?"

"Not a chance," said Edgerly. Then, reading Randall's mind: "But we don't know it's Custer, either. Can't see a blame thing," he muttered.

As they watched, the mass of riding Indians far ahead of them ceased its constant motion. The cloud of dust around and above them hung in the air. The whole prairie started to ooze, to heave slowly, like a giant carpet being pulled and shaken by some unseen hand beyond the horizon.

A trooper called from behind them.

"My God, look at them ponies. It's the Indian pony herd. Must be a million of 'em!"

Perhaps not a million, but thousands—twenty thousand, maybe more. Off to the left, beyond the river, the huge herd was moving away. Nearer at hand thousands of Indians began to glide toward them. They were coming from the villages, from the ravines, from behind the hills. Those who had been shooting at the unseen targets two miles ahead wheeled as one and began to charge back toward the hills where they could see Weir and Edgerly and Reno and Benteen advancing.

Edgerly spoke in awestruck tones.

"Oh, Lord, they're coming back. I didn't know there were so many of them. We can't stay here. We've got to get back to the main body."

"But what about Custer?" cried Randall.

"Who knows?"

There was desperation in Edgerly's voice now.

"Maybe he fought 'em and went on out the other side to join up with Terry. All I know is we've got to get out of here."

"But I've got a message for Custer. It's got to be delivered now."

Edgerly did not bother to reply.

"Come on, men," he yelled. "Back to the main body. Don't try to hook up with the rest of D Company. They'll be comin' back, quick enough. Just take the straightest route you can."

MacLane wasn't sure even the straight route was going to do them much good. The big body of Indians was still almost two miles behind them, but there were patches of a dozen to a hundred that were coming at them from all directions, many almost on them. Their salvation, he knew, was that most of the Indians had to get close enough to use bows or spears. He hoped they could keep adequate distance to escape that primitive firepower.

It was then that Randall felt the rage burn through his

body. It had not fired him since he had beaten the summer stove into submission while his grandfather died. Now the grayness was back. It covered the prairie in a pall of dust, snuffing out life and hope. He had nothing to go back to. Now he had nothing to go forward to, either? Who were these Indians, these savages, to be whirling about in his way, keeping him from going forth, deflecting him into nothingness? He had come to deliver a message to Custer, and by God, he would deliver it!

He whirled his horse away from Edgerly and D Company and faced directly into the advancing mass of Indians. That was where Custer had to be. In his heart he knew that the famous general was dead, but neither his heart nor his head controlled him now. His mind had given way to his muscles, to his shoulders and hands and their reality of violence.

He kicked his horse in the flanks and started down the ridge. He had ridden no more than a hundred yards before he reached the first Indian. He was a young brave, working his way up a gully on foot, hoping for a big coup that would have his people telling the tale of his prowess around the campfires for generations to come.

The brave popped up from the gully and took aim on MacLane with his bow, twisting slightly at the waist as he followed the path of the plunging horse, sighting the lead for his shot. His position, however, was too straight on. He held neither a truly direct shot nor a good angle. He was also unnerved by the sight of an obviously crazy rider urging his horse right at him. He rushed the shot. It went behind Randall, slicing through the thin past that trailed in his wake.

Randall didn't even bother to slow down. He simply ran his horse right into the warrior. The boy was quick and timed his leap almost perfectly, but he guessed wrongly. Randall pulled left on the bridle just as the brave jumped in that direction. The boy went spinning from under the iron-shod hooves and landed like a bag of old boots.

A group of about a half-dozen riders angled at him, trying to cut him off before he reached the mass ahead, to get the kill for themselves. They did not count on the rage of the man they rode against, however. They did not know how his horse felt that rage through his thighs, so that it ran with the strength of terror, trying to escape the power of destruction that sat astride it.

The Indians rode only for the joy of fighting, the hope of counting coup, the respect of their people, the urge for honor. Truly powerful motivations, but they were a flock of sparrows compared with the falcon of Randall MacLane's rage.

The Indians rode flat out with all their strength but simply could not cut off the white man without a uniform. For his part, he seemed not even to notice them. Once they were behind him, they no longer counted. He was going on. The Indians pulled up with disgust. They turned around and headed for the bluecoats, to gain some advantage in the killing before the hundreds of riders behind them cut in on all the action.

Randall MacLane rode on. He pulled his rifle from its scabbard and began to fire into the wave of Indians that now rolled toward him like a flash flood. He had no time to aim; he simply fired away. One warrior went down, his horse shot out from under him. Another rode just behind him and pulled his pony left to escape the falling horse. He cut directly across still another brave. Both their mounts went to their knees and lost their riders in the scramble.

MacLane snapped off a lucky shot that scalped an older warrior who was riding with his sons, showing them he could still keep up with them. Seeing their father somersault off the rump of his horse as the top of his head flew away stirred them into a madness equal to Randall's own. They flew at this strange and crazy intruder. The other Indians swept on by them, knowing that this mad white man belonged to the avenging sons of the man he had killed.

Despite his primitive rage, Randall's brain still functioned as though it were the rational tool of an educated man. It knew his rifle was no good at the range he had closed to. It also knew he had never been much of a shot with a handgun. He shoved his rifle back into the scabbard. Then he drew the sword he had so recently strapped on.

The two screaming braves closed on him from either side. MacLane struck out with the sword at the one on his right. At the same time the warrior on his left leaped at him, slashing with his knife.

Randall's wild-eyed horse wheeled violently away from the creature that flew at it through the air, knocking the man sideways in midflight. The mount's action pushed Randall directly into the other brave, surprising the youngster with the suddenness of the move, making it impossible for him to use his knife in the overhand stab that he had started.

Randall's sword slash carried behind the brave, slicing off his single feather. He pulled his sword back in desperation, sure he did not have enough time to use it before the boy could strike him with his knife. In his wildness it seemed to him that he just grazed the back of the other's neck as he pulled the sword back toward him. His strength, however, was the strength of frenzy. The young warrior fell forward, limp as a rag doll, his spinal cord severed.

MacLane sensed more than saw the brother of the brave he had just killed. He had been knocked to the ground by the swift turn of Randall's horse. He was now up again, running, gaining momentum for another leap. Before he could get into it, however, Randall's horse reeled and stumbled and fell forward like a stone in water.

MacLane had already lost the foothold in his right stirrup. That probably saved his life. Otherwise he would have been trapped under the falling horse and easy prey for the remaining Indian. As it was, however, he barely had time to roll free from the horse as it fell, coming back to his feet with a somersault that he learned as a child in his grandfather's orchard twenty years before.

The two men were now separated by the mound of the horse. The beast twitched once and lay still. MacLane and the brave both stared at it in dull, sweaty astonishment for a brief moment. Randall just had time to register that the horse had been hit in the head by a bullet. Whether it was one meant for him or just a stray, he had no time even to consider. The other man leaped across the horse and flew at him in a mad charge, screaming a wild war cry.

Randall went down under the force of the man's assault, grappling with him, trying to get control of the knife, his fist wrapped around the other's right wrist. The brave had his fist in turn tightly wrapped on Randall's right wrist, preventing him from using his sword. They strained and rocked and grunted for what seemed an eternity, each in rage, neither able to gain an advantage.

MacLane's patience went before his strength. When it did, he saw a possibility. It was a combination that became an old but uneasy friend in years to come, impatience that led to innovation. He knew he had to give up his weapon to have any chance to win this battle.

Still another corner of his educated brain functioned independently. Even as his body strained and teetered on the brink of extinction, that corner looked on and analyzed. How odd, it mused, that man must come so close to another, either to kill or to love. How odd, that man must give up his weapons both to love and to kill.

As they rolled and hissed and fumbled at each other, MacLane waited for a moment when he was underneath the brave. Then he suddenly released his grip on the sword and let his arm go limp. The brave was pulled into him by the sudden slackening in force, but off balance. Randall got a knee into the man's gut and thrust him into the air. The warrior flew over his head and landed flat on his back with a thud. He managed to hold on to his knife but was slow in getting up, the wind knocked out of him completely. Randall scrambled to his knees, pulled his pistol from its holster, and shot the man before he could struggle to his feet.

As immediately as it had come, the rage was now gone. Cold rationality took its place. Randall MacLane knew that he was in deep trouble. He was a mile from the troops in either direction, assuming that there were any bluecoats left alive ahead of him. His horse was dead. There were thousands of hostiles from east to west and south to north. He was sore and tired and drained by rage and battle. He was now an Indian fighter. He himself was now the hero of his dreams. He had no idea what that meant.

The Battle
and Beyond

He looked up from the carnage of the little killing
field around him. He was not so much in danger from
thousands of Indians as from one particular group of about
fifteen. They sat their horses, fifty yards away, just looking
at him. They were all armed with rifles. Some wore pieces
of cavalry uniforms. One even had a bugle slung around
his neck. They began to walk their horses toward him.

One brave was obviously their leader. He was totally
naked except for a breechcloth and moccasins. He was
not a particularly large man, but he sat totally erect, giving
the impression he was much taller. He wore only one
feather in the band around his head. He didn't look at all
like what Randall assumed a chief would look like, but the
young soldier had been around a lot of army men. Some
were simply shaped like the sword of command, regardless of the number of their stripes or the color of their
badges. Before him was the kind of man who didn't need
stripes or badges or feathers to be in charge.

Randall readied his pistol. He knew he had no chance

against this group of savages. He was determined, however, almost by reflex now, to die fighting.

The Indians stopped barely twenty yards away. The chief barked out a few words. From the end of the line a brave rode out, leading a pony.

The chief rode up to Randall and dismounted.

"You get rifle," he said to Randall in English.

It made no sense. Nonetheless, Randall pulled the rifle from the saddle scabbard of his dead horse.

"Ride this horse," the Indian leader said.

Randall threw himself up onto the skittish Indian pony while the brave held the little mount steady.

The chief barked some more commands. The rest of the Indians, including the one who brought the horse to Randall, wheeled away, back toward the troops of Reno and Benteen. Only the leader remained.

"Come," he said.

Randall mounted up and rode behind the Indian, his body and brain both slumping, his boots almost to the ground. He didn't understand what was happening. He wasn't sure he cared.

They came to a little hill. There they sat their horses and watched what was left of the battle.

MacLane was confused. He knew he should be fighting, should be trying to reach the troops again. He also knew that was impossible. He couldn't get ten yards. If this Indian leader did not kill him, some other warrior would.

At the very least, though, he should not be surrendering so easily. But the chief did not treat him as a prisoner. Why did he have him get his rifle? Randall had even picked up his sword and carried it along. No one tried to stop him.

Were they waiting to kill him later, perhaps in some ceremony? Would they torture him? His ignorance of the plains Indians became agonizingly real to him.

Finally, he asked.

"Why?"

The chief did not answer immediately. He seemed to be asking himself the same question.

"Others run away," the chief said at last. "You ride wrong direction. You like Yellowhair. Ride to help him. No use. Yellowhair dead. You not bluecoat. You fight strong. You great warrior, maybe. You crazy, maybe. You live. Tell about us. We tell about you."

Was Custer really dead? Perhaps the Indian was lying? Just bragging? His heart and his gut told him it was not so. This must be the chief who led the party that vanquished Custer. That would account for the carbines and cavalry garb his men sported.

Randall was with the Indian through most of the night. He didn't ask him his name or where he had learned English. Such information seemed unnecessary. Perhaps it was because he understood he was in the presence of some sort of strange greatness. Only someone very special could have vanquished the mighty Custer. Only someone very special could have totally destroyed MacLane's own life at the very time he spared it.

After a while the chief dismounted and sat on the crest of the hill. Randall did the same. The Indian seemed now to have forgotten about him. From time to time a brave galloped up to the hill to give a report. Those messengers also ignored him.

Night seemed to fall with a black thud. MacLane could only guess what time it was. Although the Indians were known to be stingy with fuel, the night blazed with a thousand fires.

Randall thought about the troops on the hill. Had the pack train come up? Did they have ammunition? Were any of his new friends killed? He knew they must be short of water. What about the wounded? Were they hoping for salvation from Crook or Terry?

Then he thought about Custer and his men, all gone. Where were they tonight? So alive just a few hours ago. Now so dead.

What was he doing on this hill, sitting with this Indian? He was a man out of place, neither dead nor besieged like his comrades, but not belonging where he was, either. Who was he? He was no longer a soldier; he knew that even now, even as the battle continued. He was no longer a man with a message. He was no longer even a man with a dream, for his visions of being a famous Indian fighter disappeared as the day dropped into night.

Just before daybreak a small party gathered on the hill. There was a short discussion, perhaps even a little arguing, Randall thought from the sound of the voices.

The chief came to him.

"Much fighting now. You stay here. Take."

He handed MacLane a feather. In the darkness he could only feel the beads that dangled from the pinion.

"You stay here, hold feather, you live. You leave hill, you die. When we gone, go home."

As he finished Randall heard two quick, sharp rifle cracks. Immediately, in the first bleak graying of the day, the air was filled with war cries and firing. The Indians were attacking the rest of the soldiers.

Perhaps the chief meant literally what he said about Randall telling the story of this battle. Was he to be the only white man left alive, not so much because of his bravery, but because he was a handy mouthpiece for the savages? Would he be a man with a message, but a message *about* Custer instead of *for* him, a message about Custer's death? Is that what the world would hear from his lips? How twisted back upon itself his mission had become.

All day long the Indians besieged the soldiers, on what MacLane thought of as Benteen's hill but that became known as Reno Hill. He ran out of water but dared not leave the hill to go for more. All he could do was sit or pace on the top of his own lonely, little hill, burned by the sun, grayed by the dust, taunted and haunted by the firing and the cries of the Indians.

By late morning hunger and thirst and fatigue took

their toll. He clutched the decorated feather like a talis-man and felt like a child that holds a favorite doll close against the darkness of sleep. He felt vastly ashamed, at the undisciplined rage that had caused him to ride out against the Indians against all logic, at the protection the feather now gave him while other men, better soldiers, were dying. It did not seem right that the one who did it all wrong should escape. Still, he was glad he was alive. He was ashamed that he was glad.

In the early afternoon he was awakened by a sharp increase in the sounds of the fighting. A huge number of Indians had worked up close to the soldiers, on foot. They rushed out of the draws and gullies all around the com-mand. With a gasp of despair Randall was sure the troops would be overwhelmed and wiped out.

Almost as soon as they charged, however, the Indians withdrew. Just a few more minutes was all they needed to annihilate their enemy, but they fell back casually, as if they had lost interest. Without any signal that he could discern, they simply left, not in defeat but as though they had accomplished what they set out to do and were now bored with it.

About seven in the evening he could see the entire mass of Indians, children and families and travois and warriors and horse herds, all moving together on the left side of the river, to the west. In the gold of the advancing sunset MacLane imagined that it looked like how the vast herds of buffalo had moved, making the whole prairie undulate. It seemed that he had stepped back in time, that he had a view that was eternal, that predated the army and Custer and his message and the awful battle they had all just been through.

He was brought back to the moment by a ragged cheer from the soldiers, away on Reno Hill.

As night fell Randall started to work his way back to the soldiers. His first task, however, was water. He giddily drank his fill at the river, then became sick from drinking too much too quickly. His hunger grew sharper. He remembered he had not eaten since breakfast the day before.

It occurred to him, however, that to approach the troop position at night was not wise. They might well assume he was some isolated brave still hoping to count coup. Besides, how would he explain where he had been and the protection the Indians had given him? What if there really were savages still out there, waiting for a chance to strike? What if the great movement of the massed tribes was just for show, or to find grass for the herds while the warriors waited to catch the soldiers off guard? What good would his eagle feather be in the dark, away from the sanctuary hill?

Despite his fierce hunger, he decided to wait until light, not knowing that other stragglers were already sneaking into camp. Lying by the river, under a tree at last when he had no need of shade, he slept the sleep of those too weary to wonder.

He came awake with a start. The light was almost full, but it was not the light that awakened him. It was a bugle, blowing loud and clear. Not reveille, but retreat, then recall, then march, one right after another. MacLane could actually see the bugler, standing on the highest promontory of the troop position, his trumpet gleaming in the sun, turning first in one direction and then in another as he blew. It was Tuesday morning, June 27.

Lieutenant Randall MacLane looked down the river, in the direction where he knew Custer and all his command lay. Wearily he wandered the battered prairie until he found his dead horse, drawing flies.

Idly he wondered about the flies, about what they did when there was no carnage off which to feed, about why there should be so many around just one horse when there were so many horses and so many men available to them.

He pulled his saddlebags free, flung them over his back, and trudged toward the command. He still had a message, for the other soldiers this time, a message that the eternal Custer was dead. He wondered how he could possibly tell them, and how he would explain how he knew and why he was alive.

He was not the one who brought the word of Custer's death to the troops on Reno Hill after all. As he came close to the soldiers' position, he saw that almost all of them had come to the edge of the encampment and were watching him, or so he thought. The officers were out in front, passing field glasses around. He knew that he must look an awful mess, but . . . Perhaps they did not recognize him or realize he was one of them, since he was not in uniform. Suddenly an officer spurred out of the camp and came riding toward him at full speed. Randall stopped, assuming the man was coming out to give him a lift back.

Instead the mounted man just rode on by him, twenty yards away. Randall turned to follow his path. In the distance he saw a tall, pale cloud of dust down the river, in the opposite direction from the Indians' line of march. It was moving much more slowly than the Indians, surely a sign of infantry on its way. Even as he watched he saw the column of soldiers appear out of the dust and waver in the heat shimmers as they approached. It was the column to which the rider from Reno Hill was heading.

Randall turned and continued his weary trudge toward the troops on the hill. When he arrived at the group of officers, no one seemed especially interested in him, except Captain Weir and Lieutenant Edgerly. They edged away slightly from the others and made small beckoning motions toward him. His weary legs and empty belly resented the last few steps they required of him, but not enough to refuse.

"Good God, man," said Edgerly, almost in a whisper. "What happened to you? We thought you were dead for sure! Did your horse bolt?"

Randall dropped his saddlebags.

"No, I guess it wasn't the horse's fault, but it's dead now, anyway. I . . . Well, I fought with some of the Indians, and killed some . . . but most of them rode on by me, after you. . . ."

I killed some Indians. . . . It sounded like he was bragging, at least to his own ears. He didn't mean to. He was not proud that he had killed, not proud of his rage.

"You must have done some real fighting," said Weir. "What's that you got?"

Randall followed the captain's gaze, down to his clinched fist. He was still carrying the chief's eagle feather.

"Oh . . . I took it from an Indian. . . ."

It was the truth, but not quite. Another voice spoke from behind him.

"Not just any Indian. Chief's feather. Big medicine. You must fight good."

It was one of the half-breed scouts, one who had straggled into camp during the night from a hideout in the bush. He looked at MacLane with speculation. Randall dropped his own gaze and muttered.

"I'd better go report to Major Reno and Captain Benteen. I'm afraid I've got bad news."

He turned quickly and walked to the officers, wanting to get this over with as soon as possible. Just as he got to them, however, the young officer who had ridden past him so shortly before came spurring back. Another lieutenant, of the Seventh Infantry, rode at his side. They slid from their horses. The new officer snapped a quick salute.

"Lieutenant Bradley, sir," he said to Reno. "General Terry's compliments, sir. He'll be with you shortly. In the meantime, I fear I have bad news. We counted a hundred ninety-seven bodies back there. It looks like Custer's whole command was wiped out."

The words hung in the air, still, unmoving. Then they were swallowed up by a deep, bruised silence. Each man looked in his own direction, at his hands or feet, at the dust around his boots, inward. Gradually each raised his gaze until they were all focused on the horizon from which Lieutenant Bradley had ridden, watching General Terry's column advance, but really seeing Custer.

MacLane gradually released his breath in a long, silent sigh. He was both relieved and disappointed that he was not the one to speak the news of the massacre.

Finally Captain Benteen blurted out what they all felt.

"My God, man, that's impossible."

They all knew, however, that it had to be true. So they simply stood and waited for Terry, "old braid-beard," as the Indians liked to call him. His image wavered in the rising heat as he rode toward them. It seemed to waver even more the closer he came. Finally he arrived, slumped in his saddle, his face an ashen gray. There was nothing to say. No one said it.

There was still work to do, however. First were the wounded. Several men had wounds on which gangrene was advancing. At last Dr. Potter had time to do amputations. Other men were glad to work at putting the pack train back together. It took them farther away from the sound of the rasping saw and the screaming wounded. Injured and galled horses needed tending. Equipment had to be repaired. There was the unwanted task of trying to identify the stripped, bloated, and blackened bodies of Custer and his men.

Randall MacLane wanted none of this. He was no longer in the army. He knew his message would never be delivered. Most importantly, though, he knew he had no place to go. The congressman and his friends were correct. He was perfect for the job because he had no family and no home to worry about. Now his perfection was his curse. He had no desire to stay in the army, even if he could. He didn't even want to stay with these soldiers long enough to get back to what they so easily called "civilization."

He went to General Terry with his papers. Mustering out in the field was unusual but not unheard of. After all, his time was up. Nonetheless, he dreaded trying to explain why he was here and what had happened to him in the fighting. Terry was too busy and too tired to care about some wandering lieutenant, however. He signed Randall's discharge papers and told his aide to see that he got a horse.

The aide turned him over to a quartermaster who saw an opportunity to rid himself of a problem horse. The piebald mare was worn down, worn-out, and used up. It also had a loco glint in its eye. Randall had never been a "good animal man," even on the farm. He knew enough, however, to see this was hardly the mount he needed to wander out to California, or wherever he was going. He was as worn down and worn out as the horse, however. His only real interest was getting away from the Little Bighorn. He threw his saddle on the nag and rode off, without a word of farewell even to Edgerly or Weir.

As he rode away from the soldiers, the battle, the Indians, the dead body of Custer, slurping through the great void of action past and goals lost, he realized he was as alone as ever he had been in his whole life. There were degrees of solitude, he reflected, and degrees of loneliness, even for a solitary man. He wondered if it were possible to be more alone than he was right then, riding on the vast plain.

He would have been surprised to learn the Indians were already telling stories about him, about the wild and raging young soldier, the man with a sword but no blue coat, the one who, when the others ran, turned and charged by himself. The books that would be written about the great battle would all repeat the Indian stories, tales that came only from the warriors, since no other white man saw what happened. Randall MacLane would even read those accounts . . . and have no idea they were about him.

At the Wagon

Randall rode in a trance. He wandered onto the road to the town of Middle Bend without even seeing what he was doing.

The whole world was so upside-down, so unreal. Custer was dead. What was he to do now?

He obviously could not deliver the message. He had been told never to contact the men who had given it to him. He had been told not to open it himself under any circumstances, and he saw no way its contents could help him, whatever they might be. So, he knew what not to do, but what was he to do? Should he keep it, bury it, send it to Mrs. Custer?

"I'm getting crazy," he muttered as he lurched along, paying no attention to keeping a decent seat on the horse. "I couldn't send it to her. They told me it had to go to Custer himself and to no one else. I've got to keep my mind on what's going on here."

But what was going on?

He was worn down, exhausted, emptied. His body was

numb from the long journey and the furious fighting. His mind was a blank.

Who was he now? He was no Indian fighter; that was terrifying and fatiguing and mystifying, not romantic. He was no soldier; he had been mustered out. He was no messenger, no man with a mission, because Custer was dead. He was no professional, with a job waiting, no husband or father, with a family waiting. He was just an ordinary man drifting down a road, alone.

For the first time since he had left home he felt truly lonely. He had always been solitary, often alone, but never lonely. Now the walls were gone. He had held all those energy-sapping emotions in a dark, little room deep inside for so long. The fight with the Indians and the death of Custer had been the horns that blew the signal. His walls had come tumbling down.

He felt tears working through the grime on his face, driving down to the stubble on his chin. Suddenly he was crying. It had been so long that at first he didn't recognize it. His shoulders shook, his lungs hacked, his throat made strangled, terrible sounds.

He had no idea how long he rode that way or how long he sat on top of the hill watching the carnage below, with eyes that could not see through the tears of his own pain. He had always been able to look outward but see inward, unconsciously choosing which scene he was a part of.

Perhaps it was the screaming that finally broke his trance. For whatever reason, he finally came awake to what was going on in front of him.

At the bottom of the hill was a burning wagon. The bodies of two men were crumpled beside it. A boy who looked to be about ten was lying near them, but it was clear that he was alive. He was not moving, however, because his hands and feet were bound.

Randall's mind came clear quite as suddenly and unexpectedly as his sobs had come a few minutes before. He instinctively knew the whole story, just as the mind completes a partial circle to make it whole, even though the entire circle cannot be seen.

These folk were either failed pioneers heading back east, or still hopeful ones going west. They might even have been farmers leaving their land temporarily to find the security of a fort until the Indian uprising was quelled. Whatever the reason, they were in the wrong place at the wrong time.

After Custer had been killed, the Indians had broken apart and ridden off in all directions. The people in this wagon had been three days away from the battle, but one of the little Indian bands just happened across them. The Indians were still drunk on triumph. They were going to drive every white invader from the land.

The plains Indians, however, rarely killed young boys. Instead they took them and raised them as a part of the tribe. So the boy who lay trussed like a pig beside the two dead men would be spared. Not so the woman.

Her screams came in a horrible rhythm as she lay in the circle formed by the dancing, clowning braves. Each one of them was naked save for some piece of the woman's clothing. They hopped madly about, like strange birds gone berserk, as if they were changed by magic garments. One brave lay on top of her, but he suddenly jumped up and beat on his breast and crowed like a rooster. She tried to get onto her knees, but the Indian wearing her skirt grabbed her legs, rolled her over onto her back again, raised up the skirt, and thrust himself in between her legs.

Randall would wonder forever more how long it really took him to comprehend what was going on. Could he have prevented more of the sickening scene had he not been so engrossed in his own misery? Could he not have done it better when he did finally get into action?

He had spent most of his army time behind a desk, but the army at least had taught him to shoot. He did not dismount, though, as the manual called for in this sort of maneuver. He simply pulled the rifle from its boot, put it to his shoulder, and shot the brave right off the woman. He didn't consider that he might miss her tormentor. Neither did he wonder what it would feel like to the woman to have a man die on top of her. He just fired at the one he wanted to stop first.

The others were caught totally by surprise. They milled about in confusion. Some tried to take off their foreign garments. Others ran for their horses. None seemed to have a weapon readily at hand. Their confusion was probably what saved his life, for there were six of them and only one of him. He had not bothered to consider that, either.

There was no rage this time, no furious flailing as there had been when he tried to reach Custer. There was a woman to save from torment and humiliation. There was a boy to save from being severed from his own people. MacLane had a job to do, and he proceeded at it piece by piece, just as he had in learning Latin and Greek when he first went to the university.

His horse wheeled halfway around at the crack of the rifle, but Randall still had the circle of braves within the range of motion of his arm. He took aim at the one closest to the line his rifle already held, squeezed the trigger, and saw the man fall. His mind automatically computed the arithmetic—two down, thirty-three and a third percent, only two thirds of the job left to do.

His horse moved again, but back toward the milling braves. Two of them had almost reached their ponies, which had wandered off and were grazing about fifty yards away. Another had found a rifle and was sprinting for the cover of the burning wagon. Randall did not expect him to do much damage through the flames, so he lined his sights up on the Indian closest to a horse and pulled the trigger. Without a sound, the horse keeled over.

"Aimed high," he complained into the air. "Got to watch it."

Randall seldom talked to himself, but he did not want to fight this battle alone. The sound of his voice gave him company.

The Indian flung himself behind the carcass of the horse. There was no other cover. His partner was swinging up onto the other horse Indian fashion, from the right side, surprising Randall as he tried to target him. The brave tried to unsling his rifle and ride off at the same time. Randall lined him up in his sights, aimed low to compensate for his last shot, saw the man grab at his side and then slide off his mount.

By now MacLane's own horse had had enough. It was not a trained cavalry mount, just an old stray saddle mount that the army had picked up along the way and used as a pack animal. It was weary from the fighting and the traveling and the noise of the last few days. It simply decided to leave, for some destination it alone understood. With a jerk that snapped Randall's neck, it suddenly started down the hill on a dead run, straight toward the wagon. It was all Randall could do to keep astride the beast. That rash action, however, took him out of harm's way.

He heard a shot from the wagon but did not sense a bullet. The sudden rush of his horse had made the Indian miss badly. He had no idea what the now wild horse intended, but he had never been a horseman anyway. He knew he was no match for the wild-eyed, sweat-flecked bay beneath him. He wasted no time trying to control the horse. He just leaned low over the horn, squeezed tightly with his knees to be sure he stayed in the saddle, and lined up his rifle again.

Because of the horse's wild rush, he was now only a few feet from a dumbfounded brave. The man just stood, a petticoat crumpled ludicrously around his ankles, seemingly unable to comprehend what was happening. Randall aimed for his midsection, his intent being simply to hit the Indian somewhere. He was a good marksman on the practice range. He was not the best even there, however, and the headlong flight of his horse took away the possibility of any careful aiming. As he fired, the top of the man's head seemed to fly off, scalped by the bullet.

For a moment he had the uncanny and uneasy feeling that he was right back at the Little Bighorn, fighting all the same fights in all the same ways. Would that battle ever be over?

"High again!" Randall blurted out, trying to placate some ghostly and omnipresent rifle-range instructor.

The warrior was down, high shot or not, and two-thirds of the job was done. Randall swiveled in the saddle as best he could to see what had become of the Indian on the horse. He hoped the man had decided to run and was a little surprised to hear a bullet whine by his ear, followed immediately by the harsh crack of its father, the rifle.

"Son of a gun!" gasped Randall, a piece of profanity fancied by the other young officers in Washington. He was amazed at himself that he should use such an oath now when he had always been so careful to watch his language.

There was no time to consider the changes that the events of the last few days had begun to work in him, however. Right in front of him, wheeling his pony to try for another angle, was the mounted brave.

MacLane's horse did not seem to see the pony or the brave or anything else in front of it. It headed straight for the Indian, true as a homing pigeon, running flatout. Only a few feet separated them before Randall and the Indian both realized the horses would collide. Normally a horse will do anything necessary to avoid a collision, even risk a broken leg. Randall's horse, however, seemed to have gone deeply berserk, to be under a bizarre control that forced it to be some beast other than a horse.

The Indian brought his rifle down hard on his own mount's flank, trying to wheel it once again to escape the onslaught of the mad steed and its avenging rider. Randall had the advantage because he knew he had no control, that there was no point in trying to affect the movements of the horse that was no longer really his. Thus he was able to concentrate on the other man. As the horse crashed full speed into the desperate brave and his mount, MacLane swung his rifle in a short, head-bending arc. The Indian's body immediately went limp and fell from the pony like a sack of grain off the tailgate of a wagon.

Randall only had time to catch a glimpse of the falling brave before he felt himself going, too. Somehow the collision of the horses had severed his saddle's girth strap. The saddle turned from the horse's back to its belly so quickly that he did not even have time to grab for the horn. The next thing he knew, he was lying on his back in the dust, looking up at a horse that was saddled upside down.

For the crazed horse, that was the final straw. It reared on its hind legs, crashed down, and then flailed out with its back hooves in a wild effort to dislodge the thing that had suddenly grabbed it from below. Randall knew he should try to roll free, but his mind was working faster than his body. He felt paralyzed as he watched the kicking, iron-shod hooves.

The very inability of his body to move as quickly as his mind commanded probably saved him, just as his inability to control the horse had saved him when the brave had fired at him from the wagon. With the horse rearing and bucking, directly underneath it was the safest place to be. It jerked left and the frayed girth finally let loose. The saddle flew off and landed heavily just a few feet from Randall's head, crashing rifle scabbard and saddlebags down with it. Freed of its burdens, the horse wheeled once more in a tight circle and then started again into a flat-out run across the plain. Randall could do nothing except pull himself up on one elbow and watch it go.

All at once he realized he was not doing his arithmetic. There had been six braves. How many had he gotten? More importantly, how many were left? He rolled over onto his belly and began to crawl toward his saddle, his head swiveling, trying to take in his entire little battlefield at once. Who was left? Where would the attack come from now? His rifle was still in his hand. He flung its barrel over the saddle and waited. His hat was gone and he had to squint hard against the sun. Dusty sweat rolled down into his eyes.

The wagon . . . There was an Indian there. He wiped at his eyes with his left hand and tried to hold the rifle steady with his right, pointing it in the general direction of the smoldering wagon. Smoke and dust mingled and hung in the hot, dry air. Randall pulled his eyelids down until he was staring intently at the wagon through narrow slits of light. He had the disadvantage now. The wagon provided better cover to the brave than his broken saddle could possibly give him. He knew he had to wait for the Indian to make his move.

Heat images began to dance slowly in the dust that drifted between him and the wagon. Sweat ran on him everywhere, pulling his dirty clothes in tight and hot against his skin. His hat was gone. Where he had no idea, and he now longed for its shade. He tried to swallow, but his mouth was like cotton. Grit edged his teeth. His elbows hurt with the effort of holding him up taut behind the saddle.

"God, let it be soon," he breathed through parched lips.

He knew he could not go on much longer. His adrenaline had run out. A huge tiredness was coming over him, pressing down on him like a giant hand. His head was getting light while his body was getting heavy. He was giddy enough that he might do something foolish, like rush the wagon, just to get the thing over and done with. His body, however, was not about to cooperate; it was too tired. Bodies sometimes have a way of their own. They can use that way to save as well as to damn. This was not the last time he would learn that.

He waited so long that his eyes began to close, whether against the glare or because of fatigue he didn't know. His mind started to wander, taking him back to the long, dusty, hilly summer roads of his boyhood. The heat images before him became maple trees and sassafras and wild blackberry bushes beside the road. He was beginning to sink into the earth beneath him when he was jerked back to the Montana prairie by a thin, quavering voice.

"He ran away," it said.

It took MacLane a long moment to understand. The voice came from the huddled form of the boy on the ground.

"The Indian ran away?" he yelled back.

"Yes."

"Where did he go?"

"I don't know. I can't see the wagon, but I heard him running."

It was all so damned confusing! The boy was trussed up like a pig and facing away from the wagon. Could Randall trust his judgment? Maybe it was some sort of Indian trick. Randall knew the Indians were crafty. He had heard all the stories about their clever ways from the time he was a boy. Maybe the brave had just faked running away to lure him out.

There had not been much trickery at the Little Bighorn—just overwhelming numbers and a lot of courage. But that was over. What now?

MacLane felt so heavy. His rage had been drained in the attempt to get through to Custer. What energy he had left was used up in his mad charge down this little hill at the Indians that now lay dead about him.

"Please help us."

It was the boy calling to him again, his voice fluttering plaintively in the air.

Randall just got tired of trying to figure it all out. If the brave had not really run away, well, he simply didn't care. He pulled himself slowly and wearily to his feet, pushed the carbine up into the crook of his arm, and weaved unsteadily toward the boy.

Then it struck him. The boy said, "Please help *us*." There was the woman, too, the woman off whom he had shot the first Indian. In his concentration on fighting, he had forgotten about her. He broke into a stumbling run, pushing the boy out of his mind for the moment. There she lay, naked, on her back, only inches from the brave who had been atop her before Randall shot the man's brains out. Her eyes were open, staring fixedly at nothing.

At first Randall thought she must be dead. Then he saw that her hands were moving, grasping at the ground on either side of her, blunt fingers clutching at the dirt until it oozed up between her knuckles. When all the dust was gone from her hands, her fists unclenched and clutched again at the dirt on which she lay.

MacLane had never before seen a naked woman, let alone one who did not seem to be mentally in this world. What was he to do?

Looking at her stirred his dry innards with feelings he couldn't name. He raised his eyes away from her and stared at the horizon until the endless plains light burned his eyes.

No one else to turn to, he thought of the child.

He trotted back to where the boy lay, unsheathed his knife, and cut the rawhide straps that bound his hands and feet. He rested on his knees beside the small body. The boy had lank blond hair and large, deep, wide-set blue eyes.

"What's your name, boy?"

The youngster ran his tongue over his lips in a poor attempt at clearing his mouth of dust.

"Isaac," he sputtered. "My name's Isaac. You got any water, mister?"

Randall groaned aloud. His canteen was on his saddle. The idea of getting to his feet and walking there and back was more than he even wanted to consider.

"You saw where I was lying behind the saddle?" he asked the boy.

"Yeah."

"Canteen's on the saddle. Go get it, but don't drink any until we've given some to her."

He jerked his thumb in the direction of the woman.

"I'm not sure how much I've got left. She your mother?"

"Yeah," replied the boy.

He stood up and rubbed his wrists as he looked off toward the horizon, away from the burning wagon, the dead bodies, his naked mother.

"I wanted to help her, mister. I tried to fight. They killed Pa and they killed Uncle Ike. I figured they'd kill me, too, but I tried to fight, when they started hurtin' her like they did. But they just laughed at me and held me down and tied me up and they kept on hurtin' her."

The boy's words rushed out, tumbling over one another, like leaves washed down a hillside gully in an Indiana rain.

That was what the words reminded him of for some strange reason, leaves down a gully in an Indiana rain. Randall could see those leaves in his mind's eye, could almost feel the rain. He wanted to be there, back home again, washed clean by hillside rain, washed clean from plains dust and plains killing.

He did not have Indiana rain, however. All he had was a partially filled canteen. He knew it contained nothing that could wash the plains from Isaac's pained mind, from his guilt at his powerlessness, from the woman's tortured body, from his own bloodied hands. Right now, though, it was all he had. He rose wearily to his feet and put his hand on the boy's shoulder.

He did not respond to the boy's words; there was nothing he knew how to say.

"Go get the canteen now, son," he said softly.

To his surprise, the boy shrank away at his touch, as though he had been struck. He started running toward MacLane's saddle, but running like a dog that has its tail between its legs. Randall did not know what to make of the boy's behavior, but nothing seemed to make any sense to him now. He walked back to where the woman lay, still staring fixedly at the sky, still grasping at the dust between her fingers.

The Weight
of Salvation

"You're going to get sunstroke or go blind if you keep
staring like that," Randall said, more to himself than to
her.

He didn't think she could hear him. She was in some
sort of trance. He knelt down beside her and put his left
hand under her head. Her already rigid body stiffened
even more at his touch.

"Your mind may be somewhere else, but your body's
still here, isn't it?" he said, as soothingly as he could.

He had often been told that his deep voice was a blessing, that it put people at ease. He tried to use it that way
now, speaking softly, hoping that his words and his tone
would help the woman understand that her ordeal was
over.

He was not at all sure that was true. The Indians were
gone, but he had no idea how badly hurt she was. What if
she never recovered at all? What if her mind refused to
return from the lonely outpost to which it had fled? Well,
that was not his problem. She and the boy would have to

be sent to her family, wherever that might be. That was a job for government officials. He certainly was not a part of the government anymore. He was not sure he was a part of anything.

Isaac came trotting back with the canteen, slowing to a hesitant walk as he came close to them. He licked his dry lips again, looked almost desperately at the canteen, shook it once to hear the water slosh, then held it out at arm's length while his eyes sought the farthest horizon they could find. Randall had to lay the woman's head down, struggle up, and take three weary steps in order to reach the water.

"Don't worry. You'll get some," he said.

He meant for it to be reassuring, but even to himself, his voice sounded like a crosscut saw rasping into buried metal. Well, what could they expect? He knew the boy had had a hard time. Well, so had he. Now he had a naked body with no brain on his hands. His only help was a kid who couldn't think beyond a drink of water.

He almost told Isaac to go back for a blanket or something to cover up his mother's nakedness but caught himself. Better to let him have some water first.

Randall knelt down beside the woman again. He tipped the canteen to her lips. The thin trickle of water ran down her cheek and disappeared into the dust. He realized he had to get her head higher for the water to get inside her and do some good. He pushed his left arm beneath her rigid form to bring her to a sitting position.

Her lips parted and a sudden shriek of pain and rage and terror shot from her mouth, piercing Randall like an arrow. For a moment he thought he really had been shot. Perhaps other Indians had happened across them or the one Indian who escaped him had returned.

It was so physical, that scream, that he felt it go through him. It soared up into the sky, bounced off the far horizon, and came back to knife through his eardrums and into his brain.

It caught him so unaware that he lost his grip on the canteen. It bounced off the woman's rigid body and onto the ground, the precious water sloshing out as it went.

Isaac was whipped around by his mother's scream and now made a wild dive for the canteen.

"Don't touch her," he screeched at Randall as he scooped up the canteen.

Greedily he sucked at the mouth of the canteen, then lowered it toward his mother and splashed some of the water at her mouth, yelling at Randall again not to touch her. He repeated this twice more, gurgling water down, pouring a little on his mother, shouting at Randall to leave her alone. Quickly the canteen was empty. Isaac laid it upon his mother's breast.

MacLane looked at the empty canteen and felt his own overwhelming thirst. How long had it been since he'd had a drink? It must have been early in the morning. He had been trying to conserve, not sure of where he could find more water. Then he had stumbled across this bizarre scene.

He had killed. Killing takes something out of you, he thought. It has to be replaced by water. Now, though, the people he had saved by his killing had taken what he needed.

He knelt beside the woman, across her agonized body from her son, above the empty canteen, and he felt completely drained of life. He had not killed before, not like this, not coldly, mathematically, not counting up the score as he went along. It had been different when he was trying to get to Custer, when he had killed in rage, never expecting to live himself. What kind of man was he now?

The boy looked at him sullenly, his eyelids pulled down against the sun and against his memory and against the man who knelt on the other side of his naked mother. There was a dull challenge back deep in the slitted eyes.

Randall did not understand what he was being challenged to, and he was too dead tired to care. He licked his dry lips, slowly pulled himself to his feet, and set about doing what had to be done.

For one quick moment he thought about just walking away. Hadn't he done his job already, done more than could be expected, gone "above and beyond the call of duty"? He had saved their lives! Was that not enough? His body, however, was already going about the tasks at hand, as though it knew his mind's inevitable decision, and so there was no point in wasting time.

He worked as if in a trance himself, stumbling about the little battlefield. Instinctively he went first for his saddlebags and the once precious message for Custer. Whether it had any value now he had no idea. He knew he would have to decide soon what to do with it. For the moment that decision could wait. His hat meant more to him now. He was stupidly happy when he found it.

Isaac offered no help. He simply sat beside his mother as Randall continued his trek about the little piece of trampled and bloody plains ground. MacLane looked out beyond the plot of violence and thought how much this tiny piece of earth seemed like a desert island in a vast ocean, except it was the ocean that looked like the haven of safety and the island that threatened to drown him without water.

He had to take them somewhere, someplace that they could get help and water. He couldn't use the wagon. It was too badly burned.

Some of the woman's clothes were still scattered about, but she could not dress herself. He doubted that he and Isaac could get anything onto her, as stiff as she was. He found a blanket and carried it to where she lay. The boy got up hurriedly and grabbed the blanket, then awkwardly spread it over his mother.

She didn't scream at the touch. MacLane noticed that he left the empty canteen on her breast, under the blanket.

One of the Indian ponies stood off a way, standing

sideways to the scene, as if unable to decide whether it belonged here or at the other end of the plains. No other horses were in sight.

Randall wondered why this one had elected to remain while the others used the cover of human violence to make a bid for freedom. He did not care, he told himself. The horse was there; that was all that mattered. But he did care. He shrugged his shoulders and almost chuckled. Here he was, with an undeliverable message, having lived through more fright and confusion and violence in the last two days than he had experienced during the rest of his life, with a crazy woman and an impossible boy on his hands, without job or family or prospects, surrounded by dead bodies, and he still wanted to know "why" about something as minor as whether a horse chose to stay or to go.

There was this part of him that stood off, watching. It observed him and everything around him. To it, he was just an actor. The real self was the observer. That watcher kept asking, "Why?" Why was he doing this rather than something else? Why was he the one who was given the message to Custer? Why had he come across the Indians and the woman and the burning wagon? What did it mean, down to why did the horse stay?

What *did* it all mean? That was the question that had driven him to the university. He had not found any answers there, only more questions. Would he ever know? If he could not know, would he ever, at least, be able to stop asking and just live?

The pony had only a simple head bridle. MacLane walked up to it slowly. He knew if it bolted he would never have the strength to chase it down. It seemed to sense his weariness and responded in kind, as though neither of them had a choice about his fate. Randall spoke softly as

he approached, slurring his words because of the dryness
of his mouth.

"Don't worry, little horse. Just a little while now. Just a
little."

The pony didn't seem to mind that Randall had a reputation for being poor with animals. It bowed its head and
let him take its bridle. Together they trudged to where
the woman lay, each footfall of both man and horse stirring up a tiny, sluggish cloud of dust.

How, now, to get the woman on the horse? Randall
was not sure how badly she had been hurt by the Indians,
but he knew it was best not to seat her astride the horse.
He had no stomach for examining her private parts and
wasn't sure what a woman was supposed to look like there
anyway. She could be badly hurt or perfectly all right and
he wouldn't know the difference. He did not know what to
expect from the boy, either, but he was too tired and dry-
mouthed to want to argue.

"Please, for God's sake, relax," Randall pleaded with a
dry rasp.

He said it as much for his own benefit as for hers, as
when he was fighting the Indians only a little while before
and had talked out loud to give himself company. Now no
one was shooting at him, and he was with people, but he
felt more isolated than he had in the chaos of the fight. It
seemed somehow that he had more in common with the
noisy forces of violence, those Indian braves, than he had
with this silent violence of a rigid woman and her hostile
son. He understood the violence of bullets. He had an
answer for it, and so he was in control. But why did these
people he had just saved act as if he were an intruder? He
had no answer. He had to make the decisions, do the
work, but they were in control.

He felt like walking off and leaving them, but he knew
he would not. He told himself that he did not care, so he
might as well stay as go. He knew, however, that he would
stay just because he thought it was the right thing to do.

It was important to do the right thing, regardless of whether anyone noticed.

"What a man does when no one is watching, that is character."

President Wylie had said that in a chapel service at the university. President Wylie's character flew above him like a little ensign. MacLane was not sure he had that kind of character, and he was sure that if he did not have it, nothing else mattered.

As much to himself as to Isaac, he muttered, "Let's put her over the horse. She's not in shape to ride."

MacLane knelt down beside the woman and worked his arms under her. Isaac watched him with the same sullen stare. Randall nodded to him, then nodded at the woman. Isaac moved slowly, but he dropped down and put his arms under her from the other side. They began to lift, and she stiffened again.

The scene was so outlandish. Randall grew light-headed, and a part of him stood aside again to observe. He and Isaac staggered, looking like a saloon vaudeville act, a drunk and a dwarf, trying to hoist onto an increasingly restless Indian pony a live body that was as stiff as a corpse three days into rigor mortis. If the thirst hadn't already stuck his tongue to his mouth, the way old envelopes seal themselves in a forgotten drawer, he would have laughed.

Somehow they got the woman over the horse's back. The empty canteen fell off beneath the pony. The blanket bunched under her. Her arms and breasts hung down on one side, her legs on the other. Randall tried to cover her bare bottom with the ends of the blanket, but he had no way to fasten them. He finally gave up.

It was indecent, to haul her around that way, but he was too drained to care. When you're down to the dregs of your strength, a bare behind just does not seem important, especially if it's someone else's.

He found a bit of rope at the wagon and tied her wrists to her ankles, to keep her from falling off. It was wrong to tie her, to put her into that kind of bondage, especially with scorched rope from her own burned wagon, after what she'd been through, especially since her mind was frozen and she would not understand why. He certainly couldn't hold her on, though, touching her the whole way, however far that might be. He just didn't know what else to do.

He nodded at the boy to take the horse's lead braid and prepared to walk along beside to steady her.

The boy stared at him with dull eyes, his arms hanging at his sides.

"We oughta bury Pa and Uncle Ike."

Randall was too weary for anger, too weary for laughter, too weary. . . .

"We'll send somebody from town," he whispered.

He didn't know what town he was talking about. He didn't care. This was a wagon road. It had to go somewhere. In days to come, he often wished that he had taken any other road to any other town.

Finally the boy took the lead braid and started trudging off, the dragging heels of his clodhopper shoes trailing tiny puffs of dust. Isaac did not look back, at the burned-out wagon or at the dead bodies. Or at the young man who had killed the Indians or at his mother, one drag-assed and the other bare-assed, side by side, moving along behind him in the shimmering heat waves like a misshapen beast.

At some point from deep in his eyes, Randall knew that the boy would hold it against him, that he would use Randall's refusal to bury his kin as an excuse to hate him for saving his life.

Middle Bend

<hr>

It was a strange and bedraggled caravan that trudged into Middle Bend under the hot eye of the afternoon sun. The sun's eye was almost indifferent, however, compared with those of the citizens of the town. Stories had circulated quickly through the territory, stories of thousands of savages overrunning the plains, stories of the death of Custer. The town had been on constant alert for several days, hoping against hope that none of the murdering redskins would come their way, sure that their own slaughter would be complete if they did.

The first watchers saw Isaac and Randall and the woman before anyone could even tell whether they were red or white. Every man who could hold a gun was at the edge of town by the time they reached it.

When MacLane saw the crowd waiting for them, he wanted to run to them, to get within the safety of those numbers, to feel just one precious drink of water sliding down his gullet, and then another. He tried to yell out to them, to call them out from the end of the street, to hurry them down to help him with the woman, to bring water, but his throat was so dry and rusty he could not even croak. All he could do, all the boy and the pony could do, was just keep trudging on, one weary foot after another.

"Why don't they get out here?" he asked himself. "Can't they see we are in trouble, that we need help?"

He tipped his dusty hat back on his head and scanned the crowd. It was so thick across the end of the street, like a windbreak of young pines, impossible to walk through. There were no women or children in the thicket of bodies, only men, each one with a rifle or shotgun across his arms. The faces on the men were sullen, almost disappointed looking.

A shimmer of heat performed a St. Vitus dance in front of him, warping the faces. Randall's plains-cleansed nostrils began to pick up closed-in scents, the smells of a stable, of grease and tobacco and sweat, of too many people huddled together in too much fear.

Even though they were desperate for water and for the safety of the town, Isaac and the pony began to slow down as they approached the knot of dark figures, so immobile, like actors in a melodrama tableau. MacLane could feel his own steps unconsciously shortening, even against his will. His mind had been dulled by the battle at the Little Bighorn and the fight at the wagon and the thirst, dulled like an ax used to fell tree after tree without ever being sharpened. His shorter steps gave him a chance to pull his mind from the tired stump in which it had become embedded.

He thought first of the woman's nakedness. Somehow it was wrong to walk past all those men with her looped naked over a horse, even though none of them knew her and would probably never see her again. One part of his mind knew it was stupid to worry about the nakedness of her flesh, after all it had been through. He knew that her throat must be as parched as his own; better to have a drink than to be clothed. Still, she was coming naked to that knot of men before they were coming to water, and nothing now could be done about what she had already been through.

It bothered him that he was even thinking about it. It was such a minor detail in the big picture of what they had all suffered. He had been plagued all his life, however, with the inability to get the niggling details off his mind. They were like the dust that got down the back of his shirt when he put up hay back on the farm. No act of mind could make him forget them. They were there until he took some action to strike them off his list. So, he pulled his dust-laden sweat-soaked hat off his head and stuck it on top of the woman's sunburned rump.

The men of the town watched as the shimmering, dust-colored splotch moved toward them in the heat haze, lurching eerily out of the wide and dreaded plain. Even in the day's worst heat, under the unforgiving sun, the unmoving air about them loaded down with their unwashed fear, they crowded together.

"What in bejesus is that?" whispered a small man at the corner of the crowd. His abnormally large Adam's apple bobbed up and down with his breathing.

"What you think, Si?"

The speaker this time was a portly man, his considerable girth swaddled by a gravy-spotted waistcoat that came up almost to his chin, mercifully hiding a loosely tied and punishingly plaid cravat. He belonged to that race of fat men that seems to be insulated against the heat. He stood in the front row, middle, of the street's-end crowd, beside a tall and square-jawed figure. The tall man was the one he addressed as Si.

"Don't know," the tall man said. "If what we hear about Custer's right, could be redskins right after 'em, could be leadin' 'em right here. Damn."

His *damn* sounded more like disappointment than a curse.

"Looks like a little boy up front there, leading the

horse," commented a voice from the second rank of the bunch.

The voice was louder than the others had been, as though small things could be mentioned in full voice without fear of reprisal.

The little man with the Adam's apple spoke up again, above a whisper now, but just barely. His profession mitigated against raised voices. He was the undertaker, Titus Lowe, "Whispering" Lowe, as he was known to all the town.

"Bejesus. There's a body on the horse," he said.

Titus Lowe tended to notice bodies.

"Ain't no horse, really," said Si, the tall one. "Injin pony. No saddle. No bridle. Some Injin's killed hisself a white man and put the body on the horse."

The tall man was farsighted and had a bad back. He eased his back by craning his head forward, so that he always seemed to be gazing at some far and terrible spot, much as a buzzard does. The people of the town mistook his faraway look for wisdom. Actually, he just saw things before others; he did not know what they meant. However, men who are tall, farsighted, square-jawed, and named for a weapon are almost invariably pressed into leadership roles, whether they want them or deserve them.

This had happened to Silas Winchester ever since he came to Middle Bend. Consequently he had come to believe that he could interpret what he saw. Since he saw it first, he had time to think up some meaning.

The men stirred restlessly, making action room for their rifles while still hanging close to one another. If what Si Winchester said was true, they'd better be ready. The brazen "Injin" was bringing his prey right up into the town.

"I don't know, Si," said the portly man, his gravy stains rising with a sigh. "No Injin's gonna be crazy enough to walk into town with a dead white man."

Milo Rosewater understood about Si Winchester's long look. In fact, he often used it to his advantage. Being the owner of the town's leading saloon, Milo was looked up to but not trusted. So he used Si Winchester to express opinions that people did not want to hear from someone named for a barber shop perfume. Unfortunately for Milo, Si sometimes went off to thinking on his own.

"Unless it's a trick," whispered Titus Lowe, "a trick to get us all down here to this end of town, watching, whilst his cutthroat friends sneak in on our backside."

The men in the back of the crowd craned their necks around, looking for the trickers. Some turned full, shading their eyes against the horizon. One even took a tentative step back along the main street until he realized no one was coming with him.

It was just then that a rusty voice from the middle of the crowd crowed out, "My Gawd! That's a woman on that horse, naked as a jaybird. An' that feller walkin' along there just put his hat on her butt end. Look! Looks like she's got two faces ridin' sidesaddle under that hat!"

The men looked more closely at the steadily moving apparition approaching them on the plain. It was true. There was a little boy leading an Indian pony, and a man, and a naked woman, strapped over the pony. There was a dirty, black hat stacked on her bottom, which in her present position was her top.

Under normal circumstances it might not have seemed all that funny. Life on the plains was hard. The men of Middle Bend were used to seeing people dragging into town on busted wagon wheels and busted horses, with busted hopes and busted pockets. It was nothing to laugh at.

They had been on edge for three days, however, since the first rumors of the Custer massacre had drifted into town. The tales of huge bands of Indians had them clench-jawed and plain scared. When they first saw the haze-dancing specter coming at them from the flat heat of the plains, they were sure their time had come, and they had steeled themselves for the inevitable conflict. Now this—a little boy and a gaunt, young man and a naked woman wearing a hat on her bare butt. It was so totally different from what they were expecting that it was ludicrous. It exploded their tension like a ripe tomato splatting on a barn side.

"Godawmighty," yelled one of the men. "Ain't they a sorry sight."

The whole band broke into loud guffaws, slapping their knees, pounding their neighbors on their backs, staggering around like drunks, laughing until they had to drop their rifles to hold their sides.

"They better take her to the assay office," gurgled a man, just as the laughter began to let up, and that started it all over again.

"No," shouted someone else. "They better take her to Widder Bowen, the hatmaker. That hat ain't becomin' to her behind."

"Hell, that young feller can't tell his head from a butt," said another, giggling.

"This could turn the whole hatrack business upside down," roared still another.

MacLane had just plodded into good seeing and hearing range of the men when their laughter started. It made no sense to him. Just as the men of Middle Bend had been wrapped in the cloak of their fear, Randall was weighed down by his thirst and fatigue and disorientation. He had no room to think about how others might see him and his burdens. He didn't recognize that the laughter of the men teetered on the edge of hysteria, just as their lives teetered on the edge of civilization.

He could make out the words now, the coarse jests about the woman, the crude jokes at his expense. His sun-baked brain was slow, but it still worked. It could tell the difference between laughing with him and laughing at him. He felt the acid in his belly, the tightening of his guts. The anger began to build in him, anger at his grandfather for dying so loudly that Randall had made a spectacle of himself beating on the stove, anger at his father and brother for dropping their lives like cowpies on some southern battlefield, anger at the men in Washington for giving him the message, anger at Custer for rushing off into a horde of murderous Indians to escape him, anger at the woman for getting raped and for being naked and for wearing his hat. He felt like a runaway train, no engineer at the controls, just a mad fireman shoveling coal into the burners with no thought for where it was headed, just hell-bent for nowhere as fast as possible.

One part of his brain was so astonished at his anger and its irrationality that it slipped off to the side of where he walked, a little ahead of him, shakily glancing back at him, amazed that he could still generate anger after the battle at the Little Bighorn and the fight at the woman's wagon.

Randall wasn't used to thinking of himself as either a violent or angry man. He was proud of his discipline and orderliness. Now his whole life had been taken over by rage and fury. It shook him to be so out of control, but he had no idea how to get the control back. Everything that happened to him now was so different from all that he had known in his past.

The anger took on focus as he surveyed the idiotic clowns in front of him.

They have no idea what we've been through, what we've suffered, he thought. They've been sitting here in town, snug and safe, while good men have been out there getting massacred on the plains. This woman's been through hell, and they're laughing at her. They don't even know if she's alive or dead, but just because she's naked and has a hat on her behind to protect her from the sun, they act like it's a vaudeville act.

Then he realized that in the whole walk into town, he was so absorbed in his own thirst and weariness that he had not even noticed if her fair skin was being burned by the unrelenting sun. Yet he was mad at the men who had just now seen her, for not considering something he had had miles to think on. It stoked his anger at them all the more.

Isaac and the Indian pony came to a stop without even

realizing it. They were both still leaning forward, dust sculptures, almost lifelike, braise-frozen into a leaden lump by the sight and sounds of the cavorting townsmen before them. MacLane did not hesitate. He just kept plodding on, like Grant had plodded through the war. He grabbed the lead line from Isaac and kept walking, straight toward the band of buffoons before him.

He knew he could not fight them, shove their teeth down their throats as he wanted to do. There were too many of them. He was too tired, and despite the rage he focused on them like sun rays through a magnifying glass, he really didn't care about them. But he had started out to get a doctor for the woman and water for them all, and he had no intention of being detoured by a bunch of loose-lipped fools.

The strongest waves of laughter had passed by the time he actually reached the men. They were now reduced to chuckling and an occasional knee slap and a lot of pointing and nudging of one another, like twelve-year-old boys after a fart in Sunday school. MacLane headed straight for the middle of the street, which happened to be where the biggest cluster of gawkers and gigglers was. The laughers gave way reluctantly, unwilling to lose the only source of merriment they'd had in days. One by one, however, they dropped back and then sideways, surprise lighting their faces as the hard, smoldering stare of the tall, young man sought their eyes.

Only Silas Winchester and Milo Rosewater remained in MacLane's path. Randall did not waver. He went straight for them. Si Winchester held up a hand. It seemed to be part greeting, part order to stop, and part indecision. Randall ignored it and marched right on. Milo Rosewater did a little dance and got to one side of the advancing horse. Si pulled his hand into his chest and fell back.

"What in hell's the matter with him?" he muttered to MacLane's tight and narrow back.

It was then that the woman stirred, lifting her head

with a groan and an effort that caused her to slide partway around the pony, her arms riding up and legs riding down. Randall's hat slid from her buttocks and plopped into the dust of the street. Her long hair was filthy. Her white flesh was burned red. She stared at the men, stared through them, into them, with a wild and feverish glare, as if seeing them from another world. She viewed them as an angry giant sees ants working in the dust, dust that is the only world they know. Then her head dropped back against the pony's flank.

The whole street went silent, as suddenly as it had erupted into laughter moments before. The heavy air, cleaved apart by the blunt edge of their relief, now rolled back over them, pressing down, squeezing sweat and laughter together into vinegar, dripping off them and disappearing into the dust.

There is always one wit who can't let it go, who senses the change but thinks that he can bring back the good times.

"Hey, Milo, you see what she had hangin' down there on your side of that pony? She's a real cow, that one," he called .

"Shut up," hissed Milo Rosewater. "This is different."

"Whutinhell's th' matter with him?" muttered the would-be wit, in a self-conscious parody of Silas Winchester's words.

Silently then, scuffing their boots in the plains dust of the town streets, stirring up a drab, little wake, they fell in behind MacLane and the pony and the woman. Some jockeyed for position for a better look at the woman, but no one spoke. They avoided her eyes, lest she raise her head and skewer them again with her crazy stare.

They totally ignored the boy trailing along, closing upon him like a wave on a canoe, until he was finally squeezed out at the end of the rolling mass of men.

Isaac dragged along, pulled by the need for water, dulled by all that had happened to him in just a few hours.

He came to MacLane's cavalry hat, which had so recently perched precariously upon his mother's buttocks, which had caused the wild laughter of the men. They had unknowingly trampled it into the dust, their eyes not on what lay in the street but upon the woman.

The boy stooped, a small hand reaching out to pick up the hat. Then he pulled the hand back, stepped on the hat with both feet, and followed the men into town.

Two Women

Randall headed for the water tower, set incongruously between the two tallest buildings in the middle of the town. It was basically a huge barrel, with pipes running into it from roof gutters on the buildings on either side of it. Underneath it was a horse watering trough. The pony got a whiff of the water and started trotting toward it, jouncing the woman with every hoof strike, until she was almost entirely on its side instead of on top, breasts on its back, legs pulled up under its belly. Randall broke into a shambling jog to try to stay up with it. He put one hand on the woman's back to keep her from sliding on around and under the pony. The little horse went directly to the trough and began to lap up the water with a noisy single-mindedness.

MacLane wanted to plunge his own head into the trough with the pony, to feel the wet wonder of it, regardless of how many horses had been drinking there, but a little part of his brain had cleared. He remembered that he should be taking care of the woman first.

He saw the swinging pipe, used to run water from the tower to the trough. He pulled it from its hook and staggered a little as he swung it out to the side of the pony, then waited for the water to come. It gushed down in a rush, and Randall turned it on the woman, still lashed to the horse. He pulled her head up by the hair and directed some of the water into her mouth, then turned it on his own face, letting water pour into his parched mouth, stinging his cracked lips, disappearing into his swollen tongue as though it were a sponge.

As water, it wasn't much. It tasted tepid, almost stagnant. But as a miracle of life, it was awe-inspiring.

When Isaac saw the water he began to run. It wasn't much of a run, more of a limb-flinging shamble, but it was the best he could do. The men were knotted too tightly in front of him to be able to get through them, so he skirted the side of the crowd, throwing himself forward, almost falling to the dirt with every step, catching himself at the last moment, and regaining enough balance to throw himself into another step toward the precious water.

He finally lost his balance just as he reached Randall and the water. He tripped over his own feet. He dove headlong right into Randall's knee, catching his nose flush on the bone. His nose immediately began to bleed, but he held on to MacLane's leg to steady himself and lifted his face in order to catch any drop that came his way.

Randall was staggered by the blow to his knee, momentarily nauseated as pain shot up to his brain and rebounded down into his stomach. He looked down and saw the boy clinging to his leg, face upraised, nose bleeding. He couldn't move with Isaac attached to his leg, so he just turned the pipe down his leg, letting the water wash down over the boy, flooding water and blood together into his mouth. He stood there, time holding still, playing the water first into his own face and then mouth, then over the woman, then down onto the boy.

"Hey," came a rough voice through the euphoria of

the water. "Don't be runnin' that water onta the ground thata way. We ain't gotta 'nough as it is."

Randall looked back at the men. The sun glanced off their faces, making them look like a collection of tin plates that had been tossed out into the street. He could not identify the speaker.

You've heard one loud mouth, you've heard them all, he thought.

He remembered his father saying that once. Randall had ridden into town with him, on the high seat of the single-tree wagon, "Old Prince" stepping out briskly on a bright blue Indiana summer day. They had driven by Tislow's Saloon. A drunk on the sidewalk had been yelling things. Randall did not recognize the words. When he asked his father what they meant, he told him the words didn't really matter: "You've heard one loudmouth, you've heard them all." He wondered why he thought of it now. This light brown day was so different from those of his childhood. . . .

He played the water over each mouth once more, then hung the pipe on its hook, reluctant to put it back, obstinately wanting just to drop it into the dust and let the water drain dead into the street. He knew, though, that too much water at once would be bad for them.

He felt the pressure on his leg release. He looked down at Isaac, whose arms hung at his sides. Only a small trickle of blood now ran from his nose to his lip.

Randall moved over to the woman. Si Winchester stepped up to him, with a rather self-important air.

"Mister, even if that's your woman, that ain't no way to treat her. I don't know what she did, but you shouldn't be tiein' her up an' draggin' her into town naked like that."

Randall noted that the entire time the man was speaking, he was carefully staring at the woman's breasts. Randall was too tired to do anything but ignore him. He stepped over to the pony to undo the thongs that bound the woman's wrists to her ankles, but he realized that if he cut her off the horse, she would be totally exposed to the probing eyes of the men.

"Not my woman," he croaked, his throat still protesting from his long thirst. "Indians. Attacked their wagon. Killed the men. I found her and the boy. Brought them in. No water. Nothing to put on her."

Randall wasn't sure why he didn't put anything into the story about his own part in killing the Indians at the wagon. It just didn't seem necessary.

Suddenly a black cannonball with a gray bun behind shot up onto MacLane's side.

"Cut that woman loose," it demanded.

Randall half turned and saw a woman who could not have been more than five feet tall but was almost as broad. She was wearing an old-fashioned eastern dress, black from the high lace collar to the dust-covered double hem that swept the street. Her face was a round moon, like a big sugar cookie, decorated with a little lump of nose, two bright blue marble eyes, and a straight slit of barely pink mouth. She was carrying a sheet and a shawl, both draped carelessly over her arm, as though she had hooked them like a mailbag on her way out of the house.

"I said to cut that woman loose."

She fairly spat out the words this time and was directing them right at Randall.

"Yes, m'am," he said, feeling foolish, but not knowing what else to say. He started to explain that cutting her loose was exactly what he intended to do, but that he could not because he had nothing with which to cover her, and the men were all standing there. . . . She cut him off.

"Elijah!" she yelled back over her shoulder.

A man came clumping up the boardwalk along the buildings. He wore a black suit with a strange collar that had two white tabs hanging down onto his vest. He was about the same age as the woman. Randall guessed them to be in their middle sixties.

Randall cut the thongs that bound the woman's hands

and ankles while the man in black eased her off the pony. The cannonball wedged herself in between the woman and the horse and covered her with the sheet. Before the sheet hid her body from view, Randall noticed that her wrists and ankles were bleeding from the thongs, that all the back side of her was burned bright by the sun, and her front side, from breasts to thighs, was rubbed raw from the horse's hair.

He felt ashamed that he had not been able to take better care of her. At the time he had started from the scene of the wagon massacre, it had just seemed so impossible. He thought about how he might have gone around to the dead Indians and collected the woman's clothes from off their bodies and re-dressed her, but he was interrupted again.

"I need two men to carry her to my house," called the little lady over her shoulder as she finished wrapping up the woman like a mummy. "And no feelin' of her private parts through the sheet," she added.

"Hazel, really," muttered the man in black, his face going red.

She ignored him. MacLane had the impression that she was used to saying what she pleased and ignoring the consequences and the man in black as well.

"I'll help," Randall croaked.

"You've done enough already," she said without looking at him. Randall wondered just what she meant by that.

"Well, you heard Mrs. Thistle," Silas Winchester shouted in his best tall man's voice. "Let's have a couple of you up here. James. Levi."

MacLane noted that it was like asking for volunteers in the army, when the names of the "volunteers" followed immediately upon the call.

Two men shouldered their way through from the back ranks of the crowd, not particularly good-naturedly. They passed a fair number of others who looked more capable of carrying a woman. Apparently Winchester's farsightedness made it preferable to be up close to him when the call for "volunteers" went out.

The men bent to their task and, careful not to look at the woman, hooked their arms under her at the spots Mrs. Thistle carefully chose for them. Randall thought it was strange how careful they were all being to protect her modesty once she was covered up when they hadn't seemed to give a damn while she was still naked. Perhaps, he thought, it was just the presence of the redoubtable Mrs. Thistle.

"I don't know who can pay the doctor," said MacLane.

"Ha!" snorted Mrs. Thistle. "No doctor fool enough to stay in Middle Bend. We doctor ourselves around here. Costs less that way, unless you count dying. I'll take care of her. Don't worry. You won't have to pay me anything. Nobody ever does."

She said the last line as she scanned the crowd of now silent men. Few of them met her eyes. Apparently most of them had received her free "doctoring" at one time or another.

The old man in black started leading the "volunteer" woman bearers back along the boardwalk. Randall assumed that he was Mr. Thistle, from the way Mrs. Thistle ordered him around. She started to gather up her skirts to go after them.

"You'd better come with me and tell me about this, assuming you know anything."

She threw the words back over her shoulder at Randall, in a hushed voice that was clearly meant only for him. She clearly had no intention of staying out in the street with the gaggle of men longer than was necessary.

"Ma'am, this is her boy here. His name's Isaac."

The boy was slumped back on his heels, still kneeling where he had held on to Randall's leg to receive the precious water, his hands limp beside him in the dust. His nose was no longer actively bleeding, but a ragged line of blood had dried on his face.

"Well, bring him along," Mrs. Thistle said, turning an impatient gray-streaked bun on him. She took several brisk steps along the walk and then whipped around. "What's the woman's name?" she demanded.

Randall held out his hands, palms up, and shrugged his shoulders. "I don't know," he said.

"Good Lord," she said, her eyes rolling up toward heaven, as though she were really addressing the deity. "Brings a naked woman into town and doesn't even know her name."

She turned to go again.

"Hannah. That's her name. Hannah Reindorf."

The voice was thin but rough-edged. It came from down below MacLane. Isaac spoke his mother's name as though it were an act of defiance, as though daring anyone to disagree with him.

"Come," said Mrs. Thistle, and turned once again to leave.

Randall reached down to help Isaac up, but the boy ducked his head forward and scrambled to his feet on his own and started after the surprisingly quick little lady in black. Randall shrugged and took a few steps after them. Then he remembered his saddlebags, turned around, and went to get them off the back of the Indian pony. As he did so Milo Rosewater nudged Silas Winchester forward.

"Uh, mister, you say Indians attacked that woman and her boy?"

MacLane shouldered the bags.

"Yes. Them and two men. Killed the men. I came up on them while they . . . I came up after they killed the men."

"Where you comin' from?"

"You know anything about Custer?"

"Did the Injins really kill him?"

"The Injins still there when you come on the wagon?"

The questions came at him all at once, from several places in the crowd.

"Now, men," said Milo Rosewater, stepping forward and facing the crowd, his back almost turned to MacLane. "We all have questions to ask of this gentleman, but we need to get his story in an orderly fashion. Let's go over to the Palace and buy him a drink. He still looks mighty thirsty. Then he can tell us all about what happened."

"I am still thirsty," said MacLane, surprise in his voice, as though Rosewater's words had just reminded him of it.

He stepped back to the downpipe from the water tower and unhooked it again. He let the tepid water flow over his face and into his mouth once more. He wanted to keep on drinking forever, to fill himself up like the camels he had learned about in Bible class so that never again would he find himself thirsty. With his first thirst slaked, however, the water began to taste like what it was—lukewarm, not very clean rainwater that had been filtered through roof shingles.

He looked down at the little puddle in which he stood, in which Isaac had knelt a few moments before. It was drying up almost as fast as it formed. The dust of the high plains was, in its season, a jealous landlord, tolerating no interlopers from the wetlands. Little brown bubbles formed where the water stood, then worked their way out to the edges of the puddle and popped against the quickly drying mud. He looked up at the strange faces of the men and found that his mind was clear and working fully again. The water had washed the dust from his mind down into the puddle at his feet.

"Thanks for the invitation," he said to Rosewater, "but I've got other things to do."

He turned to follow in the direction that they had taken the woman. What was her name? Something German. Reindorf. That would be her husband's name, of course. What was her name? Hannah . . . That was it.

Behind him he heard the voice of Silas Winchester, with the same complaint as when MacLane almost walked over him coming into town.

"What in hell's the matter with him?"

"Not very sociable, is he," he heard someone else say, not as a question.

"Hell, we finally get a chance to find out what's goin' on, and he says he's got other things to do."

The voice was a poor mockery of MacLane's own.

What was wrong with these people anyway? They greeted him at the edge of town like he was a joke, offered no help, then got huffy when he went about his business. Even men on the plains ought to understand that taking care of your people was more important than jawing in a saloon. But, of course, they weren't his people.

The crowd had spread out into a large semicircle, one end of it reaching almost to the boardwalk in front of the buildings. Randall stopped in front of the man who was last in the line.

"That lady, Mrs. Thistle? Where does she live?"

"She's the preacher's wife. Reverend Thistle. They live down beside the church."

The man did not meet Randall's eyes. He acted like he was embarrassed to give him information in front of the others, when Randall had so curtly refused news to them.

MacLane looked along the street. Beyond the buildings of the business section he saw a church steeple, down a couple of blocks and over another. He started off to find Hannah and the boy, to be of what aid he could to Mrs. Thistle, even though she didn't appear to need much help.

He was just a little surprised at himself. After all, they weren't his to care for. Nonetheless, he told himself, whether it was a song or a book or a job, he was a man who liked to finish what he started. That, he knew, was one reason why it bothered him so much that he had not been able to deliver the message to Custer. That job was unfinished. It hung like a piece of rotting meat on a hook at the back of his mind.

Unexpected Fame

Randall found the little cottage beside the church. The two buildings were set off by themselves, at the end of a street, like a drunken uncle at Christmas dinner—part of the family but not quite belonging. Three or four women stood in a yard across the street, watching, but making no attempt to cross the chasm. They stared at MacLane openly as he walked up to the parsonage and knocked lightly on the door. It was the Reverend Mr. Thistle who opened to him.

"Come in, young man," he said. "My wife has Hannah in the bedroom, looking after her. Isaac is having some milk and cold corn bread in the kitchen. It's the best I could do on my own, I'm afraid."

Reverend Thistle gave the self-deprecating smile of the male who is no good around the house and proud of it.

Randall stood self-consciously just inside the door. He was uncomfortably aware of how unfit he was to be in a home. This was the first house he had been in since he had received the message for Custer in the home of the congressman. That seemed like several lives ago. Then

115

he had been dressed for polite company. Now he was covered with plains grime mixed with tepid town water, not to mention the smell of fear and the guilt of death. Reverend Thistle understood.

"Oh, please, do come in. All sorts of folks come here. Mrs. Thistle doctors their bodies and I doctor their souls. Come out to the kitchen and have something to eat. Mrs. Thistle would fix you a regular meal, I'm sure, if she could, but she needs to pay her attention to Mrs. Reindorf, I'm sure you'll agree."

He led Randall through the austere parlor into a small but cheery kitchen. Isaac was just finishing up a bowl of corn bread chunks in milk. He recoiled when he saw Randall and shoved his bowl away and slid out the back door.

"A rather nervous youngster," observed Reverend Thistle, eyeing the old-looking young man rather nervously himself.

A frontier pastor had no trouble recognizing the signs of violence.

"Perhaps you'd like to tell me . . . about what brings all of you to Middle Bend. . . ."

Middle Bend. So that's where he was. It seemed like he could remember someone saying the name earlier, but he wasn't sure. It hardly mattered. It was just a place to drop off the woman and the boy.

Randall recounted briefly the events at the wagon while the parson fixed another bowl of corn bread in milk. He wanted to spare Reverend Thistle's religious sensibilities, so he did not mention that he had killed the Indians. He simply said that he had driven them off.

He was as ignorant of ministers as of Indians. The man in black knew more of the seamy side of life than most people could even guess at. Like most people, however, Randall thought the parson lived behind a wall of Bibles that kept him from seeing the real world.

He sat down in the chair that Isaac had vacated and began to eat. It was extremely simple food, but it reminded him of home, and he was very hungry. He gulped it down, ashamed of his manners but unable to slow down. He was about to explain how he had happened across the wagon when Mrs. Thistle appeared.

"Well," she said, "I think she's going to be all right physically, at least in terms of her private parts. Nothing done there that isn't normal enough for a woman."

Randall and her husband both turned red.

"She certainly wasn't helped much by being hauled along on that horse in the sun, but the sunburn and scrapes are mostly a matter of salve and time. I don't know about her mind, though. I guess that's going to be up to Reverend Thistle. More his department than mine, although he's a man, and I doubt she's going to be much favorable to men for a while."

Randall gulped. He wasn't used to such plain talk, especially from a woman. He was also very much aware of the strange formality that existed in the relationship between man and wife in that house. They even referred to each other as "Mrs." and "Reverend."

"Well, I see you've eaten some. I think I'd better fix a proper supper, anyway. Won't take long. You men find the boy and wash up at the stand behind the house. Then Reverend Thistle can go over to Gladys Williams and get a change of clothes for the youngun. She's got a boy about his size. Mrs. Reindorf won't be needing clothes for a while, so I'll go around tomorrow to the women her size to see what I can do. Go on. Out of my kitchen."

She shooed them as she might a pair of crows that were too old to do much damage to the corn. They left as though they were.

The parson tried to draw Isaac out as they took turns at the washstand, asking him about his life and his family before the events on the road to Middle Bend. The boy answered only in monosyllables. The minister gave up and went off to borrow clothes for him. Isaac and Randall sat uneasily, at opposite ends of the porch stoop, waiting

for one or another of the Thistles to return to save them
from being alone with each other.

Finally the parson returned, and Mrs. Thistle called
them in to eat. Reverend Thistle gave a mercifully short
grace. They all dug in to stew and biscuits and jam and
coffee. Randall was amazed at how much he and Isaac
could eat even though they had just had corn bread and
milk a little while before.

In surprisingly short order they had shoveled in all
they could hold. The four of them sat around the table,
waiting for someone else to say whatever it was that needed
to be said. It was Mrs. Thistle who broke the silence.

"Well, I'll go see if Hannah's come back to us enough
to eat. Reverend Thistle will show you where you're to
sleep, Isaac. I suppose you men will want to talk awhile."

Randall scraped to his feet as she rose to leave the
room. Her husband and the boy remained seated.

"I thank you kindly, ma'am, for the supper, and . . . for
looking after the wo— that is, Mrs. Reindorf, and her boy,
here . . . Isaac. But I'd better be getting on now. Is there a
hotel where I could get a room?"

"No need to do that, son," spoke the parson. "We can
put you up, and I imagine you'll want to be here. . . ."

He let the idea hang there, that somehow Randall had
some continuing responsibility for the woman and the
boy. Randall figured he'd better scotch that idea quickly.

"Thank you, Reverend. It's generous of you to offer. But
you have a small house here, and I won't be staying in town.
As soon as I can get a horse and saddle, I'll be heading on."

He was already edging around the table, toward the
back door. He was caught before he could make it,
speared by Mrs. Thistle's stare. Her eyes bored deep,
looking for something, but he knew not what or why. Her
voice was edged.

"The hotel's downtown, a couple of fronts up from that
water tower . . . where I got Hannah. They serve meals.
Other places do, too."

Her husband squirmed uncomfortably on his ladder-back chair. Isaac stared at his empty plate. Randall addressed himself to some point in among the three of them.

"Well, that's fine, then. I'll be going. I thank you again. It was very generous of you to feed me."

He picked up his saddlebags from beside the door and slipped out. He headed generally back toward the main street, not sure exactly how to retrace his steps but knowing he could not get lost in a town the size of Middle Bend. He was in no hurry. Walking might help him figure out Mrs. Thistle's attitude toward him.

The walk did not help. His brain was too weary to do much figuring, and his body was as tired as he could ever remember. The big supper was swelling up and all he wanted to do was sleep. Leaving could wait until tomorrow. After all, where did he have to go anyway? Anyplace else would be fine, but anyplace else would probably still be there when he got there.

He found the hotel and checked in. The clerk made a show of reading his signature.

"Well, you've certainly caused a good deal of excitement today, Mr. MacLane," he said, displaying a supercilious smile that was punctuated by a gold tooth.

Randall did not know what reply that called for and so he said nothing.

"Uh . . . they're talking quite a bit about it, uh . . . over at the Palace. You might want to go over yourself, hear what they're saying."

He smiled again, a conspiratorial leer this time, as though he and the slumping young man before him shared a dirty secret.

"All I want to do is get some sleep," Randall said curtly.

It irritated him that almost everyone in this hick town seemed to have some idea of how he should spend his time or who he should be responsible for. Why couldn't a man simply help someone and be left alone?

He hefted his saddlebags and went up to his room. He

pulled off his boots, fell back on the bed, and was immediately fast asleep, clothes and all.

He awoke fifteen hours later, still flat on his back, stiff as a board and with his mouth as dry as it had been yesterday. His head hurt, too. He couldn't even remember when he'd had a headache before. He stumbled down the hall to the bathroom, used the thunder mug, and filled his pitcher with water from a deep ceramic reservoir. Back in his room he drank half the water and poured the rest into the basin on the washstand.

Then he proceeded to clean himself up as best he could with the lukewarm stuff. When he was satisfied that he looked halfway presentable, he wandered downstairs to the dining room, in search of food and coffee, although not in that order.

There was a plump young woman, perhaps twenty, moving between the tables, setting silver and china in place. She eyed him shyly. She hid her hands in her apron as she spoke.

"We're not open for customers right now, Mr. MacLane. Breakfast is over and the cook's gone till time for startin' lunch. 'Bout the only place to get somethin' to eat this time of day is over at the Palace."

Randall felt foolish. He hadn't even known what time of day it was, just woke up and assumed it was breakfast time. It embarrassed him that the girl should realize he had slept so long and didn't know the time. He touched his hat and excused himself and backed out of the room.

He was halfway across the street to the Palace when the obvious question hopped onto his shoulder and pecked at him like a pirate's parrot. How did she know who he was?

It was no wonder when he stepped into the big saloon. Everyone there knew who he was. His name was on every tongue.

What's in a Name

"I tell ya, he left bodies all over the place, Injins and
horses, and two white men, too. Whoever was out there
did a powerful lot of killin'. Injins had rifles—"

The voice stopped. Every eye turned to stare at
MacLane as he walked through the swinging doors. A
total silence dropped with a thud. They all knew who he
was, for sure. It was clear he had been the topic of conversation. He was embarrassed again, but he was hungry. He
was also getting a little bit angry. He strode straight
across to the bar.

"They told me at the hotel I could get something to eat
over here," he said.

"Why, uh, sure," stuttered the bartender. "Could get
some steak and eggs."

"That'll be fine. You got any coffee now?"

"Sure, sure," said the bartender. "Charley! Go out to
the kitchen and bring in the coffeepot."

A little man edged away toward a door at the end of
the bar, reluctantly, as if afraid he might miss something.

Randall wanted to check his clothes, to see if he'd forgotten to put something on. Then he remembered that he hadn't really taken anything off.

Suddenly the fat man of the street the day before heaved himself up from a big, round table in the corner of the room. It looked like he had not taken anything off, either. He was still wearing the same stained waistcoat and impossible plaid cravat.

"Welcome to my establishment, Mr. MacLane," he said, his manner a bit more grandiose than his voice. "I am Milo Rosewater. There will be no charge for your meal here. Any man who can single-handedly undo the heathen redskins in the manner you apparently did . . ."

He left the implication hanging in the air, but MacLane was not sure what it was.

"Yeah," took up another voice.

Randall recognized it as the one he had interrupted when he entered.

"Some of us went out there, see what happened on the road. God Almighty, you sure done them varmints in."

"Yeah, lotta bodies out there," said a big, sullen-looking man from the end of the bar, a jerky sort of rhythm in his voice. "None of 'em buried."

He left no implications hanging. It was clear what he was saying. The white men should have been buried.

Who did these people think they were, a whole committee appointed to judge his life and tell him no good deed was ever enough? Randall MacLane was getting sick and tired of it.

"They buried now?" asked Randall.

The big man did not answer. He just stared into his drink.

The first voice took up again. The speaker was a small, thin man with longish hair and abnormally dirty clothes. He had the look of a drifter, a man more familiar with jails than bathtubs. Randall realized with disgust that he didn't look any better himself.

"Well, uh . . . we figured we'd better git back here in a hurry . . . you know, tell everybody . . . might be more Injins 'round . . . got no shovels . . . not our job . . ."

The voice had started out in an ingratiating whine and ended angry because it knew it had said too much.

Why should a group of men from the town be afraid of Indians when one man had managed against five? Why had they complained about the white men not being buried when they had not done the job themselves? Randall was sorry that he hadn't just ridden on last night, sleep or no sleep.

"Well, now," exclaimed Milo Rosewater quickly, sensing a side argument that he did not want. He swung an arm toward the thin, dirty talker. "Josh here was only tellin' us about what he and the others found out there on the road, bodies, and a wagon all burned out, and dead horses—"

He was interrupted by the arrival of Charley from the kitchen with a pot of coffee and a cup. MacLane took them without comment and walked to a table, lowered himself into a chair, and started to drink. The coffee tasted like mud, but it was hot. The men crowded around the table in a three-deep semicircle, except for the sullen man at the bar who just kept staring into his drink.

"Well, then." Milo Rosewater started over. "Anyway, there's been quite a bit of Injin scare 'round here, so everybody's interested in what happened. Of course, we have faith in the army, especially with Custer in the area, but . . . Thought you could fill us in on the incident out there on your way into town, anyway."

MacLane kept drinking his coffee. He didn't owe this bunch any stories. He kept it brief, between sips.

"Not much to tell. I was with the army. There was a big battle. After that, I was coming overland and happened on the wagon.

Some Indians had attacked them. They'd already killed the men. I drove them off."

"Drove 'em off, hell!" exclaimed the man Rosewater

had called Josh. "Drove 'em off to the happy huntin' ground! Five of 'em out there dead as doornails."

Charley arrived again, with a plate of food.

MacLane looked around. He had given the men as much story as they deserved, after the way they'd acted when he brought the woman and the boy into town yesterday. Why was it that everyone in the town seemed to find something wrong with everything he said and did?

"There was another one. I guess he's the one I drove off," he said, his lips tight.

He began to fork in his late breakfast with real appreciation.

"Hell," spat out a man from the back row of the onlookers. "That one'll probably go tell all the rest of 'em and they'll get mad and come back and wipe us all out. Shouldn't never leave no Injin alive."

"Now, now," remonstrated Rosewater, ever mindful of the furniture and mirrors in his saloon. "Let's allow Mr. MacLane to tell the story. Did they, uh, abuse the woman? She didn't have any clothes on when you brought her in."

All the men leaned a little closer as they waited for Randall's reply. His face reddened as he remembered the brave on top of her and how he had shot him off, as he recalled the humiliation of dragging her bare-assed into town.

"I suppose you might put it that way," he said. "I had to shoot one off of her."

Immediately he regretted his words. They had come out more as a memory than as a communication.

"Goddamned savages," snorted one man.

"Wait till the women hear about this," said another, shaking his head mournfully, but with a gleam in his eyes that said he could hardly wait to start spreading the news.

"She's a good-shaped woman, what we could see yesti-day, anyhow, and a widow woman now, but who'd touch her?" remarked still another.

"Yeah, once they been with Injins they ain't no good

for a white man. Best for her and that boy to just keep movin' on to someplace don't know 'bout it, I guess."

Square-jawed Si Winchester gazed into the distance, as if seeing already the place that the woman and the boy should go.

"Yes, mister," he said solemnly, "best you just load 'em up and keep on going. Ain't no place for a woman here once she's been with Indians."

Randall almost choked on a bite of steak.

"I'm not exactly sure what you're talking about," he said. "Mrs. Thistle said there wasn't anything wrong with her."

He was really getting confused now. He had never "been with" a woman himself, so he wasn't sure what the men meant. Regardless, wasn't it early to be talking about finding her another man? Her husband hadn't even been buried yet. Worst of all, however, was the assumption that he had a responsibility to keep on caring for her.

"I don't even know her," he continued. "I just came across the wagon while the Indians were attacking them. I did what anybody would do. I couldn't leave them out there."

The sullen man at the bar turned around now and bored through the crowd with a black-eyed stare. As he started to speak the men automatically fell to either side, allowing room for his words, as though they were bodies shouldering their way through.

"You shoulda left 'em out there, 'cause we don't want 'em here. Only thing she's fit for now is squawin'. Take her out and leave her for the Injins. It's simple. You brought 'em in. You take 'em out."

The saloon went silent. Only MacLane was in a position to see the speaker. No one else made a move to turn around to look at him.

Randall didn't know what to do. There was undisguised hatred in the man's eyes. Randall didn't know why. It was clear the man was spoiling for a fight, but he didn't even

know him. He had saved a woman and her son from death
or worse. Now it was being held against him. He could
think of nothing to say, so he said nothing.

Finally Milo Rosewater cleared his throat and tried
again.

"Uh, as I mentioned, we're a bit nervous here in
Middle Bend. Injins all over the place, and such. Don't
exactly like having them around, you know. But then, it's
clear you don't either, Mr. MacLane, since you killed so
many of them out there. . . . And you mentioned there was
a big battle between the savages and the army, so there's
hardly a reason for us to be worried now."

MacLane knew he should leave it there, just ride on out
of town and forget it. With General Crook in the vicinity, the
town was certain to be safe. What had happened to Custer
wouldn't affect them. But something made him push on.

"There was a big battle, but I wouldn't stop worrying
yet. The Indians won it. Custer and his whole command
were wiped out."

There was a babble of shock and disbelief. Then it was
all directed at MacLane.

"That can't be!"

"Custer couldn't be beat by a bunch of savages!"

"How do you know about all this, anyhow?"

"You a scout? You ain't dressed like no soldier."

"I'll bet he's a deserter."

The shock was now turning to anger, the classic inver-
sion by which the messenger is blamed for bad news.

Si Winchester silenced the men by raising a hand. He
stared hard at Randall, trying to bring him into focus at
such short distance.

"Mister, you'd better give us some more information.
What is this? You sayin' the Injins killed ever'body but
you? How'd you get away?"

Randall felt that he was betraying some principle of
integrity by allowing himself to be questioned in this way,
but good sense made him answer.

"No. I said every man in Custer's command was killed. He split up his troops. Major Reno's men got beat up pretty bad, but Captain Benteen's command and the pack train were all right. The Indians put them under siege for a couple of days, and then rode off, thousands of them. General Crook showed up after that. My time was up, so he mustered me out, and I headed west. That's when I came across the Reindorf woman and the boy, out there on the road. You know the rest."

He was getting angry. He didn't care if it showed. He had been through too much to put up with being treated like a schoolboy by a bunch of scared townsmen who didn't have any idea what it was really like to be out there on the plains, killing in the fear and the dust.

He saw no reason to say anything about his own charge at the Indians as he tried to get to Custer, or about his salvation at the hands of the unknown chief. No one noticed that he referred to the soldiers as "them" instead of "us."

The big man at the bar swung around, broad shoulders squaring. He hooked his left thumb into his gunbelt and tipped his hat back with his right hand, then leaned on the bar with his left elbow and cocked his right hip out, the heavy handgun on display. It was clear that he felt it was a manly pose. To Randall he looked mostly awkward.

"I say that's a bunch of horseshit. You don't know what you're talkin' about. You never killed no Injins. If you were ever with the army, you ain't nothin' but a deserter now."

The dead silence fell once again. The men began moving quietly, stealthily, sideways, like a bunch of scurrying crabs. They left a canyon of space between the man at the bar and the table where Randall still sat behind his empty plate.

What Randall MacLane felt most at the moment was confusion and thirst. He had no idea why the man had such naked, mean, bullying hostility for him. He had never run into anything like it before. And the talk of fighting brought back the thirst of the day before. Slowly, he picked up his cup and reached it out toward Milo Rosewater.

"I appreciate the breakfast, sir, but I need another cup to wash it down with."

Someone gasped out loud. There was further shuffling as men pushed against one another in an effort to widen the gap between themselves and the idiot at the table. They knew the big man at the bar would have to kill now. No one had ever tried to face him down, but no one had ever ignored him either. Every man there knew that ignoring him was more dangerous, though.

As if in a dream, Milo Rosewater took a cautious step forward, hooked the cup, and handed it to the man called Charley, who scuttled off to the kitchen, not nearly as reluctantly as before. "I'll make a fresh pot," he whispered.

The man at the bar shifted his elbow, tipped his hat back farther, puffed out his chest, and got red in the face.

"For your sake, mister," he said, "I hope you didn't hear me. I called you a liar." When Randall did not reply, he added, "To your face."

This was something the man had never encountered before. He was used to people simply backing down before him because he was bigger and meaner and louder than they were. A skinny kid in dirty clothes ignoring him in favor of a cup of coffee was something he didn't know how to handle. He was losing status by having to repeat his insults, and explain them even, but he didn't know what else to do.

MacLane turned his head, slowly, until he had the man in his line of sight. He felt the rage begin to churn in his stomach. He thought about the way he had beaten the stove when his grandfather had died. He felt lonely for his grandfather and father and brother and mother.

"Do I know you?" he asked coldly.

The man almost spluttered out loud.

"What the hell diff'rence does it make if you know

me?" he said through gritted teeth. "But I guess a man's got a right to know who's goin' to kill him. You're goin' to be a notch on the gun of Marion Morrison."

The man closed his eyes to narrow slits as he said it. He took his elbow off the bar and dropped his hands loosely to his sides.

It was the most ludicrous thing Randall had ever seen. Was this the way of the great gunfighters he had read about and heard about and secretly envied?

He just couldn't help it; he broke out laughing. He guffawed until the tears were running down his cheeks. He slapped the table with the palms of his hands until they hurt.

"Marian?" he chortled. "A gunfighter named Marian? A tough man named Marian? That's a girl's name! Marian?"

All the tension of the last month, which had culminated in the killings of the last several days, simply broke in him. He couldn't control himself, any more than he could when he had beaten the stove to drown his grandfather's screams or when he had made the mad charge to try to get to Custer. Rage and hilarity rushed together and exploded inside him.

The other men in the saloon were dumbfounded. One or another of them might have thought that Marion was a strange name for a big and blustery tough, but certainly no one would ever have put voice to the idea. Now they watched with fascination as the young man at the table laughed until he cried. He had to be crazy, but it wasn't going to save him; they knew that.

They watched as Marion Morrison advanced in rage and frustration toward the table where Randall MacLane sat and laughed. Randall could not hear the hard pounding of his heavy boots because of his own strangled roars. He grabbed his sides to try to control himself and was silent for just long enough to hear Milo Rosewater.

"Now, Marion, he's not even wearin' a gun. . . ."

That was when MacLane woke up to the fact that he

was really in danger. He glanced up just in time to see the tough pulling his gun. With nothing better to do, and propelled still by his own laughter, he slapped his hands up underneath the table and heaved it up and out. The table was big and heavy, but Randall was infused with the strength of sudden desperation. He threw the table up high and followed it as it crashed onto the man who had just promised to kill him.

The man called Marion stumbled back. His gun went off, splintering a hole in the table. MacLane followed the table, knowing he would have no second chance. He flew over it in a frenzy, trying to get to Morrison before he had a chance to level his gun and take a second shot. The gunman backpedaled toward the bar, still off balance from being struck by the table. Randall reached him in two long strides, grabbed his right wrist and forced it up, then awkwardly jabbed the man in a glancing blow in the jaw.

He was unable to get any real force into his blow. Still, the man's head flew back like he'd been hit with an anvil. His hand went slack. The gun thumped to the floor. He crumpled at Randall's feet, an untidy pile of dead muscle and dirty laundry.

MacLane stood over the lifeless form. He had killed again, this time with his bare hands, while he was laughing. He barely struck the man. How could it have killed him? He looked down at his still-balled fist. He felt a shiver of fear, fear of himself and what he was becoming.

Neither he nor anyone else would ever know that a sliver of wood from the gunshot wound to the table had been driven back through the pupil of Marion Morrison's right eye, deep into his brain, killing him instantly.

When You've Got No Other Plans

———◆•◆———

"God, I hate killing," MacLane muttered.

It was both statement and prayer. It rode on a train of confusion and shock and despair. What in the world was happening to him? This wasn't the way his life was supposed to go.

The men in the saloon drew back even farther as they heard the words. No one before had even dared to look slantwise at Marion Morrison. Here was a skinny, young man who laughed at him, made fun of his name, then killed him with one blow to the jaw. There seemed little doubt that he was indeed the one who had killed the Indians at the wagon and saved the woman and her son. Whether he was an army deserter or not, the mark of violence was upon him. He was not a man to mess with. He hated killing? They heard him say it. The opposite was clear, however. He killed as naturally as a coyote kills a rabbit. Who had ever seen a man laugh and kill at the same time?

Milo Rosewater stepped into the stunned silence.

"Here, now. Slim, you and Dave and Mack carry Marion

over to Lamb's Furniture Store. He'll have to custom-make a coffin. Marion's too big for the regular kind. Jim, you'd better help, too. Tell him he'd better get some men started digging up in Boot Hill; it'll take a while."

There was a little grumbling by Slim and Dave and Mack and Jim. They wanted to stick around to see what happened next. They eyed MacLane warily, though, and did as they were told. No use stirring up an already violent man.

Randall didn't know what else to do, so he just stood at the bar, wondering what had happened, while Rosewater tried to put things back to normal.

Charley appeared and thrust a cup of coffee at Randall. Coffee? Now? Oh, yes, he had asked for a second cup. A lifetime ago. Marion Morrison's lifetime. It was stupid to stand around, thought Randall, drinking a cup of coffee, when you've just killed a man. But it was impolite to refuse it. After all, he had asked for it. The irony of worrying about being polite when you've just killed a man didn't occur to him.

He stood at the bar and sipped at the bitter brew until it was done. The men scraped chairs into place around tables in the corners of the Palace. They talked in muted tones.

"It's a cold man," one said, "who can kill another man with his fists, then drink his second cup like nothing even happened to interrupt his breakfast."

The coffee finished, Randall looked around the room. He spied Josh, the drifter who had gone out to the wagon with Marion Morrison. He was describing to one table of men what he had seen there. His memory of the scene was now augmented by having seen MacLane in action. Randall walked over to him. The whole table fell into a deep well of silence.

"You bring my saddle in?"

"Well, uh, yeah, uh, sure did. Figgered it must be yours. Figgered you'd want it. Sure did. Yes, sir. Brought it in jist fer you. No good for me. Cinch's ripped apart. I was gonna git it fixed up fer you."

Randall knew he was lying. So did every man at the table. He had taken the saddle for what he could get out of it. That's why he went out to the wagon in the first place, to see what he could steal from two dead men and a widow and a boy.

"There a livery stable in town?" Randall asked of the table in general.

Josh jumped in again before anyone else could answer.

"Yes, sir, mister, sure is. Down at the end of the street."

"Take the saddle there. If the horse I brought in with me yesterday isn't there, somebody'd better find it and bring it down there, too."

Randall knew he was throwing his slim weight around. He didn't care. He didn't owe this town or anybody in it a tinker's damn. He was sick of the place. He just wanted out. He stalked away, back to the hotel, to get his saddlebags.

As he left the Palace he noticed that Milo Rosewater and Si Winchester were walking over to the table he had just left.

By the time he got to the livery stable, both Milo and Si were there. They were drifting about the door in a ragged circle with three other men, like moths uncertain about where the light is. Randall couldn't place the other men. They hadn't been at the Palace just now. They'd probably been in the street when he came in the day before, but most of those faces were now just smudges on his resentment.

"Back at the Palace, they say you're fixing to ride out, Mr. MacLane," said Rosewater.

"That's right."

"You sure made an impression on the men back there in my saloon, taking on Marion Morrison that way. You handle yourself real well. Did you laugh on purpose, to catch him unawares?"

Randall felt his scalp begin to flush red. It wasn't from the noonday sun. How could he explain what happened at the saloon, even to himself? Besides, he was getting fed up with everyone else making his actions their business.

"I've got to get my saddle repaired," he said as he turned to go into the livery stable.

"Wait, Mr. MacLane," Rosewater called after him. "Please," he added. "We've been talking it over. The five of us, we're the town council. We don't have a sheriff here. Marion Morrison ran off the last one. He was bullyin' everybody till you came along. Whenever we run into somebody like that, well, we just don't know what to do about it. But with you as sheriff, well, they wouldn't even try anything. And the rest of the time, why, there's hardly anything to do. It's a real nice job."

Randall stopped, turned.

"You mean you're asking me to be sheriff here?"

"That's right. We don't know much about you, but you look like you'd be a real good lawman. Job's easy. Pay's good. You got to wait till you get that saddle repaired anyway, so there's no rush about sayin' one way or the other. Just think it over."

One of the other men cleared his throat and spoke up.

"Mr. MacLane, I'm Henry Alcorn. I'm a merchant here." He spoke like Randall should be impressed with that bit of news. "You're a stranger here. We need a sheriff, and everyone's talking about you and Marion Morrison, and how you saved that woman and her son from the Indians. But, we'd like to know a little more about you."

Rosewater glared at him but he kept on.

"Like where you come from, and what your experience is. Someone said you were in the army."

Randall opened his mouth. He had plenty he could tell, and he was proud enough of it. The university, his Washington posting, the battle at the Little Bighorn . . . Then he thought about the day before, how this town had received him and Hannah and Isaac. This bunch had no right to ask anything of him, even information about who he was.

He knew nothing about being a lawman, but he immediately saw the romance of it, walking the streets with a gun on his leg. All the exciting stories of the western frontier, those tales he'd heard since boyhood, came back to him. He saw himself striding down the middle of the street, a tin star pinned to his shirt.

He didn't like Middle Bend, but he had no place else to go. He was in no hurry. He could sheriff for a while, until he decided what he wanted. After the last few days, a job with good pay and little work sounded all right.

He wouldn't give them a thing about himself, though. He would hire out his today to them, but not his yesterday. If he stayed, it would be on his terms, and his alone.

"You know what you need to know," he said. "I can't promise I'll keep the job for very long, but I'll do it for a while, until you can get someone permanently."

"Well, now," said Henry Alcorn, "I'm not sure we really meant to offer you the job right now, before we could interview you properly."

"I said I'd take it," replied Randall, his tone cool and level.

Rosewater beamed, but a little nervously. He didn't want trouble, not with the other merchants, and definitely not with the young stranger who had dispatched the town bully with such ease.

"Fine! Fine! Come along. We'll take you over to your new office and swear you in."

He herded the little group along, like an ungainly sheep dog nipping at the heels of a slow-witted flock. They ended up at the city building in the middle of the main block.

The city building had two front doors, one to the council chambers and courtroom, the other to the sheriff's office and jail. The jail was really just the back end of the sheriff's office, two spare cells with metal bunks attached to the walls.

It was actually Si Winchester who swore him in, after

Milo Rosewater produced a tin star and the keys to the cells, from a drawer in the boot-scarred desk in the sheriff's office. The other council members looked like snakes that have just been told the toads all moved to the city. It was clear, however, that they did not intend to disagree with the proceedings in the presence of the violent young stranger.

Everyone shook hands with him after he pledged to uphold the law. All of a sudden, he was a sheriff, no more than twenty minutes after the idea first came out of Milo Rosewater's mouth.

But did he really know anything about the actual work of a lawman? What would he do if another Marion Morrison showed up? He was being swept along by his new reputation, as much as everyone else in town. He didn't know how to get off the bandwagon, though.

Well, he wasn't going to be around long enough to get into any trouble, anyway. He was especially sure of that when he found out the "good pay" Milo Rosewater had mentioned was hardly enough to keep up with the rent at the livery stable and his room and board. He had lived frugally for a long time, however. He had saved most of his army pay. He wasn't really worried about money. So he went around to the mercantile stores and bought new clothes to match his new star.

Wherever he went, people were polite but distant. He sensed a definite undercurrent of fear.

"Not really all that surprising," he told himself. "After all, they only know me from killing those Indians at the wagon and that tough in the bar. It'll get better once they find out more about me."

He began to regret his rush to show off, word-wrestling the sheriff's job away from them when Henry Alcorn tried to back off from it. That kind of action only solidified the idea that he was just a slimmer and meaner version of Marion Morrison.

He still did not think of himself as a violent man. He

thought about it, though. Even if you're not violent, can doing violent deeds actually change what you are inside? He was certainly acting differently from how he had before. Colonel Seeley and Travis Hamilton wouldn't even recognize him.

Things were going too fast. One minute he didn't give a tinker's damn about Middle Bend. The next minute he wanted everyone to like him. First he only wanted to get out. Then he wanted to stay and strut around as the sheriff.

He felt the need to talk with someone who would understand. Instinctively he turned into the side street that led to the church of the Thistles.

Some women were standing in the yard across the street from the parsonage, chatting. They looked much as they had the afternoon before. When they saw MacLane coming, they scattered quickly into various houses. Obviously his new clothes had not kept them from recognizing him.

He still was not aware of the central symbol of his new identity. From now on everyone would recognize him only by the tin star on his chest. He had forgotten he even had it on.

He started for the parsonage, but something caused him to veer off toward the church building. He went up the three wooden steps and let himself into the simple, frame building. It was very much like the little Red Oak Church, where he had grown up. The Reverend Mr. Thistle sat on the front pew, just looking up at the rough-hewn wooden cross that filled the end wall behind the pulpit.

Without turning, he said, "Come in, Sheriff. When I heard you had taken the job, I hoped you would come around again to see me."

Randall did not doubt that ministers had some special sense that came from walking more closely with God than ordinary people. Still, how did the parson know it was he who entered? It made him uneasy. He walked up the center, and only, aisle, and dropped onto the other end of the pew from Reverend Thistle.

"So, the word's already gotten around about me becoming sheriff."

"Oh, yes. Word travels very quickly in a little town like this. Everyone knows about how you killed that man Morrison, and the Indians, and about how you saved poor Hannah and little Isaac. And about what the Indians did to Hannah . . ."

Randall shifted uncomfortably at the parson's words. Unlike the others in the town, it seemed that he did owe the reverend an explanation. Or perhaps he just wanted to hear himself make an explanation, to see what it would be.

"I didn't mean to say anything about that . . . well, what happened to Mrs. Reindorf, not to the townspeople. But bringing her into town naked that way . . . there just wasn't anything else to do. I had to get help. . . . It was so . . . so . . . unreal . . . out there, Reverend Thistle. There were just thousands of Indians . . . and they wiped out Custer . . . and I went charging right into them. . . ."

Haltingly, he told the whole story. He started with the days on the plains, then skipped back to his childhood and university days. The minister listened calmly, comfortably, nodding his head, indicating that he understood. There was something about the little man that made Randall tell much more than he intended.

"I don't know what's happening to me, Reverend. I'm not a killer. I charged into the Indians to get to Custer because I lost my head. I was sure I was going to die anyway. Those Indians out at the Reindorf's wagon . . . I didn't want to kill them, but I had to save Mrs. Reindorf and Isaac. That man in the saloon . . . I wouldn't make fun of a man's name, but I just kind of exploded. Then when he came at me, I didn't have any choice. I was just trying to defend myself. I don't know how he died. I didn't hit him very hard. He must have hit his head."

Reverend Thistle raised a restraining hand, the same motion he used to give the benediction on Sunday morning.

"Easy, son. I'm beginning to understand. I knew there was something different about you. At first I thought it was because you were a man of violence. The mark of Cain was all over you. I see now that you are special in an entirely different way."

"But I don't want to be special. I wanted to once, I think, to make some great mark on the world, to be a great Indian fighter like Custer, maybe. But I've seen what that's like. To make a mark you have to hurt. To make a mark on the world, you have to leave a wound in it. I don't want to do that. I just want to be an ordinary man."

"Randall, if that's what you want, you might as well try it right here, in Middle Bend. You've got a job. There are people here who need you. If you can settle down anyplace, you can do it here. But Randall, the Gospel writer says, 'To whom much is given, is much expected.' You're never going to be an ordinary man."

Desire and a Strange Woman

MacLane spent the next week trying to get a feel for the job and the town. It was a mundane routine—meals by himself in the hotel dining room, sitting at his office desk during the day, looking over old wanted posters, walking the streets in the evening, back to his small and lonely room in the hotel.

No one seemed comfortable in his presence. Some shied away like a horse that's just seen a rattler. Others sidled up like they wanted to sell him dirty pictures. Either way made him feel ill at ease. He didn't drink, but he went into the Palace and the other saloons, to make "rounds," as he thought a sheriff should. There the patrons only wanted to talk about his exploits as a killer. Even then the talk was nervous, as though the denizens of the saloons felt they must ingratiate themselves with him or they might be the next to feel his wrath.

Even Milo Rosewater, who had been so anxious to keep him in town as sheriff, now avoided him. He he knew he had gone too far. He had to resolidify his position with his permanent neighbors by showing he was not really committed to the new lawman. Someday Randall MacLane would be gone, but Milo would have to keep on living with Si Winchester and Henry Alcorn and the rest.

Randall longed for something to read, but he knew the only person in town who was likely to have any decent reading material was Reverend Thistle. The thought of returning to see him was especially uncomfortable. He had told the parson too much, revealed more of himself than he intended. He had the impression that the man in the black suit with the curious collar tabs might actually understand him better than he understood himself. Now he was afraid of the only man in town who might really be his friend.

He finally went to see him, however, because he began to overhear things that disturbed him more than his anxiety about the minister's knowledge of him. In the hotel dining room, in his infrequent stops in the saloons, occasionally even on the streets, he caught snatches of conversations that had to do with the woman Hannah Reindorf. People shut their mouths as soon as they realized he was near, but he picked up enough to catch the general drift. It was the same old thing that had come up that day in the saloon, when he had killed Marion Morrison. She had "been with Indians," and they just didn't want her around.

The minister was not in the church, so MacLane reluctantly went to the parsonage and knocked softly on the door. It was Mrs. Thistle who answered.

"Well, it's about time. I didn't figure you were so all-fired busy as sheriff of this town that you couldn't come around. Come in."

It wasn't really a greeting, or an invitation. More like a statement, or an order. She was as tactful as always.

He entered the small parlor, hat in hand. As he did so Reverend Thistle came into the room from the kitchen, shrugging on the threadbare coat of his black suit. Randall had the impression he had been doing dishes and didn't want him to know.

A woman in a rather fancy pink dress sat on a straight chair in a corner of the room, her head bowed below a mass of auburn hair. The cut of the dress emphasized the fullness of her figure.

"I don't mean to interrupt. . . . I could come back later."

It was a very long time since he had been in polite company. He had learned etiquette well in Bloomington and Washington, but he was not sure what good manners called for in a parsonage on the frontier.

"Well, I'll be!" declared Mrs. Thistle. "You don't even recognize her, do you? Hannah, raise your head, and take a look at the man who saved you and Isaac. You probably haven't even been introduced, although that's hardly necessary after all you went through together. This is Sheriff MacLane."

A pack of confusing feelings jumped onto Randall from all directions, pleasure and embarrassment being chief among them. It was the first time he had been called Sheriff MacLane. Downtown or at the hotel, he was addressed only by his title, Sheriff, much as Reverend Thistle was referred to as Reverend or Parson. He liked the sound of "Sheriff MacLane." But his pleasure was mingled with embarrassment. Here was the woman he had dragged naked into town, off whom he had shot a man who at that very moment had been "having his way" with her. How do you carry on a parlor conversation with such a woman? And the Thistles were watching, to see what he would do. It was not a stage where a man wanted an audience.

The woman raised her head and slowly focused on him with half-vacant eyes. Randall almost jumped back. She was pretty. Very pretty. He had just never really seen her before. He had not anticipated even running into her again. He was not prepared for this. Involuntarily he tried to take a step backward, but the smallness of the room trapped him where he was.

"That's a silly dress to wear around the house, but I've had trouble borrowing something to fit her," said Mrs. Thistle, as always hewing the matter-of-fact line. "Go ahead, Hannah. You can talk. You might start by thanking Sheriff MacLane for saving you."

The woman kept looking at him but said nothing. Randall couldn't stand the silence.

"Uh, that's all right. No thanks really necessary . . . I just did what needed . . . Well, I hope you're feeling better, Mrs. Reindorf."

"Poor thing," said Mrs. Thistle, as though the other woman wasn't there. "She's too sensitive, I'm afraid. Reverend Thistle's told her it's what happens in the soul that counts, not what happens to the body, but she's having a hard time forgetting."

"I'm sorry if my coming has upset her. I just wanted to see Reverend Thistle."

"That's all right. You men go on into the kitchen and have some coffee. I'm sure Reverend Thistle is through with the dishes by now."

Randall sensed that she took a certain amount of pleasure in embarrassing her husband. It was more a way of expressing affection than anything else, though. The minister accommodated her by looking distinctly uncomfortable as he ducked through the kitchen door and waved a hand at MacLane in a "Follow me and let's get out of here" motion.

As he turned to follow the parson Randall heard a soft voice, like the plopping of raindrops on fat, fall leaves.

"He should have let them have me. I'm no good now. . . ."

What Randall heard, more than the words, was the impersonal tone. Her mind and her mouth formed words, but her heart was not in them. She said them simply because they were there, not because she felt anything. Even despair or self-pity was absent. She had not spoken to him, but to someone or anyone else, just as he had spoken to Mrs. Thistle about Hannah and Mrs. Thistle had spoken to him about her. They all spoke about one another through someone else. He felt empty as he followed the preacher into the kitchen.

"Don't worry," Reverend Thistle whispered to him. "She'll get better, I think. She doesn't mean things like that. I think it's good you came to see her. No one else visits, and I imagine she gets tired of Mrs. Thistle and me after a while. If we could just get her out some."

"Actually, that's why I came to see you. I've been hearing some things in town. . . . Uh, could we go over to the church to talk?"

The minister glanced quickly at Randall and then at the doorway.

"Yes, perhaps that would be best."

They went out the back door. MacLane was surprised to see Isaac there. His face ran a quick flush. He had so easily forgotten about the boy entirely. He hadn't even asked Reverend Thistle about him.

Isaac was listlessly playing a game of mumblety-peg with a new knife. Randall felt he needed to say something to him.

"Nice-looking knife. Where did you get it?"

Immediately he regretted the question. It sounded like a sheriff's interrogation of a suspect. The boy gave a half glance in the direction of the minister.

"It seems that he had one, but it got lost out at the wagon or on the way into town. So I thought it would be nice for him to have another."

Reverend Thistle said it as though he had to apologize for giving a boy a present. Even my friends I make nervous or guilty, Randall thought. Unable to think of anything else to say, he turned and walked the few steps to the church.

They sat in the front pew, looking at the cross, as they had a week before. The new sheriff told the old parson about what he had heard concerning Hannah Reindorf.

"There's an uncommon lot of prejudice about Indians, Randall, and there's an uncommon lot of dirty-mindedness about sex. Sex and race seem to make people crazy, that and money. You put them together, and it's an explosive mix. People came out here to try to make money. They found Indians in the way of those fortunes they sought. Out here on the frontier, civilization is just a veneer. Men's dark thoughts about women come up awfully close to the surface. So, a woman who's 'been with' Indians, people treat her as though she's evil, an untouchable, like a leper in the Bible. It's like she had a disease. Lord knows, she might have gotten one from those Indians doing what they did to her, but if so, it was something the Indians got in the first place because of what white men did to their women. Hannah Reindorf was abused by those men you killed. Now the folks here in town act like it was her fault.

"I'm sorry. I'm carrying on. It's an occupational hazard, I fear. I get inside the church here and I start preaching."

The minister laughed as he stared at the cross.

"No need to apologize to me. I'm glad to hear what you have to say."

Randall wasn't just making polite chitchat. He really meant it. Listening to the minister was about as close to civilization as he figured to get in Middle Bend.

"I just thought maybe you ought to know what people are saying. I don't know what they expect her to do. . . . Go back to her family, or wherever she came from, I suppose."

The minister shook his head, a frustrated little motion that fanned the white fringe of his hair into a woolly halo.

"Where's she going to go? How's she going to get there? She's not talking much, but from what I can gather from her and Isaac, all their family and everything else they had was lost out there. Now they're just a couple of leaves blown by whatever wind is strongest."

They sat in silence for a while. Since there seemed to

be nothing more to say, Randall stood to leave, glad that the Reindorf woman and her sullen son were the minister's problem rather than his own. It was good, he thought, that every town had a minister, or who would take care of people like this?

"While I'm here, I was wondering if you had anything I could borrow to read. Gets sort of boring in the office during the days. Not much different from being in Washington with the army."

Randall coughed what he thought was a polite little laugh at himself. He didn't want to mention the loneliness of the nights.

"I'll be glad to loan you any books I have, son, but remember that you are welcome to come around and talk when the boredom gets too much even for the books."

The minister understood why Randall had not come to see him since their last talk. He also did not seem surprised.

The sheriff took the Bible and an armload of history and philosophy books that Reverend Thistle picked out. He walked back to his office to drop them off before returning to the hotel to eat. He did not get lunch until late that day, however. There was a delegation of citizens waiting for him.

A Surprising
Announcement

◆—◆—◆

Silas Winchester and Milo Rosewater and the other
three members of the town council were there. So was
"Whispering" Lowe and four or five other men MacLane
did not yet know by name.

"It's like this, Sheriff," began Rosewater. "People are getting worked up 'bout that woman you brought into town.
You know already people aren't happy 'bout her being here.
A couple of women went over to pay a polite call on her and
they said she acted crazy, like a witch or something."

He laughed nervously. The undertaker started to take
up the laugh but stifled it quickly when he realized no one
else was doing so. The saloon owner continued.

"Well, anyway, she's not welcome here. There's nothing for her to do, and no decent man would touch her,
that's for sure. She's bad luck."

He stopped. It was clear he and the others expected
some response from Randall.

"Well, Reverend Thistle and his wife are taking care of
her."

There was a slight pause as the men looked at one another. Then Henry Alcorn, the man who had expressed doubts about hiring MacLane so quickly, spoke up.

Randall knew by now the town folk referred to Alcorn as "number two," at least behind his back. He was second to Milo Rosewater as the town's most prosperous merchant, and he did not like being second.

"The Thistles are nice people, Sheriff, don't get me wrong. But that's part of the whole thing. They actually encourage the people that don't belong by bein' nice to 'em. Then they stay around here, and they're problems. Somebody's always got to be takin' care of 'em. The Thistles are sort of . . ."

"Religious?" offered the new sheriff.

"Now, Sheriff," spoke up Milo Rosewater, pulling down on his waistcoat, "the point is that we've talked about it, and the public order is at stake. You, of course, are in charge of the public order. Also, you're the one who brought them here in the first place. So, our view is, you've got to get rid of them."

"Get rid of them? What am I supposed to do, take them back into nowhere and turn them loose?"

He laughed, the scornful ratching of a crow. Anger was becoming as natural to him as politeness had always been before. The other men backed up quickly. It reminded them of the way he laughed at Marion Morrison. Randall noticed that they gave way. Giving way did not mean changing minds.

"Be just as well," someone muttered. "Take 'em out and let the Injins have 'em."

"No, no, of course not," boomed Rosewater quickly. "Just see that they get on the stage to wherever they came from."

"There's no place for them to go. No family back east. They don't even have money for a stage. Somebody 'salvaged' all their belongings out at their wagon."

"Uh, I'm the town treasurer, Sheriff," said a balding

man. He wore an eastern suit of ancient vintage. "Oscar Shurg?" He seemed to be asking MacLane for confirmation of who he was. "The town has enough funds to pay for the woman and her son to take the stage and get on the train to somewhere."

"I'm glad you mentioned the town treasury, Mr. Shurg. You still owe me the money I advanced Mr. Lowe here for the burial costs for the Reindorf men."

"Burial costs?" snorted Henry Alcorn. "Who authorized burial for them? We can't be expected to pay for burying every busted farmer that gets on the wrong side of the red-skins."

Randall MacLane was getting mad again, but it wasn't the white-hot anger of rage. It was cold, calculating anger, the same anger that put steel in his eyes and up his spine when he went after the Indians at the burning wagon.

"You authorized their burial, Mr. Alcorn," he said.

As he spoke he felt his teeth begin to grind. His jaw clenched almost shut.

"You and every man in this town. That day at the Palace, every man there backed Marion Morrison when he claimed they should have been buried. You all wanted them buried, and by God, I got them buried."

"Well, that's not the point," Henry Alcorn spluttered. "I mean, burying them out there on the prairie is one thing. Bringing them into town and paying to plant them in the graveyard is something else."

"You're absolutely right, Mr. Alcorn. It is something else. It's called civilization. It's called doing the right thing. It's called acting like human beings. I figure the sheriff's job is to keep people in a town from acting like animals and get them to act like humans. That's why Mr. Shurg is going to pay me what Mr. Lowe charged for the burials. When that's done, I'll go see Reverend Thistle, and we'll figure out what to do about the woman and her boy."

"There now," broke in a nervously beaming Milo Rosewater. "That's fair, isn't it? Pay the sheriff, Oscar.

Then he'll go take care of this and we won't have to worry about it anymore. What's the cost, Sheriff?"

"Forty dollars."

"Forty dollars?"

There were gasps all around.

"Hell," said Silas Winchester in his most ponderous manner. "Don't cost that much for somebody from the town to get buried."

Titus Lowe shuffled his feet and danced from one foot to the other. He had assumed the amount of his charge would never come to light.

"Well, uh, I think the sheriff must have misunderstood," he whispered.

MacLane started to pull out his billfold. In it he kept the receipt he had wrangled from a reluctant "Whispering" Lowe.

"Never mind, Sheriff," said Milo Rosewater. "I suspect we all know what happened here. Titus meant to charge twenty, but he made a mistake and doubled the bill. Of course, it should have been only fifteen, what with two at one time like that, so we'll let him return twenty-five to you and Oscar will pay you fifteen out of the town treasury."

Titus Lowe glared in turn at the owner of the Palace and at the sheriff. Finally, however, he pulled a wad of bills out of his pocket. He peeled off five fives and handed them to MacLane as though he were giving up his grandchildren to cannibals. Oscar Shurg hastily wrote out a draft on the local bank for the other fifteen dollars.

Randall looked around the room and realized he had no friends there.

"Thank you, gentlemen," he said, with unnecessary emphasis upon *gentlemen*. "I have some lunch to eat, and then I'll get on with my job."

He turned his back on them and walked out, leaving them grumbling at Milo Rosewater for talking them into hiring this man for sheriff. After all, he treated them more like children than employers.

*   *   *

Randall chewed his meat. It tasted like old saddle. He selected a huge slab of pie. It tasted like sawdust. He was a man who paid scant attention to what he considered the little things of life, the looks of a table or the taste of food. He had spent too many hurried days in the university and too many boring days in the army to worry about style or decoration or taste. He had no control over them. They did not lead him toward his goals. So why bother?

Nonetheless, today he was acutely aware of how tasteless his life was. All of a sudden he was both without goals and without the little amenities that made a meandering life palatable. No message for Custer, no ambition to be an Indian fighter, no army officer ladder to climb, no family to go back to, no Eldorado beyond the horizon.

Abruptly he pushed away from the table and left his saddle and sawdust awash in spilled coffee. He couldn't stomach this town.

He automatically headed toward the church and the Thistles's parsonage. He knew he had a job to do there, although he didn't know how to do it. More importantly, however, it was the one place in town where he felt he might belong, right there with the other misfits. He decided he would invite Reverend Thistle over to the church for one of their talks and ask him how he should go about breaking the news to Hannah and Isaac that they had to leave.

The parson answered his knock. He beamed. It was obvious that he was genuinely glad to see the young sheriff.

"Come in, Sheriff MacLane," he said, loudly enough for the rest of the house to hear him. "We're just ready to sit down to lunch. Please join us."

Much more softly, just for Randall's ears, he continued, "Please do. Mrs. Thistle got Hannah to help cook the meal. It's been such a release for her, doing something familiar like that."

Without waiting for a reply, Reverend Thistle took

Randall's arm and led him into the kitchen. Isaac was already seated on one side while the women were putting the food on the table. Hannah Reindorf was still wearing her fancy dress, but she looked at home in the kitchen.

"Isaac, get up and let the sheriff have that place," said the minister. "Get that stool over there from the corner and put it beside your mother's chair. You can sit on that. We're honored to have the sheriff join us for lunch."

He smiled all around, but Randall felt uneasy at his obvious displacement of the boy. Isaac did as he was told. However, his ears reddened and his motions were stiff as an old man with rheumatism. Mrs. Thistle quickly set another place at the table. Mother and son ended up sitting together across from MacLane, as though on opposite sides in an eating game.

Despite the uneasiness that laced the aroma-laden air of the kitchen, they ate with gusto. Especially after the sodden attempt at a meal he experienced at the hotel, Randall was almost overwhelmed by the tastes of the food on his plate. It was like entering into another world, like stepping back into the world of childhood security, where good food appeared like magic on his family's table.

"You ladies are certainly good cooks," he said, with real appreciation, as they finished up the last of the biscuits and coffee.

"Hannah did most of it," said the little lady in black. "I never took to the kitchen much myself. Guess I should have been a doctor for real. About all I was ever really interested in. But Hannah, now, this woman knows her way around a kitchen. Just turned her loose, and presto. . . ."

MacLane wasn't sure if Mrs. Thistle was complimenting or insulting the other woman. Hannah herself simply sat and stared at her plate. At least she had eaten. Throughout the meal he could not help but steal glances at her. All over again he was struck with how pretty she was, how gracious the lines of her face, and how full the lines of her bosom. He felt the stirrings of desire, the old images of lust within. He had to lower his head, too, and he knew he dared not stand up for a while.

From the moment he was given the message to Custer, there had been no time for lust, in his imagination or anywhere else. Now the old urges over which he seemed to have no control were working back up into his consciousness. He felt embarrassed and ashamed. After all, he was a mature man now. He had been through the wars, literally. He was a professional lawman with responsibilities. He should not be acting like some adolescent. Besides, this woman's husband was hardly cold in the ground. And she was old enough . . . Well, probably not that much older than he, a year or two or three. The presence of Isaac, however, made her seem much older. Beyond that, she had "been with" Indians. . . .

The minister broke into his reverie.

"Uh, did you want to see me about something, Sheriff?"

MacLane felt the stirrings of anger replace those of desire. His resolve stiffened, allowing his body to relax so that he could stand without humiliation. He rose up as on a spring and towered over them.

Been with Indians, indeed! What right did this town of hypocrites have to make this woman and her son leave because she had "been with" Indians, or make her leave for any other reason, for that matter? They should be trying to help her. All they wanted was to get her out of their sight. They didn't want to think about her, and about what living in Indian country could mean.

"No," he lied. "I was just dropping by. I've got business to attend to downtown. Thank you for the meal. It was very good."

He stalked out, leaving a bewildered table of Thistles and Reindorfs behind.

"I hate to think what he'd be like if he thought the food was no good," mused Mrs. Thistle, stubby fingers twisting her graying bun.

MacLane walked down the dusty streets, bent forward, pointed like an arrow. He thought about the fine meal he had just eaten and the home he lacked. He thought about the attitudes of the townspeople and the way he and Hannah and Isaac had been so ill-received when they came into town looking for help. He realized with a start that he was now referring to them just that way, as Hannah and Isaac, rather than as "the woman and the boy" or as "Mrs. Reindorf and her son." He thought about how he was hired as sheriff because he accidentally killed the town bully. The town council figured he could keep the peace just because everyone feared him.

"Well, they'll do well to fear me," he muttered to himself as he strode along.

Talking to himself was becoming a habit.

He pushed through the swinging doors of the Palace and saw Milo Rosewater sitting at a corner table having an after-lunch drink with Henry Alcorn and Silas Winchester. He marched across the room to the table. Though he was normally a quiet walker, his boot heels pounded on the bare boards of the floor. Even he was a bit startled by the sound he made in the near-empty saloon.

"Sheriff," Rosewater greeted him, tugging apprehensively at the bottom of his waistcoat. "You're back quickly. Have you settled the situation about that woman so soon?"

"Yes, Mr. Rosewater, I have. You won't have to worry about her or her son anymore. I'm going to marry her."

A Different
Sort of Trap

"You're doing the right thing, son," Reverend Thistle
assured him.

They sat in their usual places in the front row of the little
church.

"Hannah's a good woman. Mrs. Thistle says there's
nothing wrong with her physically. I know she's being a
bit slow coming around mentally from what happened to
her, but Mrs. Thistle says the best thing is to get her back
into a regular routine. It's the way God made us. A man
needs a woman and a woman needs a man. Out here, it's
doubly true. The town won't like it, but, still, you're doing
the right thing."

Randall hoped against hope that the older man was
right. He certainly knew nothing of such things. What in
the world had made him tell those men in the saloon he
was going to marry Hannah before he had even asked
her? He wasn't even sure she wanted to be married. It was
just plain perverseness, using his own life to thwart them.
But they were so wrong.

In a daze he had wandered back to the church and

sought out the parson to tell him what he had done. Reverend Thistle acted as though he had expected it.

Together they marched with falsely certain steps to the parsonage, like men going to war against unknown forces. With an occasional elbow nudge and prompting from the parson, Randall informed Mrs. Thistle and Hannah of their plan. Mrs. Thistle acted as though she had expected it, too.

Hannah was still not asked. Nonetheless, she nodded her assent. What choice did she have? He wasn't sure she even understood what he said. She sat very still in her fancy, pink dress, her knees pressed hard together, her auburn hair like a thick shawl upon her head. He could not see her face.

"We'd better go tell Isaac now," said the minister.

Isaac! Had he really forgotten the boy? He came with the woman, no question about that. But the new sheriff was getting so much at once. Looking at Hannah's impressive figure rounding out the party dress in the gentility of the parsonage parlor, he had begun to smile at the idea of having a wife. Now he was getting a son, too. How was he going to handle that?

MacLane and the minister went out to look for the boy. They found him huddled at the end of the porch.

His lank blond hair headed off in all directions at once. He was dirty from head to foot, as though he had been rolled in the dust. His face was scratched. His nose was bleeding. He was the very picture of the boy who walked in off the plains and banged his nose against MacLane's knee at the water tower. It was as if he were destined to live always in that one thin slice of time.

"My heavens, Isaac," exclaimed the parson, rushing to him. "Who did this to you?"

Isaac shrugged his shoulders.

"Some boys . . ."

"They talking about your mother?" asked Randall.

"What do you care?"

"I care because I'm going to be your new father. Your mother and I are going to get married. Then we'll all have a place to live."

"I like living here, with the reverend and his wife."

"You can't live here forever," said Randall.

He sounded disgusted, like someone who has just stepped in a fresh cow pie with new boots. He was disgusted, but it was mostly with himself. He was handling this whole matter so poorly.

Isaac, of course, assumed that he was the cow pie.

"I mean, somebody's got to take care of you."

"I can take care of myself."

The boy looked up at the young man wearing the badge. The blankness of his stare barely masked the hatred that burned beneath it.

"Isaac! Sheriff! Hold on now," intervened Reverend Thistle. "You're going too fast. We'll get all of this worked out. First, let's have Mrs. Thistle look at these scratches."

He gently but firmly grasped Isaac by a thin and rigid arm. He pulled him up and led him into the house.

Randall sat down on the edge of the porch, only a weary sigh for company. He stared into the lone and level prairie, stretching for miles out away from the town. He wondered if a man could be any more lonely out there than he was in town. Once again came the desire to be the wind, just to blow away into the vast space of the West. He knew, though, for better or for worse, he had to be with people. Somehow, these people, Hannah and the Thistles and Middle Bend, these were the people given to him.

He heaved himself up and went into the parsonage.

Things calmed down for a while. Everyone in the town seemed resigned.

At least, thought the women, she won't be roaming the town, tempting the men with her body and her mystery.

At least, thought the men, she'll be a married woman.

We won't have to spend time wondering what it would be like to be on her, knowing you were right where the Indians had been.

Everyone accepted the marriage as inevitable. Everyone but Isaac.

Of course, there was talk as well as thought. The talk didn't get done where the lean and angry sheriff could hear it.

The women talked to other women. . . .

"They say she's crazy now, her husband gettin' killed, and all them Indians doin' to her like they did. What kind of house can a crazy woman keep?"

"How can a woman like that walk down Main Street, where everyone can see her?"

The men talked to other men. . . .

"I guess he knows what he's gettin'. So does ever other man in town. We all seen her neked."

"Yep. Can't say that 'bout any other woman in town."

"Remember that crazy eye she had, there at the water tower, when she was still strapped to that Injin pony?"

"Hard to believe she'd be any good to a white man. They say after they been with Injins . . ."

And they talked to one another. . . .

"That MacLane's sure got gall, marryin' a woman like that, an' keepin' her right here in town."

"An' she's got her gall, too, her husband hardly cold, takin' another man, livin' in a decent town."

"Ain't nothin' can be done about it, I reckon."

"Nope, not now, with that new sheriff goin' around killin' people right an' left."

"We done our best to get rid of her."

"Yep. If he wants to act so high-and-mighty about it, let him live with it, an' the boy, too."

"We ain't got no responsibility now. We done the best we could to set the thing right."

*   *   *

People were polite enough to MacLane in his official capacity. They made it clear, however, that they were interested in relating to him only as the sheriff. Hannah refused to leave the little house they rented. No one but the Thistles came to call on her. Isaac spent his time playing mumblety-peg in the yard of the rented house or hanging around at the Thistles'.

Randall existed to the town only as the sheriff, not as a married man with a boy to raise. Hannah and Isaac existed only to the minister and his wife. That is, until Isaac started to school in the fall.

The new teacher didn't last a month. A sickly young man from Ohio, he could handle neither the children nor the plains. One day he was gone; no one knew where. He had told no one he was leaving, however, so the children went to school as usual. Some of the older boys saw the occasion of the absent teacher as a grand opportunity to tease Isaac about his mother. Isaac flew into a rage. He attacked them all, guilty and innocent alike. He came home with his nose bloodied, both eyes blackened, and cuts and scratches everywhere. He was more battered and bruised from the attack in the schoolhouse than he had been from the attack by the Indians at the wagon.

Considerably worse, from the standpoint of the town, was that he had bloodied the noses and blackened the eyes of almost every other kid in town. They were the ones who ran away to end the fight. The schoolhouse itself was a total mess.

The town council came to call on MacLane at his office that afternoon.

"Sheriff, you've got to do something about that boy," said Henry Alcorn.

"Don't worry, Mr. Alcorn. I intend to."

They stood around then, glancing at one another, trying to figure out where to put their hands. They had expected MacLane to be stubborn, to defend the boy in some way. Cooperation they didn't know how to handle.

"Well, uh, what will you do, Sheriff?"

It was "Whispering" Lowe this time.

"Why, take him out and shoot him, of course. That's what you want me to do, isn't it?"

They left in a huff.

Randall slumped down into his chair. The council was right for once. He had to do something, but what? He couldn't have Isaac at war with the whole town.

He'd already asked around. Isaac refused to say what had exploded the violence out of him. The other children claimed he had flown into a rage for no reason at all. Randall was sure he knew what had caused the fight. After all, these town children were raised by their parents. He never heard the talk about Hannah himself. Still, he knew exactly what they heard at home about her.

He also knew what it was like to become so enraged that you charged into the mass of the enemy with no goal but to vent your madness. That made him ill at ease both with the boy and with his own memories.

After supper that night, as every night, Isaac went out behind the house to play mumblety-peg. This time Randall followed.

"Isaac, I've got a pretty good idea why you took on all those kids at the school. I don't blame you. I'd probably have done the same thing myself. But you can't go around doing that sort of thing."

He talked on for a while. Isaac continued to flip his knife at the soft ground, acting as though he was all by himself. Not knowing what else to do, Randall dropped it and hoped the problem would go away.

One problem that wouldn't go away was his relationship with Hannah. Not only did she stay in the house to avoid everyone else, she also did her best to avoid her new husband. It was difficult in a small house, so she escaped him mostly by just shutting herself up in her private mental world, where Randall could not penetrate.

He consulted the Thistles. They told him to be patient. He was.

Hannah did her housewifely chores effectively, keeping the place clean and cooking well the items MacLane brought home from the stores. She did the washing and mending, but more as a maid than as a wife or mother. Her own clothes, what few things Mrs. Thistle had rustled up for her after the massacre at the wagon, became more and more shabby. She refused to go out to shop. Randall took Mrs. Thistle with him to buy material for her, but Hannah didn't ever make it up into a new dress. She took no pains with her own appearance at all, except to braid her long, auburn hair.

Weeks went by. They stretched into months. Winter came, with its high-plains cold. Randall asked Hannah if he could sleep in the same bed with her, to ward off the chill. She did not answer. He knew that she felt obligated to do whatever he asked, so he didn't push her.

One night he did slip in beside her. She jerked over to the far side of the bed and left a foot of empty space between them. He could feel the warmth of her body, even through the gap. He came erect with desire and felt ashamed. He stayed on his own side, but he continued to sleep in the same bed with her, even if he did not sleep with her.

Randall was patient. He did his job, and the townspeople walked softly around him. Mrs. Thistle took over the schoolteaching, as she always did when the current teacher decided he couldn't take the town or the plains anymore. Her presence made it possible for Isaac to attend school and stay out of trouble, but not to make friends. Isaac and Randall both stayed sane by talking to the Thistles, although never together. Hannah did not talk even to the Thistles.

* * *

One day Randall MacLane sat reading in his office in the morning. His feet were propped up on the desk, his Bible open on his lap. He read in Mark of the temptations of Jesus, how Jesus was in the wilderness for forty days and forty nights, "and was with the wild beasts." He shrugged his mental shoulders.

"Sounds like me," he muttered to himself, pulling at the reddish beard he had begun to grow. "Except I've been in this wilderness a lot longer than forty days. Jesus was better off because he had wild beasts. They'd make better friends than the beasts I've got."

From that point, the day went poorly for him. Everywhere he went he saw snarling beasts, in the store, in the saloons, on the street.

He saddled up his horse and rode out of town. He longed to be able just to keep on riding, leave his things in Middle Bend and ride beyond the horizon and never come back. He actually pretended that was what he was doing. He rode for an hour to the west, knowing all the time that he would turn around and go back.

When he got there, it was late and he was hungry. As soon as he rode in, however, "Cabbage" Collins hailed him down on the street. Cabbage was always there. He lived on the streets, as best Randall could tell. "Trouble at Jake's, Sheriff," he said.

Jake's was one of the smaller saloons.

"Lonnie Ledbetter and his brother and hired hand rode in from their horse spread. They got drunk and beat up Jake and pretty well took over the saloon and won't let anybody leave."

"They must be even lonelier than I am if they're keeping anyone from this town in there with them," he muttered.

He did not notice the sideways look Cabbage gave him as he rode away talking to himself. He left his horse at the livery and walked down to Jake's. As he strode along, his boot heels echoing hollowly on the boardwalks in front of the stores, his mood darkened. He was tired and hungry and lonely. He didn't like the town. He didn't like himself.

He pushed through the double, swinging half doors at Jake's and felt his head begin to float away from him. As it rose in the smoke of the saloon, it mouthed words at him.

"You're not cut out to be a lawman," it said. "You're not cut out to be a husband or father or army officer or messenger or anything else you've been and are," it said.

He floated across the rough plank floor of Jake's, trying to get back under his head, his boots not even touching down on the dirt or puddled stains of spilled beer and dried tobacco juice.

He didn't know Lonnie Ledbetter or his brother or his hired hand, but there was no mistaking them. One was behind the bar, serving up drinks to the other two. One brandished a pistol in one hand while sloshing beer into his mouth and down his shirt with the other. The third man grinned vacantly around the room. The other patrons were clustered around the corner tables in sag-shouldered little groups. Jake himself sat slumped in a teetering chair at a table in front of the bar. A mass of dried blood covered the bald spot on top of his head and ran down one side of his face.

"Well, whaddaya know?" The man with the drawn gun sneered. "Here comes a idjit with a tin star pinned on. . . ."

His voice trailed off into a slurred surprise.

MacLane was in no mood to fool around with this trio. He just kept floating across the room, right up onto the man. A grimace of confusion spread across the man's face. He didn't expect this from anybody. He didn't know what to do about it. He had consumed a year's supply of whiskey in the course of the afternoon. That certainly didn't help his reasoning powers. By the time he figured out what the sheriff was up to, it was too late.

MacLane drilled him right in the Adam's apple with a

right cross, twisting his fist into the man's throat as his blow landed. The man staggered back, clutching his throat and gagging. His gun flew out of his hand and off behind the bar, into the face of the man serving drinks. He started to draw his gun, but MacLane was quicker. The sheriff snatched a bottle off the bar and banged it over the man's head. He turned quickly toward the third man, fully expecting a bullet to rip through him. That one already had too much time to draw his gun. The man, however, was still just staring at nothing in particular, the vacant grin plastered like wet leaves on his face. MacLane walked over to him, lifted the gun from his holster, and tucked it into the waistband of his own pants.

"Sure took you long enough to git here," muttered Jake. "You oughta spend less time with that big-tit squaw woman and pay some attention to your job."

Randall felt his teeth clench and his blood go cold. He seriously considered finishing the excavation job Lonnie Ledbetter had started on Jake's head. He was suddenly very tired, though, more tired than he had been since he rode into this hard town back in the heat of summer. Jake just wasn't worth it.

Beyond that, he had some sympathy with Jake's position. As long as he wore the star, he shouldn't be out skimming along the horizon, dreaming about riding off from his responsibilities. Jake was right; he should tend to his job. Or else he should be home doing exactly what Jake accused him of.

The Squaw

Randall slipped into the house through the back door,
quietly, as always, lest he disturb the delicate balance that
allowed Hannah and her son to exist with him but not live
with him. In fact, each of the three lived in a separate
world, even though they lived in the same house.

The kitchen was cold. It seemed to Randall MacLane
that he might as well have stayed outside, for all the
warmth and welcome that "home" meant to him. Hannah
cleaned and cooked, but increasingly she just didn't seem
to care about any of the other chores necessary to keep a
household running. Isaac positively refused to do anything, such as banking the fire so that the house would
contain some warmth when the sheriff arrived home from
his nightly rounds. He hardly ever spoke a word to his
stepfather. Nonetheless, he was communicating loud and
clear that he did not consider this to be his home.

"What a mess." Randall sighed. "Three people in a
house, and it's not a home to any one of them."

He considered stoking up the kitchen fire to heat something up for a sad, late supper. That, however, might wake

Isaac. . . . He realized with a rush of excitement that he did not want to wake the boy.

With an aching emptiness in his gut, he crept to the little room where he and Hannah slept, always far, far away from each other, in the same bed. She lay still, a large, blanket-swaddled log. He couldn't tell if she was awake.

He imagined how she must look if the blankets and her nightclothes were stripped back, if she rolled over onto her back and looked up at him, her mass of auburn hair spilling out undone all over the white pillow. Quickly he started stripping off his clothes. The handgun of Lonnie Ledbetter's hired man fell to the floor with a thunk as he undid his belt. He had forgotten to leave it in his office when he had tossed the three men into their cell, the wounds he had inflicted upon them still untreated.

Hannah stirred at the sound. Randall quickly got out of the rest of his clothes and slipped into bed naked. He could sense his wife stiffen. That told him she was awake. He felt himself stiffen also.

He pushed his way along the mattress until he was an inch from her body. Heat emanated from her, heat that should have been in the stove in the kitchen but was only in the bed. He wanted so much to be warm. He reached up and touched her shoulder. She flinched, ever so slightly, but she definitely moved.

She's been waiting for this, he thought to himself. Ever since I started sleeping in this bed, she's been anticipating it every night. Everybody in town thinks this is why I married her, and we haven't even touched since I cut her loose from that Indian pony in the heat of summer.

He reached over her and gently took her breast in his hand. It was soft and hot, even through the heavy material of her winter nightdress. She lay very still, but she did not resist. He reached under her hips and pulled the nightdress up. It was hard work. She lay like a rock in the mud on the bottom of a stagnant pond. He had to yank and tug to get the dress out from under her hips and up over her bosom. By the time he had it bunched up under her arms, he was on his knees, bracing against her back, panting harder than he had a little while before when he had driven Lonnie Ledbetter and his brother back within the lines of the law.

"By God," he said, only to himself, as a man does when he's sure he's right and still ashamed of it, "you're my wife, and it's time you acted like it. That's the law, too, the law of marriage. A man takes care of his wife, and she owes him what a man needs from a woman."

He took a breast in his hand again, not so gently this time. He felt the nipple grow against his palm. He straddled her, reaching down to grip the other breast with his other hand, heedless of the cold against his back as he flung the covers off, feeling only the warmth of the woman beneath him. He pushed and pulled at her breasts until she was on her back beneath him. He slipped his body down, found the niche between her legs, pushed his way in between the full softness of her thighs. Not really knowing what to do but feeling that primeval urge to be within her, he pushed and pounded at her soft mound with his maleness, feeling giddy and desperate and almost sick with desire.

She began to breathe hard, through her nose, her lips clenched tight against any sound. Suddenly one of his awkward thrusts met no resistance and he slid deep within her. His whole body seemed to be lost, his face enveloped in her mass of hair as she turned her head aside, away from him. His chest sank into the pillow of her bosom. His legs melted into the soft flesh of her thighs. His organs and bowels were sucked into the deep, swirling pool of her soft, hot womanhood.

He pulled out, feeling the ridge of her pelvis rake him for what was both an instant and an eternity. He thrust within her again. She gasped a tiny cry and wrapped her legs around him. He wanted to stay like that forever, pulling and pushing, feeling nothing in the world but this woman under him and around him. Just as quickly as he thought it, his body exploded. He felt himself go to jelly within her. He spurted out his world and left it inside her.

He lay on top of her, too spent to move. Finally the cold became too much. He rolled over and pulled the covers back upon them.

He reached for her hand. It was moving, grasping at the sheet below her, just as it had grasped at the dirt when he first found her under the Indian.

He knew without words that she would never forgive him. Not for taking her in the way that men had always taken their wives, but for making her cry out and wrap her legs around him at the same time that she was remembering the heat of the summer and the burning wagon.

They went on like that for five full years, summer and winter, heat and cold, without a word. When the urge or the anger or the loneliness became too great, he would roll over onto her at night and try to reach her and try to punish her at the same time. Sometimes she cried out and wrapped her legs around him and sometimes she did not.

Isaac was a constant problem. He spoke neither to his mother nor to his stepfather. He spoke to everyone else in town, to curse them to their faces. He grew distant even from the Thistles. His fights diminished, but only because the other boys avoided him like a naked man in a poison-ivy patch.

"If'n ya did'n know better, you'd swear that boy was the sherf's own, ya wud," said Charley at the Palace one day. "Just as quick with his temper, one as t'other."

The other men all nodded sagely. MacLane's own reputation for quick violence kept the town remarkably calm.

No small part of that reputation was the respect the Indians paid him.

*   *   *

The hate and fear toward the Indians had died down some as the memory of the Custer massacre faded. Also, the merchants of Middle Bend wanted to make money off the Indians as much as from the rest of their potential customers. The Indians were grudgingly welcomed as they came to town to trade.

They always kept as great a distance as they could from the sheriff. At first the townspeople thought it was just because of his star. Then it became clear that they knew him, even had a special name for him, "He-who-charges." Everyone assumed it was because of what had happened at the Reindorf wagon and the story told by the one warrior who got away. They didn't know about his charge to try to get through to Custer.

MacLane made a virtue of necessity. He told himself that he was proud of his reputation and the isolation it brought.

"I'd rather have them respect me than like me," he told the parson one day.

"I feel the same way." Reverend Thistle sighed. "My problem is that the folks here neither respect me nor like me."

Randall didn't know what to say. The words the minister spoke were true. He felt a pang of pain on behalf of the only man in town he could call a friend. He knew how much it must hurt to have neither respect nor affection.

"If fear is what it takes to get respect," he said to himself, "then by God, at least I'll have their respect."

The return of the Indians was a blessing to the merchants but not to the sheriff, despite the way they added to his legend and his reputation. Their presence inevitably brought Hannah out of the house and out to the edge of town to where they camped.

At first, people were amazed to see her. They had almost forgotten that she even existed. A few tried hesitantly to speak to her if they saw her in the street, on her way toward the Indian encampments. She sailed past them as though she were a ship on a different ocean.

She just stood at the edge of the town and stared at the camps, as though searching for something. Randall was sure she was looking for the one remaining Indian who had mounted her in the heat of that summer day six years before. He was not sure why she did it, but he hoped that this search might somehow make her better, bring her back to the real world. At least it got her out of the house. That was bound to help some, he told himself.

It did not. Each time she saw the Indians, she became even more remote from him and Isaac. When he tried to make love to her, she lay like a dead woman. No longer did she wrap her legs around him and cry out. She neglected the house and her own appearance. Randall often came into the house at night and found her squatting in a corner of the kitchen, staring into nothingness.

He brought Mrs. Thistle over one day to see her in that condition. Strangely, the older woman did not seem really interested. She looked at Hannah, but as though she were peering into some distant spot. She stared so long and in such silence that Randall feared she had gone off into the far country of the mind and joined his wife in the land of nowhere.

All she said, finally, was, "Perhaps the body knows best."

As the months went by Hannah became more bold. She began to go into the Indian camps and squat with the squaws in their work circles. The Indians at first ignored her. What was a white woman from the town doing this for? They did not know, and so they tried to act as though she did not exist. She seemed content with that. But she began to take items from the house with her when she went, using them for trading, carrying the bartered goods back to their house in a feed sack.

One day Milo Rosewater came to MacLane's office. He took off his hat as he stood before Randall's increasingly battered desk.

"Sheriff, as you know, I was kind of the moving force in getting you this job. I hope you don't hold it against me."

He laughed nervously. Randall simply waited.

"Some of the other leading citizens weren't too sure, but I knew we needed a sheriff quick and that you had what it took. Well, I think my judgment's been proved pretty good. We've grown a lot here these past five years. A town like this could have gotten out of hand pretty easy, but you've got a reputation as a hard man. That seems to head off trouble before it really gets started. Yes, sir. I guess none of us ever thought you'd stay around as long as you have. Sometimes folks figured it'd be nice if you was a mite more sociable, but you've done real good."

"Get to it, Milo. Isaac gotten into another fight?"

"Oh, no, Sheriff. You've done a good job with that boy. Seems to have settled down. More interested in girls than he is in fighting these days, the way I hear it."

Randall looked down along his legs to the scuffed toes of his boots. They were the same ones he had worn when he came to Middle Bend. He did not believe in letting something go until it was worn out. He sighed as he looked at the new pants tucked into the tops of the old boots. He had a whole box of good pants at home, but they needed mending in one way or another. Hannah just had no interest in it. It would have been too embarrassing to take them to a seamstress in town. After all, he had a wife at home perfectly capable of doing the work, except that he was the sort of husband who couldn't keep a woman happy at home. That's the way they would tell it at the Palace and along the gossip fences, if they knew, so he just kept buying new for himself and Isaac whenever something tore.

Now Milo Rosewater was telling him things about his own stepson that he didn't even know. Girls? It was news to Randall that Isaac knew any girls. Milo didn't know what he was talking about, saying he had done a good job with Isaac. He had done no job at all with the boy. Nonetheless, he was happy if the town did not know that the sheriff's home housed three strangers.

"Uh, Sheriff?" Rosewater broke into his reverie. "It's not about the boy. It's your wife. I guess people understand how she's a little, well, different, what with, well, you know, what happened to her, and all. But this business of hanging around with the redskins . . . Well, I guess they could take that, too, except, now, well, she's dressin' like 'em, and that don't seem right to a lot of folks."

"What do you mean, Milo? I know she's no catalog page, but it's just that she's thrifty. . . ."

Randall flushed at the lie. He looked back to his boots as his face reddened. Hannah wasn't thrifty about her clothes. She just didn't care. He didn't know why he tried to protect Hannah's reputation as a housewife, except, of course, that it affected his reputation as a man.

Now it was Milo Rosewater's turn to be embarrassed. He turned his hat in his hands and gazed with MacLane at the scuffed boots. He and everyone else in town guessed more about what went on in the sheriff's house than Randall would ever know.

"I guess you haven't seen her today. . . ."

Randall thumped his chair down on all four legs as he pulled his boots off the desktop.

"Of course I've seen her, Milo. I saw her before I left the house this morning."

"Well, Sheriff . . . The word is, she's been trading with the Injins, and getting stuff for herself, and today she went down there, and well, she's dressed just like one of the squaws. She's even put something on her skin, so she's as dark as they are. Wouldn't know her, except for her hair. Don't seem right to a lot of folks, what with her being treated by the savages the way she was, and you taking her in and givin' her a home, and the boy, too, when no one else even wanted 'em around, for her to be kind of throwing it in everybody's face that way. Some people even say, when a woman's been with redskins, well, they can't get along without it after that."

Milo Rosewater simply turned around and ran from the sheriff's office, faster than he had ever run before. He ran all the way to the Palace.

He had seen the look in the sheriff's eye. He had seen it once before. He didn't want the sheriff to know he even existed at that moment.

He looked back out over the swinging half doors of his saloon as he gasped for breath. He saw Randall MacLane striding down the street, steps long, shoulders hunched, going toward the Indian camp at the end of town, beyond the church.

Running

<hr style="width:40%; border-top:2px solid black;">

MacLane barged right into the Indian encampment.

There weren't many families this time, perhaps six or eight. The women sat on blankets, doing various sorts of handwork. They were in their usual circle, except for Hannah.

She squatted in old moccasins, almost a part of the circle, but not quite. Her thick, auburn hair was pulled back and greased until it was straight and almost black. She wore a greasy, skin skirt that was too small, so that it pulled up obscenely on her thighs. Her breasts protruded up and almost out of her small, skin vest. Randall recognized several pieces of her clothing on other women around the circle. Hannah was bigger than any of them.

The sight of her momentarily brought him up short. If he hadn't known she was there, he wouldn't even have recognized her. Now he stared at her with a combination of lust and loathing. He had felt that flesh in the dark of their marriage bed, but he was seeing more of it now than at any time since he rescued her at the burning wagon six years before. That, too, had been in the presence of savages.

He had possessed this woman's body, "known" her, in the biblical sense. Yet he knew her not at all. He had saved her, married her, given her a home and his name, provided for her. She had not been his for a single moment of it all. His heart longed for her. His maleness hardened for her. His pride and loneliness hated her.

Then he heard her talking to them, in Indian lingo. Randall knew no Indian language, other than a few words. She spoke in a low monotone, without break, mumbling rapidly. The other women had paused in their work and were staring blankly at her. Then Randall realized the language she mouthed was no more theirs than his.

A man stepped out of a makeshift hide shelter. It hugged the ground behind the circle of women.

"We know why you come here, He-who-charges."

He spoke in English, except for the Indian name for the sheriff. That was one of the words Randall knew.

"You know who I am?"

"All of my people know about He-who-charges. We know you come for your woman. Why?"

The question kicked Randall in the stomach. Why? Because she was his woman, just as the Indian said. What more reason did he need?

He jerked his shoulders to turn his back on the man. The jerk sent an arrow of pain from the back of his neck up into his eyeballs. Who was this savage, acting like he knew something that was hidden from a college-graduate white man?

He reached Hannah in two long strides. He grasped her under the armpits and started to pull her to her feet. Her voice never wavered, just continued to string endless nonsense, guttural sounds together. Her body, however, went slack in his arms.

Behind him he heard the Indian laugh, an arrogant snort of derision.

MacLane let go of his limp wife and whirled on the Indian. The curled-lip sneer fled the man's face faster than a red-winged blackbird can streak from a fencepost. MacLane bore down on him. The brave hesitated, as though he intended to stand and face the white man, but his face and his legs fell apart at the same time. With no attempt to save face, he turned tail and ran toward the horses at the end of the little encampment.

MacLane wanted to run after him, to beat the living hell out of him, to wipe the sneer off his face. Then he remembered the sneer was already gone. He no longer had to beat men with his fists in order to beat them. His reputation alone was enough.

While the Indian women whooped and shouted catcalls at the fleeing brave, Randall turned, retraced his steps, and hoisted Hannah once more. Half dragging and half carrying, he led her toward town.

As they reached the church Randall heard the thud of hooves and cries of dismay behind him. Grasping his wife, he turned as best he could, sure the Indian must be riding down on them.

His mouth dropped open. Instead of riding down on MacLane, the man whipped his pony through his own camp, scattering the women, whacking at them with a quirt, trampling their work into the dirt. He was taking out the frustration of his fear and the humiliation of his flight on his own people and his own home. He was enraged at those who laughed at him, just as MacLane had been enraged at his laughter.

Hannah finally halted her mumbling as they watched the destruction of the place where she had sat a little while before. The slackness left her body. When Randall took her arm and turned her back into town toward their house, she walked along with him, slouching, but under her own power.

He led her through the backstreets, ignoring the stares of the few curious townspeople they met along the way.

When they reached the house, he literally pushed her through the door. He slammed it behind them and began ripping the animal skins from her body. He stripped her naked. He threw what was left of the trades with the Indian women into the corner, then dragged her onto a straight chair.

He ran through the house, heedlessly knocking into tables and chairs along his path. He rummaged through the drawers of her dresser, found the scissors, rushed back to her. He gathered great hanks of her thick, greasy hair into one hand and hacked at them with the scissors. He threw the severed mops into the corner on top of her Indian clothing. He hacked and threw until she was nearly bald. Only tufts of dark, curled roots still lifted from her white skull in a crazy-quilt pattern. Her entire head looked like the triangle between her legs.

Randall reached down from behind her, grasped her full breasts so hard that rolls of pink flesh protruded from between his fingers. He yanked her up and dragged her into their room and flung her onto the bed. He stripped off his own clothing and fell on her. He entered her immediately. Grasping the flesh of her bosom in his hands, he buried his face in the soft crevice formed by her shoulder and neck. In vain he felt for the gentle cradle of silky hair that he had always found there before.

He pounded and pounded at her. He beat into her as if he were an iron poker and she a stove in the summer kitchen of his boyhood. She cried out, whether with pain or ecstasy he did not know. She wrapped her legs around him, but whether to draw him in farther or to ease the angle of his penetration he could not tell. He whinnied like a horse as he exploded inside her, his own animal sounds mingling with hers in his ears.

His body began to go limp. He stuck out his tongue and discovered that the crevice of neck and shoulder in which he had buried his face was a salty stream. Only then did he realize he had been weeping the entire time he had been joined to her.

*   *   *

Hannah went back to her old ways, mostly. She dressed in her old clothes and worked in silence around the house that she never left. She did not seem to notice the absence of her hair. From time to time, however, Randall caught her mumbling the guttural, nonsense language that she had used at the Indian encampment. He was no more able to understand her words than he was ever able to understand her silence.

One day he came home in the middle of the afternoon. As he passed the kitchen window he was amazed to see her sitting at the kitchen table, chatting with Mrs. Thistle. She went silent again as soon as he entered the room. The parson's wife pushed herself up slowly from the table and gave a slight nod of her head to him, indicating he should follow her outside.

"Good-bye, Hannah," she said softly. "I'll come again. Perhaps we can talk some more."

Hannah MacLane stared into some indefinite distance and seemed to hear nothing.

The lean young sheriff and the parson's squat old wife stood together on the simple porch of the little MacLane house.

"I don't know, Randall. She's never recovered from that bout with the Indians, when they . . . Well, she seems to think that she's possessed by the savages, that somehow the spirits of those men you killed entered into her body. She thinks that gibberish she talks is a lost Indian language. I just don't know."

The little lady walked slowly away. Randall knew that his hope of ever understanding or possessing his wife walked away with her.

As Mrs. Thistle turned the corner Amos Tanner brushed by her, head down, walking intently toward the MacLane house. He looked like he had made up his mind to eat something he knew would have a bitter taste. He glanced up as he neared the porch, then slowed when he saw the sheriff standing there. His intensity began to melt. He whipped his hat off while still ten yards away from the shade of the porch.

MacLane knew the Tanners only slightly. They had come to town recently, lured west by some vague hope of a better life. Amos had developed a reputation as an able worker, but he had trouble finding a steady job in Middle Bend's uncertain economy. Randall knew only that they lived simply and kept pretty much to themselves.

"Howdy, Sheriff," Amos muttered uneasily. "I need to talk."

"That's fine, Amos. I could use some normal conversation."

"Don't know, Sheriff. Guess this isn't real normal, at least not for Tanners."

Randall's heart sank with some ancient Scottish second sight.

"It's about my daughter, Clara. She's only fifteen. Guess they didn't know I'd be workin' at the liv'ry barn today. Her and that boy of yours was back in the barn . . . well, doin' things they hadn't orter."

He paused, waiting for Randall. The sheriff remained mute, so he went on.

"I guess I just thought I should let you know. You're a hard man, Sheriff, everyone says so. Says you fly off the handle real quicklike. I don't wanta make trouble, but I'd appreciate it if you'd keep that boy away from Clara. She admitted it wasn't the first time. If she gets in a family way . . ."

So this simple ordinary man is afraid of me, thought Randall. He has every right to be upset at me. I can't control my wife and I can't control my son. He's afraid I'll take it out on him. What a pretty pass I've come to.

He said the only thing he could think to say.

"I'm truly sorry, Amos. I didn't know. I'll talk to the boy. You need have no fear of me. I'm just sorry. . . ."

"Thank you, Sheriff. I'm sorry, too, 'bout what I said 'bout you bein' a hard man. I guess a man like me shouldn't be listenin' to what folks say."

"No, they were telling you the truth, Amos. That's the worst part of it. But you go on home. I'm going to try to sort all this out."

Amos Tanner left. The image of the hard sheriff he left with Randall would not go away with him.

Randall had every intention of talking right away with Isaac, but he hardly knew what to say. He knew the drives a man has. He knew how once aroused, they were all the more difficult to control. This was not a subject to take lightly.

Days went by as he waited for the right opportunity. He was putting off what he should do, because he didn't know what it was.

One morning he rolled out of bed and went to the kitchen. Isaac was sitting there, his head in his hands. Maybe this is the time, he thought.

"She's gone," muttered Isaac.

Randall thought he must be talking about the girl, Clara Tanner. Perhaps Amos had decided to wait no more for the sheriff to do what was right. Perhaps he had packed up his family and headed on, farther west.

Then he sensed an absence all around him. Hannah was not in the house. Even though she was never in to him, he could feel the lack of her in a different way.

"She's gone?" he repeated, his words sounding stupid in his own ears.

"The Indians, the ones camped out there where they always do. Left before dawn. She went with them. I saw her. From the loft down at the livery. I didn't try to stop her."

Randall looked down at the top of Isaac's head. The boy was getting close to being a man. He was sixteen now. He was a man in his body, certainly. Randall knew why Isaac was in the livery loft and who he was with when he saw his mother ride off with the Indians.

He felt a hot flush of shame. It wasn't much of a man who let his own wife run off with Indians and did nothing to protect a good man's daughter from this young man he had taken as his son. He was feared by all and loved by none. It wasn't much of an identity for a man.

MacLane understood how Isaac felt, though, watching his mother ride away with the Indians. He would not have stopped her, either. He would not go after her this time; there wasn't any point. That meant Isaac was all he had left.

"Isaac, I know I didn't do for your mother what I hoped for. You and I haven't exactly been a good match as father and son, either. But I think we need to stick together now. There's not much we can do about your mother, but Amos Tanner told me about you and his girl. I guess we've got troubles here we'd better try to solve."

The boy raised his head and looked blearily at Randall. It was the same look that washed across Isaac's face when he bloodied his nose on Randall's leg. It had been there when he tried to get under the water sluice, when they first came to town on that hot and hostile day.

Isaac's voice was dull with teenage fatigue with life.

"My father was killed by redskins. My mother's run off with 'em. Clara says she's going to have my baby. I don't want a baby. I don't want a wife."

He pushed up from the table, flung open the back door and rushed out, like a coyote willing to eat off its own leg to escape the teeth of the trap. Randall knew that if there was a stove available to Isaac, he would pound it to death.

Twice before, Randall had been sure it was impossible to be any lonelier than he was at those moments. He had twice been wrong.

He trudged to his office, did his rounds, tried to stay away from people, perversely enjoying his misery. He had tried so hard, done all the right things, read and studied and prepared himself, carried the message to Custer across half a country and against thousands of savages, saved the woman and the boy and given them a home, protected the town. Who gave a tinker's damn about a bit of it? He felt very righteous as he swam 'round and 'round in the shallow pool of his own pity.

His mind kept sneaking back to the incident at the wagon. It was more clear now in memory than it had been in the dusty confusion of the moment. He could see it all, as though he had stayed on top of the hill to watch, and someone else had charged down at the Indians, someone else had dragged the deranged woman and her surly son into town, someone else had become sheriff and married Hannah and put up with Isaac. He merely stood on the horizon of the scene and observed.

Then he remembered how Isaac, also, had looked to the horizon, there at the burned-out wagon. Randall felt a surge of love for the boy, the way a wind blows up at the end of a hot afternoon and brings that slight wave of relief.

He decided to go home, to the horizon. He would take Isaac. He was old enough. Just friends this time, each one needing the other. He could barely wait.

Wait he did, however, all day. Isaac did not come for supper. MacLane ate cold biscuits and old butter, his long frame hunched on a straight chair at the kitchen table. Then he walked down to the livery, hoping Isaac would be there and at the same time afraid of what he might find.

Oscar Shurg, the town treasurer, owned the livery, but Pully Parker ran it for him, with occasional help from Amos Tanner. Pully was named for the pully-bone set of his legs. He was on duty when MacLane got there.

"Yep, he was here, Sher'f," said Pully. "Took yore horse. Had a bedroll and all. Said he was goin' campin' fur a whiles. Sure hope it was okay to let him that horse. He's dun it afore. . . ."

Pully trailed off uncertainly and hung his head to one side, darting quick glances at Randall around the red bulb of his nose. There wasn't much bad news that didn't get around in a hurry in a town like Middle Bend. Even the livery hand was aware of the strange events swirling around the hard-edged sheriff.

"For God's sake, man, straighten up," MacLane snapped. "I'm not going to bite you."

Instantly he regretted his words. He was taking out his anger at Isaac and himself on the livery hand. As remorse usually does, however, his only made him more angry.

"It's all right, Pully," he said gruffly. "You'd probably better tell Oscar I'll be needin' to buy another horse from him, though."

He knew Isaac was gone, as gone as Hannah, as gone as his horse, as gone as his dreams for being an ordinary man.

He wandered away from the stable, got almost home, decided against it, started for his office, couldn't stand the thought of that, and decided to get drunk. It shouldn't be hard, he thought, for a man who's never had a drink. He headed for the Palace.

He stepped through the swinging doors into uncommon calm for the saloon. A few muted conversations scurried around the tables by the walls. Most of the customers, however, were listening to an orator at the bar. He was actually addressing them by facing the bar as he drank. He pronounced his opinions to their reflections in the huge mirror behind the bar.

It was William "Buck" Wilforce. He had come to town only two or three years before and had promptly tried to establish himself as a man to be reckoned with. He bought a ranch but preferred to live in town. He hired Lonnie Ledbetter and his brother to run the ranch for him. The other merchants resented him. He tried to get a piece of every business in town. He had enough money that he was successful at it, too. He bought into the bank and stores. He bought up houses as they came on the market. He constantly invested but never did any of the work necessary to make a business go. He made it clear that work was for hired hands, usually the former owner. He was resented, for sure. The town also wanted his money, so it put up with him.

"It's a damn good riddance, I say. You should never have allowed the woman in this town in the first place. So crazy for Injin stuff she had to go after it. And the boy just as bad, doin' to every decent girl in town. If a man can't control his own family, he ought not—"

It was then that Buck Wilforce saw MacLane moving into sight as he gesticulated at the long mirror. He gulped back his next words like a man trying to swallow a toad. He turned away from the bar toward the room, as though about to appeal to the assembled customers directly.

MacLane glided toward him, so smoothly he seemed to be in slow motion, but he got to him no more slowly than a rattler when it strikes.

"Now, Sheriff, I didn't know—"

Wilforce didn't finish. MacLane hit him flush full in the middle of the face. Buck went reeling along the bar, holding his hands over his broken nose. Blood gushed out like beer from a split keg. It oozed between his fingers and ran red down over his dove-gray vest and across the bar. Randall followed him down the bar. When the man tried to straighten up, he threw a mule-kick upper-cut into his belly. Wilforce sank to his knees, holding his belly with one hand and his leak-sprung nose with the other.

Milo Rosewater had heaved himself up with MacLane's first step down the bar. He reached him now as the sheriff balled his fist for another blow.

"Sheriff, wait, don't," implored the Palace's owner. "You can't hit a man just for talking. He shouldn't have said it, what he did, but you're the law."

Randall looked down at his own chest, at the tin star on his worn, leather vest.

"He ain't the law here," spluttered Buck Wilforce, spitting flecks of blood as he spoke. "He's just quick with his fists and mean with his mind, that's all. You're just all afraid of him, is all. . . ."

His words trailed off into an awful reality. He had spoken the truth. He was in more trouble than ever. He began to backpedal, ran his rump hard into the bar, fell to one side, moaning and cursing. He curled up to try to protect himself from the angry blows he was sure would come.

The sheriff, however, paid no more attention to Buck Wilforce. He was still looking at his vest. Suddenly he plucked the star from his chest and whirled toward the mirror behind the bar. There he saw reflected the faces of the citizens of his town—Milo Rosewater and Whispering Lowe and Si Winchester and Oscar Shurg. . . .

He pulled back his arm and flung his badge at the mirror. It didn't even make a dent in the heavy glass.

No Place to Go

—◆—

"No need for you to do this, Sheriff," said Milo
Rosewater.

His voice was as soft as Whispering Lowe's. He stood
in the deep dark of Middle Bend, beside the man he had
hired six years before. He had been sure then it was for
the good of the town. Now he wasn't sure. In the darkness, his bulk was diminished by the doubt.

"At least wait till morning. Things'll look different
then. You just made a mistake is all."

"No, Milo, but I thank you. I thank you for your support my whole time here. We weren't friends, but you had
the best interests of the town at heart. I always appreciated
that. But Wilforce is right. I'm not respected here, just
feared. There's no reason for me to stay here anymore."

He finished cinching his new saddle on the horse he
had bought from Oscar Shurg at the livery.

"You gonna, uh, you know . . . go looking for 'em . . . ?"

Randall peered at the big man in the dark. He sensed
that Milo really cared; he wasn't just being nosy. Perhaps,

186

at least, he had made one other friend in Middle Bend, even if only at the end. A friend deserves the truth. MacLane also needed to say the words, to confirm to himself that it was the truth.

"No, Milo. No use. What's past is past."

"What will you do, then?"

"Just ride, I guess, until I find a place. The only thing I know for sure, I'm through with being a lawman."

"We'll miss you."

Even in the dark, Randall could tell the saloon owner was looking into the past instead of looking at him now.

"I'm sorry to leave like this, in the dark, Milo, but those who want me gone will be glad. The others will understand. Tell the Thistles to get our furniture and use it themselves or give it to somebody who needs it. I just packed up everything else and stuck it in that closet underneath the stairs, there by the jail's backroom. There wasn't anything else in it."

"We'll hang on to it till you send for it . . . or come for it. . . ."

There was nothing more to say. Randall swung up onto his new saddle. Without a glance to either side, he rode away in the dark.

He simply rode west, staying with the roads until it looked like he was coming to a town. Then he would strike off around, skirting where the people lived. He had no particular plan. He just wasn't interested in meeting anybody. His decision made, his family gone, he was now solitary again instead of lonely.

It was skirting around the town of Dry Creek, though, that caused him to run into the Indians. He had camped along the trickle of water that gave the town its name and breakfasted on the last of his coffee and bacon. He had just about decided to ride into town to replenish his supplies, even if it did mean a break in his solitude, when he saw the

Indian braves skulking down the creek bed. He had no sooner seen them than a toothless, old Indian man and a young woman came walking right into his camp. The old man was limping. The woman helped him along.

"We walk long. Need help," she said.

"I'll be glad to help you," Randall said loudly, "but tell your friends to come up here out of the brush, where I can see them."

The woman started to protest that they were alone, but the old man spat a long stream of brown juice into the dust and began to string together a line of what sounded to Randall like Indian curses.

Two braves shuffled up from the creek.

"Tell the others that He-who-charges wants to see all of them."

He put the emphasis and the volume on the Indian word for "He-who-charges."

The braves stopped suddenly. Then one began to edge away, back toward the creek.

The young woman spoke.

"We not know it is He-who-charges here. Your story told around our campfires. You come to take woman back. We take you to her. We know where is."

For a moment MacLane seriously thought about it, going with them. It would be simple. He was not looking for her, but since these Indians had offered . . . He thought for a moment how good it would be if she were pleased to see him, how desperately she would need him if she had come to her senses and now was too embarrassed to return home, how they could go to another town, where no one knew about her. Then he shook his head, as though shaking a spider from the back of his neck.

"No. Leave the woman as she is. And leave He-who-charges in peace."

They slipped away, the old man walking faster than any of them. He had no idea how many others had been in the brush and trees by the creek bed.

The encounter with the Indians left him feeling sour. He decided to forget about riding into town to get supplies. Like most men, when he was in a foul mood he liked to make it worse.

By evening, though, he was facing a feeble supper. He was no hunter. His father and brother were dead before they could teach him. His grandfather lost interest when his only son did not come home from the war. Randall lost himself in books. He had read a dozen stories about hunting, from James Fenimore Cooper on. He had no idea how to go about foraging for himself on the plains, though. For all the roughness of his reputation, he was a town man.

So he felt a little weight lift off his shoulders when he struck the signs of civilization before dusk. It was a ranch road. He was glad enough just to ride along to wherever it went.

It trailed into a handful of rough buildings. The sun-bleached board sign told him it was the LAZY B RANCH. That was even better. Davis Bilyeu had once come to Middle Bend looking for ranch hands. He had taken a couple of troublemakers out of MacLane's jail. The sheriff and the rancher had both been grateful for the trade.

He tied his horse in front of the big house and walked up onto the rough plank floor of the veranda. He knocked several times before he was finally admitted by an old Indian woman. She silently led him back to the office of the owner.

It took Bilyeu a moment to place him, but his greeting was cordial once he did.

"Sheriff MacLane! Didn't recognize you without your badge! What brings you out this way?"

"You'll have to get used to recognizing me this way, I guess. It's not 'Sheriff' anymore, Mr. Bilyeu. Sort of got tired of lawing, and of Middle Bend, too, I reckon. As for being out this way, I guess I'm looking for a job."

"Well, take the weight off your feet, and we'll talk about it. Almost time for supper. Be pleased if you'd join us. I eat with the boys in the chow house. Nobody here but my wife's old Injin woman. Wife died a long time ago, but this old woman's got no place to go. I suppose I'd never keep the place clean by myself, so she just hangs around."

MacLane got the impression Davis Bilyeu was hanging around, too, waiting for something without knowing himself what it might be. They talked about ranch jobs and about Randall's experience.

"I hate to say this, Sheriff . . . er, Mr. MacLane, but the truth is you'd be about as useful around a ranch as tits on a boar. You've got a right strong reputation as a lawman, but the kind of farming you're talking about from when you was a boy, why, there's just none of that sort of thing around here. But let's not jump to any conclusions. Let's get something to eat first. . . ."

The dinner gong sounded before he could finish the sentence, and Davis Bilyeu grinned in appreciation of his own sense of timing. They walked out to the cookhouse. The rancher had no special seat, and they took places on board benches beside the ranch hands, about a dozen all told. The cook started bringing in pots of food and ladling it out onto the tin plates of each man.

"Men, this here's Mr. MacLane. Used to be sheriff at Middle Bend. Some of you might remember him from there."

It wasn't much of an introduction, and was just thrown out in general into the stream of desultory conversation that flowed around the tables. A few men nodded at Randall and two or three muttered a perfunctory "Howdy." Mostly, they were just interested in eating as much as possible as fast as possible.

Randall had never eaten chowhouse food. He was surprised at how good it was. Hannah's cooking had gotten so bad toward the end. . . .

Naming her in his mind seemed to bring her into the conversation. He heard an anonymous cowhand, acting as though he were just thinking out loud, but loud enough for everyone to hear.

"MacLane . . . Wasn't that the name of the woman what got her belly full of redskins and liked it so much she ran off so she could do it with 'em all the time?"

Randall tried to keep on eating. The food really was good, and he really was hungry, but the room began to grow quiet. The food began to stick in his throat. Davis Bilyeu looked at him speculatively.

"Shut up, you fool," he heard someone whisper. "You never seen the man in action."

Randall couldn't help looking over his shoulder to see who had spoken. It had to be the man who was making the biggest show of paying no attention to him. MacLane did not recognize him as one of the hands Bilyeu had taken out of the jail in Middle Bend.

Slowly Randall uncoiled himself from the backless bench, like a rattler stretching in the sun, lazy but still deadly. He looked slowly around the room, letting his gaze linger on each man in turn.

"I don't know who was asking about my wife, since it was said behind my back, but if you'd like to say it again, well, why don't you just go ahead now."

There was not the slightest sound. No one dared even scratch a fork across a tin plate. MacLane waited. No one spoke. Finally he sat back down and began to eat again, forcing himself to measure out each bite as though nothing had happened. Slowly, the other men returned to their meals, but conversation of any kind was clearly done for the duration of that meal. Each man got up and left as soon as he could finish up his grub. Finally only Randall and the rancher were left.

"That's some hell of a reputation you got, MacLane. I know the man that said that. He's a tough hombre. He's going to have to put up with ragging from the rest of the hands every day he stays here because you faced him down that way. Normally, he'd've not backed down against no man, but the other boy reminded him of just who you are. You got the rep, and you got the way. Nobody wants to go against you.

"Let me give you some advice, son. You'll never make a ranch hand. Punchin' cows is boring work. Underneath that calm-lookin' skin of yours is a man that can't stand routine, takin' orders, the same old thing one day after another. You're a lawman. You need the law, and the law needs you. Stick to what you know, what you're made for. I happen to know the sheriff's job is open up at Lone Tree."

"Well, you're probably right about me being no ranch-hand, Mr. Bilyeu, but I'm through with the law. There comes a time to move on...."

He let the thought trail off, because he really didn't have any idea of what moving on might mean.

"Well, go on up to the house. There's a bed for you. I've got to check around the place a bit."

Davis Bilyeu did his checking. Then he and the former sheriff sat up late. They talked in front of the fire, Bilyeu stoking his pipe from time to time.

The scene appealed to Randall. He remembered when his father had smoked a pipe in just that same way. As though reading his mind, Bilyeu spoke into the haze of burley smoke.

"You ever smoke a pipe, MacLane? Soothes the soul, even if it does burn the tongue."

"I often thought about it. Just never got around to it, I guess."

Bilyeu got up and reached a box down from the mantel. He handed it to Randall, along with his tobacco pouch.

"Brand new one. Good briar. Bent stem. Somebody give it to me. Never did like a bent stem, so I never smoked it. Stoke it up. You can have the pouch and the tobacco, too. I've got another one."

Randall felt his throat narrow until it was no wider than the pipe stem. It had been a long time since anyone had given him anything but grief. Davis Bilyeu had given him a meal, a place to sleep, advice, and a pipe, simply because they were his to give.

Randall was drifting now from place to place. Bilyeu did his drifting in only one place. The former sheriff stuffed the new pipe and put his feet up on an old stool. Solitary drifters together . . . It wasn't bad. They sat in front of the fire and smoked, just like two ordinary men.

When he rode away the next morning, he was comforted by the weight of the pipe in his pocket. His mouth was dry. It tasted like he'd been kissing a porcupine. But he felt more at ease than he had in years. He also had a better understanding of why the Indians smoked a pipe when they wanted to make peace.

As he looked down the road to nowhere that he could see, he had a strong urge just to ride off to the nearest shade tree and sit down and smoke his pipe till kingdom come.

Partners
Across the Divide

———◆———

He worked his way west and north, mostly west, not ever sure exactly where he was, finding a town when his supplies ran low. It was because he was out of tobacco that he scouted around and found the road that took him to Clegg City.

Clegg City looked like a second-rate painter had tried to come up with a copy of Middle Bend. Randall shook his head with disgust. Some petty demon seemed determined to keep him from getting away from Middle Bend, from the memories that stagnated like a swamp in the back of his brain. He decided to get his tobacco and get out of town as quickly as he could.

Then he heard sounds that prickled the hairs on the back of his neck. He had left Middle Bend. He had left the law. But he hadn't been able to escape the lawman's ear for the sounds of trouble.

In front of a store that proclaimed itself, through a big, board sign as SCHMIDT'S GENERAL MERCHANDISE, three cowboys were hoorahing a Chinaman. The Chinaman had his arms folded, hands tucked into the billowing sleeves of his kimono. He seemed resigned to his fate. The cowboys pushed him back and forth, as though he were a human spinning top.

"Hey, let's cut off his pigtail," yipped one of the cowboys, slapping his knee with glee at the very thought of it.

"Yeah, then we can cut off his real pigtail," replied one of the others, rubbing his little pot gut.

MacLane recognized the voice of real meanness in that one. He was always amazed that cowboys could develop potbellies, considering the nature of their work and food, but he had seen a surprising number who had them. He assumed they were the kind who got out of as much work as possible and managed to indulge themselves, even on the range. This man certainly filled that bill.

Randall looked quickly around. No lawman was in sight. He couldn't spot the sheriff's office. Not many people were on the street. Those that were didn't even seem to notice what was happening to the Chinaman.

The first cowboy pulled a knife and made a grab for the Chinaman's pigtail. The Chinaman, arms still in his sleeves, made a little bow to the man. It effectively swung his pigtail away from the cowboy's grasp.

"Hey, I can't git holda the greasy little bastard," the man yelped with surprise.

"Jake, you grab 'im," the potbellied one directed the third cowboy, "and Bill'l cut off that prissy pigtail and I'm gonna pull down them pajamas he's wearin'. It's disgustin', wearin' pajamas out on the street this way."

He pulled a knife from his boot and advanced on the still stoical little Chinaman.

With the reflex of long habit, MacLane crossed the street toward trouble. Still astride his horse, he spoke calmly but in what he hoped were menacing tones. In Middle Bend, he didn't need to worry about his voice. His reputation was threat enough.

"That's enough, boys, you've had your fun. Let the Chinaman go now."

The first cowboy squinted up at him.

"Who the hell are you?" he asked.

Randall realized the man was drunk. The cowboy called Jake probably was, too. Only the potbellied one with the dead black eyes was sober. That figured. He was the type to get others drunk to involve them in some scheme of his own.

"Forget about him," said Potbelly to the other cowboys.

"Leave it alone, mister. This ain't your business."

"It's my business now. I said to let him go."

He felt the first stirring of the rage. It had been a long time now. He liked life without the rage. Why had he gotten involved in this? The man was right; it wasn't his business. All sorts of nastiness went on every day, all around the world. He didn't do a thing about it, because he wasn't on the scene when it happened. Just because he was there didn't mean he had to stick his nose in it. He didn't want to feel the rage. He just wanted to sit in the shade and smoke his pipe like an ordinary man.

He thought too long about it. That was a mistake. It was just one mistake along with three others. First, he had unconsciously counted on his reputation, but to these men, his reputation didn't exist. Second, he had remained on his horse. Third, he hadn't considered just how mean some people are.

The potbellied man was twirling, with that surprising lightness of foot that fat men often have, almost as though he were executing a dance step. The knife hand was back over his shoulder, already starting forward, aiming the glinting blade at MacLane. If Randall had been on foot, and thinking about the man instead of the general problem of injustice, he might have had a chance. As it was, he froze.

The Chinaman, however, did not. With movements so fast that Randall saw only blurred flashes of the man's sleeves, his hands came out of his kimono. With a little cry, almost like a cough, he chopped Potbelly's wrist with a hand and kicked him in the gut. The knife flew from his hand. The handle caught the cowboy called Jake across the face. It wasn't much of a blow, but Jake stumbled backward and sat down in the dust with a thud.

The Chinaman followed up with a swinging sidearm blow to the man that Potbelly called Bill. It slapped him across the middle like a two-by-four. The Chinaman finished up with a downward chop on the back of his neck as he doubled up. By that time, Potbelly was on his knees, retching, holding his broken wrist against his blasted belly.

It looked like a small and selective tornado had just whirled down the main street of Clegg City.

The Chinaman's hands were already back inside his kimono. He executed a small bow toward MacLane.

Almost as suddenly as the Chinaman's explosion, the street filled with people, pouring out of stores and saloons. Prominent among them was a large, walrus-mustached man wearing a star on a fancy leather vest.

"By God, that does it!" he yelled. "We've had enough of you, you yellow bastard. You're gittin' out of town, or you're gittin' strung up."

He advanced on the small Chinaman, followed by the rest of the crowd, which strung out into a rough arc around MacLane, the Chinaman, and the three downed cowboys.

It reminded Randall of a scene from one of his college Latin books, an ampitheater, with people in a semicircle around a drama involving a warrior on horseback, some slain soldiers, and a wizard of some sort. Just as the spectators in the book stayed in their seats instead of coming on stage, the people of Clegg City held back when they got about ten feet from the scene of the action. Even the blustering man with the star was careful not to get within arm or leg range of the Chinaman. Then he pulled his gun.

"All right, Chinaman. You've done your last damage around here. Are you gittin', or not?"

The Chinaman simply executed a small bow in the

direction of the sheriff. That seemed to drive the man wild. Randall almost laughed. It was such a parody of himself. The sheriff was clearly enraged, but his rage had no focus. Obviously he was angry with the Chinaman, but the rage itself seemed simply to fly off in all directions, like sweat from a running horse. He wanted to direct his fury at the Chinaman, but some invisible shield around the little yellow man seemed to protect him, deflecting the sheriff's wild wrath up and out, like spit in the wind.

"Enough!" bellowed the sheriff. "Take him and tie him up, boys. We're headin' for the nearest tree!"

The rest of the men in the crowd growled like a pack of dogs. After a tentative step or two toward the Chinaman, however, they came to a hovering halt. They had him outnumbered fifteen to one, but no one wanted to be the first to reach him. MacLane used the moment of indecision.

Randall was shocked. How could anyone wearing a badge actually lead a lynch mob? But that's the way it was. Even on his worst days as a lawman, he hadn't abused the star so badly. The odds weren't on his side, so he tried to keep his voice level.

"It seems to me that you're stringing up the wrong man, Sheriff. That man with the broken arm was trying to kill me with his knife. The Chinaman stepped in and saved my life."

The sheriff with the fancy vest turned on Randall.

"Keep your nose out of our business," he yelled. "This is somethin' we've been needin' to do for a long time, and if you git your beak into it, you'll git it chopped off, you . . . you . . . stupid bastard."

MacLane did laugh out loud then. The man was so ludicrous! Even the least articulate of the barflies back in Middle Bend could insult a man better than that.

Randall's laughter raised the ire of the Clegg City sheriff even more than the Chinaman's bow. Without warning he jerked up his gun and fired at the ex-sheriff of Middle Bend. His anger and the fact that he was firing up at a man on a horse conspired to throw off his aim. MacLane knew he would never have time to draw his gun to defend himself, so he took advantage of what he did have, a trick that had saved him more than once.

He dug his heels into his horse's flanks and drove it directly at the sheriff. The horse was already poised to go, ears back and eyes wild from the gunshot so close in front of it. It plowed right into the sheriff and the men in the crowd behind him. MacLane jerked the reins hard left just before they came to the boardwalk in front of the store and whirled the horse in a full circle, scattering bodies in all directions.

From the corner of his eye he saw the little Chinaman swoop down on the sheriff's gun, lying a few feet from the fallen lawman. He grabbed it and tucked it into the sleeve of his kimono so quickly Randall was not sure he actually saw it disappear. The sheriff certainly didn't see it. He crawled around in a dazed circle, looking for the gun.

"I'll kill you! I'll kill you!" he yelled, his voice breaking with anger and despair as he circled his own tail on his hands and knees in the dust of the street.

The men who had not been knocked down by MacLane's horse retreated into the stores and saloons closest at hand. He had no idea how badly injured were those still scattered in the dust of the street. He did know, however, that he was in trouble, not so much at the moment, but in the days to come. He could just ride out, but that would leave the Chinaman's fate to the town. No way he could do that. He really did owe his life to the little man. He could take the Chinaman with him, but they were sure to be pursued, by a posse that would want only revenge, not justice. He had to do something quickly, to take advantage of the confusion of the situation.

"All right, you men, listen carefully," he shouted, making up with volume for the weakness of the words he was about to speak. "I'm Sheriff MacLane. I've been looking for a long time for this Chinaman. I'm not about to have you yahoos stringing him up when I've finally got him. I'm taking him for trial. Some of you are going to be called to testify, so get your stories straight. As for you, Sheriff, you don't deserve the title. You're a disgrace to the profession, if you can't shoot any better than that."

With that, he walked his horse over to the Chinaman and extended his arm. The man with the pigtail hesitated for just a moment, then took the proffered hand. MacLane swung him up onto the back of his horse.

"You got a horse or anything we need to take?" he asked quietly.

"No horse. Ride straight. We get my things at home just out of town."

Randall rode straight out of town in the direction the Chinaman indicated. He hoped the threat to make the Chinaman's persecutors come to a trial to testify, and his proclaimed status as a lawman, would keep any of the Clegg City men from pursuing them. Testifying at a trial might bring out all sorts of things they would rather not have spoken about in the light of day. Perhaps the fear of that would keep them from realizing he had said nothing at all of just where he happened to be the law. Besides, the Chinaman would be gone. That ought to satisfy them, although Randall was unsure why they were so angry with the little man, who seemed so courteous and self-effacing.

They had picked up a little bag of the man's belongings in a shack at the edge of town when Randall remembered that he had not gotten his pipe tobacco.

Loss and Learning

They rode in silence, until even Randall was embar-
rassed by the absence of talk.

"I want to thank you properly for saving my life back
there," he said, "but a proper thanks requires a name. I'm
Randall MacLane."

"Why do you search for me, Sheriff?"

The voice was dropped over his shoulder, a surprisingly
large and heavy voice for so small a man, and a Chinaman
at that. Randall gave a little start. His words to the Clegg
City crowd were a ruse. He assumed the little man understood that. He was embarrassed. He didn't want to have to
explain to the man that he had lied to get them out of a
tight spot. It was quite possible that the man felt he was
equal to the situation and did not need any interference
from a white man, regardless of how well-meant.

"Well, I'm not really a sheriff anymore, you see. I
wasn't looking for you at all. I just rode into town to get
some tobacco, but it seemed like a good thing to say right
then. . . ."

He trailed off, feeling foolish. They rode in silence once again. Randall could almost hear the Chinaman thinking. He had forgotten about his intention to thank the man until he broke the quiet with his heavy voice.

"You ask name. I am Liu."

MacLane almost asked for a repeat. The name was spoken with a rush of breath from the sides of the man's mouth. He was not sure. . . . Was it one name or two? He decided to make do with what he had. For a man even quieter than himself, to ask for a repeat would be an insult.

"Well, Lew, I thank you for saving my life. And I apologize for interfering back there. No more help than I was, you would have probably been better off by yourself. I've never seen a man fight like that before, so quick, and with those jerky motions."

The silence returned for a while. It felt more comfortable this time, like a fire that's burned down but still warm. Finally Liu spoke.

"Sheriff, or man-once-sheriff, I thank you. You not fight well, but you think well. You try help. You not like sheriff Clegg City. I think well now and think you man of trouble. You get in trouble again, I sure. You need learn how fight, for when you not on horse."

He snorted what MacLane assumed was a laugh.

"Yes, well, I think my fighting days are over, Lew. I don't intend any sheriffing anymore."

"No, maybe. But trouble come, you man. You need learn. I teach."

With that he was off the horse's back as quickly and gently as a butterfly leaves a cabbage leaf. Suddenly MacLane found himself dismounted as well, standing beside the horse. How the little man had dragged him off he wasn't quite sure.

"You try hit," commanded Liu.

"You mean you're going to teach me to fight the way you do right here?"

"Yes. You try hit."

Randall had never used his fists without the rage. He hardly knew how. Of course, that didn't matter. He had seen the little man in action. He couldn't hurt him even if he were as skilled as a boxer. He delivered a roundhouse right toward Liu's head, only to find himself immediately on his knees, his face in the dirt. Liu's slippered foot on his neck.

"How in the world did you do that?" he gasped.

"I show," said Liu.

Show he did, all the rest of the day, until Randall was so tired he was standing like a spavined horse. He figured he shouldn't be so weary, considering he had spent most of the time on the ground. Still, it was all he could do to get back on the horse and ride to a small stand of aspens where they camped for the night.

Liu trotted beside him this time, seemingly not affected at all by his exertions in teaching Randall what he called "wind fighting." The phrase didn't make much sense, but it was better than the Chinese words Liu used. MacLane could not pronounce those at all.

Liu did all the work, making camp while Randall simply sat and waited for his supper.

Liu took it easier on him the next day, but not much. Randall was already getting sore, but Liu stretched him in ungodly ways until he was not only over his soreness but feeling more limber than he could ever remember. They rode for an hour and then did wind fighting for an hour, until MacLane collapsed again at the end of the day.

They traveled that way until Randall completely lost track of how many days they were out from Clegg City. Time and Liu's limbs were just a blur. The little man seemed to be like the wind itself. MacLane began to understand the value of translating Liu's Chinese words into the catchall wind fighting.

Randall had never been much of a hunter, so it was Liu who not only taught him wind fighting, but who kept them supplied with small game to eat. He simply ran animals down. If they proved too quick even for his windmill legs, he formed his headband into a slingshot and stoned rabbits and prairie chickens and even a gopher with uncanny accuracy.

The days passed quickly. Randall became so adept at wind fighting that he began, almost, to hold his own with Liu, although he suspected the other man was holding back his own most lethal abilities in order to give Randall confidence. He was no longer sore, or even very tired at the end of a day. He was learning how to use his fists and his feet without having to be in a rage.

He did not, however, learn much about Liu. Despite their almost intimate contact as they "fought" together every day, Liu kept him emotionally at arm's length. It frustrated MacLane. He felt this man was more likely to be a real friend to him than anyone he had ever met. His sense of loneliness returned. It was worse, he thought, than if he had really been alone.

He didn't know how many days they had been on the road when they came to a town. Liu didn't want to ride in with him, but MacLane finally convinced him to go along.

"Don't worry," he told the little man. "No one will dare to bother you with a great wind fighter like me there to protect you."

He meant it as a joke, of course. He knew full well that Liu could beat him seriously anytime he wished.

Nonetheless, Liu settled back into his accustomed place, behind MacLane on the horse, as though he was much comforted by the presence of his student.

The name of the place was Rainsville. MacLane snorted out loud when he saw the dried and buckled signboard at the edge of town. If there had ever been any rains there, the plains dust mocked the name now.

He bought food and tobacco at the general store, even though the storekeeper made it plain by ignoring Liu that he wasn't happy to have a Chinaman in his place. He looked right through Liu.

Randall tilted his hat back and scratched around where his hair was plastered down by the sweatband. Why did people get so upset just at the sight of a Chinaman? Most folks simply don't like anything or anybody different from themselves, he decided. He could figure it out, but it didn't make much sense, especially on the frontier. There every person needed every other one just to survive, different or not.

Liu and Randall didn't talk about it, but they rode out of town as soon as they got their supplies. They camped about a mile on, in a little stand of junipers. Liu gathered up juniper cones to make one of his home medicines. Randall cooked up some of the bacon he'd bought in Rainsville. It was good to be away from "civilization" and back in the wilderness.

It was at dawn the next morning when the men jumped them. Every one of them sported a star on his chest, although none acted like he had much respect for the law. They were led by the sheriff of Clegg City, the big blustering walrus-mustached man who had vowed revenge for his humiliation. Randall had not taken him seriously. He had been sure the Clegg City sheriff wasn't the kind of man who carried through on his threats.

When he thought about it later, Randall realized the sheriff probably didn't intend to track them down. He wouldn't want to leave the comforts of town to do his job. Someone, though, must have found out MacLane lied. He was no longer a lawman, and he hadn't been trailing the Chinaman. More than likely the Clegg City sheriff waited as long as he could, hoping he could stall it out and avoid the rigors of the trail. Only when pressure from the townspeople got too much did he swear in a posse and half-heartedly trail along after them for a couple of weeks for the sake of appearances.

He would have given up and gone home. MacLane

and Liu were traveling so slowly, however, while Liu taught Randall wind fighting, that the posse caught up to them almost by accident. The posse probably intended to liquor up at Rainsville and then head back to Clegg City, when they heard about MacLane and Liu being only a few hours ahead of them. So the sheriff had no choice but to lead his men into a fight he no longer wanted. He did it, of course, in the time-honored way of frightened and cowardly men.

The posse gave them no warning, did not call for any surrender. MacLane heard grunting and muffled cursing vaguely. He thought it was a dream, then he wasn't sure, the way folks do when they are in between worlds. He started to sit up but couldn't. Men were holding him down. Others were beating at Liu with clubs and gun butts.

They had the advantages of numbers and surprise, but they made two mistakes.

The first was taking Liu on at close range. Even though the little Chinaman was asleep when they jumped him, and groggy from the blows they managed to get in before he could react, he was now breaking wrists and thumping throats and kicking groins in a whirl like a dust devil.

The second mistake was underestimating MacLane. They had little to go on, of course, except his totally inept performance at Clegg City. They had no way of knowing that Liu had taught him wind fighting along the way. They had detailed only two men to hold him, while the others, at least six or seven, were trying to kick the shit out of Liu.

MacLane made them pay. He jackknifed his legs and caught the man who was supposed to be holding them full in the face with both feet. The effect was more devastating from his bare feet than if he still wore his boots. Liu had taught him that heavy boots actually work to the disadvantage of a kicker. They slowed down the leg. Leg speed and knowing how and where to land the kick was what did the damage. The man went down, unconscious and gurgling the blood that ran down into his throat from his broken nose.

The man holding his arms was so surprised he actually let go of MacLane and tried to pull his gun. MacLane somersaulted backward and caught his neck in a leg vise, then catapulted his body and threw the man through the air. He used his legs to throw the man and his arms to whirl himself like a wheel. The man landed heavily, like a sack of potatoes dropped off a wagon. He didn't stir.

MacLane was up before the man even hit the dust and was on his way to help Liu. The sheriff panicked. He didn't want this fight in the first place, and it wasn't going the way he planned. He pulled his handgun and started blazing away, despite the weak dawn light that made it impossible to see a target well enough to use a short gun. It was as likely that he would hit one of his own men as anyone else. In fact he shot one of the posse through the arm but did not break any bones.

The sheriff kept blazing away until the gun was empty. Liu was dead. All his marvelous wind fighting had made no difference against a gun.

If the posse had been smarter, or better led, they would have shot both men as they slept and escaped without a scratch among them. It was only their meanness, the desire to have the satisfaction of beating personally on the little Chinaman, that had kept them from an easy kill.

Even before he hit the sheriff, Randall vowed he would learn to use a gun as well as Liu had taught him to windfight. Right then, though, hitting the sheriff was all he could do, and he did it with all the skill Liu had imparted to him. He hand-hacked the sheriff on the back of the neck and then double-handed him on his spine as he crumpled. The killing gun dropped like a stone from his limp fingers. MacLane slipped immediately into a crouch, whirling in a circle to protect himself from whatever assault might be coming. There was none. He was king of the hill. Every other man there was down, dead, unconscious or groaning.

Randall walked among the bodies, collecting weapons. He destroyed every one of them. He broke off firing pins. He stoked up the campfire and threw the weapons into it. He waited until they were hot, then bent the barrels against a large rock.

He made no move to help the men who had attacked him. At first he thought he would wait until two or three of them were able to walk and force them to carry Liu's body back into Rainsville for burial in the cemetery. If he did that, though, the people would just wait until he was gone. Then they'd dig Liu up and leave his body for the varmints of the plains. Besides, it would be an indignity to Liu to be carried by such pallbearers and buried in such a place.

When two of the men were finally able to move, he made them dig a grave for Liu right there, even though one of them had a broken arm. By the time they were finished, another man, kicked in the groin by Liu, was able to hobble around, although his face was white as a sheet. MacLane made him gather up the broken guns and dump them into the grave with Liu, along with the Chinaman's pitifully small roll of worldly belongings. Then MacLane covered the grave himself.

The sheriff and the man he had kicked in the face were still unconscious. All the posse's horses but two had run away. Only one man looked like he might be able to ride comfortably, anyway. Randall didn't even look at the men. He gathered up his things, got on his horse, and rode away.

Commitment
Without a Cause

Now he knew that there was only one more task for
him in the wilderness. That required a trip into town. He
took the first wagon road he crossed and began riding
east. It was a long way. He finally arrived at a town that
wasn't much more than a wide spot in the road. The one
commercial building seemed to be a combination everything—livery, grocery, saloon, restaurant, hotel.

"Looks like you've been on the road awhile, stranger."

The store owner's greeting was a combination of
grease to slide a sucker's money from his pocket and caution that the hard-looking man before him might not be a
sucker. It startled MacLane. It was so long since he'd
lived and acted like an ordinary man, he had forgotten
that he looked like anything at all.

"You have any pipe tobacco?"

"Well, sure I do. I mean, it's tobacco, and you can sure
put it in a pipe, if you got one."

The man started toward a row of barrels at the side of
the room.

"Never mind," said Randall. "All I really need is ammunition. I'll take everything you've got for my sidearm."

"Well, make up your mind. You figurin' on takin' on the whole fort?"

He started back behind his rough-board counter with the air of a man who has nothing to do and finds it's too much.

"What fort?" asked Randall.

"Well, you're headin' right in a line for Fort Phil Kearney. I figured you to be a scout. . . ."

The storekeeper's voice traveled up a little as he trailed his sentence off, asking, without asking, what MacLane had in mind for his own future.

Fort Phil Kearney . . . It had been a long time since he'd heard the name, a long time since his ill-fated attempt to get to Custer with the message.

"Yes. I think I'll take on the fort," he said as he gathered up the ammunition and plunked most of the rest of his cash down.

He would be out of money soon. He needed a way to earn his keep. The fort sounded as reasonable as anything for an ex-soldier.

In the meantime, on the way there, he had one more lesson to learn, one more language to speak. Liu was right. He was a man who attracted trouble wherever he went, or else it attracted him. If he'd learned this lesson earlier, Liu might still be alive.

He didn't really miss Liu. The little man had kept him beyond the line of friendship. They traveled across the plains alone together. They were bound by the bonds of lives protected and saved. Still, theirs was at most the relationship of teacher and pupil. Perhaps Liu had understood that there was no time for anything else. Randall did not berate himself for being unable to save Liu, although he wished he could have. But it was a lesson.

Rage was not enough. The fluid skill of wind fighting was not enough. If a man were to survive in the world that

Randall walked, he had to be better with a handgun than those he came up against. A bullet would have gotten to the bloated sheriff of Clegg City in time to save Liu. At least, Randall wanted to think so. Now he began to wonder how he ever survived so long as a sheriff with no real skill with a gun.

"God, I haven't shown any skill as a sheriff or as a husband or a father or a messenger or a soldier or anything else I've tried," he muttered to himself as he rode on toward Fort Phil Kearney. "All I was ever good at was reading books. . . ." Suddenly he was back in the classroom at Indiana University, listening to President Wylie.

"Divide and conquer, gentlemen. All the great military leaders understood that rule. You divide the forces of the enemy, and you divide the forces arrayed in life against you. Try to go up against all of them at the same time, and they will beat you down. Take them one by one, face them down one by one, and you shall be the winner."

MacLane was off his horse before the voice stopped, right in the middle of the vast western empire. He tied his horse to a little bush and spilled the new ammunition out of his saddlebags.

"Divide and conquer," he muttered.

Methodically he began to apply that rule to conquering his handgun. There were three tasks to learn to speak the language of the gun. Get the gun out of the holster, aim it, fire it. He had to do each of the three faster than the man against him, whoever that might be. He set out to learn them one by one.

He drew the gun over and over until the palm of his hand was bruised and the tips of his fingers raw. He aimed at bushes and animal tracks and just spots in the dust. He fired the gun until its barrel was too hot to continue.

He wasn't very good, but he got better. He wasn't very good with people or horses, either, but he was good with himself. He could set himself a task and stick with it. He had always had excellent eye-hand coordination. Those were the necessary qualities for mastering the gun. They served him well now.

Each day he reined in at some sheltered place. The gun could be heard for miles on the flat plains, but he did not intend to be casually seen. He was not sure why. What he was doing was hardly illegal. It was just . . . private.

Each day he worked until the gun got hot. Then he rode awhile and stopped to practice with the gun again. Once a day he also practiced each of the wind fighting routines Liu had taught him.

Finally he was good enough with the gun that he could shoot a rabbit for his supper. That was the night before he reached the fort. He was out of money, ammunition, food, gun barrel, and memories. He was satisfied.

"You've been a lawman, eh? You look to me like you've been on the wrong side of it."

That was the curt assessment of Colonel Meiring, the commander at Fort Phil Kearney, when he presented himself at his office. Once again MacLane had forgotten about his appearance.

Unknown weeks, even months, out of Middle Bend, most of it living rough on the plains, no wonder his looks made people steer a wide berth around him. He was thin to the point of gauntness. A wide, surprisingly dark red beard hid most of his face. He wasn't even sure when he'd started growing it. It was just there. He had paid no attention to his face since Clegg City. There were more important things to do than shave.

Besides, the colonel might be right for reasons other than his looks. In those days since Middle Bend, had he not been on the wrong side of the law? He was at least on the wrong side of the posse from Clegg City. He couldn't really blame the colonel.

"Sir, I'm a soldier," he said, with more confidence than he felt. "I was mustered out because there were too many young officers at the time. My hope is that's since changed. At the time I didn't know what I wanted. Now I do."

He almost convinced himself. After all, there were worse lives. He thought of living in decent quarters, sleeping in a bed with clean sheets, people looking at him with respect as he rode by in the blue uniform, a mess to get his meals at regular times. He conveniently overlooked days in the saddle, dust and dirt, the disciplining of recalcitrant soldiers, enemies of every hue dedicated to his death. In considering a profession, men always see it from the perspective of the front porch in the evening, feet up, running a satisfied mind back over the achievements of the day. They rarely evaluate it from the view of one caught in the swirl of the job in the heat of the day.

"Well, MacLane, you're welcome to apply for a commission again. If you've got the record you claim, maybe they'll find a place for you."

He said it doubtfully.

"In the meantime, I know you've got to do something to earn your keep. The army ain't particularly quick with these things, as you ought to know. I do need another civilian to help with the horses. It's the damned cavalry. You'd think soldiers could take care of their own damned animals, but this is the newfangled army. They're doing so much running around like headless chickens when they're in the fort they ain't got the time, and when we go out to pacify the redskins, then we ain't got 'em here."

He hadn't exactly offered a job. MacLane felt he'd better take it anyway. The colonel was right; Washington could be slow as a turtle climbing into a soup pot.

He'd been at the job only a few days when the colonel's clerk came for him and led him to the commander's office.

*   *   *

"You're about the worst man with horses we've ever had around here, MacLane."

Randall had no doubt it was true. He knew he should try to wait out the military bureaucracy in some other way, but how much choice did he have? "Beggars can't be choosers." It was the one piece of advice he could remember from his grandfather. Out of money and in the middle of nowhere, he had to earn his way.

Being around Fort Phil Kearney had also stripped him of his romantic illusions about cavalry life.

What worried him more now, though, was that the colonel's natural contempt for unkempt civilians was coming through like apples rotting in a paper sack. Before, Meiring was slightly cautious in his treatment of him, just in case MacLane had friends in high places and suddenly became one of his fellow officers. Now that caution was entirely gone.

"Of course, even not knowing much about horses, you might make a soldier," the colonel continued. "This is the newfangled army, after all. If you want to enlist and wear the blue, I can go ahead and swear you in."

What was this, anyway?

"I don't understand, sir. Has word come already about my application for a commission?"

"Yep, it sure has. I've never known 'em to make up their mind so fast. They say you were a soldier, although I had my doubts about that. They also say you ain't soldierin' no more, at least as an officer. They didn't say anything about enlisting, though, and we're always looking for a man who ain't afraid of the frontier."

Randall didn't hear the rest of it, simply because he walked out. It stung him, stung him like a slap on the face or like a yellow jacket catching him with his pants down. It swiped at him like that fiery sword at the eastern gate of Eden, the sword that cut in every direction at once so Adam and Eve could never get back in again.

Something was cutting him off from all choices about his past, and yet condemning him to live in that part of his past that he didn't want. He tried to think of what enemies he could have made in the army to get turned down so quickly. He could hardly remember anyone, enemy or friend. And Colonel Meiring, absolutely delighted to offer him a position as a trooper, an enlisted man, delighted to tell him he was out of the officers' "club" forever . . .

He left the fort without even collecting his pay. He rode south.

The first town he hit was Owensville. He rode directly to the sheriff's office. It was boarded up. He walked across the street to the saloon.

"You know where the sheriff is?" he asked the bartender, who had the air of a man who felt he belonged in better surroundings.

"No sheriff here. They ran the last one off a month ago."

"Who do I see about the job?"

The bartender gave him a long look now. It started with his worn and dirty boots and traveled up to the wild-and-woolly beard. You could tell he was just about to make some remark about it. Then his eyes locked onto MacLane's. He tried to hold the stare but quickly blinked, then gazed off toward the saloon's swinging doors.

"Reckon Cantrell over to the general store is the man to see."

Randall started toward the doors. The bartender mused out loud.

"Don't know why anyone'd want it."

MacLane turned. He stared at the man. The bartender's mouth went as dry as the dead flies on the high mantel over the bar's cracked mirror. He held his peace until the lean bearded man was gone. Then he muttered what he thought, but quietly and to himself.

Cantrell, the storekeeper, wasn't sure if he should be delighted or suspicious. Men don't just ride in off the plains and apply for a low-paying job keeping the peace, at least not men you'd want in the job.

"You been a lawman before?"

"My name's MacLane. I know the job. I did it long enough at Middle Bend."

Cantrell looked at the gaunt, deep-eyed man again.

"I reckon you did," he said. "This is a little town, Mr. MacLane, but word gets around, even to here. They say you're as tough as they come. I reckon we should be honored to have a man with a reputation like yours here as sheriff, but I can't help but wonder. . . . Why are you willing to work in a place like Owensville?"

Randall appreciated the man's honesty. He was also disappointed that his reputation had spread so easily and so needlessly. Well, perhaps it would make the job easier.

"Mr. Cantrell, I need a job. Being a sheriff is what I do for a job, whether it's Owensville or somewhere else."

They shook on that. Randall MacLane took up residence again in what became a long line of jailhouses. He also took up residence again in his personal house of loneliness.

It was the strangest thing. When he was on the plains, where he didn't belong, he lived in solitude. When he was in town, where he belonged, he was lonely. It didn't make sense. The absence of sense in life, however, no longer surprised him.

The widow Martha Granert was a good-looking woman. She was tall and willowy and blond, the opposite of Hannah in looks and temperament. She was an educated woman. The sheriff never anticipated finding the likes of her in a place like Owensville. Her husband, Adam, had been a lawyer and merchant. He had been killed in an unprovoked gunfight by one of the unrestrained frontiersmen who drifted into places like Owensville, one of the same men who had run off a long line of sheriffs.

Randall shaved off his beard. He began to go around to the widow's house in the evenings. She had two young daughters who giggled when he came and when he left and any other time they saw him. He wasn't anxious to take on any more children, after his experience with Isaac, but he decided that giggling girls wouldn't be too bad.

The inevitable showdown came with the wild young man who killed Adam Granert. MacLane shot him down before the man even cleared the gun from his holster.

That night he went to see Martha. She met him at the door. She held it open just a little way, talking to him as though she were just a head protruding from out the house.

"Randall," she said, "it's not just what you did today, what I heard about. I ought to be grateful to you for killing the man who shot Adam, I suppose. In a way I am. But you are a man of violence. You're full of seriousness and silence and guilt. You only know one way to see, and that's to look inside. Even when you're looking at me, you really are looking inward at the picture you have of me in your mind. It's not just the killing today. . . . But I can't see you anymore."

As she shut the door he caught a glimpse of the young girls staring at him from out the kitchen window. They weren't giggling.

Once again he left town in the middle of the night, with just a handshake from Cantrell for his trouble. It was becoming a pattern.

He rode on, sheriffing for a year or two or more, wherever he found a vacancy in the peacekeeping trade. He found that a broken arm or two, a crippled leg here and there, was enough to establish his credentials and start the people of the town running from him.

His reputation grew all across the territory west of the Mississippi, not from dime novels or crude newspaper accounts, but by word of mouth. Through Kirksville and Garrison and Liberty City and Ross and Thomasburg he sheriffed. At times he felt his only friend was his reputation. It wasn't the only friend he wanted.

At every stop he vowed he would have no more to do with women, that his heart would never rule his head again. In every town he found some woman who turned both his heart and his head and made him forget his vow. Then every one of them, one way or another, spoke to him the same words Martha had used to shut the door against him. Edith and Mamie and Susan and Emily and Anne . . . The names formed a litany for him, linked with the towns where he found and lost them.

He was sitting at his scarred little desk in Thomasburg. He sat and wondered how twenty years had passed with only two lists of names to show for them.

Then an obese man in a gravy-stained waistcoat and loosely tied and wildly patterned cravat walked into his office in a cloud of prairie flies.

"Hello, Sheriff MacLane," said Milo Rosewater.

Middle Bend
. . . Again

Milo Rosewater had been fat when Randall first met him in Middle Bend in 1876. Now, twenty years later, he was obese. If you put him under oath, MacLane would have to swear Milo still wore the same cravat and waistcoat as twenty years before. He knew, though, that the man before him could not possibly wear any of his former clothes; he was just too big. He seemed no older, just fatter.

With a sigh Milo tried to wedge himself into the rough office's only chair. He couldn't fit and so had to make do with leaning against the wall.

"We've heard a lot about you back in Middle Bend, Sheriff. Makes us proud, to think we got you started in the peacekeeping profession. Yes, makes us think of you as one of our own."

Randall pulled out his pipe and with an effort at calmness managed to tamp in tobacco and get it char-lighted. He wasn't just surprised to see Milo Rosewater, extra poundage and all. He was thunderstruck. He was also disturbed at how much it bothered him.

He liked Milo, was even glad to see him, but Milo's presence reminded him of too much he wanted to forget. And what was it he wanted to forget? Sheriffing and a woman. And so how had he gone about forgetting for the almost twenty years since he left Middle Bend? Sheriffing and womanizing.

He laughed out loud. Milo's mouth flew open.

"No, I'm not laughing at you, Milo. I'm glad to see you. I'm just laughing at me. Seeing you has reminded me how much has happened since I left Middle Bend . . . and how much hasn't happened."

Milo's mouth drew down into a puzzled question mark. He sighed again.

"Well, happenings is why I'm here, Sheriff. I might as well get right to it. Things haven't been going too good since you left. Buck Wilforce's sort of taken over, and that's a pretty rough element. A decent person's afraid to go down the street. We need you back, Sheriff. Thomasburg's not the place for you. Like I said, you're one of us."

"Who are you speaking for, Milo? Anyone beside yourself? I don't recall that I was all that popular when I left."

"Well, I always thought you and I had a kind of understanding, Sheriff. I didn't think it was necessary to tell anybody else I was coming here to see you."

Randall didn't know where his next words came from, or why he let them get away. They seemed to fly out of his mouth with no conscious thought behind them. Maybe Milo was right. Maybe it was something as simple as the fact that he didn't belong in Thomasburg. But then, he didn't belong anywhere. Surely Middle Bend was where he belonged least. So it seemed like that's where he ought to go.

"I like you, Milo. You believed in me and stood by me when nobody else did. But I always liked that waistcoat you wore when I sheriffed in Middle Bend before. I'll go back with you if you promise to lose enough weight that you can wear that waistcoat again."

Now it was Milo Rosewater's turn to be thunderstruck.

"Bu—bu—but, Sheriff. I don't think I even have that coat anymore."

Then he understood. You could see the lightning flashes of insight in his eyes, even though they were almost hidden by the mountains of flab that surrounded them.

"Well, I guess I could look for it."

"Good enough, Milo. I'll get my things and my horse and we can go together. I assume you have a buggy."

"You mean leave right now, without telling anybody?"

"It's become a habit. It's the way I left Middle Bend, Milo. I might as well come back the same way."

Milo didn't have much trouble persuading the rest of the town council to hire MacLane as sheriff again. Randall knew that was a bad sign. Henry Alcorn and Whispering Lowe and Si Winchester would never have him back if they weren't in big trouble with Buck Wilforce. Wilforce owned so much of the town by now he didn't even take the simple precaution of sitting on the council. He was used to getting his way through intimidation. Milo was able to call a council meeting and get Randall hired before Wilforce even knew he was back in town.

Wilforce got the word that night when Lonnie Ledbetter came riding into his ranch yard, hell-bent-for-leather. Wilforce was sitting on the porch with his feet up and a big cigar in his mouth.

He preferred to live in town, but had decided familiarity bred contempt. Even though he owned more than half the town, the citizens of Middle Bend had a remarkable lack of respect for him. He thought living out at the ranch and only coming into town when he had business would improve things. It hadn't.

There wasn't much Buck Wilforce did that seemed to improve things. Certainly forcing the council to hire

Lonnie Ledbetter as sheriff made them as unhappy as a hound full of seed ticks. But Buck wanted his own man in the sheriff's office.

"My God, Buck. He's back," Lonnie shouted before he even came to a stop. "He's back, and they fired me. Just walked right into the new city building you built and told me to get out 'cause he was sheriff now. My God, never saw anything like it."

"What you talkin' about, Lonnie? Who you talkin' about? Who's back, anyway?"

"MacLane, that's who. That goddamn squawman. I—"

"Shut up. What are you sayin'? MacLane's back, and that no-account council's hired him as sheriff?"

"That's what I'm sayin', for sure."

"They can't do that! You're the sheriff. They can't hire somebody else."

But the town council could do precisely that, if they had the guts, and he knew it. With MacLane there, they must have found some guts for the first time in well over a decade.

He kicked the corner porch post so hard that pain shot up his leg and through his body and made him giddy.

"Why'd you let 'em, you idiot?" he shouted at Lonnie through his pain. "You shoulda just told 'em to git out. Goddamn! What you think I pay you for, anyway?"

Lonnie's eyes narrowed, and his mouth curled over into a sneer.

"You're a good one to talk," he gurgled, his voice somewhere between a snarl and a whine. "Last time you saw him your nose was bleedin' like a stuck pig and you was jumpin' around cryin' like a baby 'bout how big and mean he was. Well, he's older, but he looks meaner than ever. And you know what we keep hearin' 'bout how he's cleaned up one town after another'n."

That was as far as Lonnie's speech got. Then he was sitting down in the dirt in front of the porch, holding his own nose. It was spouting blood like a mare taking a leak on main street. His head rang with the blow from the barrel of Buck Wilforce's gun. Buck was the sort of man who carried enough metal on his hip to make a wagon tongue, even when only sitting on his own front porch. Randall MacLane was one of the reasons he had started doing so. He didn't want to be reminded of it, especially by the likes of Lonnie Ledbetter.

Lonnie sat in the dust and his own blood and moaned. Buck walked off to the other end of the porch and looked down the road toward Middle Bend.

"Goddamn," he muttered. "Double goddamn."

Randall moved cautiously in his early days, recalling names, not forcing any relationships, meeting newcomers who had moved to town in the fourteen years since he left. Old-timers and newcomers alike kept their respectful distance from him, but they made it clear that they were glad he was there. They knew his reputation, from his former days in Middle Bend and from what they had heard in the last few years. If anyone could face down Buck Wilforce and his rowdy bunch, this was the man. Since Wilforce and his hands steered clear of any trouble, the citizens grew more and more at ease. Middle Bend was turning into a town again, instead of just Wilforc's private fiefdom.

MacLane liked it. His reputation was all he needed. Only Milo Rosewater was willing to come forward to be his friend, but he felt surprisingly at home. For one thing, his old house had burned, so he was not reminded of where he lived so unsuccessfully with Hannah and Isaac. For another, there was indeed a new city building, with decent living quarters built in behind the jail for the sheriff.

It was a rather imposing-looking building for Middle Bend, built at the edge of town. The old jailhouse and sheriff's office on Main Street just sat there, unused except for storage. Buck Wilforce had forced the new city building on them as a draw for new citizens and new business. Of course, his own rough-riding ways then kept out the very businesses and citizens he wanted to attract. They paid a lot of taxes for Wilforce's improvements, but there were few newcomers to add to their income. MacLane felt sorry for the taxpayers, but he thoroughly enjoyed his living space. These were his best quarters since he left the university.

He walked the streets, sat in the saloons, made his rounds of the businesses. Regular citizens breathed easy when they saw him. Wilforce's men, and the other lawless elements that a figure like Wilforce always attracts, tried not to breathe at all when he came by. They were tough men. When they got "likkered up" they could talk a good game about how "the mighty Sheriff MacLane" didn't scare them a bit. The truth was that he scared them with every movement of his body. They'd heard the stories. No one wanted to see if they were true.

One young cowboy was honest enough to admit, "If he stubbed his toe and said 'shit,' I'd git my pants down and start producin'."

He didn't have to worry about it. The sheriff never said "shit" or any other profanity. It wasn't in his nature, that was true. But it was also because of Lara Eastbrook.

Lara Eastbrook was thirty-three, an honest and forthright schoolmarm, with a smile for everyone. Her smile for children was full and beaming, like a benevolent early-morning sun. The smile she gave the rowdy cowboys as she walked by them on the board sidewalk in front of the saloons was straightforward but clear. It said, "I'll smile on you as on everyone else in this town, but don't come inside the smile." Some of the cowboys tried to smile back, or at least tip a hat. Most of them turned away in embarrassment. Her smile for women was a crescent of acceptance. "Have no fear; your homes are in no danger because of me." The smile she gave the other men in town was one of tolerance. "I know you wonder what I would be like, under this long dress, under the sheets. I accept that. Keep wondering."

Keep wondering they did, because for all her forthrightness and smiling charm, no one knew much about Lara Eastbrook. She would chat with anyone about today. Yesterday, however, was as closed as the *McGuffy's Reader*s when she rang the bell at the end of the school's day.

She was thirty-three, but she shared that fact with no one. Most guessed her to be twenty-three to twenty-seven. They assumed she had taught school back east before coming out west, because she was clearly an experienced teacher.

They had a dozen stories, however, about why she had come to Middle Bend—a shattered romance, a wealthy father gone destitute or crazy, a failed ambition to perform on the European stage, a jealous stepmother—anything that would explain the contradiction of this beautiful and self-assured young woman living alone in the middle of the plains.

Beautiful she was, although not in a conventional sense. Her mouth was too wide, her lips too full, her eyes too green, her hair too deeply red, her body too slim. It was just that combination of wide and full and green and red and slim that gave her smile its extra allure.

In the town where in his youth he tried to love an older woman, the crazy Hannah Reindorf, the woman who never smiled, Randall MacLane in the summer of his years fell totally in love with the mysterious young woman who smiled at one and all. He even found himself walking down the street, making his rounds at night, humming crazy little tunes that he made up in his own head. When he peered into the windows of closed shops to be sure no one was inside, he saw only a beaming middle-aged man winking a loopy grin above a five-pointed star.

Sometimes it made him laugh so hard at himself that he walked the round of all the Methodist houses in town, until he found the one where his new friend, the Reverend John Wesley Bishop, was staying for the night. He hoped it would be one of the more tolerant parishioners, who wouldn't mind if he smoked a pipeful while he and the new parson sat on the front porch and chatted.

Friends

————◆◆◆————

Reverend Thistle had died about two years after MacLane left town, he learned from Milo Rosewater. Mrs. Thistle stayed on, to doctor and to prod, but without her mild-mannered husband, the spirit seemed to go out of her. She followed him to the pitiful, little cemetery in the field behind the church within a year.

Whenever Randall thought of them, it was with a galling remorse that pulled at his insides like the aftermath of swallowing a hot stone. He hadn't said farewell to them before he left. They were his only friends, almost like parents to him, or at least like grandparents to Isaac. He should have found some way to see them, or have written them, to tell them how much they meant to him. He was just like the rest of the town, he thought, with a bitter swipe at the sweat along his thinning hairline. Took all they had to give, used them up, tossed them out. It was all Middle Bend did to anyone. It did it to him, and made him one of them, just like them. Milo had hit it on the nose; he belonged there.

When his evening wanderings finally brought him to wherever J.W., as he called his new friend, was lodging for the evening, he found a strange comfort. Strange, because the very presence of a new pastor in the place of his old and beloved Reverend Thistle ought to have reminded him even more of how much he had failed his friends.

Although fifteen years of age separated them, Randall found in the younger man a kindred spirit. J.W. talked like Reverend Thistle, even dressed like him, but the reminder was a pleasant one, a memory of all the good things the Thistles had been and done for the young sheriff and his family.

J.W. Bishop simply had a way of forgiving you before you even came into his presence, so that when you got there, your soul was at ease. Guilt was gone, and peace reigned. Randall MacLane sought out the younger man whenever he needed to get a fresh view of his life. He was always glad that he did.

J.W. was not the first minister sent to replace Reverend Thistle. There had been a succession, all run off by the rough ways of Buck Wilforce and his breed, or else worn down by the indifference of the town. After a while they stopped coming. The congregation sold the parsonage, the house where the Thistles had lived. It had been more of a home to Randall than his own house. Now it was occupied by strangers.

All that remained was the church building, and it was kept in poor repair. The congregation dwindled to the point that it certainly could not have supported a full-time minister, not that it had done that well even with the Thistles.

J.W. Bishop was a circuit rider. He served the churches in five other towns as well, scattered over a range of more than a hundred miles. Middle Bend was not on his circuit at first, but he asked the supervising elder for permission to add it to his round.

"No place where there are people should be without a preacher, at least once in a while," he said.

So, once a month, he was in Middle Bend for a few days. Without a parsonage, he simply spent the nights with families of the church.

J.W.'s parishioners were always glad enough to get out of providing a free meal for their pastor, so it was not hard for the two men to develop the habit of eating an occasional supper together at the hotel.

The sheriff always paid. The minister never had cash. The church members hardly ever got around to coughing up the pittance they referred to grandly as his salary. What little he did receive usually went to aid someone he felt was needier than himself. MacLane didn't mind paying for the meal. He felt it was a cheap price for good company. Moreover, it was how he got his chance to talk with Lara Eastbrook.

Lara went to church, of course. That was taken for granted. It was part of her job, even though no one would have put it that way. It meant she and J.W. were on a hand-shaking basis.

Lara lived in Widow Kelley's rooming house. The widow took Friday night off from cooking, however, and let her roomers fend for themselves. Lara always went to the hotel dining room, where she sat alone to eat a hurried supper. She was caught between contradictory impulses. She wanted to get out as quickly as possible, to where the other diners could not stare at her. If she bolted her food, however, her rude manners would be the talk of the back fences the next week.

One Friday night the sheriff and the parson happened to run into the schoolmarm on the porch of the hotel as they converged on their respective suppers. J.W. introduced Lara and Randall. She extended her gloved hand as one public official to another.

Randall was amazed at how small it was. He tried to remember all the other hands of all the other women he had known. Were they all that small? He didn't know; he could not recall just holding a woman's hand before. He turned red when he realized how long he had held on to her. He dropped the hand as though he had just been told it was a rattler.

"Pleased to make your acquaintance," he mumbled.

"Actually, we've met before," she said, a hint of mischief in her eyes. "Mr. Rosewater introduced us when you first came to town. Of course, I know you mostly by your reputation."

Now, what did she mean by that? Was it a compliment or an insult? Of course he remembered Milo had introduced them; he just couldn't think of anything else to say. . . . J.W. broke into his racing thoughts.

"Miss Eastbrook, why don't you join us for supper?"

He said it in his best ministerial tones, to be sure neither she nor anyone who overheard would think he noticed her as anything other than a schoolmarm and a parishioner. Not, God forbid, as a woman.

"I would surely love to, Reverend Bishop." She smiled. "But you know the ways of a small town. No unattached woman dares to be seen dining with a man, and the schoolmarm really shouldn't even stand on the porch and talk to one."

"Well, but . . ." J.W. stammered. "I think this is different. Yes, I've given this some thought. I mean, just now I've thought about it. First, you aren't with one man, but two, so obviously you could not be . . . that is . . . could not be doing anything improper. And second, we are public figures. I mean, Sheriff MacLane, as you say, has a reputation, and I'm the parson. So surely no one would think anything improper."

Randall was not sure just how his reputation figured into the propriety of the schoolteacher eating with them, but he was anxious enough to share a table with her that he was willing to accept any argument that would persuade her.

It was not until much later, after they had walked her back to the widow's boardinghouse, that he began to wonder about his friend's flustered behavior. After all, the man made his living with words, but he couldn't get one sentence finished before another one stumbled all over it while he talked to Lara. Surely he didn't feel about her the same way Randall did. Did ministers have those sorts of feelings?

Lara Eastbrook dropped a low hearty laugh that in a man would be called a chuckle.

"You are persuasive, Reverend Bishop. And I'm sure that if anyone dares to criticize, the sheriff's reputation will surely scare them off. Yes, I'll eat with you, and the school board be damned."

Both men reddened. Oddly enough, it was for the same reason. Neither could even imagine this refined and careful woman cursing, yet she did it right in front of them. It sounded like a declaration of independence. Neither man was sure he wanted her to be that independent.

Lara Eastbrook turned her back on them. She sailed through the doors of the hotel and into the dining room. They trotted along like a pair of puppies, hats in hand, swiping at their hair, hoping against all odds that no one noticed them.

With the two men at her usual little table in the corner, Lara Eastbrook expanded like popcorn in the fireplace. She knew all the others in the dining room were watching her, as they always did, but for a different reason this time. The two most eligible bachelors in town, known to be friends, were paying her court. That was all you could call it, regardless of the Reverend Bishop's protestations. It reminded Lara of who she was. It was one thing to be appreciated by little children, yet another to be lusted after by tongue-tied cowboys and greased-down husbands. Now, however, there was a competition, between truly worthy opponents. One was older, world- and woman-worn, a man of violence and law. The other was younger, still idealistic, a man of kindness and grace. She was the prize, but either way, she was also the winner.

The two men, of course, had no idea they were competing with each other. Each was too involved with trying not to make a fool of himself to notice the other's feverish and bumbling attempts to gain her attention in some favorable way.

Each man was also aware that it was necessary to protect her reputation, or she wouldn't even be allowed to remain in town. Where would he be then? Each realized the only way he could "pay attention" to this woman was in the company of the other. As long as they were a trio, what could anyone say? So began their odd, three-ringed friendship.

None of the three had a home. The minister lived with parishioners in six different towns. The teacher lived in a boardinghouse. The sheriff lived in the jail. Even if the two men had not been in love with Lara, they were drawn together because they were all outsiders. What they did not know at first, but what their friendship allowed them to understand and admit, was that they were not only outsiders; they were also frauds.

Months passed. Their friendships grew slowly because Reverend Bishop was in town on an irregular basis. Middle Bend was the sixth and last point on his circuit. He normally spent only three or four days there once a month. As the year went by, however, he worked the circuit in such a way that he could cross Middle Bend in the middle of the month as well as at the end. That allowed him a total of six or seven days out of thirty in the company of his friends. The other churches complained that he was neglecting them. His Middle Bend members complained so much about putting him up for the extra nights that he began to sleep in a cell at the jail. They complained about that, too. He worried about it. No minister wants his people complaining about him. But the urge to be with his friends was stronger than anything else in his life.

In the course of those months, the three ate together and walked together as much as they could. After supper, or after church on Sunday, they spent short hours simply walking and talking. MacLane did not go to worship, but he would meet the other two afterward.

One early-autumn afternoon, as they walked following their meal, Lara Eastbrook hooked her small, gloved hands through the crooks of the arms of the men on either side of her. She squinted at the copper-plated sun as she spoke.

"Autumn has always seemed to me . . . to be a time for truth." She waited for a step, three steps, five steps, then spoke on. "You can smell it in the air, the truth. It's dry, and just a little chilly, but with the sun still on it, too. I . . . I don't know for sure how either of you feels about me. I've had to guess. We've talked about everything this past year except ourselves."

She laughed one of those low chuckles that ended with a grimace.

"We know everything about everyone else in this town, we've talked about them so much. Well, I know how I feel about you, and so I've got to tell the truth."

Involuntarily each of the men pulled her hand against his side.

"Some ways," she continued, "you're almost more like family to me than friends." She felt them stiffen, and she laughed again, a full, hearty, happy sound this time. "No, don't take that too seriously. You're definitely men, the best I've ever known. But I mean . . . because you're like family, I can trust you. I feel safe with you."

They walked almost half a block in silence this time, the men waiting for her to continue, not sure they really wanted her to. Autumn might be a time for truth, but it was a time for love, too. Love and truth do not always mix as well as pumpkin and pie crust, or cider and fried biscuits.

"I . . . I'm . . . not exactly what I seem. You see, I'm not really a schoolteacher. I never went but to fifth grade in school back in Pennsylvania. Mother said I was 'developing too rapidly,' and she talked Father into sending me away to a girls' finishing school. I learned a lot of etiquette, but nothing children in a town like Middle Bend need to know. But . . . one of the teachers, the music master, used to give me private lessons—"

Her voice broke just a little. In the silence John Wesley Bishop bleated a little moan. Lara hurried on, afraid now that she couldn't tell the story if she paused even another second.

"When he found out I was going to have a baby, he just disappeared. And it was all for nothing, because the baby came too soon, and . . . it didn't live. A little girl. I named her. Naomi. I . . . thought it was a pretty name. . . . But I was so ashamed. I couldn't go home, and there was noplace else, so . . . I lied."

They were barely moving now. A child who saw them pass in front of his house reported to his mother that the schoolmarm looked sick, she was walking so slow. It looked like the preacher and the sheriff were propping her up.

"Ha!" sniffed his mother. "Propping her up, my eye. She's got those two fools dancing on a string."

"Anyway, I got a job teaching by saying I'd gone to high school and had a year of normal school. It didn't take long for the school-board president to find out I lied. He said he'd keep quiet if I'd . . . be nice to him."

Unconsciously Randall MacLane loosened the pistol in its holster.

"I—I just left. I didn't know what else to do. I wanted to be with the children. So I just kept lying about my past, and getting one teaching job after another, and moving before I thought anyone could find out about me. That's how I got clear out here."

She gave Randall's arm a squeeze. It was just a firm grasp, but he felt jarred to his toenails.

"Everyone thinks I'm happy because I smile. Everyone

thinks I'm self-assured, because I act like I don't need any-one, except maybe the children. Meeting the two of you has made me realize how hollow my smile is, and how I have so little worth of my own."

She was paying no attention to how she walked. Her toe caught at a wagon rut in the street. Normally she would have been thrown to her knees. With both men holding her, she just sailed over it, hardly aware that she had stumbled.

"We both have reputations, Sheriff. In your job, it's an advantage. In mine . . . well, I hope mine doesn't follow me. I want to be honest with both of you. With you, Reverend, because I'm a 'fallen woman.' With you, Sheriff, because I'm not sure I can risk taking a chance on an older man again. With both of you . . . because I'm just not an honest person."

They snailed on, now at the edge of town, automatically turning and walking along the fringe of the buildings, staying in sight of the townspeople lest anyone should gossip, moving toward the westering sun and its autum-nal, truth-glinting light, awkwardly hobbling like some mutant, three-headed caterpillar. Lara tried to withdraw her hands from the men's arms, but each pressed her tight against his ribs and placed his outside hand over her curling fingers as well. Finally MacLane shot a glance across her at the man in black.

"Well, you're the preacher around here," he said, like a bear that's been prodded with a stick in the middle of winter. "Aren't you going to say anything?"

Doing What You Are

John Wesley Bishop clasped tightly to the small hand in the crook of his arm. He knew how vulnerable Lara was at this moment. He wanted to find the words of hope and consolation that he knew she needed, but he wasn't sure he had them. Yes, it was time for him to speak, but not because he was the preacher. His calling was an accident or fate, anyhow. "The high calling . . ." All he knew to do in response to her story was to tell his own.

"It was my mother, or my name, or both, I guess. She named me, of course. John Wesley Bishop! With a name like that, what else could I do? Every other minister I know can tell you exactly when the Lord spoke to him, told him he was to be a preacher. It was like a lightning bolt, or they saw words in the sky, or they wrestled all night with the devil. In my case, the only one the Lord spoke to was my mother, and that was before I was born. I guess my kind of hypocrisy is the worst kind there is, pretending to be a man of God when I'm not even sure of who I am."

His voice cracked. His face turned redder than the reflection of the copper-clad sun required. He despised people who reveled in their agonies, who spent their days in self-pity, the way his mother always did. He hated himself when he was like her.

Randall MacLane squeezed hard on Lara's hand, as though he could send a message through her to the unsure soul of his young friend. She squeezed back, her gesture saying, "Yes, I understand that you want to reach him." But she needed no prompting. Her fingers curled around J.W.'s, and she silently cursed her gloves for the extra layer of distance they put between them.

"It's not that I don't like people. I care about what happens to folks. But I don't have a heart for evangelism. I can't believe people have to get saved here on earth or God will damn them to hell forever. I think you have to understand and forgive. . . . But that's just me talking. I don't have any calling. I—I . . . wish I was like you, Randall."

The word sounded strange. No one called him Randall. It was the first time J.W. had done so. The parson referred to him as "Sheriff." So did Lara, but she always called J.W. "Reverend," too. They both called her by her first name, except when others were around to hear. That was all right; she was a woman. J.W. was younger than either of them, so it was all right to call him by his initials. MacLane knew his friend was taking an important and fearful step toward him now, asking to be treated in a new way.

"Go ahead, J.W.," Lara prompted, picking up on the new intimacy. "Why do you want to be like Randall?"

"Well . . . he knows exactly what his job is. Whatever it takes to get it done, that's what he does, and that's all right. If somebody gets drunk, and he puts him in jail, he knows he's done his job. If somebody gets drunk and comes to me for help, and I pray with him, I don't know if I've done him any good, or whether I've even done what I should."

His words were picking up speed, as though his

tongue could hardly keep up with his brain. He switched from answering Lara's question to speaking directly to MacLane.

"And if you get mad, you have an outlet for it. You can beat people up and throw them in jail and feel righteous about it, because that's your job. This is a violent country, and you know how to survive in it. You help others who are weak to survive. Even me. If somebody started fooling with me, I'd get mad and want to hurt them, but I wouldn't even know how. You'd have to come fight my fight for me, like you do for most of us. I trust you, Randall, and I trust in your ways, but I'm not supposed to. I'm supposed to turn the other cheek. Underneath, I'm not like what I claim to be on the outside. This black suit hides a black heart, and I ought to get out of it, but I don't even know how to do that."

Randall MacLane shook his head. He didn't know where to begin. The only real friends he had in the world, however, were looking at him, waiting for him. . . .

"I guess we're all frauds," he said, "but we've gotten comfortable enough with our roles that none of us knows how to get out. Maybe that's why we . . . like one another so much, why we're friends. We understand one another."

He was the old one in this trio, and he felt it. They were his friends, but they were so young. They were hardly children, but compared with them, it seemed as if he had slogged through two or three lives. There comes a time when a man wants to deny his age but share his experience. It puts him in a bend. MacLane felt it twisting him now.

"I can understand why you feel my way, the direct way, is so good, J.W. But I no more set out to be a lawman than Lara wanted to be a teacher or you wanted to be a preacher. In fact, I tried to get out of it, many times, but I came back to it just because I wasn't any good at anything else."

Then he told them his story, from the death of his grandfather on.

"I suppose I should have been a scholar. It was the only other thing I was any good at. But it must not have been meant for me. Now I'm stuck as a lawman, by being in the wrong place at the wrong time, and because I couldn't control my temper."

Lara and J.W. had heard talk about the sheriff, of course. He was the most celebrated man in town. They had heard of his wife and her son—how he saved them from the Indians but couldn't hold them. They'd heard about his fights—exaggerated many times in the telling, the towns he tamed between his first years in Middle Bend and his current tour of duty in the new municipal building. They knew that just below the surface calm of Middle Bend, Buck Wilforce sizzled and brewed and waited for a chance.

The dark slipped down around them, softer than Lara's gloves, as Randall talked. It was easier to talk in the dark, and the lawman felt a little bit ashamed. He had let his friends speak in the light of the truth-leeching sun, but he had waited for the cloak of darkness.

Still, there was a peacefulness that was new to him, walking beyond the light with his friends. They were frauds. Each had known the outward mask of self. Now each knew the inner person of the others as well. Randall felt his age again. It thinned his hair and widened his middle, but it filled out his soul as well. Out of that fullness he spoke.

"Well, I guess you're a fake, J.W., since you weren't called to be a preacher. But if you're such a fake, why do people feel so good when they see you coming?

"And a schoolteacher who's not been to school. You're a fake, Lara. But why do the little children love you so? When you say, 'Read,' all they ask is, 'How far?'

"All I know is that the church and the children need you. Middle Bend needs you. I know for sure I need you."

He didn't even have time to feel the inevitable embarrassment that comes from declaring love and dependence for the first time. Cabbage Collins came scurrying out of an alley like a mouse that's seen the cat and isn't waiting around to find out if it's been seen back.

"Sheriff, Sheriff," the little man whispered hoarsely. "Beggin' your pardon, ma'am, Revrund."

They sensed more than saw the quick tip of his mangled stovepipe hat. His attention turned immediately back to MacLane.

"Buck Wilforce's down at the Palace. He never goes in there."

MacLane knew that to be true. The Palace was Milo Rosewater's place. Wilforce owned all the other saloons in town. He hardly needed to patronize a competitor. Besides, there was bad enough blood between Milo and Buck before Milo brought Randall back to Middle Bend.

"He's givin' Milo a hard time, Sheriff, him and his boys. And there's this new fella with 'em. I ain't got any idea who he is, but he's meaner lookin' than a skunk, an' got two guns strapped down on his legs."

So this was the time. MacLane knew it had to come sooner or later. Wilforce wasn't the kind to accept defeat, but he wasn't the kind to do the hard part of revenge for himself, either. The calm of Middle Bend since he'd been back was only a lull so Buck could hire some spine.

Randall didn't want to leave his friends, not right now, when they were on the verge of something new, something he'd never experienced before. But Milo was a friend, too. He'd actually been working at losing weight. Maybe, thought the sheriff, I have more friends than I know.

There really was no choice. He might be a sheriff by accident, but he was the sheriff. The accident was a long time ago. Now he was sheriff by choice. It was funny how that left him no choice.

"J.W., you'd better take Lara home. I'll go take care of this before it gets out of hand."

Even through the glove he could feel her hand go cold.

"But . . . but . . ."

J.W. Bishop could think of nothing more to say. He watched MacLane slip Lara's hand out of its shelter by his side. Without another word or gesture the sheriff disappeared into the darkness of the alley behind Cabbage. Even in the deep night, though, the pastor could still hear.

"Go home, Cabbage. I appreciate you coming to get me, but I don't want you getting hurt."

"Hell, Sheriff, I'm already home. Besides, I wouldn't miss this for the world."

The preacher and the teacher stood for a little while, ears cocked toward the darkness, frightened by the unadulterated glee in the little man's voice. Then Lara spoke, her voice a little squeaky with the strain.

"Let's go to the Palace."

J.W. knew it was the wrong thing to do, but he put his head down and started through the alley.

MacLane didn't hesitate at the swinging half doors of the Palace, didn't bother to use his height to stand there for a moment, look the place over, see who was where. He just pushed the doors open and walked on in. Cabbage Collins scurried in behind him, scuttling down the wall and into a corner.

Milo Rosewater sat at his usual round table at the end of the room. He was slumped down in his chair as far as his bulk and unusual position allowed. A thin trickle of blood flowed from his nose, down around his full lips. It dripped onto his already stained cravat.

Buck Wilforce and his boys were gathered around the table, laughing somewhat tightly as a thin, hawk-faced man MacLane had never seen before pushed the barrel of a gun up into Milo's other nostril. He was saying something Randall could not hear. About a dozen or so men were at the other tables in the room. They sat painted into their places.

MacLane didn't break stride, just moved on through the room. Lonnie Ledbetter saw him first, but not until he was almost on them.

"He's here," Lonnie whispered urgently.

They turned to find the sheriff already among them, the pipe in his vest pocket and his star so close they couldn't even focus on them. He stood less than two feet from the man with the gun at Milo's nose.

"Leave," he said, voice level and low, staring directly into the eyes of Wilforce's hired gun.

There was no kindling rage flushing his face, no quiver of indignation in his voice. The word was simply cold command.

"Well, Sheriff . . ." the gunman hissed, air escaping out the back of his mouth on either side.

Either he couldn't remember to switch from his Milo-menacing voice, or it was the only one he had. He tried to back away from MacLane, but the sheriff wouldn't let him. He stayed right with him, oblivious to chairs or tables in the way, chest out, forcing the gunman to stay face-to-face with him or back off. He could smell the man's sweat, his putrid breath, the oil on his hair. From those smells he wanted to back away himself, but he set his nose like a rock and pushed on.

The gunman was getting desperate. He had never experienced anything like this. People stayed as far away from him as they could get. Certainly people he had come to kill did not get right up into his face and simply stare at him. The sheriff's eye was rigid as flint. It stared at him like he was a fly about to be squashed. Finally he let out a hissing squeal.

"Goddamnit, MacLane. You don't know who you're dealin' with."

"I'm not dealing with anybody. You're nobody. I'm telling you to leave."

The gunman was up against the wall now, in every imaginable way. This wasn't the man Buck Wilforce and his tagalong thugs had told him about. They said MacLane was a man who boiled quickly into a furious rage, who was fearsome with his fists but never used a gun, who almost always took the time to try to talk his way through a bad spot first and only when he had been goaded to anger did he lash out in violence. Now here this middle-aged man was crowding him like he was nothing. Not a trace of anger showed, even though his friend Milo Rosewater was being humiliated in his own saloon. The gunman wanted to dry his sweaty palms on the seat of his pants but was afraid the sheriff would think he was going for his gun.

Then he remembered. He was supposed to go for his gun. That was why he was in Middle Bend in the first place. Everyone knew the sheriff was no quick draw, but even Buck Wilforce and the lout-mouthed Lonnie Ledbetter were afraid to try him. That was why they'd brought him in. The sheriff was crowding him because he wanted to use his fists and not his gun. He was a little slow in figuring it out. His speed was in his hand, not his brain. Now he had it, though. He grimaced in imitation of a smile.

"I know who you are, MacLane, even if you're too dumb to care who I am. I know why you're crowding me like a fifty-cent whore. You're afraid to use your gun, and you're afraid to let me get at mine. Back off, and we'll settle this like men."

He snarled the words, loud enough that everyone in the Palace could hear, still hissing, though, like a snake that's found a bullhorn in tall grass and can't keep from trying it out.

Randall didn't hesitate. He simply twirled on his heel, parade-ground style, like the soldier he had been. He marched halfway back across the room, until he was almost under Milo's prized faux-crystal chandelier. Automatically his boots tramped out the parade-ground cadence they had marched to so many times before. His shoulders squared as he deliberately presented his back to the man against the wall. He twirled once again to face the stranger Buck Wilforce's lust for power had brought here to die. The light from the chandelier draped over his shoulders, framing him, casting an aura of warmth around him like a new Easter sun just beginning to put the morning touch on a night-frosted oak.

As he faced the gunman once again, seeing him full for the first time, he had the uneasy feeling that there was something else in his sight as well. When he had made his turn beneath the chandelier, like a gentleman presenting his lady at the first chord of a dance, something at the door caught his eye. It was something he should be aware of, take into consideration somehow, but it was crowded out by the sight of the man in the black, greasy leather vest.

His gun was in a fancy tooled holster, strapped down low on his leg. Ivory handle grips flashed softly in the muted light at the edge of the saloon. Wasn't that the same gun that had just been up Milo's nose?

Randall chuckled softly as the recognition hit him. This man automatically holstered his gun when the real trouble started, because he lived to draw it. That was his claim to fame, that his was the fastest draw. The sheriff couldn't see if the gun's grips had notches, but he was sure they were there, the number of those who had been outdrawn. The man before him wasn't a gunman. He was a showman and a bookkeeper. The killing was necessary just so he could give his show and keep his score.

His own chuckle brought back to him the sound of Lara's laugh. He loved to hear her laugh in that chuckling way. That thought of Lara flashed the image of the Palace door to him again, but there wasn't time to try to focus it.

His humor had always gotten him into as much trouble as his anger. The gunman was offended by his chuckle.

"Nobody laughs at Brace Newman and gets away with it," he hissed.

Across the crude floor Randall MacLane could feel Brace Newman's heart. It wasn't in his snarl, not even in his threat. He was a performer with only one talent, a traveling salesman with one spiel. He was tired of it, but he knew nothing else. He was caught by his reputation and by the assumption that "the show must go on."

At least he was able to get his name in, that name he was so proud of. He so much wanted men to quake at the very sound of that name, the way they did when they heard the name of Randall MacLane.

The silliness of it made Randall laugh again. This time it was mirthless. It was really a rattle of indignation against Wilforce for bringing the man here to die. Wilforce thought he had brought him to Middle Bend to kill. He was probably one of those awed by the name of Brace Newman. Buck would be responsible for Newman's death as surely as if he pulled the trigger, unless . . .

It was Wilforce that Randall addressed as he spoke into the thick silence of the Palace saloon.

"You've given this man bad information, Buck. You've set him up to be killed. If it happens, you did it, not me."

He didn't look at Wilforce. His eyes were locked with those of Brace Newman, hoping to get his message across to the gunman before he had to kill him. But Newman's eyes were walls, not windows. There was no way to get through to him. It was up to Wilforce.

"I don't know what you're talkin' about, MacLane," snarled Wilforce.

There was no time for him to say more. Newman went for his gun, apparently thinking the sheriff was distracted by his conversation with Buck. It was the sort of thing a showman like Newman would do. Give the show, but be sure you have the edge.

He didn't have the edge. For the first time since he'd been back in Middle Bend, Randall MacLane drew his gun for real. It was automatic, just as he had practiced it for hours on the prairie after the death of Liu. Three steps—draw, aim, fire. The sheriff shot Brace Newman through the heart before the gunman even got to step two. A look of total unbelief washed across Newman's face. Then he staggered back, fell across a table, and crumpled heavily to the floor.

Randall turned to Buck Wilforce, his gun still in his hand. He locked his eyes onto Buck's and slowly holstered his gun. The challenge was clear without a word. Buck shrugged, looked quickly at the floor. Sweat began to run down his face.

"Buck, pick that man up and carry him out of here. Take him to the undertaker and pick out the best box he's got and tell him to arrange for a service. You go see Reverend Bishop and get him to say the words. And, Buck, you're paying, so give the preacher ten dollars. Then get out of here and never enter this building again."

Wilforce spoke low to the men behind him.

"Lonnie, Pete, get him out of here."

"No, Buck, not Lonnie and Pete. *You* pick him up and take him out of here. You killed him. You clean up the mess."

Wilforce shrugged again. He walked quickly over to the body of Brace Newman and struggled with the dead-weight until he got it over his shoulder. As Buck reached the door Randall saw there the white and drawn faces of Lara and J.W.

He started for the door, not sure whether he was just following Wilforce or to move back to the circle of his friends for comfort. Before he got there, they had disappeared down the street into the darkness.

"My God," he murmured to himself. "I was right on the edge of something new, out there with them. I got something new, but it was just another step in violence. It used to be the rage that made me violent. Now it's just a part of me."

He heard the tapping of short steps at his side. It was Cabbage Collins.

"By God, Sheriff, you sure showed Wilforce and that Newman something. Showed ever'body. Nobody's gonna fool with you now, by God."

"You're right, Cabbage. Nobody's going to fool with me now."

The Long, Slippery Edge of the Pit

$\bullet\!\!\blacklozenge\!\!\bullet$

The sheriff of Middle Bend dragged back to his quar-ters behind Buck Wilforce's new jail. He felt like the only tree left standing after a forest fire, sad as sin to be a survivor. He was more lonely than he ever had been in a whole life of aloneness.

Wilforce was beaten; he had seen enough of crude men in his day to know that. Oh, Buck would let it fester. He'd take it out on his horse and his ranch hands. He'd be unhappy the rest of his days. But he would never dare to cross the sheriff again.

That knowledge of victory should have been sweet and thick as chocolate in Randall's mouth. It tasted instead like he'd been sucking on the wrong end of one of his old pipes.

He'd shot a man down in front of his friends, killed him knowing he would kill him. He had put on a show for Milo Rosewater and Cabbage Collins and Buck Wilforce and Lonnie Ledbetter. He was the gunman, not Brace Newman. Perhaps if he had seen his different audience, known Lara and J.W. were at the door, watching, he could have avoided it. No, not *could* have. Would have. He would have found some way. With Lara and J.W., he was a different man. Without them, he was a rogue.

Even Brace Newman deserved a decent chance to live. He blamed it on Wilforce, proclaimed for all to hear that Wilforce was responsible, even before the act. But that was playing games, and he knew it. No one, not even Milo, knew how he had learned the fast-gun art out there on the plains. No one, not even J.W. when he spent his Middle Bend nights in a cell at the jail, knew how he practiced an hour a day to keep that draw crisp and his hand steady. No one but Randall MacLane knew Brace Newman was doomed from the start. He had done nothing to save Newman, just blamed that poor excuse for a man, Buck Wilforce. He knew that there was a wide gap between blame and responsibility, a gap wider than the Little Bighorn River.

He couldn't put off facing up to it. J.W. would be at the jail that night, perhaps already. He would have to talk to him about it. God, why had he told Wilforce to give the preacher ten dollars for doing the funeral? He made it sound like it was perfectly fine to go around shooting people down as long as the details were taken care of afterward. He had talked like his friend had no concern for a man's death except how much he made out of it.

The young minister was not at the jail, however, and neither was his traveling bag. MacLane sat up until the cold hours of the night, with a dim oil lamp flickering, smoking his pipe until his palate was raw and his tongue burned, but his friend did not return.

He woke up late, almost nine o'clock, but even then he was heavy with lack of sleep. He sat for a long time on the side of his bed, searching the dark corners of his brain for some reason to get up to face the day.

His body finally took over and dragged itself to the washstand. He poured out old, cold water into the basin and splashed it on his face. It wasn't much, but it was all he felt up to.

Combing his thin hair back with the fingers of his killing hand, he slouched out to find Whispering Lowe. The undertaker already had the coffin loaded into the back of his black hearse.

"Buck must have gotten on this quicker than I expected," the sheriff mused, half to himself and half to Lowe.

"Oh, yes," chirped the little man, his melon-sized Adam's apple bobbing up and down. "He wasn't much polite about it, but he paid the whole thing, including the ten dollars for the preacher. Got it right here."

He pulled a worn bill from his pocket and waved it under MacLane's nose. The sheriff knew there had been talk that Lowe was sometimes "slow" to pass money along from a funeral to the preacher.

Even Titus Lowe's afraid of me, thought Randall. He knows J.W.'s my friend. He doesn't want to give me an excuse to do anything to him. I'm right back where I started, in the same town, with everybody afraid of me. It used to be they feared my anger. Now they fear me just because of who I am.

"Well, excuse me, Sheriff, but I've got to get this body up to the cemetery. Preacher's set the service for ten, 'cause he's got to get back on his circuit this mornin'. You comin'?"

"Oh . . . I guess not, Titus." He glanced down at the dirty, rumpled clothes in which he had killed and slept. "I'm not really ready for a funeral."

He thought Lowe was wrong about the minister leaving town. J.W. wasn't back on the circuit for two more days.

He wandered back to the jail and considered going back to bed but decided to eat instead. By going to the hotel in midmorning he could miss the breakfast and lunch crowds both. It wasn't their regular serving hours, but they always accommodated themselves to his schedule.

He washed a little more in the cold water, changed his

clothes, and clomped over to the hotel dining room. He was welcomed by Quincy Long, the hotel manager.

"Howdy, Sheriff. Heard all about how you did in that Newman fella last night. They said you were faster'n greased lightning. Sort of caught everybody by surprise."

"I'm sorry I had to kill him, Quincy, and I guess I'm not in much of a mood to talk about it. Just want to get something to eat."

"No problem, Sheriff. Just have a seat in there in the dining room, wherever you want. Might be a bit slow today. Just got some new guests in. Cook's making up some fancy trays to take up to their rooms, but she'll get to you soon as she can."

By the time he returned to his room the funeral service was over, J. W. Bishop had gotten on his horse and left town, and there was a worn ten-dollar bill sitting on the middle of his desktop. He sat at his desk, doing nothing, until he figured the noon-hour crowd would be indoors. Then he started out to do his rounds.

That normally meant walking the streets, stopping for a few minutes in each saloon and business, just being seen. Today, though, he really didn't want to be seen. He didn't want to have to talk to anyone. What's the point of doing rounds if you don't want to be seen? he wondered. Without realizing what his feet were doing, he wandered down to the Palace.

He pushed his way in slowly through the swinging doors and was struck with how different the place looked now. It was just a big, worn, dirty room, hardly a place for Brace Newman to make his final show. Milo Rosewater sat in the same chair he'd been in last night. MacLane meandered over to the table and slouched down into a chair.

"You okay, Sheriff?"

"Just tired, Milo." It was a lie, but when had he really ever told the truth, even to his friends? "How about you?"

"I was kind of scared last night. I'll admit it. I knew

you'd come when you heard they was roughin' me up, and I'd heard about that Brace Newman, how fast he was, and all. I—I shouldn't of doubted you, Sheriff, but . . . I just didn't have any idea you could handle a gun like that."

His voice carried a blend of pride and, yes, even with Milo, fear.

"Well, I guess everybody knows now," Randall said as he folded in upon himself like an old accordion. "You shouldn't have any more trouble."

"Well, not as long as you stay in Middle Bend, anyway. . . ."

MacLane started to point out he had no place to go even if he wanted to, but there was something else in the saloon keeper's voice.

"What do you mean, Milo?"

"You mean they haven't been to see you yet?"

"Who? I've not been keeping a very regular schedule this morning."

"Well, they sure were asking a lot of questions about you, about your past, and everything. Important men, you could tell. Not just the way they dress, but the way they act. City men. Even gave me money so I wouldn't tell you they were asking about you."

Milo gave MacLane a big wink.

"Passing out money means they're serious. It's probably just as well they didn't see you last night, or they would have just dropped the questions and gone ahead and hired you."

"Hired me? What in the world, Milo?"

"Important city men, Sheriff. Here. Asking about you. Doesn't that tell you something?"

MacLane had no idea what it told him, so he just sat and waited for Rosewater.

"They want you, Sheriff. They've heard about you. I don't know where they're from, but St. Louis or Chicago wouldn't surprise me any. They've come to hire you. I can feel it. I was hoping you'd stay out your days here, but I should know better. You've always been too big for a place like Middle Bend."

Milo continued to talk, but the lawman didn't hear him. Someone was there to hire him! He was the one who'd always had to go looking, from place to place. The only time anyone had asked him was when Milo fetched him back for the second go-round in Middle Bend. Now a city? Real money? Someplace where they didn't want a fast gun but someone who could really be a lawman, have people work for him. Someplace where he could take Lara, where she would no longer have to worry about her past catching up with her.

He found himself wandering back to the jail, not sure whether he'd even said good-bye to Milo. He was listing a mental inventory of his possessions, wondering what he should take along to Chicago. Maybe it was just Springfield or Indianapolis, but that would be all right.

Then he walked into his rooms in the jail and found that someone had already taken an inventory of his possessions.

His mattress was on the floor. The wardrobe and washstand were pulled out from the wall. His clothes and books were scattered all over.

"What in the world . . ." he muttered out loud.

Who was going through his things? What could they be looking for? Who was stupid enough, especially right now? People were eyeing him like he was a grizzly gone crazy. You don't try to steal from a mad bear. Some drifter? Not likely. Buck or Lonnie or one of their bunch trying to get back at him? They'd be scared still that he'd catch them in the act, or catch them with what they stole.

Perhaps there was a clue in what they had taken. He went about putting everything back where it went—first the furniture pieces, then the items that went into or onto them. When he finished, the room looked just as it had when he left it. Not a thing was out of place; not a thing was missing.

Had J.W. come back to look for something he'd forgotten? But he kept nothing in Randall's rooms. He certainly wouldn't make a mess.

Was someone playing a joke on him? That would be the day!

Nothing was even broken.

Well, it was a mystery, but he didn't intend to worry about it for very long. Now all he had to do was wait for the strangers to get through asking around about him and to tell him what city they were from and how big his salary would be.

That waiting turned out to take more patience than he wanted to give. He sat in his office all day, waiting for them to come. His only visitors, however, were some autumn flies buzzing drowsily in the windowsills, and Cabbage Collins, who seemed content just to hang around.

He returned to the hotel for supper.

"How are your new guests doing, Quincy?"

"Well, Sheriff, it's hard to say. They've not been out of their rooms all day. Take all their meals up there. They're not hard cases, though. Don't think you need worry 'bout them."

That night he made his rounds, deliberately stopping in all the saloons. None of the strangers were around. All the regulars either avoided him or were excessively hearty in welcoming him.

"God, they're all afraid of me," he muttered as he hunched his shoulders against the October chill, while he went from store to store, trying doorknobs. "The ones who pound me on the back are just as scared as the ones who watch the walls whenever I come in. Thank goodness I'm going to have some different place, someplace big enough that a man like me won't stick out like a sore thumb."

The next day and night came and went in the same way, like a slow train to a ghost town. He kept to his office. When he had to leave, he stayed out on the street as much as possible, where he could be seen. He ate only in the hotel dining room, at the times he figured the strangers would be most likely to come down. He dawdled over coffee and pie until almost everyone else had left, but he caught no sight of them.

The strangers were in the hotel, but what were they doing? What were they waiting for? Randall didn't want to barge in on them. He knew he ought to go see them just to do his job right. A sheriff needed to know what people were in town for. But if they were going to offer him a job, he didn't want to act like he was coming looking for it. So the next morning, after breakfast, he went to the hotel clerk while Quincy Long was off duty.

"Mr. Brumfield, I understand you've got several strangers here."

"Yes, sir, Sheriff, sure do. Real high-toned fellas. Real polite. Got money, for sure. Eat in their room alla time."

"Uh . . . have they asked anything about me, Mr. Brumfield?"

The little clerk pushed his half glasses up on his nose and wiped his hands on the seat of his pants.

"Well, yes, Sheriff, they did, I guess."

"What do you mean, 'you guess'? Either they did or they didn't."

"Well, it's like this, Sheriff. You know I'm a law-abidin' citizen, and I'd surely like to cooperate, but these fellas, you see . . . well, they didn't want you to know they was askin' 'bout you. I don't know why, but they give me money to answer 'em and not to tell 'bout it, but seein' you're the sheriff and all, I guess if you want to know, I ain't got no choice. . . ."

He was prattling on, scared as all the rest, frightened of the only man in town who was sworn not to frighten him.

"That's all right, Mr. Brumfield. If you took their money, you shouldn't tell me."

MacLane considered having another talk with Milo. Maybe his fat friend had gotten it all wrong, about why these men were in town.

A sudden wave of comfortable sadness surged through him as he thought about leaving Milo.

"The fat man may be the only friend I have left," he murmured to himself as he wandered along the board sidewalks. "What a pretty pass that is."

He felt a pinch of regret for even thinking it. He hadn't seen either Lara or J.W. since the shooting of Brace Newman. He had no idea where he stood with them. If Milo were his only friend, he didn't dare think he was too good for the saloon keeper.

Instead of going to the Palace, he returned once more to the jail.

He had to fight his way into his office through a thick cloud of cigar smoke. In his chair slumped a barrel-chested man sporting a long waxed mustachio. A five-pointed star hung from his plaid shirt. He was leafing through MacLane's stack of wanted posters.

"Hope you don't mind me makin' myself at home, Sheriff. Don't have much time, so thought I'd catch up on my readin' while I was waitin' for you. I'm Daniel Simpson, marshal from Northern District. Afraid I've got some bad news for you, but I could use your help with it, too."

Randall didn't know what the man was talking about, but he liked his style. The marshal from the north didn't offer to get out of MacLane's chair or give him his desk back. He was the only person he'd encountered in a long time who just treated him like an ordinary man. Might he become a friend?

In the middle bend of his own years, Randall MacLane had begun to assay everyone he met for the ore quality of friendship.

He almost didn't hear what the man had said about bad news.

"Injin band, little travelin' bunch. Got wiped out up in my territory. Don't normally worry much 'bout dead Injins, 'specially them what don't have an Injin agent bleatin' on 'bout 'em, but turned out there was a white woman with this bunch. You'd never knowed it, 'cept for her skin. Thing is, all the Injins was just shot down. Nary another mark on 'em. But the white woman was tortured bad, like whoever done it was mighty unhappy with her 'bout somethin'. Not a pretty sight. We was gonna burn up all the stuff that was left from 'em. Filthy stuff. Not much of it, though. Them kinda Injins travel light. But one of my men found this sewed in the linin' of what was left of her rags."

He reached down to his saddlebags, piled beside the chair he had commandeered. He pulled out an old piece of newspaper. From it he extracted a dirty and much-creased piece of yellowed paper, which he poked at Randall. MacLane started to unfold it.

"Ink's gittin' faded pretty bad, but it's a marriage license. Made out to a Hannah Reindorf and Randall MacLane. Signed by some reverend named Tinsel, or somethin' like that. Asked around and found out your wife had took off to run with Injins, so figgered it must be her. You got any idea why anybody'd want her and her friends dead?"

MacLane unfolded the paper the rest of the way and stared at it. There was no doubt about it; it was their marriage license, signed by Reverend Thistle and witnessed by Mrs. Thistle and Milo Rosewater. Randall had forgotten about it completely, had no idea Hannah had taken it with her. Sewn in the lining of her clothes . . .

Simpson was talking again.

"Like I said, don't normally have reason to worry 'bout dead Injins, and 'specially not a white woman who'd run with 'em, but this looked funny. Wasn't other Injins what done it to 'em, we could tell that. Had to be white men.

Guess they might have treated her bad just 'cause she was a white woman with Injins. Lots of white men'd do that, I guess. But it still looked strange, like they wasn't torturin' her just for the fun of it. What they was tryin' to accomplish, well, I thought maybe you'd have some ideas."

Randall still couldn't get his mind on what the marshal was saying. Poor Hannah. The woman never had a chance, with the Indians who killed her husband and raped her, with him, with her son, with the Indians she left him for, with the white men who'd tortured and killed her. Every man she'd known, at least since Reindorf, had failed or abused her. No wonder she was crazy. Now she was out of her misery, but what a way.

"I came down here partways to see you, Sheriff, but partways because we picked up some sign of white men trailin' down this way from where we found their bodies. Lost the sign 'bout a day ago, but it makes sense they'd be comin' here, I guess, for one reason or another."

He looked up at Randall from under the brim of his battered, dust-colored hat. It was a calculating sort of stare as he slouched down even further in MacLane's chair. He waited.

The man before him simply stared at the worn piece of paper in his hands, at the worn memories that refused to leave him in peace.

"Sheriff, I've ridden a fur piece to tell you some news I figgered you'd be interested in, and to see if you could help me clear some of this up. It sure would help if you'd say somethin'. Surely you ain't grievin' the loss of a woman who'd run off from you and do it with Injins."

Randall looked down at the man and saw him for what he was. Here was no potential friend. Marshal Simpson treated him like an ordinary man not because he was at ease with him, but because he was too much of a clod to do otherwise. He wasn't sensitive enough to know how someone might feel, or to respect the areas of his own ignorance.

MacLane felt the first old familiar stirrings of rage. He didn't like it. He didn't like Marshal Daniel Simpson for stirring the caldron of his uncontrol.

"Get out of my chair, Marshal."

It was the first thing he had said to the man. He figured it was enough.

Simpson's mouth gaped open, then snapped shut. He picked up his saddlebags and heaved himself up out of the chair.

"If a lawman's gonna git along, he's gotta learn to cooperate with others in the profession, Sheriff. No wonder you got the reputation you do. I rode a long way. . . ."

He was almost whining now.

"You rode a long way to do your job, like you're supposed to, like you took an oath to do, whether it's Indians, or white men, or women you don't much care for, Marshal. Well, you've done it. You can be well assured that if the men you're trailing come to Middle Bend, I'll do my job. And no, I don't know why anyone would want to torture Hannah, but I imagine I'll do my job and look into that, too. If I learn anything you need to know, I'll inform you."

The sheriff sat down in his chair with a thump and swept the wanted posters into a drawer of the desk.

The Northern District marshal threw his saddlebags over his shoulder and started for the door. He barely turned his head to throw out one more sentence.

"Since you already know ever'thing, 'bout how to do the job and all, I s'pose you already know 'bout the kid calls hisself Isaac Reindorf. 'Course, pro'bly no relation to your wife anyway."

From the way he said it, MacLane knew the man had it for fact that Isaac was Hannah's son. He wasn't about to give Simpson the satisfaction of asking him what he meant. The marshal waited, poised in the doorway, and decided he couldn't stand not giving Randall some more bad news.

"Got inna buncha trouble up our way. Fancies hisself to be some sorta gunslinger. Killed a couple men in shoot-outs. Took off a couple months ago, farther west. Killed some more. Real bad case. Brags 'bout how someday he's gonna come back this way and kill the man what married his mother and made her life so bad she ran off with Injins. Have a good time doin' your job, Sheriff."

Close at Hand
and Far Away

———————— ◆ ————————

MacLane sat and fumed in sullen silence. His mouth burned with the rake and reek of too much late-night pipe tobacco. His eyes gritted with sleeplessness. The dry plains wind pushed two big ragged holes into his heart where Lara and J.W. had grown so soon before. He felt dirty from head to toe, as if he'd just been dumped over with all the accumulated dust of his past, from the roads of Indiana to the desperate memories of Hannah and her son.

What a life! He had tried so hard for so long to do what was right. Well, that was just what he'd been preaching to Marshal Simpson, wasn't it? So why not get on with it?

He stood up abruptly, grabbing a handful of determination out of the air over his desk to pull himself out of his chair. It tipped back over and landed like an upside-down turtle against the wall of his office. He just left it like that and walked out. He strode rapidly down the street to the livery.

Oscar Shurg stood in the big double doorway, over to the side, befitting his status as the owner who wasn't sure anyone took him seriously. He wore his usual ancient suit of eastern style. Surely he owned more than one, but how did he keep coming up with new twenty-year-old suits?

The sheriff launched right into it, without the preamble of small talk so dear to the hearts of merchants who are afraid to stand in their own doorways.

"Oscar, have there been any strangers in here, looking to get feed for their horses, anything like that?"

The town treasurer gulped twice, then felt for the rough support post at his left hand. He addressed the tips of his shoes.

"Understand there's been strangers down to the hotel."

"Those came in on the train. I want to know about horsemen, probably in a bunch, trailing down from the north."

Oscar Shurg shrugged, and then thought better of it. He shrank back into the camouflage of his dusty suit.

"Yep, there was some like that, Sheriff. Hard men. I—I shouldn't tell you, 'cause they told me not to, but . . . I know you to be hard man, too, Sheriff, and . . ."

The man ducked his head and the sun shone off his bald pate. Shurg's hair was only thinning when Randall first came to Middle Bend. Now his head was smooth as a billiard ball, and Randall was the one with the thinning hair.

MacLane sighed. He had known this man for so long, had protected his town and himself. Still, one hard man was like any other to Oscar Shurg. What a miserable way to live. He waited.

"Well, guess you'd find out anyway, Sheriff. They was here, four of 'em. Two of 'em just stayed here and looked at me the whole time. One went out to get a bottle. The other one went to the hotel. It wasn't long they was in town. They was real mean when they first rode in. Told me they'd hurt me bad if I was to say anything to anybody, 'specially you, 'bout them bein' here. But then the one man come back from the hotel, he talked nicer. Said they was passin' through on important business, and it might be bad for business if anybody found out 'bout it 'head of time, so that's why they wanted me to keep quiet 'bout it. He even . . . well, he give me extra money, above the horse feed, for agreein' not to say anything."

MacLane's inner eye was already roving up and down the streets of the town. What sort of business could men like these be involved with? This story Oscar told was starting to suggest a pattern, and he didn't like the design. What was it that was so important almost anyone else in town could be let in on it, to talk about him, but he wasn't supposed to hear a word of it?

The sheriff whirled about and started down the street to the hotel. It was time for some answers. He was so intent on his mission that he didn't even thank Oscar Shurg for breaking the silence to which he was sworn. He didn't see the livery owner spit on the ground as he walked away. Shurg's aim was off a little; most of the spit hit his shoes.

As he turned the corner and headed toward the hotel, his heart skipped a beat. Lara Eastbrook and J.W. Bishop stood on the board sidewalk in front of the hotel, in an intense conversation that required many quick little hand gestures. Automatically Randall stepped up his pace. As he did, J.W.'s head came up.

The preacher saw him striding toward them. He spoke quickly to Lara, clamped his black hat onto his head, turned on his heel, and walked away like a man who wants to make good time but isn't sure where he's going. Lara turned toward Randall and started toward him at a brisk walk, then slowed, and finally stopped, clasping her bag in both hands as she waited for him to come to her.

Without intending it, MacLane's own pace slowed. A jab of jealousy punched him in the stomach. He hadn't even known J.W. was in town. Here his two friends were meeting without him. Did this mean Lara had made a choice that left him out forever?

He grimaced as he thought of his foolishness. Ever since Milo had told him the strangers were asking about him, he'd been going all over with a cloud of hopes buzzing around his head like gnats in summer. A job in Chicago? He'd take Lara. A train ride to Indianapolis? Lara would be along. A whole force of lawmen to work under him? Their eyes would tell him he was a lucky man as he introduced Lara to them.

She looked exceptionally small, standing there on the rough boards, holding so tightly to her bag. Randall wanted to reach out and take her into his arms, but she was so tiny she might just slip through his fingers. There was no smile on her face today, only the hard line of a set jaw. That line ran clear up to the top of her head. It pulled her scalp tight and turned the spun red gold of her hair into twisted cables of iron.

He came up to her as though walking in molasses. He instinctively stepped down from the sidewalk into the street, bringing his eyes closer to the level of her own. They stood in silence for a long moment, the sounds of the town around them muted by the intensity of vagueness. Randall had seldom been uneasy with silence, even in the presence of a woman, but breaking, even silences, was always a responsibility that seemed to fall to him.

"I didn't know J.W. was in town."

"He got in late last night. He rearranged his schedule so he could come through. He stayed at the hotel rather than come in so late on you or one of his members. He has to ride out again in just a little or he'll get hopelessly off schedule."

She seemed exasperated, talking rapidly. He wasn't sure if her offensiveness was a schoolteacher's frustration over J.W.'s lack of orderliness or because she had something else she wanted to say and was getting his subject out of the way as quickly as possible.

She looked at him as she talked, but it wasn't a look that came from inside. Her eyes were mirrors, reflecting back to her the words she waited to use.

"Lara, isn't this a school day?"

"I didn't go today. I couldn't. I feel . . . so . . . Something odd . . . More than odd. Something downright damnable . . ."

The frustration in her voice grew fierce, like a blacksmith swinging harder with each blow of his hammer. Randall was shocked at her choice of words, but he concentrated on the feeling in them.

"Randall, someone's been in my room. The widow claims she doesn't know anything about it, and I believe her, even if she is a nosy old. . . I mean, someone searched through everything I own! Oh, Randall, it's happening all over again. Someone's found out about my past, and they're looking for evidence to get me fired, or . . ."

Somehow she managed to look even smaller and more vulnerable than before, a sparrow shrinking into its feathers. Still, there was steel in her backbone. She fought the shrinking, pulled herself up, stiffened her spine.

He felt himself stiffening, too. He fought down a surge of disgust that threatened to turn him inside out. God, he thought, this woman who touched him so deeply needed him so much now, and his middle leg was about to pop his buttons! He was glad he had stepped down into the street. Maybe it was low enough that she wouldn't notice. He was so confused he didn't realize she was waiting for him to speak. She got tired of waiting.

"I came looking for you because it's illegal, isn't it, for someone to go through my room, even if they are looking for something like that? I ran into J.W. coming out of the hotel, and we went in to have coffee. While we were there, some creepy-looking man I never saw before came down the stairs and looked at us. He just stood there, and stared. Then he went over to Mr. Brumfield, the clerk, and talked to him, and kept looking over his shoulder at us. When he went back upstairs, J.W. spoke to Mr. Brumfield to find out what was going on. He claimed the man didn't talk about us at all, but you could tell he was lying. We decided we'd better tell you, and that was when you came down the street."

Randall felt the jab of jealousy again. J.W. and Lara had coffee together. He was never able to have her to himself in that way. And hadn't J.W. run off when he saw him coming? That surely meant he felt guilty, that he was trying to snare Lara for himself. He was so busy with his feelings about Lara that he almost forgot Lara herself. Then he remembered why they were talking.

"Well, we'd better go over to your house and take a look at your room, see if we can figure out who might have been in there."

He was trying to be the sheriff. All he could think of, though, was the thrill of being in Lara's room. He hunched himself over and walked a bit bowlegged as they started off.

He didn't notice that they were being watched both from the window of the hotel lobby and from one of the rooms upstairs.

They couldn't go into Lara's room alone, of course. The Widow Kelley went along. That dampened down Randall's excitement.

He couldn't get much of a feel for how the room must be when Lara was in it by herself because of the mess from its earlier ransacking. At least he was able to relax and straighten up.

"Can you tell if they took anything?"

"I don't think so. They must have thought I have jewelry or something. Whoever it was doesn't know much about a schoolteacher's pay."

She tried to laugh a little, to carry off the deception for their unwanted chaperon, to keep the landlady from learning her real fear. MacLane walked around the room, inspecting, but his mind wasn't into it. He kept remembering the disorder of his own house when Hannah was his wife. That, of course, made him remember Hannah and her desperate life and anguished death. Going through this young woman's room made him feel limp and cold and old.

It was so much to sort out. Was he up to Lara, even if

he could win her? Who had murdered poor Hannah? Despite the speech he had given Marshal Simpson, did he care enough to go after them? What about the specter of Isaac, playing at being a gunslinger? Who were these strangers in the hotel? Were they ever going to offer him a job? Had he lost J.W.'s friendship forever? Even if they could put that friendship back together, could it stand the strain of their mutual interest in Lara? Who had searched her room? Was she really in danger of being found out? For that matter, who had searched his rooms?

It didn't occur to him to ask the questions in a logical sequence, to see if they were related. They just tumbled around in his brain like peanuts in a rolling barrel.

"Lara, you'd better straighten things up so you can see for sure if anything is missing. Then you'd better come to my office so we can fill out a report."

In a town like Middle Bend, who needed reports? But it meant he had a socially acceptable reason for seeing her again.

As he started back to his office he saw J.W. ride out of the livery and start down the street. Impulsively, he stepped off the boardwalk and waved him down. J.W. reined up, but it was clear he didn't want to be there. Randall pushed back his hat and looked up at the man he hoped was still his friend. He searched for something to say.

"Uh . . . Lara told me about her room. I went over and had a look. Couldn't tell if anything was taken. I don't have any idea who might have done it."

"Yes . . . well, I hate to go off when she's feeling like this," said J.W., "someone trying to expose her and all, but I have to keep to my schedule. . . ."

His friend wanted to talk. Randall felt it. But J.W. didn't know any better than he himself did how to do it.

"Well, I'd better get going."

Randall didn't want to let him go, wanted to say something, anything, that would keep him a little longer.

"Where are you headed now?"

"Why, back on my circuit."

"Yes, but you're off a little. I'm not sure where your next stop is."

Anything just to hang on a little longer, maybe have the time to find the words to apologize for being a killer, instead of whatever it was J.W. wanted him to be, some way to apologize for ten dollars.

J.W. seemed perplexed at having to figure out where his circuit took him next. He consulted some internal calendar.

"I guess it's Ringwood now," he said finally.

Randall MacLane didn't consider the consequences of what he did next. It was just a way of keeping the conversation going, of holding on to his friend for a little longer.

"Oh, good. Come over to my office with me a minute. I have to send Sheriff Trumbull some wanted posters. You can deliver them for me, if you don't mind."

"No, I don't mind. I will have to hurry, though. . . ."

J.W.'s voice trailed off as he trailed his horse behind MacLane to the city building. Randall wanted to invite him in, but J.W. didn't get down from his horse. If the minister wanted to talk, too, it was clear that the moment had passed.

MacLane had little choice. Trumbull would probably think he was crazy, but what could he do but go through with the charade? He went into his office and grabbed a handful of wanted posters. He stuck them in a big envelope, took them back out to the street, and handed them to the parson.

J.W. took the envelope, pushed it into his saddlebags, promised to make the delivery, and rode off.

The sheriff was still unaware that he was being observed. This time a well-dressed man watched them from the front of the hotel, then hurried off toward the livery as J.W. rode out of town in the other direction.

Why Do They All Go Away?

—————— ◆ ——————

Lara hadn't come to the office by suppertime to make her report, so MacLane walked over to her boarding-house. After all, he had a job to do, didn't he? Widow Kelley met him at the door.

"Nothing was taken. I helped her clean up, and we could see that. She's resting now. Poor thing's been through too much already. She doesn't need to see you, too. I don't either. I've got supper to get."

She disappeared toward the kitchen in a cloud of flour that rose up from her apron like a whirlwind.

He didn't feel like talking, so he walked on by the hotel and went to the Palace instead. Milo's bartender would be willing to rustle up a little food before the evening drinkers came in. He shoved it down and left.

He slouched around town on his rounds. It was get-ting cold earlier in the evening as the autumn wore on. The autumn chill stalked the space between him and everyone he knew. He stuck his hands down deep into his pockets, hunched up his shoulders, and went back to his room at the jail. There he scorched his throat with smoke. At least it was warm.

He peered into the cloud of tobacco smoke and tried to see his life there. I have a reputation most men would envy, he thought. My name is recognized all over this part of the country. Everyone who hears it either respects it or fears it, and those two impostors are about the same. I'm the most educated man in these parts. I have a profession that puts me on the side of right.

"Where's all that gotten me?" he mumbled at the smoke. "I spend my days and nights walking around a town that is scared to live with me and scared to live without me. My closest friends don't know me. Am I a killer, a madman? No, but they don't know that. I'm surely not what I set out to be. All I wanted was to be an ordinary man."

Even before he heard it, he knew the October rain had started. The thick purple smoke of his pipe curled over the rim of the bowl and oozed down toward the floor. Some smoke had already spiraled its way up toward the rafters. It now began to settle like a personal cloud around his head. The rain had a way of making everything pull down into itself.

He sat in the dark, alone, staring out at the town through the rain. The rain always made him think of the green hills of Indiana, so far away and so long ago. At the university in Bloomington he had listened to the other students complain about the rain. He could not understand it. For him, the rain had held the promise of action. Hidden somewhere in the dark and the wet was the promise of adventure.

The rain still kept its pledge of action and adventure, but he did not have to search for it. He knew it would seek him out, as it had so many times before—on a Montana hill, at the burning wagon, in a dozen lawless towns where he had worn the badge no one else dared to wear. It was the kind of night and the sort of rain that meant adventure if you were twenty-five, and action if you were thirty-five. But when you were forty-five it only meant trouble.

At forty-five, when staring through the rain, sensing the feeling in your increasingly creaky joints that action means trouble, even a solitary man begins to feel lonely. At forty-five you worry about your belt having no more holes and about your throat being raspy every time you puff your pipe and especially about the spots that float in front of your eyes on a sunny day. You wonder if you're too old for the job. You ask what else you can do, and you get no answers. Those, at least, are your thoughts if you are an ordinary man. More than anything else, Randall MacLane longed to be an ordinary man.

How, though, could a man ever be ordinary when he had been sent with a message to the world's hero, but had arrived too late? How could he be ordinary when he had tamed a dozen towns and killed a hundred people and saved a thousand more? How could he be ordinary when he was the one man an entire territory feared and trusted more than anyone else? That wasn't an ordinary life. Randall MacLane was not an ordinary man.

At least he could take refuge in the rain. Rain has always been the friend of solitary men. When you are not an ordinary man, however, you sit in the dark, alone, and stare at the town through the rain, and you know that the trouble will come.

It came the next morning with the strange sight of Milo Rosewater dragging a reluctant Lonnie Ledbetter into his office. Milo started right in without a single comment on the rain. It was a bad sign.

"Sheriff, Lonnie's got something to tell you, and he made me come along 'cause he was afraid you'd think it was him. He assures me it's just as he tells it. I'm inclined to believe him. Otherwise I don't think he'd have come in at all."

"Goddamn it, Rosewater, what kind of man you think I

am? I wouldn't leave a body out there—" Lonnie broke off and cleared his throat, then continued as though it was his idea to be there in the first place. "You see, Sheriff, I was ridin' back to the ranch along afore sunup this morning. I'd been kind of late in town last night. Figgered it'd be more pleasant stayin' with one of the town women instead of ridin' in the rain, if'n you know what I mean."

He started to giggle, then remembered where he was and what he had to tell. He went sober very quickly.

"Well, anyhow, I was ridin' out when this rider come up the road at me. 'Cept it wasn't no rider at all. It was just a horse, with saddle and bridle and all, comin' inta town. I thought maybe I recognized the horse, but it was kinda dark. I caught it easy enough, and looked through the saddlebags. You know, to see whose horse it was. But there wasn't nothin' at all in the bags, which seemed mighty strange. So I turned it around and started back-trackin', which wasn't easy acause of the rain, but I figgered it prob'ly kept to the road anyhow."

MacLane rose slowly out of his chair. Lonnie shrank back toward the door.

"You better git on with it, Lonnie," said Milo. "He doesn't need to know every detail."

"Well, I found him, anyhow. Been shot. Three or four times, I reckon. Stuff from the saddlebags all over. I picked it all up and stuffed it in the bags, but it was all pretty wet. Light enough by then I'm pretty sure I got all of it, though."

Randall MacLane knew what Lonnie Ledbetter was going to say next. He didn't want to hear it.

"He won't get around to it ever, Sheriff, so I'd better," said Milo. "It was your friend . . . the reverend. Lonnie took the body directly over to Whispering Lowe's place, which seems to be the proper thing to do since he was afraid to come here."

"Hell, I wasn't afraid to come," Lonnie started to say, but then he remembered that both of these men knew him well enough that there was no point in it.

MacLane sighed. He didn't notice it. His shoulders slumped.

"I'm sorry, Lonnie. Sorry you had to be afraid to come to see me, but I appreciate you taking the trouble to back-track and bring him in. If Buck gives you any trouble about being late to the ranch, just tell him you were work-ing for me. Better go get yourself some breakfast over at the hotel. Tell them to put it on my bill."

Lonnie's face broke into a gap-toothed grin. Wilforce wouldn't dare roust him now. And a meal at the hotel? All he could normally afford was a cantina, or maybe Max's Café. He lit out the door like a dog with a firecracker tied to its tail.

"Come on, Milo. Let's go to Lowe's place."

Randall went out the door and down the street without waiting to see if the fat man was with him.

In Titus Lowe's back room they spread out all the items from John Wesley Bishop's sodden saddlebags, along with all the things from his pockets. The pastor's money was gone, but he never had much anyway.

"Damn," said Milo. "Why'd whoever did it have to go and shoot him? He would've given 'em whatever he had. Just like old Reverend Thistle that way."

Randall continued to look through his friend's meager possessions. Everything else seemed to be there—his change of clothes, his Bible, his hymnbook.

MacLane was getting irritated about something, though, and he couldn't tell what it was. He wasn't feel-ing the grief yet. That would come later. Right now he was just numb, going through the motions. The infernal whistling of Whispering Lowe as he worked on the body in the next room didn't help his mood any. Then he got it.

Without a word to Milo he whipped out of the under-taker's establishment and down to the hotel. He strode right up to Lonnie Ledbetter. The ranch hand got ready to dive under the table.

"Lonnie, keep your wits now, because I need for you to think straight. Are you sure you picked up everything where you found J.W.'s body? Was there anything else around? Some papers maybe, blown around by the wind?"

"Hell no, Sheriff. There wasn't nothin' I could see. Like I told you, it was light by then. I'da seen papers. Besides, papers woulda been sogged down by the rain. There wasn't nothin'."

"All right, Lonnie. I'm sorry I disturbed your breakfast."

As he turned away from Lonnie's chair he saw three well-dressed men sitting at a table by the window. One was seated sideways but had twisted in his chair so his back was solidly to the sheriff. The other two were watching the exchange between Lonnie and MacLane with keen interest.

Just then, though, Mrs. Osborn, the hotel's combination hostess and cook, caught hold of his elbow and started walking him toward the door, trying to get out of earshot of Lonnie.

"Sheriff, Lonnie Ledbetter's eatin' about three breakfasts and claims he can put it on your expense."

"It's all right, Mrs. Osborn. I told him he could do it. He did a favor for me . . . and for a friend."

By the time he had mollified Mrs. Osborn, they had reached the door of the dining room. He forgot about the men at the window table. He didn't see one of them get up and walk over to Lonnie's table.

Whoever killed J.W. had taken his pittance and the wanted posters as well. Why? They were old posters. MacLane wasn't even sure they were current, just some pulled out of a drawer to have something to give to J.W.

Working it in his mind, turning it over and over the way a raccoon washes a doubtful meal, he walked over to Lara's boardinghouse. How would he tell her?

As it turned out, his dread was unnecessary, as it so often is.

"Somebody's already been here to tell her," Widow Kelley informed him. "Miss Eastbrook's resting in her room, and she doesn't want to be disturbed."

As he slipped away, the full emptiness settled down over him, like a damp fog. Only Lara could understand what the loss of J.W. meant, and he didn't have her to share it.

It was beginning to look like he might never see her again. But he needed her now, not just as a woman, but as a friend. His competition for her was gone, and he wanted it back.

"Goddamn it," he snapped. "Goddamn the soul of whoever did this."

He said it again, louder and bolder, aware it was the first time he had ever taken the name of the Lord in vain, and hoping it was not in vain. He really wanted the soul of the killer damned.

He pulled himself up until his backbone tingled. He squared his shoulders and executed a parade-ground about-face. The tears began to rush down his cheeks. He opened up his raw throat to a deep rush of cold, October after-rain plains air, and he marched back to the Widow Kelley's.

He didn't knock, just threw the door open and walked in. Up the stairs, toes only, like a dancer.

He had known which room was Lara's long before he went there the day before. He had so often seen her stand in the window to watch him and J.W. walk back to the jail after they had reluctantly seen her home. He had just as often detoured down this street on his nighttime rounds, simply to look at her window, like some cowlicked schoolboy.

He grasped the knob of her door and flung it open.

She sat on the footstool of her big chair, huddled down against the cushion of the chair. When her door exploded open, her head jerked up.

She saw a red-eyed giant, sobbing soundless heaves of grief. He fell to his knees like he was shot and crawled toward her.

She stumbled over the stool, got her legs caught up in long skirt and petticoat, started pulling herself toward him only with her arms, like a paralytic. Her hands grabbed fistfuls of rug for leverage.

They collided like two birds intent only on the same dragonfly. They clutched at each other and held on, rocking back and forth in a heap in the middle of the thin rug on the floor of Lara's rented room.

Isaac's Return

Widow Kelley was strangely understanding when she
found them. She fluttered around like a mother hen, finally
shooed them down to the kitchen.

"Can't have anyone else coming in on you two up here
in this room," she clucked.

She set coffee and biscuits and a huge pot of apple butter before them, then left them alone. She swept around
the rest of the house, finding work to do to use as a barri-
cade against intruding upon their grief and hunger.

Later they walked the streets, just the two of them
now, unconsciously tracing the regular route they used
when J.W. was with them, unconcerned about whether
they were seen and what the watchers might say.

Lara tucked her small hand into the crook of Randall's
elbow. Her right arm, the one that so recently held the
other half of her double man, hung at her side as if broken.
Even through MacLane's coat and her glove, she could
feel his tension rising. She squeezed his arm. He understood what she was asking.

"Yes, I'm going after him, or them . . . whoever did it. Not just because it's my job, although it is that. The rage is back in me, I know. Just like it's always been. But it's different this time. I'm not going to lash out. Sometimes the rage was there. It took me over, like when Grandfather died, or when I charged those Indians as I was trying to get through to Custer. Other times it was cold and calculating, like when I came down off that hill and killed the Indians who had Hannah and Isaac. It's just as real this time, but it's . . ."

He faltered as he rummaged around for the right words. Was he explaining this at all right, so she could understand? He ached with the importance of it. She simply had to grasp what he was saying. Only that would erase the picture she had seen as she stood in the saloon door while he gunned down Buck Wilforce's hired killer.

"This time it's more like a commitment, almost like the calling J.W. felt he never had. It's not blind rage. It's not cold fury, either. It's just the awareness that whoever did it has to be brought to justice. I think J.W. would approve of that."

He smiled as he thought of his friend. For a moment he had the uncanny feeling that J.W. was right there with them, walking along on the other side of Lara. It was a good feeling. Then he chuckled.

"It seems almost ridiculous to say something like this at my age, but I think I'm actually, finally growing up. Isn't that what maturity is, when—"

There was no chance to finish his thought. Milo Rosewater, with Cabbage Collins right on his heels, careened around the corner with his remarkable lightness of foot.

It brought up in MacLane's memory a picture of the potbellied cowboy who had danced around in Clegg City, trying to hurt Liu. The memory was like a bruise. It spread out and began to cover the presence of J.W.

Milo puffed to a stop in front of them, like a runaway

train that thought better of it when it began to get short of coal.

"Sheriff, I hate to bother you at a time like this." He tipped his hat to Lara. Cabbage hastily did the same with his mangled stovepipe. "But that durned—pardon me, ma'am—Henry Alcorn . . . He's getting everybody stirred up. You know, he never has cared much for you, ever since the first time we hired you and he thought we were going too fast. Well, he's going around saying you're neglecting the job, running around with Miss Eastbrook here—pardon me, ma'am—and if you were doing the job right, there wouldn't be all these killings and strange things happening around here."

Milo ran out of steam. Randall sighed.

"I suppose I'd better go talk to him."

Why did he put up with these people, anyway? He tried to serve them well. He had done so for years. But they cared nothing for competence, for loyalty, for sacrifice, for the difficulties and dangers the job posed. Their only question was "Do we like him?"

If they liked you, you could do no wrong, regardless of how incompetent you might be. If they didn't like you, you could do no right. It was a way to power, of saying "The most important thing in the world is whether I like something, which means the most important thing in the whole world is me."

"Well, actually you can talk to him and the rest of the council, too," said Milo. "They're all down at the city building, hashing it around right now. They didn't want you to know."

"Cabbage, will you escort Miss Eastbrook back home, please? Milo and I need to attend to some business."

The little man actually skipped to Lara's side, grinning like a busted watermelon.

She squeezed Randall's arm again, and spoke in a low murmur, for his ears only.

"Remember what you said . . . about the maturity. . . ."

He patted her hand and smiled down at her pale face.

"Don't worry. I've got the cards, and there aren't any more jokers in this hand."

He watched her walk off beside Cabbage. They reminded him of a fairy queen and her toad companion, a picture he had seen a million years ago, as a child, and hadn't thought of again in all that time.

As he walked to the city building with Milo, part of him wondered why such images of childhood should arise now. It would not be long before he would frown as he recalled telling her there were no more jokers in the hand.

They had walked only a block when a bartender from the Palace wheezed out of an alley. He glanced at MacLane and shied away from him like a horse that had just seen a cougar. He pulled Milo down the alley and whispered in his ear while dancing from one foot to the other. Milo's face went mottled red as he listened to the man, then went pale as he turned back to MacLane.

"Sheriff, Homer there just told me . . . Lord, I hate to put this on you, too, but . . . Isaac, he's back. He's all grown up and dressed like a gunslinger. He's over at the Palace, acting mean, and talking funny about you. I heard some stories about him before, but I didn't want to bother you with 'em. I'm sorry. I don't know what to do."

The sheriff felt a surge of appreciation for the fat man. In all his lonely days, Milo Rosewater had been a friend, and he was too absorbed in himself ever to realize it. He didn't deserve that kind of loyalty and concern from Milo, because he never had returned it. Now, though, he was filled to overflowing with gratitude for that friendship.

"It's not your problem, Milo. But I'm eternally thankful to you for thinking that it is. Well, first things first. We started to meet with the council, and we'd better do it."

Milo Rosewater nodded. This was what he had expected.

MacLane understood for the first time that part of what bound the two men together was Milo's admiration for him. To a man like Milo, the fearsome and taciturn sheriff was all he would like to be. J.W. had been like that, too, admiring Randall's ability to take decisive and direct action.

All the time, Randall MacLane himself had no intention of being an admirable figure. His reputation was just an accident, one accident upon another that added up to a tale that he really had no voice in telling. He just wanted to be . . . but then they were at the city building.

The town council was in full, raucous session when the sheriff and the owner of the Palace walked in. All immediately went silent as they caught sight of MacLane. He walked straight across the spacious room toward Henry Alcorn, now the town's number-three businessman, since Buck Wilforce had emerged to take the position as the most prosperous man in town.

As he moved through the room Randall was again aware of that curious division in his mind.

Part of him was admiring the town hall, so well built and generously appointed, built by Buck Wilforce, at the taxpayers' expense, as a monument to himself.

Part of him was feeling sorry for Henry Alcorn. The poor man had always longed to be number one. He had moved out from back east to find a pond small enough that he could be the biggest fish. Milo had beaten him out with a big belly flop. Then Buck pushed him farther out toward the stagnant edge. No wonder the man was so cantankerous.

Still another part of his mind was admiring his own maturity and congratulating him at the generous way he felt toward Alcorn.

Yet another part of him made the decision to do what he did. He didn't seem to have any control over his brain or actions.

His hand pulled the badge from his coat and stuck it out, straight arm, at Henry Alcorn.

"If you gentlemen don't like the way I'm doing this job, you're welcome to it." He turned from Henry Alcorn. His eyes swept the assembled men. No one dared return his gaze. "I know there have been a lot of strange doings around here lately, and there have been killings. I haven't gotten to the bottom of it yet, but I definitely intend to, whether I'm the sheriff here or not."

As he spoke the door between the council chambers and his own office slowly opened. The council members were seated with their backs to it, so only MacLane and Henry Alcorn were in position to see it.

As it swung full open a thin young man emerged. His hat was pushed back, revealing lank blond hair. He was dressed like a combination gambler and cowboy—cloth vest, striped dress shirt with a string tie, faded jeans stuffed into handworked boots. He was a generation older and looked a foot taller, but there was no mistake about who he was.

"Hello, Isaac," MacLane said.

Every bottom in the room swiveled toward the door. Someone gasped. MacLane wasn't sure who, and he didn't care. He simply stared at the thin blond man. That was what he was now—a man. Still, he looked so much like the boy Isaac, the boy Randall MacLane had longed to make his own son, had tried so hard to reach. He hadn't been much older then than Isaac was now.

Isaac Reindorf looked around the room, his eyes standing briefly on each man in turn. The eyes showed disappointment. The corners of his mouth turned down, like he had expected to enjoy this moment and found it turning sour. The eyes of the leading men of Middle Bend saw him no better now than they ever had.

Milo Rosewater heaved himself up out of his chair.

"Is that really you, Isaac? So many years . . ." He shook his head. His jowls flapped like sheets in the wind. "We've heard about you, stories . . . wondered if they were true."

Milo didn't finish his thought. Instead he looked the younger man up and down and found in that appraisal the answer for his question. This, indeed, was a gunman, more than Brace Newman and his kind ever dreamed to be.

"I've got business with the sheriff," Isaac said flatly.

His voice had changed more than his face. MacLane hardly recognized it. But the boy had never said much anyway. Who could remember a voice so seldom heard?

"Well, this here is a town council meetin'," blustered Henry Alcorn. "We're discussin' things with the sheriff—"

He broke off under Isaac's hard gaze. It wasn't the hard gaze of a man used to looking out over the plains, even one who watched there for trouble on the horizon. There was an internal flintiness to his eyes, like he had turned his eyeballs inward and been brushed there with sandpaper.

"Well, I imagine we can take this up some other time," Milo almost shouted, with the false heartiness of a cemetery lot salesman in the charity ward of a hospital. "Come on, men. The sheriff and his, uh, Isaac haven't seen each other for a long time."

MacLane understood Milo's motivation. A saloon keeper sees plenty of Brace Newmans. Milo knew that gunmen need audiences. He intended to deprive Isaac of his stage.

Milo began to fan at the room with his hat, herding the other members of the council up from their chairs and toward the outer door.

"This isn't a social call—" Isaac started to say. He gave up when he realized his voice was being lost in the scraping of chair legs and general thumping. All of a sudden the council members had decided it was a good thing to leave the two men alone. They weren't dallying. Even Henry Alcorn hunched his head down into his shoulders and made for the door like a turtle on wheels.

Randall and Isaac were left alone. Isaac continued to stand in the door to the sheriff's office. MacLane lowered one haunch down on the corner of the table in the front of the room, still holding in his left hand the star he was thrusting at Henry Alcorn when Isaac appeared.

His right hand automatically hovered near his gun,

down along his leg, out of sight of Isaac. What if the boy actually tried it, even without an audience? Could he really draw on Isaac? What else could he do?

He decided against silence. Silence gives the mind too much opportunity to give the hand directions.

"You haven't filled out very much, Isaac."

He was falling into the same old patterns, the same old traps. It sounded too much like criticism, too much like where their relationship had broken off years before.

Isaac didn't notice. He looked off to a far corner of the room. His eyes twitched up and down, although his head did not move. He was torn between anger and something else. . . . Guilt? Hope? Sadness?

"I guess you've heard about my mother?"

"Yes."

It wasn't lost on Randall that Isaac spoke of Hannah only as his mother, not in any way as MacLane's wife.

He thought of telling Isaac what he had learned from Marshal Simpson, about trailing the men who'd killed Hannah, almost to Middle Bend. But that might set Isaac off. He was the law in Middle Bend. He still held the proof of that in his hand. He didn't want Isaac riding off to do vigilante vengeance. That would bring them into a confrontation for sure.

"I want her things, if there's anything left."

The words were harsh, but the tilt of the young man's head betrayed the little boy within. Isaac was always such a strange mix of sullenness and hope.

MacLane was surprised by a curious lump in his throat. This boy-turned-man surely had come for vengeance of some kind. He had not become a gunman by accident. If he'd been talking in the Palace of killing the sheriff, then he'd have to try it. Reputation and audience, those were everything to a gunman. Still he couldn't resist the temptation to talk about his mother first, to ask for some memento of her.

MacLane ran over the mental inventory of his own

possessions. He had seen them all recently enough, putting them back into place after his rooms had been ransacked. Little stabs of guilt prickled his skin. He had kept no memento of his wife for himself.

"I'm sorry, Isaac. I've moved around so much since I left here after . . . well, since I left here the first time. I've had to travel pretty light. I'm afraid I don't have anything left that was hers."

The younger man's shoulders dropped. MacLane went for his gun. It was out and leveled before he realized what had happened.

Isaac stood stock-still, his mouth gapped open.

The sheriff's belly burned with shame and disgust.

"I'm sorry, Isaac," he muttered.

This apology was beginning to sound like a refrain. That disgusted him, too.

"It was automatic. I . . . I thought you were going to draw. Like Milo said, we've heard stories, but . . . that's not really it. It's just that whenever anyone makes a shoulder drop like you just did, I think he's drawing, and . . ."

It sounded more stupid when he said it than when he thought it.

To his surprise, a slow, grimacing grin turned up over Isaac's chin.

"You may have saved me a big mistake later, MacLane. If I'd tried what I've been saying I'd do, I'd be dead now. I'm pretty good. I've seen some of the ones with the big reputations. But I've never seen a gun clear leather as fast as that. I had no idea. I've heard stories about you, too, but I remembered you as a rifle-and-fists man."

The older man fixed his eyes on the floor as he holstered his gun. It was strange to hear this kind of praise from someone he'd tried to father.

"Well, it's something I picked up."

He wanted to tell Isaac about the Chinaman and about his own determination to learn how to use a handgun, about J.W. and Lara, to tell him how stupid it all was, all the killing and the loneliness. Then he realized how stupid he was. Isaac had never paid any attention to him. He was not likely to start now. So, what was there to say, except . . .

"I'm real sorry about your mother . . . about Hannah. . . . I do wish I had the things she left so you could have them now, but there wasn't much, and I left in such a hurry."

Then it hit him like a whack on the head. The *old* jail! That was where he had stored the things that were left over when he slipped out of Middle Bend after Hannah and Isaac had gone their separate ways.

"Wait. Maybe I do have something. When I came back, the new city building was up. I didn't even think about the old jail, it had been so long. Underneath the stairs, in that little closet . . . I wonder if anyone ever moved that stuff out? I doubt it. Come on."

Decision Time

◆◆◆

Randall strode out of the city building and started down the street toward the old jail. He felt like his feet and his heart had wings. Maybe he could actually do something good for someone, without bringing pain to himself or to anyone else. What a difference that would be! It wasn't much, a memento of Hannah for Isaac. He and Isaac were hardly friends. But at least they hadn't killed each other. That was worth something.

Behind him Isaac hesitated. The moment of indecision and uncertainty widened out his narrow features. He had come to kill the sheriff; he was sure of that. He hadn't tried, and he was relieved. That surprised him. There wasn't a snowball's chance that he could ever beat Randall MacLane in a gunfight, he could see that now. So he didn't have to try. That actually pleased him. And what a draw! He was almost proud of the man.

Then his eyes pinched down onto his nose again. He hurried after the sheriff, almost trotting in order to catch up.

As Isaac burst through the door he saw that almost

everyone in town was out on the street. They were watching the city building, but discreetly, shrunk back up against the buildings, or standing stiff in doorways.

He frowned. They thought there would be gunplay, that he and Randall MacLane would have shot it out by now. They were there to see who came out, alone. He was sure they were disappointed to see both men emerge and walk down the street together. For all their talk of wanting a peaceful town, there was nothing the average citizen enjoyed as much as seeing other men gun each other down.

His eyes were quick. He saw the little group of well-dressed men in front of the hotel window. He noted that they were the only ones who seemed more curious than disappointed. His immediate impression was that they did not fit the scene, were out of place. Then he had his back to them as he jump-stepped after MacLane.

Thus he didn't see one of them hurry down the street toward the livery while the others followed after him and the sheriff, slow and easy, oozing along the other side of the street, like water moccasins along a creek bank.

Isaac caught up at the door of the old town hall, where the sheriff was fumbling with the keys.

"This place is hardly used at all now. I'm not even sure about the key."

Even as he spoke, however, the right key meshed with the tumblers of the old lock. He pushed the door open. It groaned painfully on rusted hinges.

Isaac followed him into the musty old building, without bothering to close the door.

"I'll be surprised if there's anything left," said Randall. He didn't want to get Isaac's hopes too high. "There wasn't much, even then. No telling what all happened in the years I was away."

He felt his way back through the ancient gloom. He finally found the door to the little closet under the stairway. It was where he had just dumped anything he could not carry in a saddlebag, so many years before. He squeaked the door open.

It had been years before, but as he began to pull things out of the closet, it seemed as though it had been merely a few days. He could remember it all so clearly. Yet he hadn't thought about that day in all those years. Why was it so real now?

There was a small box and a carpetbag. Isaac fell on his knees and began to go through the bag like a dog digging for a bone, like he was looking for something special but wouldn't know what it was until he found it.

"This bag came with us, didn't it, from the wagon, I mean? I remember it from when I was a little kid, and then in the house . . ."

His voice trailed off. Either he didn't want to think about the house where the three of them had lived, not quite together, or else he didn't want to talk about it. He pulled out an old dress of Hannah's, a Bible, a hairbrush, a long, flat metal box.

"This is funny. I don't remember this."

He held the box so the sheriff could get a better look at it. Randall MacLane knew it at once. He had forgotten all about it, yet it was once the most important thing in his life. He had almost lost his life because of it.

Before he could speak, another voice knifed through the daylight darkness of the old building.

"We'll just take that, boy. No need to bother the sheriff with it. He wouldn't know what to do with it."

Isaac froze, the box in the air, stuck there between him and the man who once tried to be his father. Without moving his head, he took in the scene.

MacLane saw it all as he stood there, too. The strangers from the hotel, the well-dressed gentlemen, had followed them. He and Isaac were so intent on the items from the closet that they hadn't heard them come in.

Now the gentlemen stood arrayed before the open door and the dirty windows that flanked it, fortified by a brace of toughs on either end of their little line. MacLane had never seen the toughs before, but he had seen plenty of their type.

He had not seen the man who spoke before, either, not in Middle Bend, at any rate. He knew immediately that this was the leader of the pack, the one who never left the hotel room, while the others ran around to do his bidding. Randall could not see his face, except in outline, but he could smell the power and self-confidence that rose from him, like the odor of musty money and fresh horse droppings.

There was something about that voice, though, just those few words. They took him back once again, to another room. . . .

He stood in that other room, a young man in a military uniform. He was surrounded by important men, men so important he didn't even know their names. They handed him the box and told him to take it to Custer. But there was one man there he did know . . . and suddenly the voice made sense.

His young friend, the congressman, Lafayette Luquire. He'd grown older, just as Randall had, but the pounds around his middle were the outgrowth of power.

For the first time since that terrible day, when he tried so hard to deliver his message to Custer, and failed so completely, he wondered. . . . Why hadn't Luquire tried to contact him? Why hadn't he told him what to do with the undelivered message?

He had explicit instructions never to contact the men in Washington again, but he had never thought about it, anyway. From the Little Bighorn, to the burning wagon, to Hannah and Isaac, to all the days that followed, he'd never had time to consider Washington again. It was so many lifetimes ago.

Why now, after all these years, was this coming up? Why all the secrecy, all the hiding out of sight in the hotel, the gunmen? Why hadn't they just come to his office and asked him for the message case?

Then something clicked into place in his mind, like the first tumbler in the big lock on a bank safe. Someone had come to his office, looking for something. Someone came when he wasn't there.

Isaac continued to hold the message case toward MacLane. He had made a serious mistake, an error no gunman should make. But he'd been so confused about whether he wanted to kill MacLane, so absorbed in thinking about his mother, so anxious to find something.

Now these men were looking for something, too. He didn't have the slightest idea what it was all about. He knew that if MacLane didn't tell him to give the box to the man who's asked for it, he would have to use his gun.

All he could do was hope no one else had noticed his mistake. He was holding the message box in his gun hand.

MacLane gave voice to his wonder.

"Why now, after all these years?"

He said it to the man in the middle of the line of strangers, as if they were the only two in the room.

"Why not just come in and ask for it? Why all this masquerade? And why wasn't there a single word from you in all these years?"

Isaac was more confused than ever. MacLane obviously knew the man. Whatever had happened between them had to be a long time ago, before MacLane had come to Middle Bend, before he had rescued them at the burning wagon. What did he mean by masquerade?

Whoever it was, Isaac now felt the same surge Randall experienced right after the fight at the wagon, when the two of them had first come together.

Somehow they were linked. Isaac knew whose side he was on.

The gentleman from the hotel acted like a man who was used to asking questions instead of answering them. He brushed a nonexistent piece of lint from the front of his coat, then hooked a self-satisfied thumb over the gold watch chain that looped across his belly. His voice gritted on the edge of annoyance.

"You've actually caused us a great deal of inconvenience. However, this young man fortuitously appeared. It was not to our advantage to kill you, at least not until we determined whether the message still existed. It is the message, not you, Sheriff, that is the important item here, you see. That's the way it always was."

Pure scorn poured out of his mouth.

MacLane was mystified. Why? He and the congressman had been friends. He had done what he was asked to do. He had delivered the message to Custer as nearly as anyone could.

"Tell this young ruffian to hand it over now. It no longer concerns you, either of you. Cooperate, and perhaps you will be spared the fate that befell your—"

The man from Washington clamped his mouth shut. In his disdain, he had said too much. He broke off and motioned to the well-dressed, younger man on his left to go forward.

"Just give it to my man here."

The voice now held the "wrinkled lip and sneer of cold command." Perhaps that was it, thought Randall. The man simply had too much power. He had gotten used to ordering people around.

In earlier days, he had manipulated people, like the

young Lieutenant MacLane. He had gotten his way through false friendships. Now he simply told them, regardless of who they were. But what was it he was saying about fate? *The fate that befell* . . . Who was he talking about?

Then the next tumbler of the lock clicked over, and another, and another, until the door to the safe of secrets swung wide open. This was why his rooms had been searched, and Lara's as well. This was why Hannah had been tortured, why J.W. was shot down and killed after they had seen the sheriff hand him something that could look like a message.

They were after the case, or at least the message in it. If they'd known this old building was the jail of his first career in Middle Bend, had they just looked here first . . .

Then the door to understanding swung shut again. It clanged with a sharp finality that walled him off from his love for Hannah and J.W., as surely as if a part of his body had been hacked away. What was in this old message case? What could be worth robbery and torture and murder?

The scene in the dark and musty old jail building wavered in front of him, as though seen through the same plains heat mists that had filtered his vision from the time of the Little Bighorn through the past twenty years.

There was the no-longer-young congressman, grown gross with power, holding out his hand for the message case, as though it was his right to take anything for which he reached. There were his citified minions, satisfied to do his bidding simply for the chance to be on the side of power. There were the hired hard cases—wary, scarred in soul as well as body, no doubt the ones who actually took the knife to Hannah and the gun to J.W. Just before him, long now in that muscle-knotting crouch, still holding the message case, was the man who came as close to being a son to him as anyone was ever likely to be.

Then MacLane saw it, too. The case was in Isaac's right hand, his gunhand. Unless he told Isaac to give up the case, there would be a gunfight for sure. Isaac would be one bullet behind while he dropped the case and drew. That one bullet might be all it took to wipe out everything that was left of MacLane's past, wipe out all of Isaac's future. Better to let them have the silly case. It surely could not be worth Isaac's life. It had cost too many, already.

That was when Randall MacLane remembered who he was. He was thinking like an ordinary man, and he was not an ordinary man. He was the sheriff of Middle Bend. He was the one man an entire territory feared and trusted more than anyone else. He was the only chance for justice for Hannah and J.W. He was the man who had told Lara Eastbrook that he would avenge their friend, not out of anger, but just because it had to be done.

As the fury came upon him it was totally devoid of heat. In its iced coldness, he knew that Isaac could never respect him if he backed down now. He didn't know what was in the case. He knew, however, that it had been the death of the woman the two of them had loved and lost, one as a son and one as a husband.

He would finally lose Isaac most surely if he tried now to save him. Isaac wasn't looking to him for protection. He was looking for a sign. So Randall MacLane gave it to him.

He stared at the man across the room, but he spoke to the young man just in front of him.

"Isaac, when Marshal Simpson came down from the north to tell me about your mother, he gave me something that she'd been carrying in the hem of her dress all that time. It was faded. I could barely read it, but I would have recognized it even without the words. It was our marriage certificate, signed by Reverend Thistle. I reckon these men here with us in this room saw that certificate, too, but they didn't think it was worth keeping. That's why it's in my pocket now. I think you know who these men are."

The puffed-up power of the man he stared at began to leak from his well-creased edges. There was something in the sheriff's voice that spoke with more authority than his words. This wasn't a Washington boardroom, the proper venue for a man of power. This was a smelly, musty, rough-planked court of justice where the gavel was the gun. Here it made no difference if you owned the railroad. All that mattered was the guts to stoke the boiler. There was coal in the sheriff's voice.

Lafayette Luquire suddenly realized that he was no longer dealing with an impressionable and rootless young lieutenant. The man before him had been shaped by the plains into something he had never encountered in the corridors of political power.

"Now, Sheriff, you're making this more difficult than it—"

His sentence never found an end. The gunslingers at the ends of his little line knew exactly what the famous sheriff was saying to the young man who was still anxious to make his reputation and to avenge his mother. They were the ones with whom the young Reindorf had a score to settle. Their only chance was to be first.

MacLane saw the knowledge in their cruel eyes, even in the gloom of the unused room. There was one more thing he had to say, say to them, but for Isaac's ears.

"Don't be idiots," he snapped. "You haven't got a chance. This is Isaac Reindorf you're dealing with."

The one on MacLane's far left went for his gun first, so he was the first to die. The sheriff's gun thundered a second time, at the second man on his left, as he realized that Isaac had to take the right side of the line. It was the younger man's only natural field of fire. He could drop the case, draw, aim, and fire—all in one motion—if he could shoot in the same direction he was already facing.

"Right, Isaac," he cried against the blasting echoes of his own gun in the small room.

If Isaac wasn't fast enough, they were both in trouble. The guns of the other hired killers were already coming up. MacLane knew he could never sweep right, aim, and shoot fast enough to drop both the men on that end before one or both of them got off shots.

Besides, one of the congressman's dandified henchmen had come prepared. He was digging inside his suit coat at a shoulder gun. Another was diving for his ankle. MacLane had to assume he had a lady gun strapped above his shoe.

He didn't want to kill them. He knew they were only pawns to the man they served, just as he had once been. He also knew there was time for only one shot for each. He couldn't risk going for a shoulder and ending up with a slug in his own gut. He killed them both and swept his gun on, but it was too late.

Isaac had dropped the box and drawn. His aim was good. Both the men on the right end of the line were down. But he had stood as he fired. That gave them too good a target.

It irritated a back acre of the sheriff's mind. Anyone who aspired to be a professional with a gun should know better. The congressman's hired thugs had gotten off shots as well. One just managed a reflex pull at the trigger. His shot hit the message box. It had broken open and scattered its pages on the splintered floor.

The other, however, had gotten his gun up into killing position as Isaac pulled his own trigger again. The slug caught Isaac in the chest, just over from the heart, through the lung.

He crumpled back into the kneeling position. His gun dropped from his fingers onto the scattered contents of the message case.

Randall's brain closed out all the rest of the scene. The congressman, the other dying men, the message case—they meant nothing now. He dropped to his knees beside the man whose boyhood had so troubled both of them. He put his arms around him, easing him on down toward the floor.

Isaac's light blue eyes found MacLane's face, but still as though they were searching for some far horizon.

"That was just . . . a way . . . say thanks . . . for at the wagon . . ."

Rose-red blood bubbled up between his lips as he tried to speak.

A way to say thanks? It was only then that MacLane understood why Isaac had so stupidly stood as he fired on the men on the right. He had created a shield for the man he could never decide if he loved or hated. Right to the end, thought Randall MacLane, I didn't understand him.

Isaac's mouth twitched into his grimacing smile, and the frothing bubbles of his life again turned into words.

"This is Isaac Reindorf . . . you're dealing with. . . . Thanks . . . for the wagon . . . and thanks . . . for waiting. . . ."

That was all. Isaac's eyes finally found that horizon for which they had searched so restlessly and so long.

Another Message

There was no time. Randall MacLane sat from the beginning and forever on the floor of the old jail, holding against his chest the heavy weight of the young man who was finally his son, holding him as a dead man in a way he never could in life. Not that there had been a choice, for either of them; he knew that. The grayness had always been between them. Now it had settled over Isaac and taken him away, just as surely as it had taken his grandfather, and his father and brother, and his mother, and yes, his wife as well.

Out of his personal darkness he finally heard a familiar voice and saw the shadow of a friendly bulk beside him.

"Sheriff," said Milo Rosewater, in little more than a whisper, "I . . . I . . . think maybe you should get up now. . . . Titus is here, and . . . well, Miss Eastbrook is outside . . . and we've got that city fella . . . put him in the jail."

Randall MacLane looked up at his old friend. He had wept with Lara for J.W. Now the tears began to flow for his whole life.

"I'd like to get up, Milo," he choked, "but I don't think I can."

298

Milo scurried away, like some huge, benevolent mouse, and returned with Whispering Lowe. Lowe laid a blanket on the floor. Together they pulled Isaac from his arms and laid his body on it.

Then Milo stood behind him and grasped his friend and weeping hero in a bear hug and pulled Randall MacLane to his feet.

The sheriff smelled the saloon keeper and realized that for all their time together, he had never before been close enough to the man to catch his scent—old food, stale beer, tonic water, sweat, sawdust, fat. He had never smelled his friend before, and yet he would have known immediately, had the wind blown that smell to him even in a foreign city, that Milo Rosewater was there.

"I . . . I don't think I want Lara . . . Miss Eastbrook . . . to see me like this, Milo. . . ."

Milo continued to stand behind him, one hammy hand on his shoulder, bracing him. He spoke, almost as though muttering to himself.

"You need her . . . doesn't matter how you look . . . She needs you . . . doesn't make any difference . . ."

Something in Milo's voice drew MacLane up out of himself. He saw Lara Eastbrook standing in the doorway. Their eyes met. She flew across the room to him, faster than a bullet, it seemed, her frail figure crashing into his chest with an even greater impact than a bullet could have made upon him. He stood there, hugged by Lara and supported by Milo.

For all his sorrow, he couldn't remember when things had seemed so right. There was something else, finally, inside him in place of the rage. For a very long time that seemed like no time at all, they stood there together. Then Randall MacLane knew it was time to go on. He straightened himself.

"Let's find out what this is all about," he said. "Let's look at what's in that damned message box."

They hunted around in the late-afternoon gloom of the

boarded-up building until he was satisfied they had found all the papers that had spilled from the message box. Then he led them back to the jail, Lara with her small hand in the crook of his right arm, Milo trotting along beside him on the left, carrying what was left of the case itself.

They spread the papers out on the desk and MacLane put them into what looked like the right order. Then he began to read. It was indeed a message to Custer, but nothing like the message he thought he was carrying, twenty years before.

"My God," he gasped. "What they were trying to do! And I was their messenger boy!"

Milo and Lara simply stared at him and waited for him to explain. He read on, though, clear to the end of the document, looking for something that would tell him it was all a mistake, but nothing came. It was for real. As he finished he dropped down into the chair behind his desk with a fatigue greater than he had ever felt before.

"This is a message for Custer, and a contract. You know how some people have been saying Custer got into that fight because he wanted to be president, how he thought if he won a big battle against the Sioux, the Democratic convention in St. Louis could be stampeded into voting for him?"

Lara and Milo nodded.

"It made some sense to me, because on the way out here, I had to take another message to a man at the convention in St. Louis, even though it slowed me down in getting to Custer. But this . . . this is just unbelievable."

He put his head in his hands, then ran his fingers through the papers again, as though he could change their meaning by shuffling the pages.

"Custer . . . of all people . . . I trusted him. I almost got killed because of him. . . . A lot of people did get killed because of him."

"What is it, Randall?" Lara asked softly.

"We'd better get him in here to listen to this, too," MacLane replied, rising slowly from his chair and heading back to the prisoner cells.

He returned with the man he could still think of only as the "young congressman." The man from Washington still oozed authority and power, even as a prisoner. Lara recoiled from him, far more than necessary.

"Hadn't you better handcuff him?" she asked, her voice tremulous.

MacLane read what she was trying to do. It pleased him inordinately. Not only did he understand this woman, as no other woman he had ever known, but she was thinking ahead to try to protect him.

"No, Lara, it's not necessary. He won't try to escape, because he doesn't think he needs to, and I'm not looking for a chance to shoot him while he's doing it. Neither one of us is the man he used to be. In my case, that's an improvement."

Lafayette Luquire saw the contents of the message box spread out on the desk. He made a step toward it.

"That message is none of your business. You have no right—"

He was cut off by MacLane's glare and Milo's heavy hand on his shoulder.

"I have the right, not because you killed my son"—he didn't even notice that he'd called Isaac "son"—"but because I'm the law here."

You could see the congressman begin to deflate, like when a puff weed's been riding high on the breeze and falls to the ground and starts flattening out. He looked around him, his heavy sense of self-assurance already spreading out on the floor. This wasn't his world, a world where the law was written down in books that the rich and powerful could bang over the heads of the poor and ignorant. Here the law was just one man, and Luquire was definitely on the wrong side of the law.

"It seems the message my old 'friend' here used me to

take to Custer wasn't about Custer becoming president of the United States. It says the time was right for him to become 'emperor' of a whole new country, all the territory west of the Mississippi right up to the Pacific Ocean. What were you going to call it, 'Custer Country'?"

"You're a fool," the man said, savagely but softly. "You're in over your head. You're dealing with powerful people. Drop it now; that's your only hope."

He sounded as if he were talking to himself as much as to MacLane.

"No, I guess 'Custer Country' wouldn't do, because it wasn't really going to be his, was it? He was just a figure-head, useful because the western troops would follow him and become the new army of a new country. He loved the glory more than the power. That would probably be enough for him, to have an emperor's outfit to wear and ride in parades."

"You don't know anything," the man muttered.

"I'm only guessing about Custer, but the rest of this contract is clear. You and the rest of those men in your house the night you sent me out here were the real powers behind the scheme. You were going to make the real profits and have the real power, a cabal, or oligarchy, if you will."

Milo Rosewater cleared his throat and lifted an eyebrow. MacLane understood.

"An oligarchy," he said to the room at large, "is just a little group of power-hungry men who run a country by themselves for themselves and have it fixed up so they'll always be in power, regardless of what the form of government is. In this case, they weren't going to use any front except Custer as emperor. His contract with them shows that. And the timing was perfect. The country was weak and divided after the Civil War. The army was under strength."

"What's happened in this country since then shows we are right. Democracy is a fool's paradise, too weak and slow to act decisively about anything," declared Lafayette Luquire.

"And men like you always think 'decisive' is a good thing, don't you?"

It was clear the man who was the law did not expect an answer, for he went right on.

"Custer was decisive when he went after those Indians at the Little Bighorn. It got him and all the men with him killed. He never figured those 'inferior' Indians could win a battle against white men, regardless of how many they were. That was part of your idea, according to these papers."

He waved his hand at his desk.

"Idea?" asked Lara.

"Perhaps philosophy is a better word, although it's not put like that in this message. Custer was told to drive out from the new empire all the nonwhites, the redskins, the black cowboys and settlers, the Mexicans, the Chinamen who came over to work on the railroads. There are plenty of people out here who would be glad to help with that, glad to make it into what these papers call a 'white man's paradise.'"

His eyes fixed on a spot out beyond the walls as he remembered Liu and Clegg City.

"The western part of this country has vast mineral resources. Plenty of good agricultural land, too, but small farmers can't exploit raw materials for industry, and they can't even raise their crops and families with the riffraff of the world overrunning the place," huffed the man from Washington.

"The riffraff you're talking about was either here before the white men got here, or was brought here by them," countered MacLane.

"Ridiculous," puffed the man from Washington. "How can darkies and Indians and the like know anything about building a modern country? We're talking about civilization. That means white people."

"It means some white people more than others, doesn't it? What an irony! You say democracy is a fool's paradise.

Yet you drew up a contract to start a new empire according to the laws of the democracy. And you've not really given up on your idea, have you? You're just going to work at it from a different angle now."

Luquire reddened and began to swell.

"I don't know what you're talking about. That whole idea failed when Custer got himself killed, the idiot. Now we have to be resigned to the continent as it is, not as it might have been."

"Seems to me that for men resigned to things as they are, you certainly went to a lot of trouble right now to get back a message box that is irrelevant, as you tell it. And you killed a lot of people—Hannah, Isaac, J.W.—"

"Now, listen," the man said, in the way of politicians the world around when they're about to tell a lie. "I had nothing to do with that. It was those stupid men my associates hired. They went far beyond what they were ordered to do. I think it's time we cleared the air between us, Sheriff. We were friends once, and you took a real risk trying to do the right thing in bringing that message to Custer. We owe you for that, and we're ready to pay that debt. All you need to do is hand over that case and those papers so we can tidy things up and get all that behind us. In return, I can promise you almost anything you want. Money enough to take you anywhere you want to live and to support you in style for the rest of your life. A law job— chief of police—in any city in the country. A job in government. Back in the army, even—general—"

MacLane waved him to a halt. He knew the army and police-chief positions were blown smoke. No one could deliver on those promises, and they wouldn't dare let him live in one of those positions with what he knew. That went for Lara and Milo, too,

Not only had he had a hand in the deaths of everyone else who had been important to him, now he had endangered his last two friends by having them present while he sparred with this man without morals.

The money, however, might work. If he got it up front, and they got out of the country quickly enough, they could live like regular people. Maybe in Central America . . . Milo could run a saloon, and he and Lara could ranch. . . . Well, no, he was no rancher, but surely there was something. . . . Or he wouldn't have to do anything, if he had enough money. He could just be an ordinary man. . . .

The man before him, and the invisible ones behind him, hadn't actually pulled the triggers that killed Isaac and Hannah and J.W. Those men were dead, at his own hand, or Isaac's. Surely that score was even. What good would more revenge do his soul? Wasn't it more important now to protect his last remaining friends, the ones he loved?

He picked up the case and scooped the papers into what was left of it. The man before him eased. He was used to this scene, the power of money having worked its way.

Randall MacLane saved out one paper. He handed it to Lara.

"See that name, the first one in the list of the oligarchy that was going to run the western empire? Do you recognize it?"

"No," yelped the man from his past.

"Why, yes, of course," gasped Lara. "He's running for president!"

"That's what I meant when I said they hadn't given up. They're just coming at it from a different angle. That's why they had to get this message back, after all these years, no matter what it took. They couldn't afford to have his name come up now in connection with this scheme."

"Now look," said the congressman. "You're wrong about that. We're not planning anything like's in those papers. He's going to be a good president. It's not too late for you to get in on it. Just keep quiet about this. I can still get you more money than you could ever spend."

MacLane turned to his friends.

"All I ever wanted was to be an ordinary man, to have

friends, a woman to love who loved me. I have you, Milo, and I have you, Lara. You are more than any man deserves, but I also have a past and a badge."

He took Lara in his arms and kissed her. While she still clung to his arm he shook hands with Milo Rosewater as rivulets ran down the man's fat cheeks.

"Don't let anything happen to her, Milo."

Milo nodded. Randall kissed Lara again.

Then he picked up the message case and took by the arm the man who had given it to him years before.

"Come on. We've got a train to catch to Washington. I've got a message to deliver."

J. R. McFarland is a husband, father, author, cancer survivor, and all-star third baseman in the slow-guys league—an ordinary man.

HarperPaperbacks *By Mail*

**To complete your Zane Grey collection, check off
the titles you're missing and order today!**

❏ Arizona Ames (0-06-100171-6)............................. $3.99
❏ The Arizona Clan (0-06-100457-X)....................... $3.99
❏ Betty Zane (0-06-100523-1).................................. $3.99
❏ Black Mesa (0-06-100291-7)................................. $3.99
❏ Blue Feather and Other Stories (0-06-100581-9)....... $3.99
❏ The Border Legion (0-06-100083-3)...................... $3.95
❏ Boulder Dam (0-06-100111-2)............................... $3.99
❏ The Call of the Canyon (0-06-100342-5)............... $3.99
❏ Captives of the Desert (0-06-100292-5)............... $3.99
❏ Code of the West (0-06-1001173-2)...................... $3.99
❏ The Deer Stalker (0-06-100147-3)........................ $3.99
❏ Desert Gold (0-06-100454-5)............................... $3.99
❏ The Drift Fence (0-06-100455-3).................... $3.99
❏ The Dude Ranger (0-06-100055-8)................. $3.99
❏ Fighting Caravans (0-06-100456-1)............... $3.99
❏ Forlorn River (0-06-100391-3)....................... $3.99
❏ The Fugitive Trail (0-06-100442-1)................. $3.99
❏ The Hash Knife Outfit (0-06-100452-9)........... $3.99
❏ The Heritage of the Desert (0-06-100451-0)....... $3.99
❏ Knights of the Range (0-06-100436-7)................ $3.99
❏ The Last Trail (0-06-100583-5)............................. $3.99
❏ The Light of Western Stars (0-06-100339-5)........ $3.99
❏ The Lone Star Ranger (0-06-100450-2)............... $3.99
❏ The Lost Wagon Train (0-06-100064-7)............... $3.99
❏ Majesty's Rancho (0-06-100341-7)....................... $3.99
❏ The Maverick Queen (0-06-100392-1)................. $3.99
❏ The Mysterious Rider (0-06-100132-5)................. $3.99
❏ Raiders of Spanish Peaks (0-06-100393-X)......... $3.99
❏ The Ranger and Other Stories (0-06-100587-8)... $3.99
❏ The Reef Girl (0-06-100498-7).............................. $3.99
❏ Riders of the Purple Sage (0-06-100469-3).......... $3.99

- ❏ Robbers' Roost (0-06-100280-1)............................. $3.99
- ❏ Shadow on the Trail (0-06-100443-X)..................... $3.99
- ❏ The Shepherd of Guadaloupe (0-06-100500-2)..... $3.99
- ❏ The Spirit of the Border (0-06-100293-3)............... $3.99
- ❏ Stairs of Sand (0-06-100468-5)............................. $3.99
- ❏ Stranger From the Tonto (0-06-100174-0)............ $3.99
- ❏ Sunset Pass (0-06-100084-1)................................ $3.99
- ❏ Tappan's Burro (0-06-100588-6)............................ $3.99
- ❏ 30,000 on the Hoof (0-06-100085-X)..................... $3.99
- ❏ Thunder Mountain (0-06-100216-X)....................... $3.99
- ❏ The Thundering Herd (0-06-100217-8)................... $3.99
- ❏ The Trail Driver (0-06-100154-6)........................... $3.99
- ❏ Twin Sombreros (0-06-100101-5)........................... $3.99
- ❏ Under the Tonto Rim (0-06-100294-1).................... $3.99
- ❏ The Vanishing American (0-06-100295-X)............... $3.99
- ❏ Wanderer of the Wasteland (0-06-100092-2)........ $3.99
- ❏ West of the Pecos (0-06-100467-7)....................... $3.99
- ❏ Wilderness Trek (0-06-100260-7).......................... $3.99
- ❏ Wild Horse Mesa (0-06-100338-7).......................... $3.99
- ❏ Wildfire (0-06-100081-7)....................................... $3.99
- ❏ Wyoming (0-06-100340-9)...................................... $3.99

$1,000.00

FOR YOUR THOUGHTS

Let us know what you think. Just answer these seven questions and you could win $1,000! For completing and returning this survey, you'll be entered into a drawing to win a $1,000 prize.

OFFICIAL RULES: *No additional purchase necessary.* Complete the HarperPaperbacks questionnaire—be sure to include your name and address—and mail it, with first-class postage, to HarperPaperbacks, Survey Sweeps, 10 E. 53rd Street, New York, NY 10022. Entries must be received no later than midnight, October 4, 1995. One winner will be chosen at random from the completed readership surveys received by HarperPaperbacks. A random drawing will take place in the offices of HarperPaperbacks on or about October 16, 1995. The odds of winning are determined by the number of entries received. If you are the winner, you will be notified by certified mail how to collect the $1,000 and will be required to sign an affidavit of eligibility within 21 days of notification. A $1,000 money order will be given to the *sole winner* only—to be sent by registered mail. Payment of any taxes imposed on the prize winner will be the sole responsibility of the winner. All federal, state, and local laws apply. Void where prohibited by law. The prize is not transferable. **No photocopied entries.**

Entrants are responsible for mailing the completed readership survey to HarperPaperbacks, Survey Sweeps, at 10 E. 53rd Street, New York, NY 10022. If you wish to send a survey without entering the sweepstakes drawing, simply leave the name/address section blank. Surveys without name and address will not be entered in the sweepstakes drawing. HarperPaperbacks is not responsible for lost or misdirected mail. Photocopied submissions will be disqualified. Entrants must be at least 18 years of age and U.S. citizens. All information supplied is subject to verification. Employees, and their immediate family, of HarperCollins*Publishers* are not eligible. For winner information, send a stamped, self-addressed №10 envelope by November 10, 1995 to HarperPaperbacks, Sweeps Winners, 10 E. 53rd Street, New York, NY 10022.

Harper Paperbacks

would like to give you a chance to win **$1,000.00**
and all you have to do is answer these easy questions.
Please refer to the previous page for official rules and regulations.

Name: _____ Sex: M $_{01}$ F $_{02}$

Address: _____

City: _____ State: _____ Zip: _____

Age: 7-12 $_{03}$ 13-17 $_{04}$ 18-24 $_{05}$ 25-34 $_{06}$ 35-49 $_{07}$ 50+ $_{08}$

We hope you enjoyed reading **An Ordinary Man.**

1 a) Did you intend to purchase this particular book? Y $_{09}$ N $_{10}$
 b) Was this an impulse purchase? Y $_{11}$ N $_{12}$

2) How important were the following in your purchase of this book?
(1 = not important; 3 = moderately important; 5 = very important)

word of mouth	1 $_{13}$	3 $_{14}$	5 $_{15}$	advertising	1 $_{31}$	3 $_{32}$	5 $_{33}$
cover art & design	1 $_{16}$	3 $_{17}$	5 $_{18}$	plot description	1 $_{34}$	3 $_{35}$	5 $_{36}$
cover glitz	1 $_{19}$	3 $_{20}$	5 $_{21}$	price	1 $_{37}$	3 $_{38}$	5 $_{39}$
cover color	1 $_{22}$	3 $_{23}$	5 $_{24}$	author	1 $_{40}$	3 $_{41}$	5 $_{42}$
floor stand/display	1 $_{25}$	3 $_{26}$	5 $_{27}$	length of book	1 $_{43}$	3 $_{44}$	5 $_{45}$
contest offer	1 $_{28}$	3 $_{29}$	5 $_{30}$				

3) In general, how do you find out about the books you want to read?

_____ $_{46}$ word of mouth   _____ $_{50}$ author publicity
_____ $_{47}$ book reviews   _____ $_{51}$ reader's clubs
_____ $_{48}$ libraries   _____ $_{52}$ advertising
_____ $_{49}$ store browsing

4) Where did you buy this book?

Store Name: _____

City/State: _____

5) Have you ever listened to a book on tape? Y $_{53}$ N $_{54}$

6) How many of the following do you buy each month?

mass market paperbacks	0 $_{55}$	1-2 $_{56}$	3-5 $_{57}$	5+ $_{58}$
large format paperbacks	0 $_{59}$	1-2 $_{60}$	3-5 $_{61}$	5+ $_{62}$
hardcovers	0 $_{63}$	1-2 $_{64}$	3-5 $_{65}$	5+ $_{66}$
spoken audio products/books on tape	0 $_{67}$	1-2 $_{68}$	3-5 $_{69}$	5+ $_{70}$

7) What types of books do you usually buy? (check all that apply)

_____ $_{71}$ mystery/suspense/thriller   _____ $_{77}$ romance/women's fiction
_____ $_{72}$ science fiction/fantasy/horror _____ $_{78}$ self-help/inspirational
_____ $_{73}$ true crime   _____ $_{79}$ entertainment/Hollywood
_____ $_{74}$ westerns   _____ $_{80}$ young adult (age 13+)
_____ $_{75}$ reference   _____ $_{81}$ children's (ages 7-12)
_____ $_{76}$ business   _____ $_{82}$ nonfiction/other

please return to:
HarperPaperbacks, Survey Sweeps, 10 East 53rd Street, New York, NY 10022